Fell Too Deep

Patrice L. Guyton

authorHOUSE®

AuthorHouse™
1663 Liberty Drive
Bloomington, IN 47403
www.authorhouse.com
Phone: 1-800-839-8640

© 2012 Patrice L. Guyton. All rights reserved.

No part of this book may be reproduced, stored in a retrieval system, or transmitted by any means without the written permission of the author.

Published by AuthorHouse 3/9/2012

ISBN: 978-1-4634-1247-0 (e)
ISBN: 978-1-4634-1249-4 (hc)
ISBN: 978-1-4634-1251-7 (sc)

Library of Congress Control Number: 2011908230

Any people depicted in stock imagery provided by Thinkstock are models, and such images are being used for illustrative purposes only.
Certain stock imagery © Thinkstock.

This book is printed on acid-free paper.

Because of the dynamic nature of the Internet, any web addresses or links contained in this book may have changed since publication and may no longer be valid. The views expressed in this work are solely those of the author and do not necessarily reflect the views of the publisher, and the publisher hereby disclaims any responsibility for them.

My Intelligent, Beautiful and Amazing daughter,

Kamiyah Elise Jones

Thanks for always making mommy smile!

My oldest and kind-hearted brother

Damian Maurice Tucker

"Gone but Never Forgotten"

February 2nd 1983- August 18th 2003

ACKNOWLEDMENTS

First and foremost, I would like to thank the man that made all of this Possible. My Lord and Savior, Jesus Christ. God has been so good to me and I will never be able to thank him enough. But GOD, I stand as proud as I know how, thanking you for life and this amazing opportunity. Thank you for always looking pass my faults and seeing my needs. I love you and I will always and forever lift your name on high.

The late, great Rosie Bell (Big Ma) Guyton. My great-grandma and the Rock of the family. Thanks for always loving me. No matter what I went through or the mistakes I made, you were always there uplifting me. Though, you didn't like the fact that I cut off all of my hair, you found a way to grit your teeth and say, "It's ok." I love you dearly.

My Support System: She has been here for me since the day I was placed on this earth. She is with me when I'm right and stops me when I'm wrong. I thank God daily for blessing me with such a beautiful and inspirational woman. When everyone, I mean everyone turns their back on me, she is always there. She is the head and I'm the body so without her, I'm clueless as to where to go, I don't know what decision to make and I simply can't make it in this life without her. She is more than a mom; she is my friend, my backbone and when in need, my provider. Mom, I absolutely love making you proud and I can't wait until I tell you the words, "You no longer have to clock in." Her name is Patricia A. Baldwin and she belongs to me. Eddie (Big John) Guyton. That guy there is the best. He's there comforting me when I'm down and always praising me when I'm up. He is and forever will be the first person to read any of my material and he is the first to hear all of my ideas. That's only because he supports every positive thing that I do. He has been there and no matter what, he will always be there. My brother and nonetheless, by biggest and number one Fan. Janie, though we argue a lot, she is always there when I need her.

Tari, her husband, thanks man for pushing me. Thanks for giving me money and telling me, "You don't have to pay me back." I love it when I don't have to pay someone back. Mark, thanks cousin for the small things. You are the best. Lavuntae (Butter-ball), when I need a few words of encouragement, you are always there. I can call you at 3 A.M. and you will always pick up the phone. (You maybe a little irritable but still you answer) You sing to me when I'm down and you make me laugh when I'm hurting. My Best Friend for 13 years and counting. I look forward to our future and I love you more than you will ever know.

Keziah: my sister and friend. Thanks for cursing people out for me because I'm not as convincing. Thanks for always having my back. Thanks to you and Mike for taking me in when I was in Cali. Thanks for feeding me when I was too broke to buy groceries. Thanks for being there for me even when I'm wrong. Uncle Tony- Aunt Angela Guyton, thanks for always pushing me and encouraging me to stay in school.

Daddy, you are the best dad that I have ever had (literally). You are a powerful man of God and a darn good preacher. I'm your princess and you are my King. Thank you so much for giving me a heads up on men. You always tell me, "You are the cause of your own self-inflicted wombs", so I try to think before acting. Thanks for being a role model in my life. Ma Brenda, thanks for always pushing me and letting me know that nothing in life is Free. Thanks for taking my dad's credit card and maxing it out on everything that I needed for college. Curt, thanks for pushing me (even though you would love for me to enlist in the army). Thanks for accepting my brother and I as your own.

Pastor Matthews, thanks for being a friend and a true man of God. Thanks for breaking down the sermons every Sunday in a way that I can understand God's word because if not, I'm lost. ☺

Tynisha, thanks for always being an ear when I need to talk. You let me speak before commenting. We have an understanding so you dislike the people that I dislike. ☺ Just one argument with you and April, fortifies my day. You have never discouraged me. Good friends since the 6th grade. Neesy, thanks for coming back into my life. I love you girl. Thanks to you and your mom, Mrs.Sara for always being there for me but mostly, thanks for loving me for who I am.

My senior Pastor Gus Walker and First Lady, Mrs. Walker. I pray for you daily and I love you so much. Pastor, keep the faith because I believe that you will be up and walking in no time. The church that made and raised me, DIVINE HEALING TEMPLE and later turned into Kingdom Vision International Church: the church that changed me. Grandma Rosie, thanks for taking me in as your own. You always send a card full of love on every holiday and birthday. I love you more than life itself. Chanel Smith, my roommate in college, partner in crime and one of my favorite people. My God-parents, Lisa and Tyrone Cunningham. I love you guys so much. You will never know how much the two of you mean to me. My second grandma; Annie Stewart and the Lashley family, thanks for the unconditionally love. My loving aunt Brenda and Uncle Quinn. Special thanks to Ms.Juanita Robinson. Soleeta –Lulu (my sister, best friend and believe it or not: you are one of my role models), Nickesha Brown (my partner in crime), Patrick Neal, Aunt Rosie, Aunt Lena, Aunt Mary Ann and the Entire Guyton family. Ruby Jackson, thanks for always supporting me in everything that I do. Marilyn Sherrod. Kelvin and Jessica Driscoll (my favorite married couple and friends) Caterrika Lashley. and Tiara Conner, (two of my favorite girls) Shandrell, thanks for the times that you were there for me. Uncle Otis, Aunt Shirley, Uncle Carl, TT Shirley, TT Paula and the entire Harris Family. I love you all so much. The Colvin family. Cousin Gloria, Wood, Boot and the Watson family.

The best high school around, Columbus High and the best class to graduate C/0 2005. I love and miss everyone in my graduating class. To my track coach, Bernard Jones, thanks for always being there and pushing me pass my limits. B-white, My barber Keith Jordan and the Dreamteam Barbershop. To my entire family and friends, I love you all you will ever know.

Lastly but definitely not least, I would like to thank all of you that has supported me by purchasing my first book. This wouldn't be possible without you. Thanks for the Love, the Prayers, the Hugs, the Letters and the Encouraging words throughout this process. A special shout out to my hometown, the city of Columbus Mississippi. Enjoy and God Bless. Much Love-Patrice Guyton.

Prologue

WHAT'S THE DIFFERENCE BETWEEN A MAN GOING TO JAIL FOR COMMITTING MURDER PHYSICALLY THAN MENTALLY? HONESTLY SPEAKING, "THERE ISN'T". THIS MAN RAN OUT OF MY LIFE, LEAVING MY HEART DAMAGE. MY HEART IS IN CRITICAL CONDITION AND BARELY HOLDING ON. AS I SIT HERE IN THE "ICU", THE DOCTOR COMES IN., "I'M SORRY MA'AM , BUT I DON'T THINK THAT YOU WILL EVER BE ABLE TO RECOVER FROM THIS HEARTACHE. THIS MAN HAS CUT YOU SO DEEP THAT YOU WILL NEVER BE ABLE TO LOVE NOR TRUST AGAIN.

AS I SIT AND LISTEN TO THIS DEVASTATING NEWS, I NOTICED THAT I CANT EXPRESS ANY FEELINGS. I CAN'T SMILE, I CAN'T FROWN. OH MY GOSH, I CAN'T FEEL ANYTHING ! HOW CAN A HUMAN BEING TAKE AWAY EVERYTHING THAT YOU HAVE?

THE DOCTOR LEAVES AND THE PHONE RINGS…."HELLO ?' I ANSWERED. IT'S MY MOM. SHE'S SOUNDS TERRIFIED. SHE'S ANGRY AND CRYING. "MOM, WHAT'S WRONG?" "BABY, I'M SO SORRY TO TELL YOU THIS…..." "MOM, CALM DOWN. WHAT'S WRONG?" I ASKED. "SOMETHING TERRIBLE HAS HAPPENED AND IT'S ALL OVER THE NEWS, CHANNEL 7 TO BE EXACT. THE HEADLINE READS, "A MURDERER WAS FREED TODAY FOR BRUTALLY DAMAGING A WOMAN'S HEART." SHE CRIED.

YOU HAVE GOT TO BE KIDDING ME. I'M SITTING HERE IN THIS BED, THE DOCTOR HAS GIVEN UP ON ME, I'M BARELY HANGING ON AND THIS MOTHERFUCKER WAS FOUND "NOT GUILTY?" (NO

25-LIFE AND NO COMMUNITY WORK?) WHAT DOES IT TAKE FOR A JURY TO RULE FAIR AROUND HERE?

THERE GOES ANOTHER CASE WHERE NO JUSTICE IS SERVED! WELL RIGHT NOW, IT SEEMED THAT WAY BUT HE FORGOT ONE THING. THE FINAL VERDICT LIES IN THE HANDS OF THE JUDGE. SO YOU SEE: I, JUDGE HARRIS, SERVED HIM WITH "25"….25 TO KARMA THAT IS, BITCH !

What goes around will eventually come around

CHAPTER 1

How it All Began

I cannot wait until the last day of high school is finally here. These teachers are really stressing me, or maybe I am stressing them but who cares. I really need to give this college thing another thought because I can't take too much more of sitting in a boring classroom learning absolutely nothing. But, you know how parents are. I think they all say the same thing, "Baby, nothing in this world is free: you must have an education to become successful. Mostly all restaurants require at least a diploma. At the end of the day, you must attend college to make it in this world." Yea, yea I have heard all of this before but is college for me? I barely made it through high school so how will I survive college? I even heard that you will be expel if you are caught cheating. What? How do you suppose I passed all of my finals?

One good thing that came out of this is the fact that I run track. I've been running since the eight grade and now it has became a part of my life. This is something that I could actually see myself doing for as long as my body is able to perform. My track coach, Robert Jones, mentioned to me about a month ago, that I should start applying to universities that have both good track and field teams and a great physical therapy program, being that my major is Physical Therapy. My list of schools consist of Long Beach, University of Memphis, UCLA, University of Arkansas, LSU and Long Beach City. UCLA was number one on my list but I'm sure that they will be the last to respond. I always prepare myself for obstacles since I can't predict the future but someone has to accept me, or at least I was hoping and praying that I will get in somewhere.

I have always wanted to live in California and that is mainly because my dad lives there. I have not seen my dad since I was about fifteen. He isn't a bad father nor did he neglect my brother and me. He just decided to move away from Mississippi about six years ago. He wanted to leave and experience a new life and that is how I feel right now. I would love to leave Columbus and adventure out so what better place to go than California. My younger brother and I went there to visit our father when I turned fifteen. I knew the moment I stepped off of the plane, Cali was where I was going to live, find my husband and start my family. Yep, I can see my future now. But for now, I have to wait and see who is crazy enough to accept me.

Time is running out and I'm becoming discourage. It's been three weeks now and I still haven't received a letter from Long Beach nor UCLA, which are my top two choices. What's wrong? Did I fill them out correctly? Did they receive it? Hell, what was I thinking: I should have known better. No one is interested in me. I am going to give it one more week and after that, I'm hanging this up. I might as well go and look for a job. There is only one month of school left so I need to start preparing myself for what ever is going to happen. So, just in case I'm not accepted anywhere, I must prepare a back-up plan.

As the final days of school drew near, I have started to eat my own words. I don't think that I'm ready to graduate. I am going to miss everyone, especially my classmates. I'm pretty sure that I will never see some of them again and that worries me. The mighty class of 2005 is so close. We have the best personalities and have the most fun. I'm popular so I knew all of my classmates and the undergrads. This school will never be the same once we leave; sad but true.

I still had no clue as to where I was going to continue my education. I have been receiving nothing but "Denial" letters. I only have a few days left so I didn't want to give up just yet.

It is 1:36 p.m. and my sixth period class is over. I am standing outside of Mrs. Lanmaster's class; the most evil art teacher at this school, waiting for my friend Melissa to come out. Melissa, one of my best friends, is a girl that I've known since the 5th grade. Melissa is a down-to-earth and very intelligent person, though she doesn't look it. She is a good friend but many females dislike her because they assume that she is arrogant or conceited but once they get to know her, they will see that she is a sweet person. But don't get me wrong because at times I want to slap the taste out of her mouth. I will take now for example. She is my ride home so we meet here in the same spot every day. I am already pissed because she is running extremely late and I just checked with my coach to see if he had heard anything from the universities that I applied to and his answer was no, just like the previous days. Finally, she walks out with the biggest smile on her face; singing and dancing and shit.

"Damn, what took you so long? You act as if I do not have shit to do?"

"Girl please! Do I have to remind you everyday that you are riding with me? I can take hours if I want to. For someone that does not have a car, you are really ungrateful." "Melissa, you feed me that same line everyday. I know that I have to ride with you but sometimes, try being considerate." "Considerate my ass, you should consider giving me some gas money. Times are hard." "Gas Money? Well, in that case, girl take as much time as you need." "Yea, I thought so." "Whatever! I am not having a good day so I will let you win this debate. Please, just get me to my house. I could use a nap right now."

Once we arrived at my house, I also noticed the mail man pulling up. As always, I thanked Melissa for the ride and she drove off. I was surprised not to see my mom standing outside waiting on Mr. Smith, our mail carrier to arrive. Now usually, I will ask him how his day was going but today, I didn't care. I asked for the mail and nothing else.

He handed me a stack of mail so in my hands held bank statements, sales papers and coupons, but on the bottom was a big brown envelope. I flipped it over and automatically everything but that envelope fell out of my hands and onto the ground. It was sent from, Barbara Sanders, the girls track and field coach from LBC. As I ripped it open, my heart started racing.

Dear Parker Harris,

My name is Barbara Sanders and I am the girls' track coach here at Long Beach City.
(I already knew who she was because I practically go online everyday just to check the girls track records, look at their pictures and read up on them) The letter goes on to say......
I have been reviewing your newspaper clippings online. It appears to me that you are a very talented young lady. I also know that you applied here at Long Beach City. I am sure you know that you must obtain at Least a 2.5 GPA and other requirements in order to be accepted here. It would be a pleasure to have you on my team but Unfortunately, you only have a 2.4 GPA and Long Beach takes education seriously. I then started to do more research on you and decided to personally go to the admissions here at the school and see if I could help them choose to bring you in. After an hour meeting with them, we all came to an agreement. I knew how you would react to this decision so I wanted to personally send you this letter. Attached you will find the ACCEPTANCE LETTER from Long Beach City College along, with your Full Scholarship in Track and Field, certificate letter. Congratulations Parker, because everything is paid for! Just bring yourself on August 21st for orientation. We will see you soon. Enjoy your Summer.

Barbara Sanders

NO! Is this a dream? As I pinched myself, I read it again. FULL SCHOLARSHIP, EVERYTHING PAID FOR, JUST BRING YOURSELF.... Oh Jesus, it's real.

"MAMA, MAMA!" I screamed as I ran in the house. "Girl what is your problem? Why are you breathing so hard? I am trying to catch up on my damn soap opera!" "Mama I got accepted, to Long Beach today and I received a Full scholarship in Track and Field." "Oh Lord," she yelled. "Mama is so proud of you baby. I knew this whole time that you were going to get accepted somewhere. Congratulations", she screamed as she fell to the floor. My mom is 6'2 and weigh about 240 pounds. Now, I know that she is overly excited for me but I am not about to help her ass up. She always get into the shouting spirit and I have to end up picking her up or fanning her off. "Come on and help your mama up baby, you know that I'm getting old." "Mom you're only 43." "Just do like I ask and help me up." I ate my words and grabbed her arms.

Fell Too Deep

She was in the spirit but I was trying to refrain from screaming, again. I was beyond excited. I feel like going to the highest rooftop in Columbus and shout to the world this amazing news.

"Parker" my mom called out. "Ma'am". "Let's change clothes and when your brother gets home we can all go out to eat and celebrate together."

I was going to change clothes but to hell with that, I'm too happy. I went into the bathroom to wash my face and then reapply my make-up. My mom stood at the door, "I just want to tell you again how proud I am of you. You were sad and depressed thinking that you weren't going to be accepted anywhere, but I had faith in God and I knew that he was going to work it out for you. So right now, I want to pray with and for you. You have a long journey ahead and you must remember to keep God first because he is the one that has paved the way for you. C'mon and close your eyes."

Dear LORD,

I thank you for everything that you are doing in my life. I thank you
for sunny days as well as those cloudy days. I come to
you today, giving you thanks for everything that you have done. By
your grace and mercy, you allowed a full track and field scholarship to
be given to my daughter and Lord I just want to thank you on today. Lord you didn't have to do it but you did. Lord you could have given it to a another girl name Shalita but you gave it Parker. Lord, you have done so much and for that, we will not complain Lord God and we shall not complain. Lord I ask that you watch over her as she adventure out into this world. Lord, keep her safe and focused. Lord, give her the strength and peace of mind to fight off any enemies that may try to harm her. Again Lord I thank you for giving her this
opportunity. I thank you for what you are doing in my life as well as my family lives on today. In these many blessings I ask in your son Jesus Name.

Amen

"Whew! Mama feel like shouting again." "Well, let's hold off on that for right now, I'm hungry."

CHAPTER 2

LAST-MINUTES

With only a week left until I leave for college, I am starting to realize how much I am going to miss this place. My mom was washing up my last set of clothes that I am taking with me. I love her so much. She is such an amazing and kind-hearted person and always looking to help someone else first. She thinks that I do not notice it but I do. When I leave, it is not only going to affect me but it is also going to affect her. I am finally leaving my mom's nest. I am not sure as to what to expect being that I am going alone with no parents, family or friends. My dad and step-mom lives in California but its damn near two hours away from where I will be living. I've never been separated from my mom for a long period of time. I know that it will be ok but I will still miss home.

As I put some of my clothes away, the doorbell rang. "Get the door", my mom called out. "Who is it"? "It's Cherell girl, and I'm coming in." She is also a good friend of mines, we are best friends to be exact." "Hey bitch, what time are we leaving tonight?" "Uh, Parker is the name slut and I will leave my house at10:30. When I come blowing, please be ready."

This will be my last Saturday night in Mississippi so we decided to hit up the club and have some fun.

"Aight, I have some groceries in the car so I have to go but I promise you that I will be ready."

Yeah right, she moves slower than I do and that is not possible. We always make it to the club late but I wanted to enjoy the entire night this time.

I tried on my black skinny jeans, with a black and white checkerboard vest and my six-inch black pumps but I can't forget my big-framed eyeglasses that are trimmed in red. Without a doubt, my butt is my best feature but that is because it's so damn big. It's sits high whether I'm wearing sweats or jeans. As I look in the mirror, I noticed how fine I am, Damn! I have itty bitty titties, a small waist and a big ass but let's not forget the pretty face, with the exception of a few bumps. I have the body that many bitches dream about everyday.

However, I decided to wear my mustard, spandex turtleneck dress with my dark brown chocolate six-inch pumps. I figured if I was going to do it then I should do it right. This will be the last time that I can hit up the club in Columbus for a while so I wanted to leave out with a bang! I was running out of time so my mom volunteered to iron my clothes while I took a shower.

It is 10:25 and I am here at Cherell's house blowing the horn like a maniac. See, I knew that I should have told her ass to be ready at 10:00. She takes hours to get dressed and comes out the house still looking the same. She had her cousin yell out the door to give her a few minutes but I yelled back to let her know that she only had a few seconds to walk her skinny ass out of that house or I am pulling off. After I laid my foot down, she came out of the house looking foolish and being sarcastic. It would not be Cherell if something ignorant weren't always coming out of her mouth.

"Just get your ass in the car. You already know that the club is going to be packed tonight while you moving like molasses."

Moments later, we pulled up and the parking lot was exactly how I had expected it to be. It was extremely pack and I had a feeling that they are already filled to capacity on the inside. I couldn't solely blame her because I left the house late myself. I glossed up my sexy lips and headed to the line where we saw many of our classmates standing. Cherell had a friend to do us a fake ID so unlike some of the other classmates, we were about to get wasted.

We talked our way to the front of the line and moments later, we were in the club. I headed straight to the bar to order a Bahama Mama. I didn't want to overdo it but this is my last night in Columbus so to hell with that, I'm treating myself to unlimited drinks all night!

I just downed my second shot and I am feeling lovely honey. I have a few drinks in my system so I'm ready to hit the dance floor. There are some fine brothers in here tonight and I am going to back my ass up on at least one of them. With only an hour and a half let, I have to make sure I got at least two more shots and take pictures with some of my classmates that showed up tonight. "Bartender, another shot please." Suddenly a voice behind me said, "Is that you Parker?" I turned around to my high school crush of 3 years: Dallas Hill. He is one of the most handsome men that ever walk this earth. I was mesmerized and speechless, but only for a split second.

"What's up sexy? How are you? He asked

"DALLAS! I have not seen you since you graduated last year."

(I ran track with him for three years at C-Town high school. We started something a while ago but that was not a success because he was solely focused on track and sleeping with all of the girls. He was a very nonchalant and down-to-earth person. We used to engage in conversation all of the time. I wanted to take it a little further with him but I knew that he was going off to college soon. He still looks the same: Tall 6'1, dark brown skin, nicely trimmed low fade, size 13 shoe, white teeth and the thing that really got me is that athletic body and that wonderful six pack. Oh, I can melt just thinking about his sexy ass.)

I'm headed to California next Saturday. I received a scholarship in track at Long Beach City."

"Yeah I was reading that in the newspaper last week, Congratulations!." He said

Well go ahead and enjoy your night and I will get up with you afterwards. Maybe we can go and grab something to eat and catch up on good times."

He is such and hoe but what the hell, all he wants to do is talk and there is no harm in that. We then gave each other a hug and exchanged numbers.

"Ok, it is the last song of the night, She Got A Rump" the D.J. said.

The club went crazy, well mostly the girls and so did I. This is my shit. Of course, the rapper made this song for me because my Rump is so big. I can't exactly sit a cup on it but I'm getting pretty close to doing so. I went to the middle of the dance floor to get the spotlight and there was this girl with no ass standing there dancing with a crowd around her. She is looking busted and fucking disgusted so there was no reason for her to be in the center. So being the person that I am: I politely went in front of her to take over the show that she thought she had going on. So, here I am getting it. I started shaking my ass as fast as I could and for a minute, I thought I was having a damn seizure. I mean I was working the hell out of that dance floor and all of the niggas were drooling. Out of nowhere, this hoe pushes me. I guess she was mad because I took the attention from her skinny ass. (You already know what happened next: I gained all of the strength that my drunk ass had left and punched that bitch right in the face. The minute she starts wobbling, her click runs up because they knew exactly what she had coming. I was going to beat that bitch to sleep.

Some girls I fuck with (including Cherell who was practically missing the entire night) ran up. Seconds later, it was a big altercation on the dance floor. Bottles were being thrown through the air; curse words being exchanged, females, and even some dude were fighting at this point.

"BREAK IT UP, BREAK THIS UP!" about five security men screamed as they stormed through the crowd. One man folds my arms behind my back but I was still trying to get loose. "Yea Hoe, what you thought I was not going to strike back? I' don't play that shit. You better rise up." "Ma'am, we are not going to let you go until you calm down." I continued to tug and try to pull away but those men weren't budging."

By this time, my blood pressure was high and my nerves are on edge. I am so drunk and I need everyone to get out of my way including this overly weight security guard.

As I try to convince the club cop to let me go, Dallas walks up. "Sir, she is with me. I'll take her." He said. I snatched away, pulled my dress down and we walked off. "Parker, are you cool? Man you are wilding out right now. What happen? Well it is not even important. What's up? What are you about to do?" I was thinking, "I'm about to screw you with your sexy ass." He had that seductive look in his eyes but like I said: he is, well he was a hoe back in the day so there is no telling in whom he has slept with and I can't deal with that. "Dallas, I need to head to my house before I get into more trouble tonight." I was no longer drunk because this chick has ruined my high but I still have a buzz. "Would you like to at least go and grab something to eat?" he asked. He was being very tempted so I gave in. "Yes, I'll go but I have to find Cherell first so I can get my keys and follow you." "Oh no, I don't think you are able to drive. Why won't you ride with me and I can bring you back to the car after we eat. I'm sure you will be ok to drive then." "That's fine, but I still have to find her so I can have the keys."

When I finally located her, she was leaning out of her boyfriend's car, throwing up. She can't even hold down a wine cooler without vomiting. I grabbed my keys, locked my door and hopped in the car with Dallas. I thought I was about to be riding in some kind of beat up Oldsmobile but his car was very nice. It smelled fresh and it was clean.

We arrived at "Waffle Town" and of course everyone and their cousin's little sister was there. The moment we walked in, it was all eyes on us. I can hear the little mouths whispering, "Are they talking now? What are they doing here together? Damn how she get him?" Curiosity kills. They will never know that we are just here to eat and chill out, so I will let them do their assuming while I enjoy a meal on Dallas. Yes, he is paying because he did the inviting.

Dallas says, "It is too many people in here. Do you want to get our food to go and chill at my mom's house for a minute? Afterwards I will take you back to your car and trail you home." Yea, Dallas thinks he is slick. He is trying to get some booty but I wouldn't dare and especially not at his moms house, ugh. However, I will play his little game. "Yea that sounds good but you do know that everyone is going to be talking about us tomorrow right? "Yea girl, I saw them leave Waffle Town last night and this and that. I swear this city is too small. Everyone knows everyone business and it's ridiculous.

Once we ordered our food, we headed to his mom house where I was scared to cough because I didn't want to wake his mom. I know if my mom woke up and found some random guy in her house at 2 AM, she will flip out. After we ate, we sat and talked for a while. "Have you seen the movie <u>Handsaw III</u>?" Dallas asked walking to his 55 inch flat screen TV. "Oh My Gosh, NO! I did not know it was out DVD. <u>Handsaw III</u> is the best sequel scary movie ever. "No, I have not seen it yet so you can go ahead and pop that in. But wait, what time is it? "2:05" he said. I have to call my mom and tell her that I'm staying at Cherell's house because it is too late to be walking in her house. I mean I am about to go off to college but I am not grown so I have to respect her rules. "Ok baby love you," she said. "I love you too mom good night." I make it seem easy to lie to your parents but it's not and it even hurts a little. I shouldn't have to lie but she will not approve of me being at someone's house this late. I am staying the night at Cherell's; I'm just not there yet.

"Now where were we?" he asked

"Um... I think you were about to put your arms around me and press play." Now I am sitting here squirming in my seat and feeling a little freaky. Either its from the alcohol in my system or his big, muscular, nice smelling body up against me. Ok I really need to calm down and just watch this movie. I said to myself. Besides, Part III is supposedly the best one. However, all I want is one kiss. What is the harm in a little peck? So as I was about to kiss him; he must have read my mind because he turned my face to kiss my lips first. Oh, I loved it. It taste so sweet and his lips were so soft and big. Hell, his lips are drowning mines but again I love it. He gently pushed me back and laid on top of me. He then starts to breathe in my ear and softly kiss on my neck.

Wait! WHAT AM I DOING? I don't know who he has been with or what he has been doing. I could be going about this all wrong but it feels so right. Well I am going off to college in a couple of days so what's the harm in having a little fun tonight.

As he starts to caress my body, I felt myself getting weaker by the moment. It felt like we were a grown couple in a sex scene in some kind of porn movie. I am only 18 and I am pretty sure that I am not suppose to be feeling the way that I am feeling right now. His tongue played with my tongue and then his tongue moved down to my navel. He was doing things that no one has ever done before and might I add, he is good at it. He is rubbing his hands through my hair while I am gripping and leaving marks in his back. I feel like I am about to, YOU KNOW: but I can't. Not now. I have so much more to put in. He moved down to my vagina and tried to lick me dry but I was becoming wetter by the second. He sucked on my lips and went deep into my hole. I couldn't help it. I screamed to the top of my lungs. He was serving me and he was doing a damn good job. He pulled his tongue out and placed his penis out. A sexual sensation raced through my body. I have never had anyone to do my body this way. He knew exactly where to go. As he pushes further I can feel him in my stomach. It was pleasing pain and it was feeling so good. "Fuck me Dallas." I whispered in his ear. "I'm about to…" he started to say and then he pulled out.

I know damn well this ain't all he got. He is three years older than I am and this is all that this punk ass nigga can give me. Oh hell no, I wanted to get a knife and cut his shit off. I knew better than to sell myself short like this anyway. I have just pulled a hoe move. I wasn't in need of sex that bad. I can't believe I did it and with no condom. If I die from any sexual transmitted diseases then it's no one's fault but mines. He is fine as hell but he can't fuck and that is a major turn off for me. I'm beyond pissed, I'm furious. Minutes later, I heard him snoring like his ass had put in hours of work. Yes he ate my pussy like none before but he lacked the most important part; grinding and slow winding. The appetizer was good but the dinner didn't have enough of seasonings. I threw my clothes back on, grabbed my things and started walking back to the club where I left my mom's car. It was about a fifteen-minute walk but I made it there in no time and that's only because I was full of steam and rage.

Chapter 3

Saying Good-Bye (for now)

"Parker, you need to start putting your luggage in the car. You are going to miss your flight because you are around here procrastinating. Now get off of that phone and finish getting your bags together before you leave something." "Ok mama calm down before you have a heart attack. I was on the phone with Cherell saying my good-byes."

I am really going to miss her, Melissa and Tony. They are my three best friends but we all knew that this separation isn't going to end anything. We had to go off and get this career thing started so we could all make some money. Cherell wants to do hair and become an elementary school teacher, Melissa is going to school to become an accountant, and Tony wants to do hair as well. Aqua, another very close friend of mine, also received a full track and field scholarship but she will be attending Coppin State in Maryland. I had a different bond with each one of them and no one can break it.

My plane is leaving at 2:35 p.m. from Alabama and that is about a two and half hour drive so we have to leave early. "Alright ma my luggage is in the car and I am ready". "Ok but we have to wait on your brother. He rode the bike to his friends' house to get his IPOD. But while we wait, I want you to know again how proud I am. This is a big step for you so I want you to take advantage of it. You go run and jump your best at that school and most of all, GET YOUR DEGREE. I am going to miss you but I know that you are about to go and better yourself. Don't loose sight on your goal and don't let a man come in and sweet talk you. I have been there and it's not worth it. You will have good days and you will have bad days but as long as you keep God first, everything is going to work out in your favor." "Aw mama, that was sweet. I am going to make you, my dad, my step-mom and myself very proud so don't worry." "The King Is Back" my brother said as he walked back in the house." "Well it's about that time, now come on lets get on the highway."

I couldn't believe that I was actually about to go to California and run track. I have so many butterflies and I have not made there yet. This is going to be an exciting experience for me. I have to get acquainted with a new set of girls and at times, that can be complicated because I do not trust too many people especially females. The girls track coach called me last week to Confirm that I did not change my mind about coming to California. She also informed me that I would be staying in a house with SEVEN other females. I thought she was kidding at first but she wasn't. How is that possible? Eight females in one house, that can't be possible. It was only six of us at first but she said that her assistant coach came across two girls from Texas who is extremely talented. One girl is a sprinter and the other runs fifty-one seconds in the 400-meter dash. Along with the two girls from Texas, there will be one coming from Miami, two from New York, one from Jamaica, and one originally from Trinidad. Coach believed that we have a good chance on bringing the school a championship this year. I know all of us will have different attitudes and maybe even different beliefs but eventually we will work it out. The house has three bedrooms and two baths. There will be two girls in each room. Everyone will also be living rent and utility free. The homeowner was a good friend of our coach and she was willing to allow all eight of us to live there.

"Parker", my mom called out. "Yes mother." "Call your dad and tell him that we are almost at the airport and he needs to make sure that he has the right time so he will not be late picking you up. I don't want you at that airport by yourself at night." "Mom it's probably not going to be dark anyway, California is two hours behind us. "Parker I do not care. Call your daddy and just make sure that he will be there on time." "Ok mom." Damn, she is so scary. "My poor mama" my brother said laughing.

"I don't care what y'all say. People now days are crazy especially in California. I remember when I could walk… "Oh Lord here we go" my brother and I both said.

"NO I am being serious y'all. When I was young, we could walk the street at 2:00 a.m. in the morning and no one would ever bother us. You can't do that in this day and age and that just doesn't make any sense. But y'all can keep laughing. I can't tell you anything but you will learn now call your daddy right now I said!"

"Ok ma." One minute she is playing and the next she is serious. "Ma, he said the plane lands at 6:10 so it will be after 8 o'clock in Mississippi when I arrive. He said that he will make it there around 5:30 just in case it comes early. Well all right daddy, that's all I wanted. We are about to stop and eat before we go to the airport. "Ok baby, I love you and tell your brother I love him also. Have a safe flight and I will see you in a few hours." "Alright daddy we love you too."

"We were a few minutes behind our schedule so the drive-thru it is. Y'all order quickly because we have to go. Go ahead and eat your food now because once we get to the airport, I am going to drop you and your brother off at the door so you can check your bags in and I will go park. Make sure you have your I.D. out with your confirmation number so the process can move along smoothly.

This is where I get frustrated: having to stand in these long lines especially if I am running late. I have about thirty-five minutes to check-in, say my good-byes and prepare for departure. My mom needs to hurry up. I was hoping that she had already found a parking spot and was on her way in here. I was standing there daydreaming and almost didn't hear the attendant call me up to check my bags. She handed me my boarding passes and confirm with me that instead of my plane leaving at 2:35, it will not be departing until 3:15. "What a relief?" My mom walked in breathing heavy as if she had been running for hours. "I thought that I was not going to find a place to park. Have you checked in? Is the plane on time?" she asked, "Yes ma I checked in and thank God my plane is running late.

My plane isnt leaving until 3:15 so we sat by the security gate for a few minutes. "Well here we are kids. Where does the time go? It seems like you two were just babies yesterday and today Parker has a track scholarship in California and you D.J. will be graduating from high school in only two years. I am so proud of the both of you and I just can't say that enough." "I know you are mom and for that I am going to do my best not to let you down: Though everyone makes mistakes, I will try and make as few as possible. Well y'all its time for me to line up and mama please don't cry. You know I am going to call you every single day and I will be home for Christmas. This is not a good-bye only a see you in a few months. D.J don't stand over there trying to act all tough. Come on and lets do a group hug. "I love you guys so much and I will call as soon as I land." "Ok we love you too."

At that moment, I realized that this is it. I am walking into a new life and I have to start this one right. I have to stay focus and as much as I say that, it is one of the hardest things for me to do. I always seem to get around the wrong crowd or meet some dude to fill my head with sweet lies, but not anymore. No longer will anyone deceive me. I have never felt so positive about anything in my life so Let's Go Get It!

Once I landed, I did what I had promised and that was to call my mom. She was relieved to know that I made it safely. I reunited with my dad; which was a great feeling. He was happy to see me and I was more excited to see him. Once we grabbed my luggage, we left and headed out to his house. I move into my new house tomorrow along with the other seven females. I was wondering if any of the other girls had arrived. I wondered what they looked like. I hope I do not end up in a room with someone I can't get along with because that will be all bad. But I am going to stay positive about everything because that was one of the things I promise to myself. My dad and step-mom has agreed to buy me everything that I need for college: From an iron to a new bed. I guess he figured that it was his time to give my mom a break and for him to step up and do a little more. I didn't mind at all because I deserve everything that I am offered. Once I got home I was going to talk to my step-mom for a minute and then head to sleep because I have another long and exhausting day tomorrow.

Chapter 4

Moving In

I got a phone call from my Coach this morning and she told me that the team was going to meet at the field. She along with the other coaches decided to have a cookout so we can get a feel of the track and meet one another. I am a very shy person especially around people that I do not know. We are here at the school and it is time for me to meet my teammates and my roommates. I was hoping that they didn't judge me before actually getting to know me.

As my dad and I began walking, my legs started to tremble. The first person I spotted was this girl standing by the water fountain. I figured that she was someone's sister because she was too short to be out here running track. But I walked up and introduced myself anyway. I told her the basics, which was that I am from Mississippi, ran the 400-meter dash, and did the high jump.

Her name was Chanel and she was one of the girls that came from Miami. So, she actually does run track. She is about 4'9 and it seems weird that she is a college student. Her voice is very high but as loud as a whistle. She did all of the sprints so I applaud her for that. We had the same name; well my first name is her middle name. We clicked and agreed to have each other's back. We also decided that we should be roommates. Besides, we were both from the south so it was only right. After I introduced her to my dad, we walked over to the grill where we saw Coach B standing. Once I introduced myself to the Coach, my dad took over the conversation by first thanking her for giving me the opportunity to be a part of this school and this track team this year. My dad is very corny so of course he entertained everyone with his jokes. It wouldn't be him if he didn't try and steal the show.

Keziah and Meka, the girls from Bronx New York, Lele: the girl from Trinidad and Nicki: the girl from Jamaica walked to where I was standing and we all introduced ourselves. Within about five minutes, all six of us felt comfortable with one another. The girl's first impression seems to be good. I just hope it stays like that.

After we ate, we headed to our new house, which was in Carson. That's about a twenty minute drive to and from school every day. We pulled up to this beautiful house and my dad and I was stunned. It was a two-door car garage with beautiful green grass. I knew that if the outside was beautiful, the inside was going to be fabulous. Chanel helped us unload the car because I had a lot of shit. I basically had everything I needed but my bed; it's going to be delivered in a few hours. After we had everything squared away, my dad prepared to leave.

"Well baby I am about to go. I am going to stop by your grandma's house before I get back on the highway. Don't forget that she is only a few blocks up the street so call and visit her sometimes. She would really love that". (That is my step-mom's mother but I do not refer to her as step-grandmother: she is my grandma) "I will definitely do that. Call me when you make it home. Love you daddy." "I love you too."

It was heartbreaking seeing him drive off because we had just reunited with one another. However, I thought about my life and where I am headed. I am independent now and its exciting and scary at the same time. I am going to be living on my own with no one to look after myself but myself. I deserve to be here. I deserve to be standing where I'm standing right now and that is in front of my house. I know it's going to get tough and at times I may feel like giving up but I have come to far to give up now. I looked at my neighborhood and then I turned to look at my house. My journey begins!

CHAPTER 5

You Remind Me

I woke up feeling better than ever. I had slob on my face and my head scarf was on the floor. Chanel was already dressed and lining up her brand name glasses when I rolled over. I forgot to tell her that my snoring was loud enough to keep her up all night but oh well; there was nothing she could do about it now because we were already roomies. She told me that she and her dad were about to head out to see some of their family in Pasadena. Keziah and Meka was at work, they have been out here for two weeks and they already have jobs. Nicki was at her boyfriend's house and Lele went for a jog. "So I'm going to be here by myself?" "Yes, unless you would like to roll with me." I thought about it but I changed my mind. I didn't want to sit at someone's house that I knew nothing about. "I'll just sit around here today. I can watch DVD's or play on my computer." "Ok, well have fun with that. I will see you later." "Alright."

It was nice to have some peace and quiet for a moment because I knew that within a few days, the "Female Turmoil" is going to begin. I still had to unpack all of my things so I'm sure that will take up my entire day. I got up to wash my face and brush my teeth. When I made it back to my room, I popped in a CD and turned on my radio. My music was blasting because there was no one here to complain about it. My heart dropped when I heard a knock on my door. I thought I was here by myself. Chanel was supposed to have locked the door so I didn't know how this person on the other side of my door was knocking on it. I opened my door to a caramel brother that stands about 6'1. He is skinny but muscular. He sort of reminds me of the dude on that BET countdown show. "Hey how are you? I'm Mike, Keziah's boyfriend." "Oh hey, how are you? I thought

I was here by myself." "Yea I did too until I heard your music. Are you about to do anything?" "No, I'm just unpacking since everyone is gone." "I'm about to go to the mall to take Keziah some lunch so you can roll with me if you like.

I looked him up and down. I was trying to see if he had "Rapist" written on his body. I hesitated because I don't know him. Who knocks on a stranger's door and ask them if they would like to go to the mall? No one does that. "Diamond!" he yelled out. In walked this beautiful little girl. "This is my 3 year old daughter, Diamond." I'm guessing that he was trying to show me that he wasn't going to hurt me because he has his daughter with him. He made a good statement by introducing me to her. I knew that he wouldn't do anything to me while his daughter is with us so I volunteered to go. "Give me about an hour to take a shower and find something to wear and I'll give you a holler when I'm done."

This is good I thought. I was meeting new friends already. I was finally geared up so I walked outside to wait on Mike. I'm looking around for the car but there was no sign of one. Mike walked outside and said, We are walking because I don't have a car, I hope you are cool with that." I was ok with walking because I'm in shape but I was curious as to how far this damn mall was. He came out of the house, talking like he does this shit everyday. "Hey, the sun is out, let's walk to the mall."

We were only talking and walking for a few minutes and we were full of conversation. We were telling jokes because he has a personality similar to mines. I'm always laughing about something. Many people often say that "I should grow up" but I often say, "Live Life and Laugh." They can turn on the news if they would like to be serious because it's a lot of serious and crazy motherfuckers on there. Mike even shared with me a few secrets about his baby's mom, and no, it was not Keziah. Speaking of Keziah, I hope that she does not think that I want her man. One, he's not my type. Two, he walks to the mall during his spare time and three, he is already like a brother to me. In this short period, Mike and I had already built a relationship. I'm not physically attracted to him and I wasn't in love. It wasn't that type of relationship. It was more of a brother-sister bond. I'm not the person that trusts easily but I knew that I can confide in him.

He reminds me so much of my older brother. I always wanted an older guy in my life that I can look up to. I need someone to go to with my problems when I am having trouble with men or even when I need advice on how they think. My older brother used to comfort me in that area: Until he passed away in the year of 2003. That was a tragic lost for my entire family and it's a day that I will never forget

(Usually when I get home from school, I will see his tall and lanky body sitting on the couch watching TV or in the refrigerator looking for something to eat while asking me "What did you learn today?" Eating was one of his specialties but just like me, we never gained any weight. If he was not at my mom's house, his dad's, or his trifling ass bitch ass girlfriend house then I would try to call around and see if anyone had seen him. He called himself a "Vicelord" from Northside so he and his gang were always beefing with the "Gangsters" on Southside so I had to keep up with him at all times. On this particular day, I called his dad's house and that's where he was. Just like any other day, we talked for a while. He then told me that he was tired and that he wanted to take a nap. "I'll call you as soon as I wake up sis" He said. I remembered watching some videos and his favorite rapper; "Slim" had a new video out. I wasn't sure if had seen it so I called him up.

Mrs. Ruby, his step-mom, answered. "Hello." "Hey how are you? Is Maurice still sleep?" I asked. "Yea he still in there knocked out." she replied. I told her to tell him to call me as soon as he wakes up. It was only about twenty minutes later when my phone rang. I glanced at the caller ID and it was him. *I thought, "Some nap."* I answered. "Hey Maurice." But instead of him on the other line, it was Mrs. Ruby asking if my mom was home. "No ma'am" I replied. She is at the store. "Ok," she said. Tell her to call me when she gets back because something is wrong with Maurice." I was thinking if something was so wrong with him, why couldn't he call? The hospital is only a minute away so if he was sick they could have took him there. I called my mom and told her that Mrs. Ruby wanted her to call. She had just dropped my aunt Brenda off. She was passing by the neighborhood where my brother's dad lived so she said that she will stop by to make sure that everything was Ok. I didn't think anything else about it because I figured if it was something serious, Mrs.Ruby would have told me while we were on the phone.

After a while, I did worry. I realized that the world around me was quiet. There was no movement and no sound. I looked out the window and the sky was white. "Something is wrong", I thought. Something is wrong with my brother. My phone rang and it was my aunt calling. My heart dropped at the silent discomfort on the phone. Something happened. My aunt had been crying.

"He's gone." She said

"Who is gone?" I screamed. I knew damn well that she wasn't talking about my brother. He was just going to lye down for a nap and I have never heard of anyone dying that quick. I ran outside again but this time I was screaming to the top of my lungs. My neighbor, Mrs. Betty, was walking over to where I was standing. My mom had obviously told her the news because she said, "Come on Parker, I have to take you to your brother's house."

When I pulled up, the sight of ambulances and police cars damn near scared me to death. I spotted my mom and a coroner truck at the same time. I knew then that this wasn't a dream. My brother was gone. I jumped out the car and ran as fast as I could up to the crowd and that's when the police stopped me and said, "Sorry ma'am, we can't let anyone in at this time." I explained to him that the man in the house was my brother and not some friend off the street but that pig still didn't budge. I ran to my mom for answers but that didn't help at all. She only said that Mrs. Ruby went into his bedroom to wake him for dinner but he didn't move.

(Many people on the street have said that he overdose and when his aunt found him: his penis was in his hand and his eyes were the same color as the rain. From my understanding, his step-mom was the one that walked in and tried to wake him up. Some even said that his aunt gave him the pill that supposedly killed him. My mom told me that his heart was enlarged and it burst while he was asleep but I know there is more to the story. Maybe he had a heart problem and those pills that people say he swallowed was too much for his heart to handle but I'm sure that he didn't overdose .

My mom wanted to keep the truth away from me because she figured that I wouldn't be able to handle it. Since the streets have been talking then I figure it's only right that I find out on my own "The Real Story" of my brother's death. I am going to go over and beyond to find out if anyone did anything to take my brother's life away from him. His aunt wasn't too fond of him and a number of fake ass gangsters wanted to see him down. So how did my brother die and why did it happen so soon?)

The coroner then came out and ask the immediate family if we wanted to come in and see him one last time and like an idiot, I told him no. I didn't do it because I couldn't stand the thought of seeing him lye there so restless with not one ounce of breath in his body. That day, I thought the easiest thing to do was to not go in that house but I have regretted that terrible decision ever since. I often ask myself why didn't I go look at him? Why didn't I go hold his hand? Why didn't I whisper in his ear and say "I

Love You"? Why didn't I go and pray with his soul one last time? Those questions will forever be unanswered because I chose not to go in and see his body. I must live with that for the rest of my life. He was the only older sibling that I had. He was my rock. He was the one that taught me how to play "Slap Box." When I told people that he was my older brother, they would back down. He fought for me and my life isn't the same without him. I could walk the streets with no fear in my heart because I knew he had my back. We always picked on my younger brother who was considered the crybaby. We all bickered and fought but that showed the love that we had for another. I think of him all of the time. He is truly missed and he will Forever have a place in my heart !

R.I.P MY BROTHER
DAMIEN MAURICE TUCKER
GONE BUT NEVER FORGOTTEN

CHAPTER 6

Getting the hang of things

It's been three months since I have made that major move. Things are running a little smoother than they were in the beginning. All of the down-south girls tried to stay together but that wasn't working to well. Chanel and I have become the best of friends but we have somehow formed a rivalry with Anesha and Teri: the two chicks from Texas. One of them can't figure out if she wants to be with man or a woman and the other one is the whore of all whores. We still did things together like go out to eat or party. But it fails, every time we step out; you can see the envy on the females face wishing they could be us, and the lust in the dudes' eyes wishing they could get with us.

About a week ago, the four of us went out looking for jobs just to have something to do. We all applied at this huge Retail store, I was the only one that received a call for an interview, and days later, I got the job working as a cashier. My parents were the ones who first thought of the idea. They figured that I will soon want more money than they could give me. The idea of me working was hilarious. I have never had a job nor have I ever thought about working. I feel that parents were placed on this earth to cater to their kids along with all of the other major responsibilities that they have. Honestly speaking, I needed to focus on my schoolwork and track. I didn't have time to be dealing with managers telling me what to do or rude customers waiting to be slapped. However, since I did get the job, I figured that I would at least try it. I agreed, to myself, that I wouldn't let this job stress me. If I feel that I am being "overworked", I'll quit and it's just that simple. This was actually my first job so I was very excited and nervous. I was excited because I can finally put something on my resume and I will have extra cash in my pocket. I was nervous because this was retail and I have heard that this was one of the worst fields to work in.

With about three weeks of training, I was still making careless mistakes but I was getting the hang of things. I bring home about a $350.00 check every two weeks. Hell sometimes I think that I have rubber band banks. No but seriously, being 19 years old with no kids, no bills with a nice paycheck make me very happy. The money that I earn all goes to God and me. I don't have any extra baggage weighing me down and that is a huge blessing. So far, I have been able to juggle school, work, and track at the same time but it was getting a bit challenging. Eventually, I may have to let one of them go but for right now everything is going well.

I was on the verge of failing my "World History" class because the teacher's voice is so dreadful. I can never learn anything because I am always sleeping. No matter how much coffee I drink or how long I slept the night before, I can never stay awake in that class. I have tried tutoring with advanced students after class hours and I even sent emails to the professor but nothing is sinking in to me. Maybe because I could care less about what happened 500,000 years ago? My coach talked me into dropping the class instead of failing because it looks better on your record. I was failing myself at the end but I'm winning at the moment.

Track was coming pretty fine. We workout everyday, except for Saturday and Sunday, for two hours. Within those couple of hours of practice, it felt like I went to hell and back. Though I know nothing about Hell, dealing with this shit everyday gives me a pretty good idea. When I was in high school, running track was different and shame on me for thinking that college track was going to be the same thing. We had our little workouts back then but this shit right here was something that I would have never expect. We start with a mile jog then stretch and drill exercises. That's only the warm-up but after that I'm usually ready to head home and go to sleep. I have started to tighten up my form up and lower my times. Track season usually doesn't start until the end of January or the beginning of February so I still have close to three months left to really get into shape.

Chanel recently met this dude off the football team so she is hardly ever home. He seems laid back and drives a nice dark blue impala but he may have to work on his looks a little bit. (I'm just throwing it out there) She was not feeling him the way he was into her right off because for one, he is a cornball and two, his physical appearance needs a little work. Don't get me wrong now, he isn't dog-faced ugly nor is he drop dead gorgeous but he is a sweetie pie and I think that is what got her. She was really falling for this dude so if she loves it then I like it honey.

Patrice L. Guyton

    Keziah and Mike are always out with each other but they are always together. He was now trying to find another car and a place to live. He was living with a friend but some personal problems occurred so he had to move out. He then started to live out of his car until one night he was stopped for speeding: he found out that his license was suspended. In Cali, if your license is suspended, they will impound your car. I feel so bad for him simply because we have grown so close to each other. He is my brother and I hate to see him go through that especially since he has a child. There wasn't much that Keziah could do because she works, goes to school and run tracks. No matter what, she is always by his side and that's what I love the most about them. I hope that one day I have a relationship very similar to theirs.

CHAPTER 7

Meeting # 44

"Parker! Come on. We are going to be late again and it's always because of you."

"Chanel, not once did I tell you to wait on me. I simply told you that I had to turn in the rest of my paperwork for my financial aid. You were the one that decided to stand here and wait." (She was tripping and worrying about making it to practice on time. I was worried about it as well but checks go out next week and I'm not trying to miss out on my money honey.)

"And you were the one that said that you only have to drop it off and it will not take long," she said. "Well you saw for yourself how long the line was and you still decided to stay so I have nothing to do with that. However, we will be late if we keep going back and forth on something that is already done.

We made it to practice in time with two minutes to spare while her ass was doing all of that crying and shit. We have been practicing on a huge field that is full of grass, holes and lumps. I have no idea why but they claim to have a good reason to do whatever it is that they do. The team was always begging them to let us practice on the track but they didn't want to get the girls sidetrack because the track is also where the football players practice. Coach said, "Everyone had been asking, "When are we going to start working out on the track?" Well I say, What better day to start than on "Terrible Tuesday?" I want everyone to line up so we can get started. Automatically you heard grunts because we had been complaining about working out over here but out of all the days in the week, she had to choose Tuesday. Tuesdays are the days that they give us a workout from the devil himself. They have us running up and down the bleachers, doing exercises that I have never thought of and they make us run miles at a time. However, I was glad that I decided to wear my spandex workout jumpsuit today. While I sweat, I wanted to give the football players something to focus on. I didn't mind entertaining them for those two hours that I will be out here. Practice started:

"Parker, Tuck those damn arms in and run. This is a sprint girl not a jog. You do not want to be the reason we start this practice over, now get a move on it, NOW." Coach screamed. He was the assistant coach. He is originally from Miami, Florida so he does not play any games and he has the loud voice to go with it. I was too busy trying to show off that I lost track of what I was supposed to be doing. I can't be the reason that we start practice over because I will never hear the end of it from my team mates. I was in a good mood so I didn't need anyone ruining that for me. I gathered myself and finished practice strong.

"Ok everyone, bring it in. You guys and girls had a good workout today but Parker you have to work harder. Our first meet is approaching and you are out here playing and not taking this shit serious. I don't know how it is in Mississippi but in California, these chicks don't play. You will have to go heads up with some talented girls that have very good times in the 400 so if you don't tighten up, you may have your spot snatched. You didn't come all the way out here to cheer on your teammates; you came to run. Show me what you are capable of." Coach said. "I got you coach and I got this. I will not let my team down." "Show me that you aren't all talk. All right, huddle in team. Long Beach on three, Long Beach on three, **1-2-3 Long Beach**. See everyone tomorrow.

Today I am riding with Chanel and her boyfriend so we may not leave until another 30 minutes or so because he was still out there practicing. That was fine with me because I want to see the men in action. I love the sight of tights and shoulder pads on the football field. I was checking out number 4, 23 and 44. All of their butts look so cute and they all appear to be star athletes. The three of them stood out to me though I couldn't see their faces. Chanel told me that her boyfriend told her that mostly all of the guys, especially the star players, were up to no good. He said either they only wanted sex or they were solely focus on football.

I didn't care about what he thought because he was a cornball. He was a great player but still a cornball so he may think the same about everyone that have sex. I was wondering if I should even get involved with a football player. I wasn't worried about him rejecting me because no one rejects me.

I am concerned about my reputation. Will I be the talk of the school? Will everyone suspect that since I am dating a football player that we are only sexually involved with each other? I didn't want to go through that. I only wanted a dude that I could kick it with, have fun and go out with every now and then. I have too many other important things going on to get in too deep with a dude right now but I would like a friend-guy to rescue me from this house full of females sometimes. While walking back to the field from getting something out of my bag, I noticed that practice was over. I spotted number 44 talking to his coach. By the looks of things, it appeared to me that they were having a very heated conversation. I wasn't sure if they had gotten into an argument or if practice was going bad. Whatever it was, this was perfect timing. I waited until his coach walked off to introduce myself. I didn't know if he had a cute face nor did I know if he was upset or not. I took my chances.

"Man, he was going pretty tough on you. Are you o.k.?" "Yea I'm good; I'm used to all of that and more actually. Today was not a good day for me." "I can feel you on that because I have many of those but I hear that you are one of the star football players on the team." He smiled. "Well I'm not going to brag but if you heard that then who am I to say otherwise." (Enough with the small talk I thought) "So does the best football player have a girl?" "Not at the moment. I really don't have time for a girl. What about you? I know you have a dude as fine as you are?" Aw thank you but actually I don't so I guess we have something in common." I have to leave his mind wondering so I ended the conversation. "Well, you probably have to go but it was very nice to meet you. Mr ?".. I glanced at his jersey as if I hadn't done so already. "Mr. 44" I started to walk off.

"Hold Up! I didn't get your name." (I had him right where I wanted. You have to know exactly how to play the game and that's what I did) "Oh I'm sorry. My name is Parker."

He took off his helmet and said, "My name is Timothy but everyone calls me Tim. So Parker, how about we exchange numbers and then I can find out a little more about you." "I thought you would never ask." He had a few bumps on his face but who doesn't. I didn't care about those bumps honey. If he can give me some alcohol and a cotton ball, I will pop the hell out them. However, shortly after that, I had forgotten about the other two dudes that I was trying to get with. Tim gained all of my attention and I couldn't stop looking at his number in my phone. I was kidding myself.

This dude is the star football player and claims to be single. I know there are many chicks on his dick but I'm not worried about that. I was looking for friends to mingle with so it's not like I'm trying to make this thing permanent. With every person that I meet, I must at least give them a chance to prove themselves before I bounce their ass. The look in his eyes told me he might be a cool kid. (Let's just hope so)

    I walked over to Chanel to tell her that Tim and I exchanged numbers. They have a meeting after practice every day so that gave us time to talk for a minute. I didn't know if I should call him or wait and let him call me so I asked for her opinion. She said that I should call but I didn't. I decided to wait on him to move first. I had to play my cards right. I didn't want him thinking that I was all over him. One thing for sure: You can't let a man know that you are thinking about him all of the time. If he doesn't call, so be it: Move on to another bait that is waiting and hoping to be caught.

Chapter 8

Mike and Keziah have finally moved into their new house. I was happy for them because they needed their own space especially with Mike having his daughter. It's nothing like having your own shit. They were having a house warming party/ bar-b-que today so they invited me over to eat and play cards. There were a few guys from the track team there and some of their friends outside of school. For Keziah to be from New York, she has a lot of southern hospitality. Mike is the very similar. Whenever I need a shoulder to cry on or if I'm in the need of a good laugh, I can count on them. Chanel is still my buddy but she is always with her boyfriend so its basically Keziah, Nicki and I that are always together.

Tim and I were doing fine. Even though I said that I didn't want to be in a relationship, I've talked to him about taking things a little further or even putting a title on this thing that we had. He made it clear that we are friends and nothing more. We have been on a few dates but most of the time; he just comes to my house so we can watch movies and enjoy each other's company. I have the room to myself now since Chanel is always gone.

It's been almost a month now and I still haven't given in to that lustful temptation. I am definitely proud of myself because as sad as it is: If a man was treating me good and doing all of the right things, within two or three weeks I'm usually dropping the panties and jumping on something. I have slept with a few men along my path and I have done some terrible things. However, I am trying to move pass my past. I'm not proud of the deceitful decisions that I have made. I repent and made a vow to myself not to ever repeat those actions. With that being sad, I didn't want to move as fast and

I definitely didn't want to give up the goodies. This football player has to put in some work but I'm in no rush. I just want to keep the friendship going for now and have fun later. We actually clicked with each other very quickly. We are both messy as hell. Every time we are on the phone, his ears are always glued to my background. One day he overheard Lele talking about a douche that was left in the bathroom on the side of the tub. He wanted to know exactly who did such a nasty thing and me being the messy person that I am, I told him who it was, Nene big nasty ass!

    I was in the back playing a game of spades when Keziah told me that my Timmy was outside. I text and told him that I was over here so I know that he is popping up to see if I was with another guy. He only had on a pair of sweats and a t-shirt but he was so damn fine. I introduced him to everyone and once I made him a plate, he left. A prime example of Eat and Run.

Chapter 9

One day at a time

I am in class on a test day with a blank piece of paper in front of me on my desk. There are always little cheat sheets going around and Nene was holding the answers. If I fail this test because of this black Bitch then there is going to be problems. I should have done like every other average student and studied. But it was too late for shoulda, coulda's. Anesha gave the answers to Tim first. The word around school is that she had a little thing for him. But what kills me is how she is always trying to get what I have and that ranges from clothes to now my man. I never really paid any attention to it but now I am more cautious of her. After Tim completed his test, he grabbed mines and completed it for me. I felt special and at that moment, I knew that he would do anything for me: might I say that I was very impressed. I honestly do not think that I would have done the same thing for him but he finished it and that is the only thing that matters right now.

One day, after practice, he took me to the cheesecake factory and we went on a stroll on the beach. Tim is so sweet and can be very tempting at times. We have been together for almost two months. I told myself that I wasn't going to fall in love again and here I am doing the exact opposite. I am in love with a guy that does not want to hold a title with me. I should consider going to speak to someone because I fall in love entirely too quick; or is it lust? I was afraid of being alone but on the other hand, I did have a very low self-esteem. When I look in the mirror, some days I see pretty and on other days, I see ugly. My face breaks out with these huge bumps and I have terrible marks and rashes that come on my hands, chest and sometimes my neck. My nose is so big that it seems like I have been telling lies since the day I was born. (Get it?) Sometimes I feel like I need guys in my life to tell me how beautiful I am and that is not good thing. I really can't explain it. I'm not happy with my looks. Yes I have a nice body but until I get to that point where I am fully confident with how God has created me, I will forever look for other people to tell me how pretty I am, especially men.

However, when I am around Tim, things are different. I am able to be myself because we are so much alike. We like the same things, we act the same way, eat basically the same types of food and we know how to have fun. I mean is that a match or what? I did love him but I tried to stop myself from getting too involved because I didn't want him to eventually leave me because of the hounding. Therefore, I tried to fall back and see how far it will take me.

CHAPTER 10

And it Happens Again

"Ok mama, I love you too and I will talk to you later."

I think between me and my mama phone calls, we call each other about 20 times a day and it not just a hey and bye, it's a full conversation every time we speak to each other. I love her to death so I don't think that I can ever talk to her too much.

I called and asked Mike if he could come and rescue me from this boring ass house. I am always arguing with the Texas chicks because they have this twisted way of thinking that everything they say goes and that is so far from the truth. When I'm in the need for a good laugh I will usually call my younger brother Big John and my best guy friend Tony. They always seem to give me a good comedy show over the phone every now and then. They are the closest guys to me but they can never get along. I find it quite hilarious and cute when they try to fight over my attention. I can always count on them to lift my spirits.

Keziah, on the other hand, was at home cooking so I hope the food will be prepared by the time I get there. For the record, she is by far the best cook in this world I think. I never ever put anyone's fried chicken over my moms' but this girl is amazing when it comes to chicken and a list of other dishes. Whenever or wherever she is cooking, I'm always the first person in line. Keziah is only 19, the same age as me but she is more mature than I am. She speaks and acts as if she's a mom or a full grown adult. She says the right words at the right time even when I don't want to hear them and that's why I like her so much. While I waited on the food, I couldn't help but drift off into space thinking about Tim.

Just a couple of days ago we were doing so well. It even seemed as if we had gotten closer but here it is November 10 2005 and it now seems as if we don't have that connection that we used to have. We talk about everything so if he was having personal problems then I am sure that he can come to me. He is doing well in school and football so I have the slightest idea of what could be wrong. I fell for this guy and maybe I was becoming old news to him. I hope it wasn't the end of us. He sent me a text asking if we could meet tonight because he really needed to talk to me.

I didn't know what this talk was going to be about. I went to Mike and Keziah for answers but they left me very confused. Mike thinks we spend too much time together so maybe Tim wanted space but Keziah thinks that Tim was about to break it off with me. The food was good and the advice was helpful but I had to go home and get dressed. I didn't know what kind of night this was going to be so I had to prepare myself.

• • •

I am fresh out of the shower looking sexy and smelling good. I had on my pink and dark chocolate bra and panties set. Tim sent a text to tell me that he was on his way. I wanted to stay here and model for him but if that's what he wanted, I'm sure he would have said something. As far as sex, we haven't made it to that point just yet. We will tease each other every now and then but that was it. I heard his truck pull up outside but I waited a while before I walked out. When I got in the car, he spoke to me and gave me a gentle kiss. Moments later, there was silence and suddenly he started to talk.

"Look Parker, I don't want to beat around the bush any longer. You are an amazing friend and I can talk to you about almost anything. We laugh and joke every time we are together .I know you have been wondering, when are we going to take this relationship to another level, but I've made up my mind and I think that we should remain friends. We have a good thing going and I don't want to lose that but as far as a relationship, you deserve better and you deserve someone who is going to be there for you, make you smile, and treat you like the queen that you are and right now I can't do that. My focus is football, not a woman. I will not be able to put you first." "Remain Friends Tim?

Are you kidding me?" "Parker it's not your fault, its mine. I led you on knowing that I didn't want to be in a relationship. I just got out of one about three months ago and I can't imagine jumping into another one this quick."

Yes, I was pissed but I was even more upset at the fact that he didn't tell me that he was recently committed. This girl is before my time so I can't dwell on that but it still would have been nice to know. I can't jump from one relationship to another. I need that time to heal and try to fix all of my errors. He told me that this girl had broken his heart and that he still had some repairing to do. He also added that he still cared about me but he knew this could not work because he simply wasn't ready. I couldn't believe what I was hearing. Who wouldn't want me? I have a job, in school and running track. I thought that we actually had something going on. I thought that this was going to work because it felt so real. The only good thing that came out of this is that he told me now and not later.

That's exactly how many relationships and marriages go wrong. One partner's love drastically changes for the other and the feelings aren't there anymore. But because they have been together so long, it seems only right that the unhappy person stays in a relationship that he or she doesn't want to be in. I'm not congratulating Tim for breaking my heart just when I thought I had found happiness but I'm glad that he told me how he felt before my feelings got any deeper.

Well Damn, another heartbreak. I swear this makes number thirty and I'm only 19. I could seriously have a record in the Guinness book. When I go against my words, those consequences are always there to remind me. Being involve in a relationship was suppose to be the last goal to accomplish but when I met Tim, I immediately wanted him whether it was sexually ,mentally, physically or all three combined. There I was stuck and clueless on what was going to happen next in my life. I thought about giving up on men all together because with them comes so many headaches. Tim tried to soothe my pain by supposedly encouraging me. He told me not to ever look for a man. He said I should allow a man to come to me because when that happens, it's always "Heaven Sent". He was acting as if he didn't just break it off with me. I was trying to hold all of my emotions in until I got home. I was in love with him and the entire time he only wanted to be friends. I guess everything happens for a reason so I decided to remove the bad, replace it with the good and keep it pushing. My pastor once said, "Every time some one ends up in a mess, it's usually because they need something". I will take my situation for example: I am always in a mess with men so it is something that I am looking for a man to do. I feel like I need a man to complete me. I must admit that I am in a terrible state in my life, mentally. Turning to man when I need to be turning to GOD. I mean he is the only one that can fix me. Once I find the thing that I'm lacking, I can move pass this.

Chapter 11

Moving On

Sometimes I really hate coming to work dealing with these ignorant ass people in here. If a person can work in the customer service then he or she can do any job there is. Every now and again you will come across someone trying to pull a scheme. I can use today for example: this black lady walked her cheap costume jewelry, long nappy weave wearing ass to my line trying to return a stroller that she bought about three months ago. She didn't have her receipt but she wanted to return it because her son no longer needed it. I love my black people because that's who I am, but sometimes I wonder what goes on inside of their heads. I apologized about her son no longer being able to use the stroller but she had exceeded the maximum amount of days to receive a refund.

After speaking with the manager, her request was denied because it was obvious that the stroller had been used. The stroller was about thirty dollars and she gave the manager thirty dollars worth of curse words. She couldn't understand why she couldn't get her refund. As much as I wanted to stay and laugh at this woman making a complete fool out of herself, my time was up at this place. This has been a long day and I was ready to go home.

I was glad to see Chanel and Dan outside and on time. They are usually about 10-15 minutes late every time I need them to pick me up so I was very grateful because today is not my day. I have been thinking about Tim lately and I miss us hanging out. We have gone from five conversations a day to about once a week. Of course we still speak at school because we are always coincidently (so he says) running into each other but we both knew things had changed.

I figured that he had already moved on. We were still friends and I hope that it could remain that way. As much as I miss him and his personality, I think that I am missing that black, sexy body the most. My heart melted every time I rubbed my fingers across that ab-licious stomach. "OH My!" You see when I was in high school, I heard that football players are always packing but the couple of ones that I have been with were more like unpacking honey. I mean their dicks were no bigger than my hand and that ain't shit.

They didn't give me anything to work with and even when if it's not that big, you should still know how to stroke it: but hell none of them knew about that. It was only stick it in, pump pump and pull out. Now I know that the myth about football players having a big mumba jumba is not always true.

But Tim on the other hand, was different. I can see his manhood through his pants and I've even grabbed it a few times so I know that he is big but I wanted to know if he could stroke it with the motion and give one hundred percent. I was getting excited just thinking about him but I didn't say that I'm going to give any. Hell, I am barely getting a phone call out of him so sex is definitely out of the question: for now.

"Girl you and Dan were reading my mind because I was praying that y'all made it on time today." "We have to go pick up Dan's god-brother from work. But it seems like you had a long day, so we will take you home first."

"Yes I have girl and thanks for being so considerate." I'm about to take a shower and relax. I also have a taste for some Jiff cornbread so that's my dinner for tonight. I just want to chill out and calm my nerves so I will be seeing you guys tomorrow." "Well if it's ok, we were going to pick him up and bring him back over here for a while because he lives the other way in LA. I know you probably don't feel like having extra company in our room right now but Dan doesn't want to take him home just yet." "Yeah, it's whatever. Thanks for the ride and I will see y'all in a bit."

I didn't know why the taste of cornbread has been in my mouth and on my mind all day but that's the only thing I felt like eating. I took a hot steamy shower and went to lay across my bed for a minute to gather my thoughts. Sometimes that's the only thing that I need to reduce stress because after a shower, I feel like a totally different person. I felt myself drifting off to sleep so I sat up and started moving around. I tried calling my mom while I was at work but I took a nap on my break. I'm pretty sure that she is asleep but I still have to tell her good night or I wouldn't feel complete before I go to bed.

I had reached her voicemail, "Hey mom, this is Parker. I'm just getting off of work and now I'm about to make me some cornbread and don't ask me why", I laughed. I just want to tell you goodnight and I love you. Ok. I'll talk to you tomorrow, Bye."

All right here we go: I gather my eggs, milk, dough, sugar, butter and set the oven to 400 degrees. I'm always humming or singing to myself all while I'm cooking. I think it's natural to carry out a tune while waiting on your food. Now I'm not the best cook in the world because I chose to be outside instead of at home in the kitchen watching my mom cook but I do know how to feed myself and survive. Everything was mix and spread out in a greased pan. In about 20 or 25 minutes, I will have the best tasting Jiff cornbread that anyone could eat. I sat in the kitchen to enjoy the peace and quiet of the house when suddenly I hear that squeaky voice, "Parker we are back. Where you at?" So much for the peace. "I'm in the kitchen honey, what do you need?" In walked Chanel, Dan and I'm guessing his god-brother.

"Parker this is Alexander but we call him "Alex" and Alex this is Parker." Dan said. "Hi Alex, please excuse the way I look. I'm just getting in from work so these are my relaxing clothes." "It's cool; you are at home so you should be comfortable." Alex said.

First impressions are everything and this guy looks a hot ass mess. Well no I will not say a mess, he just has a little too many things going on at once. He had on a white-collar shirt that was entirely too big. He wears his hair like every other guy out here in California does and that's with jerry curls. They add some type of curl activator and gel to their hair so it can have that wet and hard look to it. (Such a tragedy) Today I noticed that he probably used too much gel because right on the neck of his collar was a brownish black line. (Still a tragedy). I really didn't stare into his eyes but when I glanced at him he appeared to be crossed-eyes. (Oh my!) He had these big ass headphones on his ears, he was using it as a wireless earpiece because it was connected to his cellular phone. They were big enough to use with a c.d. player or an i.pod but this idiot had it connected to his phone thinking that he was fly. If I tried to tell him otherwise, he probably would have bit my damn head off. I tell you the truth; these damn Californians are something else.

"Hey Alex, I'm about to be in the room if you need me. Are you straight?" Dan asked

"Yes Dan he's cool." I added. "I'm not going to hurt your brother." By the look of things, he have already hurt himself. I mumbled.

"So Parker, that is your name right?" "It is." "What you got cooking over there?" "Uh, nothing really. I've had taste for some sweet cornbread all day so I decided to cook some." I said as I took it out of the oven. "When it cools off may I taste it? It smells good." I only gave him a piece because I wanted a second opinion on how great my cornbread is.

I hope you like it but if not, just throw it away. Trust me, I won't be offended. The more I talked the more he heard my country accent. I knew it wouldn't be long before he said something about it. He told me that he has heard southern slang but it wasn't as strong as mines. He applaud me on my cornbread, either that or he was most definitely trying to score major brownie points. We started talking and the subject "Track" somehow came up. He told me that he also ran track as well as play football at Los angles Southwest Community College. He was not the cutest guy that I have seen but he seems to have a sweet spirit about him and he made me laugh a lot.

Well Alex, it was good talking to you but I'm about to go to sleep because I have another long day at work tomorrow. If you don't want to be in here by your longsome then you are more than welcomed to come in our room and crash out on the floor." "Yea that would be cool because Dan was supposed to be taking me home but he is already asleep." I gave him a pillow and we both said "Good Night."

Chapter 12

When you wake up drenched from slob: it usually means that you had some good sleep. That cornbread last night really hit the spot and I probably gained like five pounds because I ate a pan full and went to sleep. I paused for a second because I knew that I went to sleep to three people in my room last night and now it's empty. Chanel then came in the room brushing her teeth and trying to talk at the same time.

"Parker you left Alex on the floor by himself with no blanket or anything to cover up with while you slept peacefully and snored all night." "So is that why they left?"

"No Dan had to take his mom to the store and Alex had to be at work at 10:00. Well damn, what time is it?" "It's 11:30." "11:30! Are you serious? I really did sleep well."

"Yeah you were snoring all night nonstop." "Oh well that's my room too you know so if anyone had a problem with that, they could have left out including you." "Aw, look at you getting all defensive. No one was tripping, I just said that you was snoring all night. That's all Parker." "Oh well say that then. You know my blood pressure be jumping up and down honey." "So, What did you think about Alex?" "Shit, what is there to think about?" "Well do you think he is cute? He is single you know and you are too." "Chanel, don't try to play matchmaker because I wouldn't dare get into another relationship right now (Hell I am still trying to give my goodies to Tim) But seriously, Alex is a pretty cool guy. We had a lot to talk about until I got too sleepy to continue." "Well me and Dan are going to Alex's church tonight. They are having a youth service and Alex has to dance, you should come with us." "Uh no, I'll pass. Me and all the other girls have made plans to go out tonight." "Since you have gotten closer with the other girls you don't even acknowledge me anymore or invite me when y'all go out."

"Chanel, don't come to me with that shit because you know that I always ask you first and include you in on whatever is going on. Besides, you are hardly ever here. When Dan comes around he is all that matters but I don't have a problem with that because he is your man. When I ask if you want to hang out you always say, "I am going to be with Dan", so knock off whatever you are trying to start with me because you know I am right. I'm pretty sure that he is on his way over here right now and I won't see you again for about three or four days or whenever you need some more clothes.

"Yea he just texted me and said that he was down the street. We are going to the beach" "Exactly you have just proved my point." "Well you know we can't be apart too long." "Yea, yea have a good day and a wonderful night. Pray for me while you are at church and wish Alex good luck for me." I laughed, "You are making jokes before you get to know him. He is a nice and respectable guy so just give him a chance?"

"Give him a chance? You are acting as if he tried to holler at me and I turned him down. That isn't the case. He is cool but I am not trying to take it there. I don't even want a guy-friend right now because I am tired of falling for men and ending up heartbroken. Besides he does not seem like my type, well I will rephrase that: his looks does not meet my standards but his personality does." "Parker, looks are not everything. I get sick and tired of females judging guys on their looks before they could give that person a chance and that's not fair to them."

"Chanel, guys do the same thing when it comes down to females: It's natural. If a dude tried to approach you looking all busted, are you going to give him a chance? NO because a first impression is what a person sticks with and remember. My friend you are right, looks are not everything because I have dated some fine brothers and they have turned out to be DOGS. I at least need something to work with. I want to have kids one day and I can't be giving birth to aliens honey. That's not going to work at all. Now don't get me wrong, I'm not saying Alex is busted but he just didn't catch my eye at first. We can be friends if that's cool with him but I am good on that girlfriend boyfriend thing." "Well alright, you said what you had to say. My baby is outside so I will see you later." "Bye girl."

I'm home, by myself, once again. However, I look at it as a good thing because I go to work today and I need some time to myself. I wish I could lean on my parents for my finances but that is out of the question. But why is that? They want to teach us how to be responsible and to let us know that nothing in life is free. My parents' favorite line, "If you want something, you have to work for it." Yadda yadda yadda. All I'm saying is that if you have it then spread a little love to your child. I don't think it's fair that I have to go to school, run track and work. My only focus right now should be to get my degree and run track: not dealing with stupid customers every day. However, I do love the paychecks every two weeks and all the money I receive because that goes to me and only me. I am pretty blessed right now so I won't complain about having a job though I still think that parents should provide us with our needs and wants until we at least turn 21. I could say that my parents, which includes my Mom, Dad, Step-mom, Step-dad didn't give me exactly everything that I wanted while in high school but they did a hell of a job providing me with my needs. They really did prepare me for the world after high school. My mom said that I was a woman now so I have to start acting like one. I couldn't call home every day with every single problem that I had. I couldn't whine and complain about life or how at times it feels like everyone is against me. I have to stand up for myself because my parents could no longer do so.

The professors don't play that shit either. If you are late, trying to clown around in class or failing your work, they are not going call you to the side and say, "I've noticed that you are slacking a little and if you need a little extra help just let me know". If you don't go to class they could care less so it's your responsibility to get up and go.

I had to learn that on my own because I didn't take it to serious when I first arrived here. I was finally feeling free from my parents and loving the independent life. I no longer had any curfews and there was no more checking in and telling lies about where I was. I am now experiencing that fun college life that everyone talks about. This is all new to me and I want to see it all. I know that I am still immature when it comes to certain things such as love, men, spending money wisely and not taking my work as serious as I should. But I am only 19 years old so what do you expect. Its hard trying to get through a 19 year olds head (whether it's a girl or boy) because being free from his or her parents' throne is exciting and it's new.

Life is full of temptations that we all want to experience. It's sad to say but unless something terrible happens to us such as getting pregnant or going to jail, we are going to continue to party and do whatever we want because that's the dream life of a teenager especially when there are no parents jumping down our backs. I have grown some but I still have a long way to go and I'm in no rush to actually grow up right now.

Speaking of maturing and taking responsibilities, I have to be at work in two hours and I am catching the bus today so I have to leave earlier than normal. Mike and Keziah are working and Dan and Chanel are on their way to church so the bus it is. It usually takes an hour on a bus but in a car it's only fifteen to twenty minutes to get to my job. I hate asking and depending on other people to do things for me. It irritates the hell out of me. At the beginning, things are cool but after a while people get tired of being nice and going out of their way to help you. I really need a car so I should definitely think about putting that on the top of my "Things to accomplish list" because this whole catching the bus thing is not for me.

CHAPTER 13

Theft

I'm only working 4 til 9:30 today so thank God for that. My job is laid back but every so often, a customer or employee brings out the bitch in me and then I am not as friendly. But on most days it's cool and sometimes goes by in a breeze. I arrived at work fifteen minutes early so I decided to go ahead and clock in. As I swiped my badge, things felt different. It was very gloomy outside from the rain earlier this morning and as I looked around, none of the co-workers that I laugh and joke around with is working today.

It wasn't as busy, which is a first. I thought, "Today would be a great day for some drama", such as someone getting caught stealing and trying to get away from the police, or an employee being fired or even a loud, rude and upset customer going on and on how she demands to see the manager. Still it was nothing. I even thought about calling Anesha up here to steal me some more clothes and other miscellaneous items.

I let her do it once before and we ended up with over three hundred dollars in stolen merchandise. She was able to get me jewelry, workout clothes, a few casual clothes and about two purses. Stealing isn't appropriate but why pay for something when you can get it for free? But it's easier for her to come on our busier days because our secret shopper wouldn't know exactly who to keep an eye on. Hell, the process went along so smooth that I was sure that she had stolen before. You never know with her because she is a little schemer. I bet she stole all sorts of stuff in Texas. I think I played it off smooth as well.

(I had her to wait until every employee had a customer before she came to my line to check out because if not, they would have called her to their lines and our plan would have been a no-go. Once I noticed that every employee including myself had at least one customer, I gave her the signal to come to my line. I then treated her as a normal customer and started the transaction by greeting her and asking if she found everything ok today.

Of course her response was "Yes I found everything that I was looking for." I said to myself, "I bet you did with all of the shit you have at this register." I started ringing up one item and placing about five or six items in the bags. I tried not to look around as much or have the word "Guilty" written all over my face even though I was terrified of being caught.

While Anesha stood there cool and collect with not one care in the world, there my ass was sweating, shaking and trying to move as fast I could before another customer walked up to my line and caught me putting free items in these bag. "Ok ma'am, your total today is 267.42." I had to call out a fake price because if I had said the real price (which was only 8.52 dollars for about fifteen bags full of shit) someone would have been questioning me. I told her before she came to pay with a debit or credit card since I didn't ring everything up.

I knew the total was going to be extremely low so handing me a ten-dollar bill for everything that she stole would not have been a good look. I gave her the receipt and told her to have a nice day, just as I would have done any other customer.

Our mission was not yet completed. She had to make it through the doors before I quietly did the victory dance. I spotted Mrs. Wallace (the door greeter) heading towards the door. This old ass woman looks for every item on the receipt. She really does take her work seriously. Anesha was on her way to the door also, so I had to think of something quick so she could turn around and Mrs. Wallace would not be able to read the receipt.

I had to get her attention and tell her to go through the mall entrance because at this moment, no one was standing over there checking baskets or receipts. "Quick Parker! Think." I said to myself as I grabbed a customer complaint card.

"Excuse me ma'am." I yelled. "Is your name Anesha?" She turned around with the biggest shock on her face. Her facial expression read, "Parker, what in the hell are you doing?" She said, "Yes, my name is Anesha." With my eyes, I told her to follow my lead. "You left your debit card at my counter" "Parker what are you doing?" she whispered, "I'm trying to get your ignorant ass out of here.

That woman at the front door checks receipts to make sure that every item in your bag is on your receipt so go through the mall entrance and get the hell out of here."

I can still remember inhaling and exhaling when she made it through those doors and the alarm didn't go off. I was even happier when she text me saying that she had made it out. (It felt as if we had just robbed a bank or something)

I was happy and disappointed in myself because my parents taught me better than that. I grew up on the saying "If you don't have enough money to buy it then don't touch it because most likely, you don't really need it" I felt guilty every time I wore something that Anesha stole for me that day. I know that stealing is a very awful thing to do but deep down I wanted to do it again. I was thinking that since I got away with it the last time that I could easily get away with it again but I can't. I wouldn't be able to live with myself.

"Parker! Snap out of it. What are you daydreaming about? You are supposed to be working or looking like you are doing some kind of work. You can take your fifteen minute break now." That was Ronald (the front-end manager.) He is the man over all of the cashiers and the coolest manager in the store. He is also a sexy lil something but he is too old for me and he is a newlywed. He doesn't trip on the small things so I decided to take an extra ten minutes to drop a load off in this good ole restroom and enjoy me a cup of coffee before I head back out to the floor.

Now if you are not constipated this could be a very relaxing time. I outlined the toilet rim with tissue and sat down. I then heard: BANG, BANG! Some strange person is hitting my door as if they wanted to come in. It is four more stalls available so whoever it is could easily walk to another one. The main door closes so I'm guessing they went out.

Whoever it was really gained my attention. My break is almost over and I didn't accomplish anything in here. When I walked out the stall, there stood two stiff bodies dressed in all black from head to toe and their face is covered with a mask. They literally scared the shit out of me. Then one said, "I know you are wondering why we are here. You must understand that we are not here to hurt you Parker. We are here to rob the store and we are coming to your register to do it."

I tried to scream for help but one of them had his arm in the coat. I assume that he is carrying a gun. I wanted to run but I knew that I wouldn't be able to move two inches before they would stop me. How did he know my name and how did he know that I was in the bathroom?

"We have been watching this store and have noticed that you are the newest cashier so it's only right that we choose you."

I have to catch the bus home tonight so I don't want to give them a reason to sit and wait on me outside. They did say that they have been watching me. They also knew that I was a new employee so that along let me knew that they already had too much of my personal information.

"I want you to listen closely because I am only going to say this once. You will walk out of this restroom and go back to your register. My brother and I will only be a few feet behind. You will open your register, give us everything in it and we will walk off with no one getting hurt."

I know that the manager is going to roll the camera back to see exactly what happened and when they did so, they are going to see me giving the robbers money and without any questions ,I would be fired and most likely in jail. I couldn't do that so I had to think of something before I went back to my register and quick.

"Parker do not mess this up for us. We both have guns and don't have a problem with using them but we'd prefer not to. Now again I will tell you how this is going to work. You will walk back to your register as if nothing is wrong. You will keep the same smile and act as you normally would.

We will come to your line; you will empty out your cash register and give us every dollar you have." I asked, "How will I take other customers? What if they would like change back?" "That's not our problem. You will have to figure all of that out once we are out of the store."

How in the hell am I going to pull this off. I am so scared. I didn't have a clue how I was going to get out of this nightmare. It was obvious that they already had this planned out.

Maybe, I could go along with their plan and go straight to a manager once I leave out the restroom. But what if they catch me doing it? From the looks of things, they have been following me for a while now. This can't be happening. This is something that you see in the movies. I would have ever thought in a million years that I would be in this type of predicament.

Ok here is what I have to do. They said that they were going to wait a few minutes and then come to my register. Therefore, once I leave out I will act normal as they said. There is always a Team Leader in the front by the cashiers at all times. They are there to give out breaks and to assist us with any problems that we have. My life was on the line so I had to tell someone. I must go straight to Melinda (the Team leader) and let her know what is about to happen. I had to be quick with it because I know that the two mystery men are coming soon.

"Melinda! I don't have much time but I was just pinned down in the restroom by two guys dressed in all black. They said that they are about to come to my register and hold me at gunpoint until I give them all of the money I have. They also told me not to go to anyone with this information because they have guns and are not afraid to use them. Please Melinda you have to help me because I am afraid and I do not know what to do.

They said that they have been watching me.' "Parker please calm down. Where are they? Do they know you? Why are you just now coming back from your break?" "Are you fucking serious right now? I'm telling you that there are two guys that is about to rob this damn store and you have the audacity to ask ignorant ass questions right now. You need to help me because my life is on the line and so is this store."

"Ok this is what you have to do: Walk over to your register and go along with their plan. I will go get the store security and call the police. Do not worry; I will take care of this." She said

I felt like fainting right there on the floor. I trembled with every step I took because I don't know what is about to happen. I am so nervous because they specifically told me not to mention a word to anyone and I went against their word. What if the men saw me talking to Melinda? What if I have just ruined everything? I didn't hear any sirens nor did I see any sight of security in the store. This is all bad. I was just wishing earlier that I could see some kind of drama to make my day go by faster but this was the last thing that I wanted to happen. I guess you should be careful on what you wish for or in this case, never wish for it all.

Before I could prepare myself for what is about to come, the two mystery men were already in my line. "Parker just as planned, grab these bags and fill them up." I grabbed the bags and started to throw the money is as fast as I could. I only had about eight hundred dollars in my drawer but definitely no more than that. I can't believe that these two men was doing all of this for only a little amount of money. I still didn't see Melinda nor the cops.

I hope that ignorant woman didn't think I was joking around because I wasn't. I continued to fill the bags but I became more and more nervous as the seconds flew by. Suddenly, about five cops came from behind the men, threw their heads down on the floor and read them their rights. I looked up and the whole store is now filled with cops. I am happy that no one got hurt but even happier that they were caught.

"Parker you are a brave young lady and if you didn't step up and tell someone when you did, the store would have been short on money and you may have gotten hurt by these thieves." A cop said. "I'm just happy that it's over but are they going to be able to get out on bail? Now that I have turned them in, they may try to come back and harm me." "No! Bail is not an option. I think these are the same men that have been stealing from the other stores. If they are, I will make sure that stay behind bars for a very long time." "The show is over everyone. Let's get these men out of here. Thank you Parker, you pulled a brave move in a short period of time.

    I can't describe the feeling I felt when the police escorted those men out of the store. I felt so relieved that this whole incident was over. I wanted to call my mom but it's too late in Mississippi so I'm sure that she is asleep . I didn't need to wake her with this news because she will be worried all night especially if she knew I had to catch the bus.

    "Parker I know that you are probably a bit shaken up from everything that you have experience tonight so I want you to leave early and you will get paid for it. It's only about thirty minutes until 9:30 so you really won't miss too much time." The manager said.

    I took the offer and clocked out because I definitely do not have any energy left. Ok people, I will see you Monday because I'm off tomorrow and Sunday. I have to make it to this bus before 9'o clock because that's the last one for the night." "Uh Parker its about five minutes until 9 now so you need to get a move on it." Melinda said. "Yea you're right. Bye you guys."

CHAPTER 14

First Date with Alex

From the sound of things, Chanel woke up in a happy mood because she is up singing and tugging at my blanket. Beside the fact that it's too early for excitement, I am not in a playful mood.

"Parker! Parker! Roll over and wake up. It's a new day so it's time to try new things."

I said to her in the nicest way that I knew how. "Chanel, I am going to say this one time and one time only. I don't have to pull the covers off of my head because you can hear me loud and clear. I had a crazy night and now I have a migraine so I am sorry if I come off as a bitch this morning but I am not in the mood for your cheerfulness right now."

"Girl I could care less about what you are not in the mood for. Its' going on 11:30 and you need to wake your lazy ass up: besides I have some interesting news that you may want to hear. It's about Anesha and what she got caught doing yesterday. However, since you are so upset and have this terrible headache, then I won't tell you."

Before she could finish her sentence I sat up as quick as I could because I'm always up for some news honey. I don't care if it's late at night or early in the morning. What happened last night was over and like she said, this is a new day and a day that starts with gossip is always a good day for me.

"Girl What Happened? Tell me please because I'm all ears. Did she get caught by that dude from Mt.Sac or was it that dude from Cerritos? I knew her ass would get caught while she was walking around like she some Top Notch Bitch. I tell you, when it comes to Whores: They never win. "Look at you" Chanel said. "You are so damn messy. Just a few seconds ago you was acting like a bitch but when I tell you I have info, you hop your ass up with no problem." "You damn right." Now tell me what you heard."

"Sorry to be the one to tell you this but I didn't hear anything. I knew that would be the only way to get you out of the bed and that's so sad." "Well, it worked. I hate being last on drama so I wanted to know something. Anyway, I got your ass. What are you up to today besides being Dan's shadow?" "Parker, don't do that but I'm glad you asked because me and Dan had this idea. Alex does not have to work tonight and neither do you so we were thinking that you know…" "Uh, you know what? Do not invite me to go anywhere because the answer is NO."

"Parker don't act like that. It's not like we are trying to set you up on a blind date. It's more like a double date because Dan and I will be there as well. You should be more open to life and the beautiful things that awaits you outside of this house and away from your job."

"Yea Chanel whatever. I will go but you can kill the" expand your horizons" speech. For a heads up, the next time you and Dan feel like playing matchmaker, include me in on the idea first so I can tell you, Hell No. Y'all better be glad that I don't have anything else to do tonight. After last night, I need some kind of excitement in my life. Anyway, what time are we leaving and where are we going. I need some details honey if I am going to be doing volunteer work."

"Girl whatever. You don't need any details. We are leaving around five because I want to eat at the Bub Gump's restaurant and take a stroll at the Pier. Parker, he really is a nice person so go on this date and see how things work out. I also heard through a reliable source that he strives for long-term relationships so that should tell you that he is not a player. One date is all I ask and then you can kick him to the curve or do whatever you please but give him a chance and try to make the best out of this even if you are not having a good time."

"I said that I would go but if yo ass keep pressuring me then I will change my mind so let me be. I need three or four more hours of sleep since I was just waken up out of mines. You said that we are leaving around five so if you could wake me up at 3:30, I would highly appreciate it. Good day." "I'm headed to the store to find me something to wear so I'll see you later on."

As I lay down to rest my eyes for a couple of hours, I start to think about Alex. Why am I giving this date thing such a hard time? I am over Tim and there isn't anything stopping me from dating. My problem is that I am still wishing for something that I just could not have. I laughed because a singer once told me a while back that "It be's that way sometimes." Tim and I will only be friends so I have to deal with that.

"Parker! Parker."

Damn, if this girl calls me one more time as if she has lost her mind while I am sleep then something very dreadful is going to happen in this room. "What Chanel?" "Its 3:33 so that means you overslept. You already know how long it takes you to get ready so get up. You should be well rested by now because you haven't did shit."

I want to be positive about this situation so I sat up and began to make a move. What am I going to wear? The first and last time he saw me I was just getting home from a long day of work and in my pajamas so that wasn't such a good first impression. I will most definitely make up for that tonight: but with what? I wanted to be comfortable and sexy but the only thing that is in my closet and fits into both of those two categories is this blue jean tube top jumpsuit. It fits in all the right spots making it very sexy and appealing and I can wear a nice pair of flip-flops to give me that comfort that I need. I can see it now. He is going to be squirming in his seat with this fit.

I was fresh out of the shower with the sweet scent of Luxurious Spell body wash all over me. I am starting to get excited about this date after all and I haven't really kicked it with him like that. I have maybe talked to him once or twice on the phone but for the most part, we text the world's famous text "Hey, What u doing." Maybe I could learn some new things about Alex tonight and that way we will feel more comfortable around one another.

"Parker, Dan just text me and said they were outside. Are you ready?" "Yea here I come."

I was dressed and ready but I never leave the house without looking in the mirror from the front, the side and the back. I have to make sure that the face is beautiful; my stomach is still flat and that the ass is sticking out. Once the checklist was completed, I grabbed my purse and we headed out of the door.

With every step that I took toward the car, I started to wish that I didn't agree to this. I wasn't in the mood anymore. I wanted to take my lazy ass back in the house and go to sleep. As I contemplated on getting in the car or going back inside: I hear Chanel baby talking ass voice say, "Hey Alex, you remember Parker from the other night?" "Yes Chanel. You are acting like we haven't been communicating, even though it's been mostly through a text message."

I actually didn't tell her that we had been texting because the conversations are always dry so it really wasn't anything to brag about. As much as I didn't want this to happen, I put a smile on my face and shook off the many negative thoughts I had.

"Hey Alex. It's good seeing you again. Oh. Hi Dan. You know that we don't get along all of the time so don't act all friendly in front of company." "Hello Parker."

While Alex's first impression wasn't all that great, He is looking kind of handsome tonight. He still had those curls that I oh so hated but this time his fit was on point. I am starting to get hipped to the way that the guys dress out here. It really confused me at first because I was seeing dudes with skinny leg jeans, shirts as tight as mines, and these skateboard looking shoes.

I was thinking every guy that I saw dressing like that was straight up GAY: But in most cases that was not true. While down south in Mississippi, I was so used to the sagging of the pants, the Jordan or Nike tennis shoes and a white t-shirt that is always about three sizes to big but I really love this change in environment. Alex has on a white and black polo shirt and a pair of dark blue jeans that were tucked into his...HOLD UP!

I was startled. I know damn well that this boy do not have his pants tucked into his white ass socks. Oh my, he does. You see, that is exactly what I was talking about. They have their own way of dressing out here. I was about to give him his props because he was looking spiffy until I looked down at those feet honey. No sir, that is not going to work. I can't believe that I am about to actually be seen with him and those socks. I didn't know if I should scream or jump out of the car. I blinked twice, wiped my eyes and they were still there. but then again, many guys do the same thing so maybe it wouldn't be too bad. Everything else was fresh so I'll at least give him an 8 tonight with the exception of those pants and socks that may have my attention all night.

"Parker, are you ok? You looked as if something is bothering you." Alex asked. Trying my hardest not to burst out with laughter I replied, "No, I'm fine. If I can keep my eyes on him and not those shoes, then I will be ok. "So, Alex tell me something about yourself. What do you like to do?"

Before he could answer, Dan said, "We are here now so you two lovebirds will have to save that conversation for your one on one time because it's time to eat." That damn boy really irks me at times. He reminds me of my younger brother and that's a bad thing when you are twenty years old.

As I reach towards the door handle on the car, Alex says, "Don't you dare open that door! I'm your date so let me take on all of those responsibilities. You seem a little uptight so I have to get you to loosen up. You look very nice tonight and I would love for you to have a good time. But before we go, I would like to make a bet." "A bet?" I asked. What kind of bet?" "If you enjoy yourself tonight: we do this again tomorrow but it will only be the two of us. However, if this becomes one of the most boring times in your life: you can feel free not to ever speak to me again and you can go on with your life and pretend as if you never met me.

Do we have a deal?" I couldn't believe that he was making a deal with me. Is my negative energy that noticeable? Ok, I can do this. Besides, I'm sure that is will be a terrible night so I won't have to see or hear from him ever again. That is what he said. So I agreed, "Uh, Ok. I guess." "Cool, let us go then."

Chapter 15

The Hoe Move

I think this is the first time that I have ever waken up before 9'o clock in the morning when I didn't have to go to work. But hey, that's what a night full of fun will do to you. I had an amazing time last night with Alex. I seriously did not want to come home.

(We had a never-ending conversation that started from our interests and ended with us sharing secrets. I was able to be myself around him a little too much that it almost scared me. It was like a picture perfect movie. The "Bub Gump Shrimp House" was the best restaurant that I have eaten at and I have eaten at quite a few places. He said that I could order whatever I wanted because he was paying for everything. I had my own money just in case his ass was cheap. I wanted to go after those crab legs so bad but I was trying to be cute and there is no way that I could have eaten crab legs cute, so I went for the shrimp and fries: Something that was tasty but not too messy.

After we ate, we went and sat on the beach and all I could remember hearing was the soothing sound of the waves and his sexy voice. The winds were high so I could feel my hair flowing in every direction. As we continued to sit there engaging in conversation, he slowly pulled off my sandals and began to massage my feet. He asked if he was taking me too fast and I told him "No, not at all." Besides, I will never turn down a massage. This date did not go how I intended it. I only went to get out of the house and to shut Chanel's mouth but I was blown away with all of the fun that I had. We held hands while we walked alongside the beach. He even offered to hold my shoes so I could feel the sand go through my toes with every step that we took.

At the end of the night he said, "So Parker, now is the moment of truth. Did you have a good time tonight or was it just a waste? Before you answer, I would like to tell you that I had an amazing time. Once you opened up and let your guard down, everything just came natural. I could see us hanging out often. I would like for us to go on another date but either way, I will respect your decision."

I couldn't say no to this guy even if I wanted to. He didn't have to try and push so hard for me to have a good time because like he said, everything came natural with us. He looked deep into my eyes the entire night. He mentioned that whenever he talks to someone, he have to look them in their eyes because he feels that we are no longer slaves so we shouldn't look down or away from the person that we are talking to. (That is definitely a bad habit that I have. I can't look anyone in their eyes and that is because my confidence is not at the level where it should be.) He made me look into his eyes the entire night and that meant a lot to me. It confirmed to me that he could be trusted and that he likes me.

"Um, I'm waiting on my answer. What's it going to be?" He asked.

"Well this date was quite interesting so if you are asking me if I would like to do this again..., I would have to say most definitely yes. Alex, I had a wonderful time! "Are you doing anything tomorrow?" he proudly said, "My schedule is open, let me take you out, just the two of us".

He was ecstatic , basically acting as if I said yes to marrying him. I could really tell that he was interested but so was I. As we stood there holding hands, we discussed how we did not want this night to end. I wanted to reach over to give him a kiss but I wasn't sure if this was perfect timing. I mean, I could tell that he was feeling me but kissing on the first date may be a bit too much.

As soon as I erased that idea out of my head, he turned my face to his and said, "I hope that I am not overstepping my boundaries but I have wanted to do this all night." He then leaned over towards my face. Then with our lips being only about an inch away from touching, I heard the most unpleasant voice ever. "Hey y'all, we ready to go. I have football practice in the morning."

I couldn't believe what just happened. "Are you serious?" I know you did not just ruin the kiss that I was seconds away from enjoying. Damn you Dan. Damn you. I bet his ass knows how to ruin a wet dream. "So much for that. My brother sort of came at the wrong time but it's all good because maybe it wasn't meant for us to share a kiss tonight. Our time will

Fell Too Deep

come and it will be so perfect that no one will able to ruin it." He handed me my shoes and we walked off.

Once we arrived back to the house, he opened my door, walked me to my room and gave me a hug. He told me that he was excited about our second date and made me promise that I would not stand him up.)

So yea, that was our night. I must say that it ended on a good note. Now I'm sitting here on the edge of my bed bored and ready to go. My dad is coming today so we can hang out and go and eat.

I really love when my dad and I have father/daughter time. He is such a comedian and swears up and down that he and Samuel L. Jackson have the same features. If we are in the mall, he will have me say "Oh my gosh, is that Samuel L. Jackson?" and then people will look around as if the actor was really there. We sit back and quote different scenes from our favorite TVs shows and movies.

"Hello my favorite daughter" my dad said as if I had another sister. "Daddy! It's almost two o' clock, where are you?" "I'm pulling up, the freeway was crowded. Are you ready to go because I'm very hungry?" "As a matter of fact, I am too." "Ok and bring all of your dirty clothes. I am going to take you to a laundry mat so you can wash them. I would take you to your grandma's house but she just left with Mrs.Francis, they are headed to the casino." "Ok, that's fine. I'm just glad that you said something because I would have went another week without washing my clothes." "Do you need any help?" "Nah I can manage." "Well I'm outside." "Ok, I'm on my way out."

I am always happy when my dad comes to visit. I just love to be around him because he always has something crazy to say to make me laugh. I could tell by the look in his eyes that he is very proud of me. I would absolute hate to let my mom or my dad down. They have a lot of trust in me so I am basically doing all of this for them. My plans are to finish school, obtain my degree and make as much money as I possible can so they would never have to work another day in their life. I have big plans and dreams and I am not going to stop until I have fulfilled them all.

We ate lunch at this famous fish restaurant (Louise's House) out here on the west coast. The name will make you think that it is black owned but actually it is owned by a Chinese couple: Very strange because some may question, what could Chinese people possibly know about fish, especially fried but I had to give them their props because the food is great.

I always cherish the times I spend with my dad because due to his work schedule and me juggling track, school and work, we hardly get to spend a day with each other but today and at this time, my mind is elsewhere. I have been thinking about Alex all day. Of course, we have been texting and talking on the phone for most of the day but I was ready to see him again. My dad kept telling me to get off the phone but I couldn't.

Alex is at work bored and he wants to get off so that he can come and hang with my dad and me. I stopped him right in his tracks because this is not the time for him to meet my pops. He is cool but meeting the parents this early is a big No, especially my dad. He will interrogate the shit out of someone." What are your intentions? Who are your parents and where were they born?" I'm like daddy enough with all of that. He thinks he knows everyone in the United States. Anyway, I was reminiscing about last night and started to get excited about tonight. He wasn't sure as to where we should go but I told him that I didn't care as long as we could chill the way we did last night.

It was getting time for my daddy to leave and every time that happens, he tends to move and drive slower than normal. I know we have a lot of fun together and sometimes we don't want our night to come to an end but unfortunately tonight I was ready to go back home. I am done with my last load of clothes and I noticed that Alex had not called back to let me know exactly what we were going to do. I started to think that I had been stood up because it was now 7:30 and he gets off at 8:30 so I didn't know what to think. Maybe I was too excited and was jumping the gun too early.

My dad sighed as we pulled into my driveway "Ok, you are back at home and now I have to go. Is it me or did this visit go by very quickly?" "Yea somewhat, but you are acting as if I am in prison or something. I am only an hour away and maybe I can come out to you guys house next week or the week after instead of you driving over here all of the time.

You know it will be so cool if I had a car and that way I could see y'all all the time." "Oh please girl. You can get a car when you save up enough money to buy one and besides, you don't have your license yet so you can erase that thought out of your head for right now. But if you get a car, you will not come and see us, so don't lie. We will probably see you like once every two or three months." "Now daddy you know that I will not do that to y'all," I said as I gave a fake grin. "Yea ok, we will see. But let me get out of here before your mom starts to miss me. I love you and I'll call you tomorrow." "Ok, love you too and tell ma that I said hey."

I grabbed my clothes out of the car and waved good-bye as he drove off. I always hate when my dad leaves but not so much right now. The only thing that was on my mind was getting in this house; taking a bath and chilling with Alex before another long day of work tomorrow. When I walked in the house, I went straight towards my bedroom. Anesha has company in the living room and I didn't stop to speak simply because I'm not obligated to besides, speaking is not my primary focus at the moment.

I am worried because Alex hasn't called me back with more information about tonight. Before I could even make it to my room: I can hear Chanel arguing with Dan over the phone about playing a game or something. I started contemplating on whether I should sort all of my clean clothes now or wait until tomorrow to do it. Somehow, I always have the hardest time deciding on the smallest things. But, I knew if I didn't do it right then that I would never do it.

"Why are you at home? I thought you and Alex was going on a second date tonight." Chanel said "Didn't I just hear you yelling at Dan? You just went from being loud and ghetto to calm and collect. I swear sometimes I think you have major mood swings and that really needs fixing. Anyway, I'm waiting on him to get back with me to let me know what we are doing tonight. Why were you and Dan arguing as if I wasn't already ear hustling."

"Because all he do is sit around and play that damn video game with his brothers. He would rather do that than to go somewhere with me." "Oh wait, Alex is calling me so hold that thought."

"Hello," I said trying to sound peaceful and as if I haven't been waiting on his phone call." "Hey what's up? I have a change of plans tonight but I wanted to make sure it was cool with you first." He said

I hope that he is not about to tell me that he can't come tonight. I knew this was too good to be true. There I was rushing along my father and daughter date with my dad and get home to him telling me that something came up and he is not going to be able to come.

"What's the change?" "Well I'm still at work because we are busy due to the Thanksgiving and Christmas holidays that are coming up. They have us working overtime so I will be here another thirty minutes to an hour. I was wondering if I could just come over and chill with you instead of us going out somewhere because I had a long day at work and you have to work in the morning. I went and rented a couple of new releases and I could stop and get you something to eat if you are hungry."

Even though we aren't going anywhere tonight, I am relieved. I got all worked up thinking that he was going to stand me up. I knew that there was something different about this guy. If it was any other dude that was just getting off of work: he will want to go home and go to sleep but not Alex. I realized that he was willing to do whatever he had to do just to make me happy.

"Yes, that will be good because I'm just getting home myself. I'm still putting my clothes up and I have to take a bath so just call me once you are off." "Ok Parker, see you in a minute."

"Ok Chanel back to you. Oh he says my name so sexy. P-A-R-K-E-R I could see his lips now honey. Woo, It sends a shiver through my spine. I didn't mean to cut you off just now but I was trying to see what was up with him. Unfortunately, we are going to have to finish chatting in a minute because I have to go get in the tub. "Yea whatever, when you want to talk about Alex or whoever, I will make sure that I'm busy as well." She said

Usually, I will sit down and listen to her problems because she listens to mines but during this whole day, my mind has only been on Alex and now I am trying to get myself together as well as clean my room before he gets here. I walked into the bathroom first to see if anyone was in there or if anyone had left it dirty and surprisingly, the coast was clear and spotless. It's so many females in this house so the only way to be fair is to call out for your turn in the bathroom and if you are not in there at that time or if you woke up late then you are out of luck. It's crazy because every other time I really need the bathroom, someone is in there or next in line but tonight I was able to get in. I started the water and prepared myself for this hot and bubbly bath. I will normally take a shower but I wanted to soak and relax tonight.

My phone rang from the other room but I didn't get it. I am already in the bathroom so whoever it is will have to wait. I knew it wasn't Alex because he had his own ring tone.

As I look in the mirror and undress my self slowly, I start to fantasize about Tim. I haven't spoken to him in a few days but for some reason, I want him. I wonder what would happen if he were standing here with me while I'm in total nude. What will he do to me and how will he do it? I already have it pictured in my head.

He would start down at my feet rubbing his hands up my legs, to my inner thighs and then up to my ass squeezing it as hard as he possibly could. He would then start too slowly but passionately kiss my lips. From there I could see myself throwing him on the floor and having my way on top of him by riding him very slow and making sure, I don't miss a

Fell Too Deep

beat. I don't know what it is. I have never wanted anyone this bad. I want to call and ask him if he would like to engage in a wonderful yet lustful one-night stand.

But I can't. Hell, like I said, we have not communicated in a long time. I still can't understand how our communication became so dry towards one another. After he broke it off with me, he didn't waste any time. He stops talking to me and move on without thinking twice about how badly he hurt me. Hell who am I kidding; he doesn't deserve these goodies anyway. So, I killed that fantasy.

As I place one foot in the tub, I hear my phone ring again. Whoever it is must have an emergency so I grabbed my robe and went to go get it. Instead of my phone being on the charger, where I left it, it was in Chanel's hand. "Why in the hell do you have my phone in your hands?" "Girl Tim has been blowing you up for the pass five minutes. Girl I wonder want he wants." You already know I had to get smart with her ass for going through my damn phone. "Well you know if he wanted you to know, I'm thinking that he would have called or texted your phone."

But I was just as curious as she was because he has never called me back to back like this. "Chanel, I am going to take this in the bathroom so I can try and finish my bath. I will let you know what happened when I get out." "Ok but hurry up because you know I'm nosey."

I notice that Tim sent me three texts messages. The first one said what's up? How u been," the second read "Did you get my message?" and finally "R u there?"

Damn, I got out of tub for this shit. I thought that maybe something major had happened by the way that my phone was going off. But since I had just mesmerized about having sex with him, I decided to play a game, you know: tease him a little bit. So I text him back, "My bad, I'm in the tub and my fingers were a little busy: if u know what I mean." Normally it takes him forever to send something back but not this time. I couldn't help but laugh when I saw his response. "Now Parker u know u need 2 have someone doing that 4 u and even more." It seems like he is volunteering to satisfy me so I am all for it.

"Tim, we both know that u r not ready 4 me. Right now u only want 2 be friends but once I put it on u, u will want to make me your wife." As I waited for his response I thought about how good it is now days that we have the ability to text because I could not have said these exact same words over the phone or face to face. He responded, "Damn u get down like that? Well let me come get you. You talking but I want to know if u can hold up." "K, that's what's up but let me finish cleaning my body and I will call you when I'm ready and don't chicken out on me Mr. Tim." "Oh no, never that. Just call me when u ready because I am about 2 leave now and just chill ova my home boy crib. He lives down the street from your house." "Ok"

I cleaned my body twice because I had to make sure that my girl was extra fresh. As I dried off, my light bulb came on. Oh My Fucking Gosh. What have I done? I was too busy running off at the mouth and so caught up with this fantasy about Tim and I having sex that I totally forgot about Alex. Damn! I want to chill with Alex but I will love to finally fuck Tim. I need a lie to tell Alex but it has to be convincing. I'm terrible at lying but that chick in my room is the best. She can lie her ass off and can make it sound so real.

I rushed out of the bathroom and into our room with my body still wet and my towel hanging halfway off of me. "Girl what the hell is wrong with you?" "Chanel I need you. I just pulled a foul move, well more of a hoe move. "What now?" "I just told Tim that......Well basically he is about to come get me so we have sex but, that's not the best part. Alex is about to get off work in like five minutes. We are suppose to be chilling tonight here at the house. Who should I be with, what should I do? Well, let me rephrase that, what should I tell Alex because I am most definitely about to leave with Tim." "Parker that is wrong on so many levels but it's obvious that you have your mind made up." "Yes I do so are you going to help me out or what?" "Well um, just tell Alex that your grandma is sick. Go on about how you are the nearest relative and that everyone has called and told you to sit with her until your uncle or someone comes in the morning to take her to the doctor. "Damn, you good. I couldn't have came up with anything better. Now shut the hell up while I call him."

As I dialed his number, I could hear Chanel over there on her bed mumbling under her breath about how wrong I am. I know that this is not right but I can't help myself. I am going with my head and not my heart. I feel terrible but I know that this could be my only chance to have sex with Tim. Yes, it's all lust but it's good lust. At least I'm not about to go and fuck some random person. I can't pass this up. I haven't had sex since Dallas and that was earlier this summer.

Alex finally answered after six rings: "Hey I'm about to get off so ill be on my way in a few minutes." He said. As much as I hated to do it, I had to. "Well I hate to tell you this but something just came up. My grandma is sick and I have to stay the night with her since I am the closest relative. My uncle is supposed to be coming by in the morning to take her to the doctor. I am so sorry and if you want, you could come over to my grandma's house for a while and hang out." (I only offered because I knew he was going to say no. If he would have said Yes, I would have been screwed.) "No, that's not necessary. Take care of her and we can always get together another time. But if you could, call me when you get there and get situated." "Ok Alex, thanks for understanding." We both said "bye" and that was it.

After I heard how disappointed he was, I began to have second thoughts, but not for long. I phoned Tim within the next two minutes to tell him to come and get me. Since he was only right down the street, I quickly lotion my body so my skin will feel silky smooth and smell powder fresh.

Finally he text me and said that he was outside. He parked on the side of the house because I didn't want Nene nosey ass in my business. "Ok Chanel. I'm out of here and if you are not here when I get back then I will provide you with detail by detail in the morning just the way you like it." "You damn right! She laughed." Have fun." "I will. Bye"

I spot him as soon as I walk out of the house but this ignorant ass boy starts to honk his horn as if he is insane.

"What the hell is wrong with you? I don't want people to know that I'm leaving with you." He starts to laugh like the shit is funny. It was obvious that he wanted the girls in the house to know what was about to go down but you know how guys are: they love to show off when they are about to have sex and just like women, they love to brag afterwards. "Tim that shit wasn't cool at all." "Parker get in the car and calm down. It was only a joke but damn, you are sexy as hell when you are mad." "Oh whatever, just pull off. I am trying to keep this on the down-low but it seems like you are trying to do the opposite."

When I'm trying to sneak and do something, I don't need the world knowing about it. But on another note, he is looking very sexy over there in that drivers seat. He has on a white muscle shirt, a fitted L.A. hat and red basketball shorts. I couldn't see the type of shoes he had on because it was dark and quite frankly I didn't give a damn. "What you over there thinking about Parker?"

I wanted to say that I was thinking about how I wanted him to pull this Eddie Bauer over so I could go ahead and hop on top of him but I didn't want to seem desperate.

"Nothing, I'm just chilling. Why you ask?" "You seem a bit tense or like you were in a deep thought." "Oh no, I'm good".

I noticed that he had a bottle of wine in the backseat so I reached over, grabbed it and opened it. Clearly, it is for us to sip on to maybe loosen up but I didn't need that extra boost. I am already horny. We agreed on having sex in his truck so we drove around to find a clear and open spot. I was cool with the idea of us getting down in his truck because I've done it once before, during my teen years. Anyway, we have only been riding for about twenty minutes and I already have a buzz from whatever kind of wine he had.

I was tired of riding around in circles so we pulled up to an elementary school that sat next to a park.

"Good job Parker. Thanks for telling me to park here." Here we have two adults about to have sex in a car on elementary soil. Talking about setting a good example for kids: shit we were way off. He turned the car off and put in a CD that had nothing but baby making songs on it. He then climbed to the back and lied across the blankets that were placed on top of his seats. "Dang Tim, I see you were prepared." "Yes I was. Are you surprised?" "Oh, I'm not surprised; I just see that you aren't trying to waste any time." "Hell no, Time is precious so bring yo sexy ass back here."

I wore a dress with nothing underneath because for one: I wanted to be able to hop on top of him without having to stop and pull my panties to the side. Two: I didn't want to leave any evidence behind. I moved to the back and sat on top of his shorts. I wanted to get a feel of what I was about to work with.

Damn, he is rock hard and I haven't started yet. I guess it's just the touch that I have. "So what's up? How are we going to do this? Do you want to start on top or do you want me to start?" I asked. "Well, since you are already up there, you might as well stay."

Why did I know that he was going to say that? As I slipped my dress over my head, he took his shirt and shorts off. Damn that body was off the chain. I slowly rubbed my hands up and down that sexy ass chest and stomach of his. I was unsure of exactly where to start because it was so many places that I wanted to put my lips on. Therefore, I decided to start at the top and slowly lick my way down. We kissed passionately for a while and that along was making my pussy very wet. I moved down to his neck where I didn't want to stay too long because I was ready to get to all of those abs. His nipples are standing out the same way girls nipples do when they are wearing a wet t-shirt. "Damn Parker, this shit feels good." "I know it does so just lay back and let me finish pleasing you. I hate being interrupted."

He didn't part his mouth to say another word. That's how I knew that

I was giving him the business. I made it to my favorite place on his body and I had to take my time with them because they are so precious to me. I think I counted about eight of them. I then slid my tongue over to his side. The side is a very common hot spot on most guys so I decided to test his water. I would say that I was over there for about five seconds when I felt him jump. "Did I hit a hot spot?" "Hell yes. You know you did." "Ok I'm done with all of this licking and shit. My tongue is getting numb. Do you want me to ride you or are you ready to switch?" "Switch?" But you ain't done." "What do you mean I'm not done. What else do you need me to do you, hell I done licked every part of your body." "Well not exactly every part, you did miss a spot." He said

(So we kissed, I sucked on his neck, sucked on his nipples, licked on his abs and sucked on his side. What more does his ass want? I hope he didn't think that I was about to suck his toes or something because I don't engage in that type of 12 play shit honey.)

"What you mean I missed a spot?" "Oh you weren't going to…you know? Since you was already down there I figured you wouldn't mind getting it out the way."

I gathered his information and it sounds like he was asking me to give him head (as they would call it) I have never done that but whenever I had enough guts to actually do it: I wanted it to be special and with someone that I truly loved. As good as this night is going; I still don't feel too comfortable with doing that: Especially when I don't know what or who his ass has been doing.

"Well sucking your dick was not in my plans tonight. But to be honest, I have never done it."

"Are you serious? Damn, it seem like you can get down with that. Well….I mean….I will show you how to do it if you want me to."

He is very surprised at the fact that I don't suck dicks. Hell no I don't and I didn't want to start tonight on his ass but then again, I didn't want to go out like a punk so I volunteered. "Well if you want to show me then I'm down to do it."

When I said that his ass lit up like a light bulb.

"Parker, it's similar to sucking a banana because all you have to do is put your mouth on it and go up and down but in a passionate and affectionate way. Oh and try very hard not to use your teeth because that shit hurt. And that's all to it. Just pretend like you are auditioning for a sex scene in a movie and the only prop they gave you was a banana."

When he broke it down, it didn't seem as bad. I imagine myself in this porn movie sucking a banana. I slowly ran my mouth up his penis and back down but remembering not to use my teeth. I became comfortable by the minute and so did my mouth. My tongue took control because all I can hear is "Oooh, Ah." I knew I was serving his ass up. Then he stops me.

"Damn girl hold up. Are you sure this is your first time because it sure as hell don't feel like it." "Yea this is my first time but as my teachers used to say, "I'm a quick learner." It only last for five more minutes because I had to stop. My damn jaws are hurting. But I am ready to get down to the real deal. Fuck all of this oral sex. "So you done already?"

"What do you mean already? I was down there for ten minutes and that's too long if you ask me. We have done too much talking and interrupting. If you don't know, I like for it to be quiet while I'm having sex. The only thing that I need to hear is the sound of the man that I'm fucking, moaning in my ear telling me how good my pussy is. "Well you did good and I am very impressed but now, it's my turn to return the favor."

We switched positions and as much as I like to ride, it is my time to lie on my back. He started sucking and pulling on my nipples with his soft lips while rubbing his strong masculine hands up and down my body. I was in heat and coming every two minutes. If I didn't know any better, I would have thought that I had pissed on myself. His next move was to my inner thighs. As I licked his neck, he licked his way down to my overly wet vagina. I was uncertain if he was going to eat me but I am so happy he did. Though this was not my first time receiving head, he was trying to make sure that his name was at the top of my list. I was trying so hard not to bust but it was feeling good. I was biting the hell out of my lip, moaning and screaming his name as if we were long term intimate lovers. He reached to the front seat to grab his condom and then he placed it on.

"I'm really trying to hold this nut so can we please get this show on the road. I've done the normal position so let's try something more exotic." He said " I guess I can let you hit it from the back. "Well turn this big ass around then."

Oh my Goodness. That has to be the best position ever, well to me it is. As soon as he was inside of me, I wanted to scream. I could feel him rub against my walls. Damn, this shit is feeling good. He starts to grip my sides and pulls me back and forth going deeper and deeper. I could tell that he is about to come because he starts to pump even faster. The slow lovemaking is cool but I love it when they beat it up.

"I'm almost there so can I take the condom off? I promise to pull out when I feel myself about to nut. I just want to feel the real thing. Can I please feel the real thing?"

I was in my own zone so I didn't care what he did at this moment. As long as he fucks me until he catches a cramp. "Ok Tim but you better pull out."

He took the condom off and started his engine back up. A few seconds later, I feel him tense up so I man-pushed his ass off me. Before he could get a word out, cum was everywhere. It seems like it's been stored in him for a few months.

"Damn you didn't have to push me." "I'm sorry about that but you were acting like you weren't going to get up." "Whew, anyway that felt so good. Girl you were great." "Yea I know. I've never had any complaints." "I'm sure you don't, but I'm still amazed at the fact that this was your first time giving head." "You say it like it's a bad thing." "No, not bad at all, just still shock."

We laid there for a while because he had to gain enough strength to take me back home. Overall, I would say that we handled our business. We switched from teenagers to older, married adults because we laid there naked and talking. We also debated on who played the biggest part in this one-night extravaganza. We talked about where we stood as friends. We agreed that we would remain friends no matter what, even if one of us moves on and find love elsewhere. We realized that we are suppose to be friends and nothing more. On the way home, it hit me that I was never in love with Tim. It was only lust the entire time.

However, even though I have been dreaming about this night for a while now, I couldn't help but think about Alex and what I had done to him. I will admit that the stunt that I just pulled was foul but I guess you could say it was foul in a good way. I finally got what I wanted from Tim. I should be good on sex for a few months, Hopefully !

Chapter 16

Could it Be ?

Two more hours and I'm out of here. It's December so that mean long days at work. I recently received my second financial aid check so I don't have a clue as to why I am still working. The only reason I see is for the extra money but I think that's the reason everyone works. So once again, I have to suck it up and get the job done. I have been contemplating on whether I should keep my job or quit. What I really need is for a man to come and sweep me off my feet and tell me these words, "You no longer have to work my African Princess." A rapper once said, "You can have whatever you like". What I would give to have a man say those words to me? But I couldn't tell my mom that without her cursing me out. I can hear her now. "Parker, a man will only give you so much before he wants something in return." And she is most definitely right but the thought didn't hurt.

With Christmas being only a couple of weeks away, I have to work harder and pull more hours. I have so many gifts to buy this year. Lets see we have my mom, step-dad, brother, dad, step-mom, grandma, a line of cousins, uncles, aunties and my nephew Roderick (We aren't related but we are attached at heart. He turned six this pass August and I wasn't there for his party so I have to make up this Christmas for that. It's weird how we are not related but yet we are so close. I have known and loved him since he was a newborn. I think I loved him more than anyone else did and that's because he was always with me. I had my own Minnie me.) So I definitely had to get his gift out of the way first. I wanted to make sure that I got everyone a gift since I was financially stable this Christmas to do so. It would be nice to buy a man something for a change. I made a vow that night after Tim and I had sex that I was never going to go after a guy again. Yea I know that I have said it many times before but this time I am so serious. I am tired of having sex with no strings attached.

I would like to be held at night, go to the movies, out to eat or maybe taking long walks on the beach. I have realized that I only want the simple things out of a relationship. I am trying to control my hormones because I believe that is what ruins my relationship every time. I would like to find that significant other and take it one day at a time so if that means just sitting back and allowing Mr.Right to find me then that's what I have to do. I have to learn how to look pass the outer appearance and go for what's on the inside because you could never loose to someone with a pure heart.

Alex and I finally had our movie night at my house the other day. It was nice and very relaxing. It was something about him that I found attractive. I don't know if it's the way he carries himself or the way he treats me but whatever it is, I like it. Before he left my house last night, he volunteered to pick me up today from work which will be in a few minutes. "Parker, you can go ahead and take your draw out while your line is down and when you take it to the back, just go ahead and clock out."

I guess the cashier manager thought he was giving me a break by allowing me to leave five minutes earlier. I wasn't complaining because I was ready to go anyway. Therefore, I grabbed my draw, jacket and bottled water and headed to the back to check out. "Excuse me miss, Are you off of work?" I turned around and it was Alex. "Boy you scared me. You made it right on time because the manager just let me off." "So this was perfect timing huh?" "Yes it sure was but let me clock out and I'll be right back out."

As soon as I went through the doors, nosey Mary (co-worker) came up to me. "Is that your boyfriend? He's a nice one." "No Mary damn, can you enjoy your break and stay out of people business?" "So he is your boyfriend?" "No he is not but I'm sure you will know when he is. Bye Mary, see you later."

When I walked back out to where Alex was standing, he had this weird facial expression.

"Alex, why you looking like that? What happened?" "I heard you telling that lady back there that I wasn't your boyfriend." "Damn, I don't know who is the nosiest, you or her. But you aren't my boyfriend." "You are right, I'm not. But this day isn't over." He said

I didn't know if I should blush or ask him why was he eavesdropping. I can possibly see us being long-term but I think it's too soon to know for sure. He is cool and always impressing me so it is something to definitely think about.

Chapter 17

Hanging with the girls

Keziah and I are meeting up today for a girls day out. We decided to get our nails done and then grab something to eat so we can catch up; preferably talk about our boyfriends. I don't exactly have one of those but Alex and I act as if we are a couple. We are doing great but I still can't rush things. We have been seeing and talking to each other on a daily basis but I still get butterflies when he comes around. I guess we have that puppy love because when we are in each other's presence, we are constantly laughing and acting like kids. It feels so right.

He sent me a text this morning telling me how he also enjoy being with me. He then said, "I don't want to put any pressure on you with this question but I have to ask it." Before I could text him back, he was calling my phone. The conversation went like this.

"Hello" "Parker, this is Alex." as if I didn't know that. He cont. "I love being with you. We have endless conversations and nothing but good times when we are together. I know this is sudden and I may be jumping the gun too fast but I was wondering if I could make you my girl." That was very sudden and I needed time to think about this because I promised myself that I wouldn't be caught up in a man again. It's different this time because I always go out looking for a man but this time, he came to me. Basically, he fell in my lap so that has to be a sign right?. He did have many of the characteristics that I like in a guy: well he was missing a few (he's shorter than I am, he doesn't have any swag and I hate those curls in his hair) but who's counting?

I was in a mime ministry back home and the leader (whom we call Mama J) told me something very important a few months before I came out here. She probably don't remember but I have kept those words with me and I always will. She told me to write down everything that I wanted in a Man, basically, "What I wanted my dream husband to be like". From his appearance, personality, beliefs, sense of humor, likes and dislikes and so on. My number one must-have is how he treats me. He must know that I am a Queen and I need him to treat me like one. Mama J told me that my man should meet all or most of those qualities on that paper, if not, I'm settling.

Alex fit into almost every category, which is a huge plus. The fact that this guy could possible be too good to be true also had me thinking. I have to consider everything including the even and the odds. I want my next relationship to be long-term; No one night stands, No, "I'm just kicking it: Straight long-term. Before I give him an answer, I told him that I have to think about it and I will get back with him later on today. This is where Keziah steps in. She is having problems with her relationship and I am having problems trying to figure out if I should get into one.

Keziah yelled from the front door, "Parker I'm outside! Are you ready?" "Sure am. I'm on my way out now." She waited until I was outside before she walked back to her car like I needed her assistance or something.

"Parker don't even look at me like that because everyone that know you always take forever to get fully dressed".

"No ma'am. See Keziah, that's what you are not going to do. You are not going to act like you know me honey. There have been times when I come right out like today for example, so don't do me." "Yea, and I bet that was the first time it has ever happened." "Whatever, I figured since its already pass lunch time that we can get something to eat and then go get our nails done." "That's fine with me."

We decided to go to this restaurant called "The Apple." I have no idea where that name came from because the only apple recipe that they have is their apple crisp turnover dessert. I usually get the sampler which includes Buffalo wings, mozzarella sticks, onion rings, loaded quesadillas and mini cheeseburgers but today I was craving their New York steak, seasoned veggies, loaded potatoes, garlic bread and their famous raspberry lemonade. My mouth was watery just thinking about it. I eat a lot and I believe that will never change but the good thing is that I could eat and not gain one pound.

I'm blessed. But on another note, I could tell that something is bothering Keziah and that same something is also bothering my brother Mike. They are having a trust issue because he is always gone due to work, commercials and plays. She thinks that he is cheating. Mike and I talk about a lot of things but he never really open up to me about his relationship/girl problems and I can understand that because Keziah and I are close friends as well.

When the server came, Keziah ordered a bottle of wine. "Damn Kez, is it that bad?" "Well maybe it's not as bad as I am putting it but I'm starting to think that Mike is sleeping around with other women because he is never home. He say that he is always at work but for some reason when it come time to pay the bills, we are always broke." "Well if it helps a little: He hasn't told me anything but I would know if Mike was cheating on you. I think he will act different and he acts the same to me. Some dudes know how to cheat. They can stand there, look you in the face, say I love you and sleep with another woman all at the same time. It's just what they do. I also believe that you don't think he's cheating. Maybe you just need more attention."

I seriously didn't know what to say to her but "I don't think he is sleeping around." At this specific time, I don't want to give any advice. I want to receive it. So, even though her topic was more serious, I wanted to throw in my issue with Alex. I was still stuck on the fact that he wanted to make me his girl.

"Ok Kez, I really think that the both of you just need to sit down and talk it out. Let him know how you feel and why you feel that way. But listen, I received a call from Alex this morning and he want us to be together. You know: Have a title. I thought about it but I want to live the single life for a while because I would hate to go through all of that stress and drama: Perfect example, you and mike. I mean the committing, cheating, lying, trust and so forth. I really don't need that right now. Girl we are too fly and too young for all of that extra baggage honey. On the other hand, I'm thinking that maybe I do need to settle down because going out and clubbing all of the time will eventually get old to me. It would be nice to have a boyfriend because it's been a while since I have actually had one. So should I or shouldn't I.?"

"Well Parker, this is similar to what you told me, that's a decision that only you can make because I don't know if you really want to be single or in a relationship. It sounds like an easy choice to make but it sometimes isn't. You have to ask yourself is this going to be long-term or short-term. Could you see yourself with him ten years from now or do you just want him to be a friend with sexually benefits. You have to take all of that into consideration and once you do that, you will have your decision."

And she was right. I couldn't come up with a decision so quickly about something so extreme. But our food had finally arrived and usually I try to put all conversations to the side because I seriously can't think or talk while I'm eating. My main concern is usually my food but for some reason I couldn't let off the thought that Alex wanted me to be his girl. I felt like he had asked me to marry him. That's how serious I was taking this, but why? Maybe because I wanted to be with him and I wanted this to be real. Who knows, this is probably the relationship that I have been praying for.

I took maybe one or two bites of my steak, sipped on my lemonade and out of nowhere, I started to get butterflies because I was now seconds away from calling Alex and telling him that I would love to see if this relationship thing could work out.

Keziah said,"Parker, I can tell that this is what you want so go ahead and call the damn boy."

I dialed 310, the first three digits of his number, truthfully about six times and closed my phone and when I was going for the seventh time, Keziah snatched my phone and said, "What are you trying to do break a record or something? Just call him already and stop acting like a child. Be a grown-up about the situation".

Before I could part my mouth to call her a few nasty words, she was already dialing his number. I didn't know what to think or what to say because he was already on the phone.

"Hello." "Hey. What you doing? "Waiting on you to call me with an answer."

He just came straight out with it so I'm guessing I had him waiting long enough.

"My answer is Yes Alex. I am willing to try and see if this will work out. You are someone that I could see myself dating and like I told you before, I really enjoy your company." Well then, it's official. Parker and Alex. I can call you my girl now right?" "That's right".

And that was it. At that moment, I was in a relationship and hopefully a good one. This could actually work once we learn a little more about each other but that keeps the relationship interesting, finding out the good and bad things about your significant other. Some of the things I know about him right off is that he runs track at LA Southwest college, he dances, and works at Radio Spot, his birthday is on Christmas and above all, he is truly a gentleman. He hasn't really opened up to me on any personally issues: like his parents or his past so I don't know anything about his family but I'm guessing he will fill me in when he feels the time is right. I have learned that you really shouldn't tell your mate everything right off because sooner or later they could use that information against you. I had to learn that the hard way but I'm not worried about Alex.

He seems trustworthy but you never know when it comes to a man. Now, I will not be alone for Christmas but I have to add his name to my "gift list" and if he doesn't know: he has to add my name to his. I'm excited because I have never spent Christmas with a man because they usually break up with me a few days before or buy me something really cheesy like an ugly shirt or a cheap ass watch. If Alex only takes me out to eat, I will be satisfied because we are going to have fun regardless of what I get or what we do.

• • •

Days went by and our relationship grew stronger. We were beginning to become inseparable. We have shared secrets with one another but of course, I knew not to say too much too soon. I didn't want to run him away, especially about my past.

CHAPTER 18

I Miss My Mom

It was about four in the morning when my phone started to ring off the hook. At first, I thought that I was in a dream but the ringing didn't stop. Who could this be and what could they possibly need with me this early in the morning. Usually I would not answer but with it being so early and me not thinking straight, I did.

Without opening my eyes, I said very angrily, "Hello." Strange, I can't hear anything. I repeated, "Uh, hello, it's entirely too early for the games. Who is this?" As I prepared to close my flip phone and roll back over, I heard the sound of someone crying. I suddenly came up with the cleaver idea, "Read the name on the Caller ID," which was something that I should have done before I answered my phone. When I realized that it was my cousin Elise I rose up so quick that I became slightly dizzy. It scares me when close relatives call me at crazy hours of the night or very early in the morning especially when I answer and get an awkward silence like now.

"Elise what happened? Are you Okay? Talk to me." She finally gained enough strength to talk or in this case mumble a few words. She told me how sorry she was for calling me so early but I wasn't even tripping on that because she is family. She was feeling depressed because today marked the second year that her mom passed away. This was also a tragic lost for our family. My aunt was the most kind, sweetest, humble and down to earth person that you could ever meet. She was the baby of her siblings but she was the one that held everything and everyone together. She was like "The Rock" of our family and on December 20th [2004], God took her away from us. She was the only person that my cousin really had. I called them salt and pepper because my aunt was bright skin and my cousin was a little on

Patrice L. Guyton

the chocolate side. They were always together. You didn't see one without the other. I was so upset with God the day that he took my aunt away. We all needed her more than he did. He had enough angels in heaven so one more was not going to make a difference. However, later I learned that God does everything for a reason and he makes no mistakes. I turned my hurt and anger to joy because I knew that she was going to a better place. A place where she will not have to take any more pills and a place where she will not have to go through pain pertaining to her having lupus. I am so grateful that she went peacefully because not everyone is fortunate enough to go that way.

TT Diane Guyton Gone But Never Forgotten

CHAPTER 19

We took it there

With only a few days before Christmas, our store is packed and it seems like we are to the maximum capacity. Waiting to the last minute to buy Christmas gifts is something that everyone including myself is guilty of. I don't know why we, the American people, procrastinate. Now I have to deal with the long lines and long hours because the customers just realized that Christmas is December 25, always have been and always will be. But I wasn't upset because my mind was on one thing well one person and that was Alex. I tell you, this boy is slowly sweeping me off my feet. I already feel comfortable around him. We are becoming more attached by the day and I love it. I know that the first stage is really the best stage in a relationship but I am on cloud nine right now and I didn't want to come down.

I pulled a double shift today so I was exhausted. Alex was already outside so once I clocked out that was it for me until the day after Christmas. I walked out of that store and didn't look back. We decided to grab some take out from the Chinese restaurant and go to my house to chill for the rest of the night. I had to keep reminding myself that I was going to take it slow. Things felt so right when I was with him. I have never had these feelings for any other guy. Maybe I'm not moving too fast. It's possible that I have finally found my match and when you find that person the rest just falls into place. The plan was for Alex to come over and chill for a few minutes but that turned into hours and the next thing we knew, it was two in the morning.

"I should get going because I don't want to fall asleep on the freeway." Alex said

"Yeah we definitely can't have that. But are you sure that you can drive? You already look sleepy to me." I was trying to give the hint that I wanted him to stay.

"I could sleep in Chanel's bed and you can sleep in my bed if you want. I can wake you up in the morning so you could go home, shower and go to work." He paused and gave me this weird look as if he didn't want to stay. Men are similar to women; they want you to beg. I ask one time and that's it honey. "Yea that sounds good to me. I was going to ask, but I didn't want you to think that I was intruding."

"Ok, I'm going in the bathroom to take a shower and if you are still up, I'll see you when I get out and if not, Good Night. We gave each other a long and compassionate kiss. I was only going to the shower but we were acting as if this was a good-bye. At that moment, I knew that I was falling in love.

I left out of my room and rushed to the bathroom because I didn't want to leave his side. Damn, I'm sprung. He hasn't mentioned the topic "Sex" and for once, I haven't been thinking about it. That along is a major accomplishment for me because like I have said, I am terrible at managing my hormones.

Am I a slut because sex is all that I think about? Am I a whore for wanting to fuck every fine man that I see? I don't have sex with them but I damn sure think about. I have to keep my body healthy if I ever want to have kids so it only remains a thought.

I did one last wash and rinse because its getting steamy in here. Christmas is in two days so I would love for my hairstyle to remain fresh. I hopped out the shower, dried myself off and brushed my teeth.

When I finally made it back to my room, which seemed forever, Alex was already asleep. He look so peaceful but I want another kiss before I close my eyes for the night. Obviously, he was pretending because when I leaned over to steal a peck, he grabbed a hold of my lips with his lips and he did not let go. Our lips were a perfect match for each other. I thought that Tim was the best kisser but Alex had him beat by a long shot. With his arms tightly around my waist, I began to melt. I tried pushing myself back but I couldn't. The moment felt right but the timing was so wrong. It was still too early for us to take it there. We were doing so well and I didn't want sex to ruin our relationship because it always does. But once he started kissing on my neck and rubbing on my body, I could no longer resist. That's when I got on top of him and put his dick in myself. Not thinking twice, not stopping to put on a condom or asking if he was ready to go there with me. I had done it again. I let my hormones get the best of me. We haven't been in this relationship for a month and I am giving it up.

"Wait, I can't do this." he said "Why? Is it me?" "No it's me. I can't help but hear my mom's voice telling me not to have sex with a girl until I am married or have really true and deep feelings for her. I am not a virgin but I try not to sleep around. I hope you don't take this the wrong way because I really do like you and when that time comes: I want it to be special".

Wow! I have finally found a man that wants more to a relationship than sex and that is exactly what I need. I must admit that I felt so low. I could not believe what I had done but then again I could. Somehow, I always tend to mess things up. I had to let him know that I was not that type of girl. Yes, I did fall short but I really like him.

"Alex I am so sorry and I hope that you don't think less of me. I should have never crossed you in that way. You seem to be a very mannerly guy and so I do apologize."

"Parker don't do that. I kissed and grabbed you first so I take full responsibility and things will not change. I really like you and I want this to work." As the word, Shame, appears on my face, I politely walked over to Chanel's bed, which was supposed to have been the plan at first. "Good night baby." He said. I laughed, "Good night Alex."

• • •

I woke up the next morning wishing that what happened last night was a dream but unfortunately, there was reality lying over there in my bed. I tossed and turned all night thinking about the dumb move I made. I couldn't help but to think about how I have ruined this perfect relationship. How could I be so stupid? Maybe I really am a sex addict and need to seek professional help or maybe I just need to get a grip on life and start realizing that sex isn't everything. Right here and right now, I stand on my word and I vow, to myself, to stop giving in to temptation. Seriously, this is something that I have to pray about because I can't go on doing the things I do.

I got up to wash my face and brush my teeth and once I made it back in my room, he was raiding my mini refrigerator.

"Good Morning, I see that you are hungry. Well you are welcomed to whatever is in there. That may not be much because Chanel and I have to go grocery shopping soon. Look Alex, about last night...

Before I could apologize yet again, for what happened he put his finger over my lips and said "Look everything is cool so could you just drop it because I'm not worried about that." "Well in that case my lips are sealed and I will never mention it again." "Yea you better not. But I need to get out of here because I could stand here and talk to you all day. I really don't want to work this eight hour shift today on Christmas Eve and the eve of my birthday but it has to be done." "Well better the eve and not on the actual day."

"Yea you right but I'm going to go home, take a shower and grab me something to eat since it wasn't anything here." He laughed. Have a good day and I'll call you when I get off." "Ok baby, I'll talk to you later.

As I flopped on my bed in awe, I realized how happy I am with Alex. He is the perfect guy, minus those things that I want him to change. He must kill those fake ass jerry curls and switch up his swag.

Once I correct those, we will be good.

Fell Too Deep

Meanwhile, I get this disturbing phone call from Keziah. She tells me that she is damn near two months pregnant. I could have cursed every piece of hair off her head. I seriously think I called her every name in the book. What did she mean she was pregnant? She didn't seem a bit nervous or frantic when she broke the news to me so I was thinking that this did not bother her in the least bit. I on the other hand, is pissed. She is the best hurdler that I have ever seen and now she has to sit out this year. With the way that our girls track team has been practicing, I think that we are really good and with a little more commitment we are bound to be "State Champions" this year. Now we have lost major points. A new life is coming into this world but right now, I could care less. She makes the second girl to become pregnant on our team and that's not good. Hell it felt like pregnancy was becoming contagious but as long as I wasn't anywhere around it or the water they are drinking, then I'm good.

Me, Kez and Chanel decided to go out to eat tonight. They were celebrating but I wasn't. I was only going to eat and do nothing more, no toasting or giggling because again this is not an amazing occasion to me. I don't think she is ready for a baby and my brother mike is not ready for a second child right now. I am not the one to judge people especially my friends, but damn. If you are going to have sex, protect yourself. (Says the person that hopped on Alex and Tim without a condom.) If they can work it out then it's fine with me but I still can't be happy for them right now. I just think that this situation could have been prevented. I'm not having any kids until I graduate college, find a stable and well paying job and married for at least two years. A child is a blessing but as I've seen, your life turn around and you have to head in a completely different direction. But I guess it's my dough and their cookies honey. Meaning, my bitterness is their sweetness.

Chapter 20

Christmas Bells

I woke up to a phone full of texts and they all said the same thing, "Merry Christmas!" Any other time this will be just another day to me but I was feeling different. I had a man and I was happy. Despite me being in love and full of joy, I was still a bit unhappy because I wanted to be with my mom and all of my family back home. When we all get together, we have the best of times. Especially when my cousin Elise and my brother are side by side, because all they do is argue and it's so hilarious. We try not to get on her nerves too bad because she has a squeaky voice that will drive a deaf person insane. And please don't let her curse. That's one of the funniest things ever. When she curses, she sounds out every syllable and says it very proper so who ever she is cursing will never take her serious. Then we have my two guy cousin who I just absolute love Mark and Cory.

Mark is serving in the United States Army and currently deployed in Iraq. I really wish that he didn't have to go overseas and fight because most of the soldiers really don't know the real reason why they are there. All they know is that they are making their country proud. When I think about it, 80 percent of the Americans could care less about our soldiers and the lives being taken every day. But I thank God daily that he is safe and still alive.

My cousin Cory goes by his rapper name Capone. No, he is not yet a rapper but trust me, his day is coming. He is very talented when it comes to beats and lyrics and I'm not just saying that because he is my cousin. I know most people support their relatives even when they have no talent. For example, you tell your relative that she can sing like B' but you know damn well that they don't stand a chance at a karaoke bar. But seriously, I believe that if he runs across the right person at the right time that he will most definitely make it.

Their sister Lisa is the total opposite. She is extremely quiet, smart and has the most humble spirit. I have been around her since birth and not once have I seen her dance, curse or talk loud (which is definitely the opposite of me.) All she does is laugh. I mean she laughs at the craziest things. I have never seen her stress out of about boys, money and life in general. Being content is a good thing but only to a certain extent because you will eventually burst from keeping everything bottled in.

Then we have their mom, Aunt Bren, the outspoken one. If it's right or wrong, funny or boring she will let you know. She is struggling with a kidney failure right now, so she does have a lot on her plate to deal with. She has been on the waiting list for years and still no one knows the day that she will receive that call. I know that she has God on her side but I still wish there were something that I can do. My uncle, who we all call Bone, is the drill sergeant of the family. He has retired from the US Military and is now married with three kids and three step-kids. He lives in Oklahoma, which is a ways from Mississippi but he tries to drive down on the holidays. We have a small immediate family and that's good because we all are so close: Sometimes it feels like we are sisters and brothers and I love that. Of course, we argue and disagree but in a matter of days, we are back smiling and laughing again.

• • •

"Merry Christmas! Hey mom. What you doing?" "Hey Baby, Merry Christmas to you as well. I'm about to cook some breakfast for your brother and Curt. What do you have going on today?" "Uh, .Alex's birthday is today and he's having a party later tonight at his house." "Oh ok. I still haven't talked to him so when y'all meet up, call me. He seems nice from the way you describe and talk about him but I still need to be sure." "I guess, Ma. But you will like him. He still haven't spoke with daddy either." "Oh Lord. Don't let your daddy scare that poor boy away." She laughed.

"You are right, but I have already filled Alex in on how my dad can get, especially when he starts asking questions. Who are you? What's your dad name? What side of town were you raised on?" "Yep, you have your dad down to the T." she laughed.

"I'm going to get up and start this breakfast and I will call you later. I love you baby." "I love you too mama." "Oh wait your brother and Curt said "Hey and Merry Christmas." "Ok tell them Merry Christmas and tell my brother that I will text him later on when I get out of this bed." "Ok Baby."

I really hate that I can't be in Mississippi with them but it's a part of this adjustment that I'm trying to get used to. There will be many times that I will not be able to make it home during the holidays so this is a start to prepare me for the future.

Next on my list is Alex, but he was already calling me.

He called to wish me a Merry Christmas and to make sure that I am still coming over to his house later tonight. He told me that they have a celebration at his house every year on Christmas. He wants me to come early to help him set-up and meet his family. I'm extremely nervous but also excited. I don't know what to expect from them. I hope they don't judge me before they actually get a chance to know me. That's exactly what most families do when a relative brings home a new girl/boyfriend. I know because my family does the same thing.

While we were on the phone, I told him Merry Christmas but I didn't wish him a Happy Birthday simply because I wanted him to think that I forgot. He kept saying, "I'm excited for you to see your gifts", but I never said a word. He wanted me to share with him what I had bought but I didn't."

I blew him a kiss through the phone and hung up. I really hope that I didn't hurt his feelings because I was only trying to throw him off.

With only an hour left, I wanted to go ahead and get ready. Being that today is his day, I did not want to procrastinate. However, I am ready to see what he bought me. I know I told him that I wanted a pair of cowboy boots that I saw in the mall. They are gold with a hint of cream. But he thought that they were dead awful so he probably didn't buy them. I bought him a pair of van shoes, 14 carat stud earrings, a Jamaican shirt with the face of Bob Marley on the front and a LA fitted hat. I spent the most money on him and my mom this year but I wasn't complaining because my mom deserves the best and more and Alex deserves a few nice gifts because of the wonderful gentlemen that he is.

We made it to his house at exactly 7:30. The moment we exit off the freeway, I knew that I was officially in the hood of Los Angeles. There were kids outside running barefoot, men and women on the coroners gambling and smoking weed, loud music playing, spinner rims on raggedy cars, people arguing and some fighting. I didn't know if I should call 911 or start praying. I was seconds away from telling him to turn this damn car around and take me back to my side of town. My life is so precious to me and I need to live as long as I can. I'm guessing that he noticed how scared I was because he promised that he will let nothing happen to me. Let's just hope so.

Once we made it closer to his house, the environment changed. I started to see colors again where at first, I only saw smoke and black and white. It was five cars outside and I could hear the music playing from inside of the house when we arrived. He was talking about helping them set-up but apparently, the party had already started. I really couldn't see exactly what he had on in the car but once he got out and walked over to open my door, I got a better glimpse of him. He was very handsome in his black Jordan sweat suit that was trimmed in light blue.

As always, my fit was well put together. It was my first time meeting his family so of course I had to come correct. I wanted to dress casual so I wore a nice pair of gray slacks that fitted this fat ass just right. I wore a black turtle neck that drooped low in the front, a pair of black flats with the tiny heel and since it was a bit chilly outside, I completed my outfit with my favorite black, gray and white pea coat.

I still didn't mention anything about his birthday even though I know he saw this big ass bag in my hand when I walked out of my house. Seconds later, he walked to his trunk to get something out but I had already guessed that he was going to get my gifts. I mean it didn't take a rocket scientist to figure that out.

I walked back to the trunk as well and watched him pull out a huge beautiful bag with colorful strings all over it. As I reached for it, he tapped at my hand the same way you do a toddler when they are reaching for something that they shouldn't have.

"Uh, what are you doing?" he asked. "Baby stop playing, let me see what you got me." "Why do you think that this bag is for you?" he said laughing. "Who else will it be for?" "Oh no, see this is for my aunt. This is just a token of appreciation to thank her for planning this party."

I didn't see any other gifts in the car so if this wasn't mines then that meant that he didn't buy me anything, which only means that he isn't getting this bag out of my hand.

"Calm down baby. It was only a joke. This is for you, Merry Christmas gorgeous." "See you play too much." I said as I grabbed the bag out of his hand.

I opened the bag and found my gold and cream cowboy boots, a gold belt, a pair of gold Coach Earrings and a card with 200 dollars in it. I knew about the boots but the belt, earrings and money was a shocker. I was very impressed at the fact that he took that extra mile to buy accessories. Most men wouldn't do all of that.

"Aw baby, Thank you so much. You really did surprise me." "Well I'm glad you liked it. I still can't believe that I went into a female store looking for jewelry. I did get a little help from a young lady out of one of the stores. She said that you would love them. I'm glad to know that I have good taste." "Yes you do baby but we have been out here long enough. I'm ready to go inside, meet the family and eat."

"Ok." he said glancing down at his bag that was still in my hand. I made him wait long enough so I finally gave him his gift.

"Happy Birthday baby and Merry Christmas. You know I did not forget about you. I hope you like it but we are really missing your party standing out here in this cold weather." "Ok, but one more thing." "What is it?"

"I want a kiss."

Before I could pucker up and lean over, he was already in my mouth with his tongue to the back of my throat. I was thinking please stop. I was seeing a re-run of this same episode with Tim and I in his truck and that can not go down again: not here and definitely not now.

"Ok Alex we have to stop this before it gets out of hand. We don't want one thing leading to another because a lot could happen in a split second.

I had to say "WE" because I didn't want to make it seem like I didn't want to have sex with him. Hell to be honest, I could have him right now if he was willing to take it there, but I knew he wasn't. He was trying to be true to himself and his mom and I can understand that so I eased up, but don't get me wrong because if I really put in enough effort: I could get any guy to sleep with me including Alex.

"Ok baby, that's enough for right now. Let's go inside and have fun."

Chapter 21

A Look Back

It is only a couple of days left in this year and I am happier than ever. I spent this past Christmas with my boyfriend and I am going to bring this year in with him. Things were going so perfect and smooth that I had to question myself on if this was real or not. I only wanted to be with him. I only wanted to talk to him. If he is away from me for more than two hours, I am miserable and forlorn. I am definitely becoming attached. It was his personality and the way he treated me that had me going hay wild. I was starting to get jealous when other girls came around.

For instance at his party, on Christmas he had a few friends from his church to come over and a couple of them were females. One girl was a redbone with long pretty hair. She had a pie face but she was cute. She was a small and petite chick, the total opposite of me. She had on a long red maxi dress with a black and red scarf. The other girl, well hell I wasn't worried about her. She looked like a monkey by the face but one good thing that she had going for herself was her shape: still nothing like this coca-cola bottled shape diva. They had a close relationship and was hugging all night. I really didn't think anything of it because all of them were fun to be around and very outgoing but I was now his girl and I wanted all the attention. I want all of him to myself so there could be no room for anyone else.

I don't know what happened to me in these last couple of weeks because I was getting hooked and it was happening too fast. I had to be careful because I could not let this ruin my goals and the main reason I am out here, which was to run track and graduate college.

On yesterday, Alex called to inform me that his car had been reposed.

His brother borrowed his car to run a few errands but he was pulled over for speeding and his license was suspended. Alex spent the entire day trying to find enough money to get his car out of the impound but hadn't yet came across that much money. I knew that I didn't have enough to help him out so I didn't offer. While on the phone, he also told me that he was transferring to my college in January to run with our team.

I was not too thrilled about the idea. He didn't ask me how I felt about it. I honestly don't think it's a good move but it's already done. I guess my words bit me in the ass because I just said that I wanted to be around him everyday. Now, that has changed. I didn't want us to be around one another all day and every day because when that happens, the bond eventually starts to drift away. Same school means most likely the same classes then off to track practice and from there to each other's house and that might be a bit too much for me.

Of course, everything is good at the beginning but I don't want our flames to go out.

Besides, I would not be able to flirt with Tim as much I do. I still call him every now and then to check up on him. (The Word of Mouth says that he has a lil girlfriend.) "Hell I could care less." I laughed. "She will never be me!" I have a boyfriend and I'm on the verge of falling in love but I still had feelings for Tim. I really don't think it's a crime to be in love with one guy and care deeply for another. I was however, praying that Alex never finds out about Tim nor that night I left him hanging to go and engage in that rendezvous. I wasn't hiding it from Alex; I just wanted to avoid any drama that it may bring. Besides, we weren't a couple then.

Rewind:

I was surprised at how well his family took me in the night of his party. His aunt: Jeanette, stood about 5'12, weighing about 220 pounds with gold and black micro braids. She has two daughters by the name of Amiya (19) and Sheila, the baby girl, (12) The moment I walked in they welcomed me with open arms. "Alex, Is this Parker?" His aunt said with such glee. "We are so happy to finally meet you and you are really pretty." Amiya added. I gave a small smirk because I already knew that I was the shit but I was delighted to know that they thought the same.

Amiya called me in the kitchen so we could get acquainted with one another. We started a small conversation while she fixed me a coffee-chocolate shake: something that I have never heard of before but surprisingly it was very tasteful. The rest of the night was a breeze.

Fell Too Deep

We talked, laughed and did one of my favorite things to do: eat. We had everything from meatballs, pizza, rotel dip, bar-b-que chicken and chips. I felt like I was already a part of his family but what I loved the most was that I did not have to fake my personality or pretend to be someone that I wasn't just to fit in. I was totally myself and was pleased with how much fun we had.

Chapter 22

Catch UP

Alex invited me to attend his church on New Years Eve. They have a program at the end of every year to bring in the New Year. There will be dancing, praying, singing, eating, and just praising the Lord as the new year rolls in. I need that more than anything and what better way to bring in a year than with the Lord and your man. I have heard that Alex was a really good praise dancer but I still have not seen him perform so I was very excited about that. I knew that the New Year had many good things in store for us as a couple because we were going in it the right way. I was going to make a promise to him that I will try my best not to ever intentionally hurt him but no human being on this earth is perfect.

I was in love with this guy and nothing or no one could tell me different or tell me that we were not meant to be. I am hoping that he is feeling the same way because it never works when one person is putting in more than the other, it has to be mutual.

I never thought that I would fall for him this hard and this soon, but hey, it happened. Many people often say that you should never just put your all in another person because you will always end up heartbroken. I haven't given him my All just yet but I'm almost there. I am confident that he will never do anything to hurt me because he is too much of a sweetheart to cause harm to anyone.

Chanel and Keziah have wanted to hang out with me for a few days now. I'm starting to sense that they have been getting irritated with me because my response every time is "Go ahead. I'm going to kick it with my baby today." I've tried to get them to understand that when I was at home bored and out of my mind, they were out with their men so now that I have one, they want to flip the script and try to trip.

Chanel, Dan and myself was running late to the New Year's Celebration Program at Alex's church. We took the wrong exit and were not able to get back on the freeway due to traffic. It's so sad that black people are always late. If you want make it anywhere on time in California, you must leave at least 2 hours prior to the time that you have to be there. Alex sent a text telling me that he was next on the program but we were still a few minutes away. Dan pushed the pedal to the floor and got us there. Luckily, there was an empty parking spot right in the front. I noticed how big and crowded this church was. What if I missed him? What if I can't find a good seat?

They had the loudest and biggest speakers that I have ever seen sitting outside of the church. I'm guessing that they were trying to let the entire neighborhood hear what was going on inside. Once we got out of the car, the first thing I heard was the announcer saying "Next we have a powerful young man who goes by the name A.J."

"Chanel! Dan!" I yelled, Alex is up. He is about to dance right now." We all took off as quick as we could running as fast as our legs could go. Once we made it to the door, we were out of breath. The ushers didn't know what to think. "Sorry. So sorry Ma am." I said breathing tremendously hard. "We were trying to make it here in time to see the next performer dance." "Oh well you made it just in time. There are a few seats here." She said pointing towards the front. "You guys be blessed and enjoy the rest of the night." We all said "Thank You." and walked to the empty seats.

The announcer went on to say, "This man has been dancing since he was forced to join our all-girl dance class. This was supposed to be his punishment for running around in the sanctuary, when he was younger, and accidentally breaking a glass vase (so he says).

You could hear the crowd laugh including myself, because I could image him running around, bad as hell and knocking that vase over.

"But it turned out to be an incredible thing because this boy can dance like David danced. I hope he bless you all the same way he has and continues to bless us here at Zoe fellowship church. So come on everyone and let's give a warm round of applause for A.J."

The audience clapped their hands and the lights drew dim. I was so nervous for him. I didn't have enough time to prepare myself. My hands were sweating and I just knew that I was about to vomit in any second now. I was really acting as if it was me up there about to dance in front of all of these people. Chanel was beside me laughing at how I was making a complete fool of myself. I just wanted him to do well. But everyone was talking about how good of a praise dancer he was so I had nothing to worry about. I even heard a woman sitting behind us say to her friend, "He is the only reason I came here tonight." There was nothing else I could do but hold my breath, sit back and watch him minister.

After the program was over and the countdown to the New Year was complete; Alex, I, Chanel, Dan and few of his friends decided to go out to eat. His best friend Kevin and fiancé Jessie said that they wanted to see what the "New Girlfriend" was about. Twenty minutes later into this dinner date, I found myself still laughing harder than I have probably ever laughed. These guys were hilarious. Everything that came out of their mouth had me cracking up. The manager kept threatening to put us out of the restaurant for the excess noise. Alex text me and said, "Don't I have the perfect set of friends?" and I replied "Only because you haven't met mines." It seemed like we had just made it there but the night had already come to a rapid end. I guess all of the laughing made the time go by.

After we paid for our food, we stood outside a few minutes playing around. You could tell that none of us wanted to go home because we were having such a good time but good ole Alex had to take the spotlight by bussing out with some of his Michael moves. His dancing at church tonight stunned me but he had now thrown in some hip-hop and I was even more impressed. There is this type of dancing out here in Cali called the "Krump" and he did it very well. That has to be one of the hardest, wildest and craziest dances ever and he had it down pack, and to top it off, he was sexy. What more can I ask for?

"Ok Alex, we know you someday want to be Michael but now is definitely not the time." Kevin said. "Only my friends will hate on the best." He said. "Baby don't worry about them. You as well as everyone else know that you are untouchable in dancing." I added.

We said our goodbyes and headed home. I was still upset at the fact that Alex no longer had a car but there was nothing that I could do about that. So until we come up with an idea or come up with enough cash to get his car out: Dan has agreed to be our taxi if we provide him with gas money. I have started to save my money because I need my own car. I didn't want anything too luxury but as long as it gets me back and forth from school to work, then I'm good.

So here, we are sitting in the backseat of someone else's car holding each other's hands. How high school is that? We can't complain because we could be outside walking, so for us this was a major blessing. I wanted to ask Alex if he would stay with me tonight: only because it felt appropriate. You know, finish bringing in the New Year with your sweetheart all cuddled up and wrapped in blankets, sipping on Sparkling Cider pretending its wine and watching movies until we fall asleep. That would be the perfect way to end it: If you ask me. We have been riding in this car for a while and he still haven't given me a hint or sign that he wants to stay the night with me. Chanel was staying at Dan's house so I had the room to myself, again.

I didn't know if the other girls was going to be home but I was assuming that since most people are in the club on new years that they will be out also, especially with the way that we party. I can't remember the last time I went to a club with the girls. Alex and I have been spending so much time together that I don't have the urge to go like how I used to. As we pulled into my driveway, Alex said, "I hope you don't take this the wrong way but I'm crashing at your place tonight and I came prepared this time... "Could he be talking about having a condom?" I said to myself "I have my clothes and necessities in the trunk." He said. Damn, he wasn't talking about a condom.

But I couldn't be any happier. I guess we were in the stage now where we didn't have to ask unnecessary things anymore like "Could I stay at your house tonight?" or "Could you buy me something to eat?" I guess like the old saying goes, "My house is your house" and that's the type of understanding we had.

"Alright y'all. Thanks! We should go somewhere tomorrow: maybe the movies or eating since coincidentally we are all off of work." "Ok we will let you guys know!"

I was happy that he decided to stay with me tonight. He was reading my mind. His company is always welcomed with me anyway. We went straight to my room and started a senseless debate on who was taking their shower first. I was telling him that since this was my house and my room that I should be the one to go first, and then he came right behind me saying " Since I am a guest and you are suppose to honor any guest in your home." Please! If someone comes to your house more than once, my mom said, "They are no longer a guest". Her motto is "If it's here and you want it, go get it. I'm not your slave pass two visits." She even have that posted on her front door so everyone that comes in would already know.

However, since I was in a good mood and he was practically begging me, I decided to go ahead and let him shower first. Guys really don't take a long time to shower anyway: Just a squirt of body wash on a sponge, wash their neck and their balls and they are out so I don't have too much time to wait. I pulled out my new pajama set that I bought from my store during the holiday sale. It was a lime green tank top and boy shorts with assorted colors and stripes. I wanted to wear something attractive and cute but not so wild and provocative. I wanted him to be like "Damn my girlfriend bad and her body is banging" not more so "Damn, I wanna fuck her right now". I knew he wasn't that type of person but sometimes the clothes you wear and the actions you make speak up for the type of person you are, and since I have been trying to change those old ways, I can't put myself out like that anymore. Things have been going well for me and I can't mess that up tonight. Well let me rephrase that, I wont be the one to start anything but if it is started, I will most definitely finish it.

He made it back into the room where I was patiently waiting. I glanced at him and grabbed my clothes. I'll be back in a minute and this time, don't fall asleep." "I'm not. As late as it is, I'm not sleepy just yet. Besides I have something that I need to talk to you about." "Well in that case, I won't prolong the time."

I left out of the room anxious. I didn't know what he had to tell me. We were doing well thus far so I hope that we were not about to have that "Let's Just Be Friends" talk. Whatever it was had me worried. I was falling.... well to be honest I was in love with him. I had a feeling a while back that I was moving too fast but I didn't think about it because I assumed he felt the same. Now, I'm in the shower thinking about everything that a guy can tell his girlfriend. I wanted to prepare myself with whatever news that he was about to hit me with. I think this was the quickest shower that I have ever taken. I don't even think I dried myself off completely. But after thinking a little deeper into this mystery conversation, I figured that if he wanted to break it off that he would not have volunteered to stay with me tonight. He came prepared with clothes so maybe I shouldn't worry as much. Maybe he wants to take it a step further.

I stayed in the bathroom a little while longer because it was a little too soon to go back in there. I stared at myself for a while and, Damn, I look good. My ass was getting bigger but these small ass breasts weren't. It's no wonder why I had those guys tripping over me back in the day. I turned my butt to the mirror again and tried to do that jiggling thing but it was not happening. I practice those moves damn near every day but I just can't get it. Guess I'll have to watch some more of those videos that come on at 3 a.m. in the morning. Now those women can definitely shake their asses. How can you keep one cheek still while the other one wiggle up, down and all around? I don't know just yet but I will learn.

But back to earth now. My mind constantly drifts off from one thing to another in seconds when I am supposed to be focused on something else.

I sprayed a little more "Pleasure P" all over my body trying my best not to miss a single spot of this beautiful frame. I put on my PJ's, brushed my teeth, flossed and swished around some mouthwash. I put on lip-gloss, looked in the mirror and headed back to room where I found Alex watching an episode of Martin.

"Damn baby. I thought you got lost in there. I was about to go to sleep once this episode went off." He was watching the one when Sha-nana sued Tommy for damaging her bumper. Personally, one of my favorites.

"I told you I had to talk to you about something." He said sitting up with a serious look all over his face. I moved from Chanel's bed to my bed where he was lying, smelling good and looking so fine. We were now so close to each other that our nose was practically an inch away from touching. I just wanted to suck his lips right off of his face. It was so tempting but I remain cool. I wanted him to pass the first move because that would have let me known that he was ready. It was still too early in our relationship, so I was not expecting us to have sex.

I just wanted to cuddle. He then grabbed my hands and said, "Parker, I've known you for a short period of time and I find myself thinking about you everyday. I have never fallen for someone so quickly. I, I just can't figure out what it is. If I could be with you all day everyday, I would. You make me laugh at the corny things you say. I love the fact that you aren't normal." He joked. "I know for a fact that I have found my soul mate. My heart has been broken a few times so I figured that I would never find anyone to care about me as much as I care about them. Parker, I want to tell you that I love you: No, let me rephrase that, I have fallen in love with you. You are everything to me and I am going to try my hardest not to hurt you. I would be a fool to hurt someone that God has personally sent to me.

" Damn, I was shocked. Wow, no one has ever felt this way about me. If they did, their feelings never showed it. This moment is unexplainable. If I could hold my tears, I would.

I have never had anyone say such profound words like that to me. It was the sweetest thing but I couldn't show too many emotions.

He continued, "From this New Year and on, I promise to be the best boyfriend that you have ever had. If you ever need anything, come to me first. I wanna be you friend, your soul mate and most of all: I wanna be your lover."

My eyes lit up like an alcoholic at a liquor store. (I'm talking about those alcoholics that praise you whenever you give them just enough change to buy one of those cheap ass beers). Did he just say lover? Could this possibly mean that he was ready to have sex? I thought.

"Most guys have sex with their girls but I want to make love to you. I want to feel the passion when we are making love and I want feel that compassion in our relationship."

His words aroused me. He knew I wanted him and I wanted him right at that moment. I'm not well at hiding my facial expressions so if something is bothering me, my face tells it all.

"Did I startle you?" "No Alex, not at all. I'm glad to know that the feelings are mutual. I want you to know that I love you just as much. You should never have to question my love for you. I too, will remain faithful as long as we are a couple." He grabbed my face and started kissing my neck. "We have both shared our feelings so just be quiet. This isn't the time for talking." Damn, he was already taking over his role as a man and I wasn't going to stop him. I closed my mouth so he could do his thang.

He gently laid me back and turned me over to my stomach. He pulled off my Pj's and tossed them to the floor. "You didn't need these anyway." He said. I was so caught up in this beautiful moment that I didn't notice that he was already completely naked. I knew when I felt his bare chest on my back and his dick slide up and down on the crack of my ass. Oh my, this is great. This is pleasing to my body and I'm well overdue. He licked me from head to toe but making sure to give my ass cheeks much attention. Things were getting heavy between us and I knew that because I had already came twice. The main course wasn't served to me just yet. The room was silent and that's the best way to engage in Love Making. He turned me around and now we are face to face looking deep into each others eyes. "I love you Parker." He said.

"I love you too Alex." My breasts weren't big but they were the perfect size for his mouth. By the way that he licked my breast and pull at my nipples, I knew that he loved them. I attempt to suck his neck but I couldn't, all I could do was moan and dig my nails deeper into his back. I tried to give but he wanted me to receive. It was so much heat between us that my body caught a chill every time his hand left a spot. As he rolled his tongue down my stomach to my navel, I tried to keep my composure. He opened my legs with his knees and rubbed his hands down my inner thighs. "Alex." I moaned. "Baby". Before I could say another word, he had his face in my overly wet vagina. He pulled his tongue out, blew in my

Fell Too Deep

hole and stuck his tongue back in. He repeated that act time after time. He came back up to my face and whispered in my ear, "Baby can I put it in?" I only had enough strength to say, "Yes baby."

The room was so stuffy but of course, that's exactly how I like it. The moment he slid in, I gripped his dick with my pussy muscles. That was to let him know that I wasn't going anywhere. "Alex, oh you feel so good." He was the hand, I was the glove and together, our bodies made a perfect fit. He pulled out for a split second, just to turn me over to my back again. He then pulled my ass up so that my body could make a perfect arch. I have a lot of ass but he was able to deal with it. "Damn baby". He said positioning both of his hands on my hips. Moments later, he was pulling my ass back and forth as if he was playing a game of tug of war. I didn't want him to stop but once I felt myself coming again, I pulled up until he was completely out of me. "Baby, what's wrong?" he asked. "Nothing at all: everything is right but it's your turn to be pleased. It was now time for me to give my man a feeling that he has never felt a day in his life.

I leaned down so he could feel my breasts on his chest. I aimed for his neck where I knew was his weakness. He must have tensed up every time I moved my tongue to a different spot. That is exactly what I was aiming for. I wanted to show him everything I had to offer but I had to save some of my special features for another time. With that being sad: I eighty-six the idea of giving him head (at least for right now). I cuffed his dick in my hand and stuffed it inside of me until I felt him in my stomach. I could feel my juice pouring out on his manhood. He was squirming and moaning so I knew that things were going great. I went into in the "Chair" position (when both of your feet are planted on the bed with your elbows on your knees) and starting grinding on him in a circular motion. Ten minutes and two nuts later, he was now at the edge of his breakthrough so I hoped up as fast as I could. We were both in the moment but not so deep that I couldn't force myself up. We both laid there breathing hard as ever.

"Damn this is funny!" he laughed "The fact that the both of us run track and we are sitting here out of breath, is hilarious. We don't breathe this hard at track practice."

"Yea that is kind of sad once you think about it." I agreed.

We laid there talking for few minutes not thinking about getting up to wash ourselves off. I guess we felt that since we had gotten this close that it was no biggie. I didn't feel like getting up anyway. After an experience like that, I would not be surprised if I am glued to this bed for the next couple of days. After having sex for the first time with your new partner, you always have to ask the questions, "How was it? Did you like it?" He was sounding like he was about to fall asleep any minute now so I asked first.

"Parker, I have to be 100 percent honest with you right now. That was the best time I have ever had. I feel like we shared something special and I will never forget it. Even fifty years from now, I will remember this night and this experience." "And that's exactly how I feel. Alex, I love you." There was a silence. "Alex, Alex! Did you hear me?" I glanced over to find him sleep with his mouth open. I'm the one who is always falling asleep in the middle of a conversation but I see that he has beaten me to that. I guess that's another thing that we have in common. I placed my thigh between his legs, wrapped my arms tightly around his waist and kissed him on the cheek. "Good job." I thought. I really put it on him tonight.

Chapter 23

"Play Hard or Go Home"

"COME ON PARKER, YOU NEED TO GET YOUR SLOW ASS TO THE FRONT OF THE LINE! IF YOU CANT HANG WITH THE BIG DAWGS THEN MAYBE YOU NEED TO GO BACK HOME AND RUN FOR YOUR HIGH SCHOOL AGAIN."

My coach was becoming pissed as I lagged further and further behind. *Hell I will get up there when I get there.* She was trying to make me do something that I could not do. We were doing this drill called the "Indian Run" that everyone hated to do including myself. I wanted to say so many times "Get your ass out here in this 90 degree weather and do a damn Indian run."

We had this big ass track team and we were practicing with the men so how in the hell was I supposed to run pass everyone and get to the front of the line. I knew the price I had to pay when I took the offer to come out here and do the whole track thing. I have heard many people talk about how much pressure and anxiety a person can go through while running track in college, but I figured that some people were adding a little drama to it. I am here with a hands on experience so I could say that the information that I was given was very true.

"Parker you need to push yourself harder. I know you didn't come all the way out here to stay at the back of the line every damn day. We have a track meet in a few days and it appears to us that you are not ready. I know you want to run because this is one of our major meets." Angie said as if she was frustrated with me. She is something like my own personal motivational speaker and trainer. She ran track here the previous year and will be finishing this year.

She puts you in the mind of a tomboy: Well she is a tomboy. Her hair is short but it's styled in baby dreads. She is one of the faster girls on this team, I couldn't catch her if she had on a pair of heels. Instead of panties, she wears boxers. Her wardrobe consists of tennis shoes; Preferably Jordan's, button down polo shirts and baggy pants. She would try to dress up a little by wearing a pair of fitted jeans and a tight fitting shirt: but that's all you are getting out of Angie.

She sees more capability in me than I see in myself and that is not a good thing. It's like I know that I can do well but I perform better when other people tell me that I can do it. My self-esteem is so low but again that is something I'm still working on. Whenever I feel like quitting and going home, she says only a few words to rejuvenate me. I don't see her as much as the other girls because she doesn't live in or near our track house but we do communicate on an everyday basis so it's the same.

You would think that I would be trying to show off in front of Alex since he was now running with this team but I was not. I was very tired, lazy and didn't have a care in the world for whoever was watching. Many people have said that "Having Sex" is one of the best ways to ruin your track career, besides getting caught on steroids, and we have been having sex almost every other day and that's exactly why I am out here moving so slow. But Alex, on the other hand, is doing pretty good. I thought sex can slow down a guy as well but it doesn't seem to be bothering him as much. Poor thing was over there running his little heart out trying to stay in the front with the big dogs: and I do mean DOGS because we have some killers on this team. They practice and run as if they are trying out for the Olympics or something. My Alex may not be the fastest but he definitely isn't the slowest guy on this team, I don't think.

Finally, coach called for a water break and I swear we never get enough of those. They won't be satisfied until we fall out or die from a heat stroke in this hot ass sun. One swallow of water out of these tiny toddlers cup and we were back on the field.

"Alright, we are going to do this last thing but only if everyone does it correctly and exactly how I want it done. If not, we will start practice over." Coach said. I looked up and suddenly everyone cut their eyes over at me. Hell I was probably not running at the speed that they wanted me to run but I was on it.

"I want everyone to get in one single file line and every time I blow the whistle, someone will take off. I will give each of you enough time to get some length before I send the next person after you. The person behind you should not catch you but if that does happen, practice starts over. Please don't try and slow up to avoid not passing the person in front of you because I am timing you. Parker, you are up first then Teri you are up behind her."

"Who is up first?" I asked. No this Bitch didn't. See, this is the shit that I constantly talk about. I hate when she does stupid shit like this. Lord I could barely breathe so how could I pull this off especially with Teri coming right after me. Coach's words were, "Not to let anyone pass you" and there was no doubt in my mind that Teri is going to pass me even if she gave me a two hundred yard lead, being that she is the fastest girl on this team.

"Come on Parker, you can do it." My teammates cheered

"Let's go Parker. You're up" Coach said.

All of the attention was on me once again but this time, I didn't like it as much. Somehow, I was able to bring out that faith in myself that I had hidden. She blew that whistle and I took off finishing first and in time with no one catching up to me. I applauded myself when I crossed the line but I already knew what I could do it. I was just nervous.

After everyone finished, practice was over and I couldn't have been happier. Alex walked up to me and told me how good I did today acting like a proud father or something. Now that football season was over, we didn't wait around anymore because Dan was always ready to leave right after our practice was over. The only time that Alex and I ride with Dan is when we are going to my house.

Otherwise we would ride with Mike and Keziah and stay at their house. I was in the process of saving so I could go and purchase my own set of wheels. I had my own money. I didn't have to ask anyone for anything especially a man. I never have and hopefully, I never will. It feels to be independent. My dad taught me that I should keep a job and a nice amount of money in my savings account so when my husband comes along, he will have to offer me more than money to keep me. And besides, my money adds interest because my dad gives me whatever I want.

Speaking of parents, I had to call my dad and step mom to see if they were still coming to my track meet. This will be the first time my dad gets to see me run! I'm so excited! He was gone long before I realized that I even loved track: so he was thrilled about coming. Our coach had the team selling calendars for one of our fundraisers and he wanted to showboat so he sold every single calendar I had and wanted to sell more. My coach gave out LBC hats and shirts and since my dad was so supportive of the team, she gave him clothing as well. He proudly calls me everyday to tell me that he has on his red LBC clothing cruising in his red Corvette.

"Hello" "Hey daddy, this is Parker. What cha doing?" "Nothing parker, I just gave you some money." "See daddy, that's why I don't call you because when I do call, you think I'm asking for money." "Well most of the time you are." He said sarcastically "Anyway, I was calling to see if you and ma were still coming to the track meet this weekend." "Uh yea I was going to call you about that; I have this engagement to do at a church so we won't be able to make it."

I was excited about them coming. He even said that they were going to place all of their plans to the side so they could come out and see me run but obviously, things had changed. I didn't let on to the fact that I was disappointed but I knew he could tell because there was a sudden silence. "Hello, hello." He said repeatedly "Yea daddy I'm here." "What's wrong?" (Besides the fact that you and ma are complete liars) I thought. "Nothing is wrong." I replied. He started laughing so hard as if I had just said something extremely funny.

"Now you know I was just teasing you. I wouldn't miss this meet for anything in the world." He knew that was a good way to stop all communications with them but I was relieved. Most of the girls wasn't from Cali so they didn't have any family members here but I was blessed enough to have my step-mom, dad and grandma so I most definitely wanted that support from them. Besides, I usually perform great when I have family members at my track meets because I like to show out in front of them. I hope that I do well this weekend because I just love making my parents proud.

"Aight daddy, you made your joke for today so I will talk to you later.

"Ok baby, don't practice too hard this week." "Bye."

Chapter 24

First Track Meet

"It never fails Parker. If we are rushing or taking our time, you will always be the person that everyone has to wait on." Keziah said. I think I fell asleep talking to Alex last night and now I had overslept. We agreed that we should sleep in our own beds and in our own homes because we both needed our rest for today's track meet: We had to focus. But by the looks of things, we did the opposite. I can't remember exactly how we got off the phone last night but here I was minutes away from being late. I woke up running around like a chicken with its head cut off. I couldn't find anything that I was looking for. Mike is outside tooting that damn horn as if he has no sense and Keziah is nagging in my ear about how I'm always late.

Hell I know that I am very slow when it comes to getting dressed so I didn't need her reminding me. Finally, I had everything I needed but it still felt as if I was forgetting something because I always leave something behind. But if I forgot it today then it was left because there is no way Keziah and Mike was about to let me go back in the house to do a double check. Once I was in the car, I realized that I hadn't spoken with Alex this morning. I hope he got up in time because he has a longer drive than I do. I could call but I wanted to avoid doing that right now because I woke up frustrated and with only about five hours of sleep in me. I love my baby but I know how I am. If I saw him right now or talked to him, we would be out here clowning around and losing our focus. I am in three different events today, the 400-meter dash, 4x4 meter relay and my specialty, which is the High Jump. I was never too fond about running but jumping is what I live for,

Patrice L. Guyton

I love it: It's the reason I love track so much. In high school, I consider myself a good jumper, you know slightly above average but I am running against college girls now and competing with them is no joke. I just hope they don't beat me too bad.

No lie, Mike was really tripping. I have never seen him drive so fast to get somewhere. Hell he don't drive like that when he is late for work. I didn't have time to calm my nerves or get myself together because we arrived at the school approximately ten minutes later. When I hopped out the car, it was like I pulled up to a big block party.

There were cars and people everywhere. I heard that track meets out here are like nightclubs, because people get all dressed up to come here, but I didn't imagine that it would be this many people. I could smell the aroma from the bar b que on the other side of the field, the announcer was over the speakers testing out the microphone, and a gunman trying out his gun. Teams were already warming up and doing their drills and here we were just making it to the school.

Keziah and Mike threw me the keys and rushed out the car. I wasn't completely prepared for this meet. I had my shoes on but the laces were untied and my uniform was wrinkle as hell. I sat in the car debating if I was going to go in or not. I had so much anxiety flowing through my veins. I just wanted to go out there and perform: I want these girls to leave here with a little fear in their hearts. I need them to be in the mindset of "Stepping their game up" every time they see me. I want to be known as the High Jumper that came from Mississippi and took over. Finally, I walked to the track and found the entire team impatiently standing there waiting on me. I knew I was late and I knew I was going to make it up at practice the following week and Coach didn't hesitate on reminding me.

What she said went in one ear and out the other. I couldn't let her get to me. Hell, I was already nervous so her being mad and threatening me was the least of my worries. With only thirty minutes until the start of the meet, we had to jog a lap and do our stretches. I was so far in a dazed that I didn't notice Alex until we were finished with the warm-up. I saw him walking towards me out of the corner of my eyes. "Baby you forgot about me this morning didn't you?" he said. That's the voice that always sends chills down my spine whenever it speaks to me. Just one word makes my day. I turned around with the biggest smile on my face matching the same one he had on his. We were acting like we didn't just see each other last night. But then again, that's the way love goes. I hope he didn't think I was avoiding him because I really didn't see him when I walked in.

"Bay, I'm sorry for not calling. You see what kind of morning I am having don't you? I overslept and was hoping that you didn't do the same." "Babe its cool. Let's just focus right now and we will talk once the meet starts."

Coach didn't like seeing couples around each other on Meet days because she figured it will cause them to lose their focus, but she was right so we agreed to keep our distance until later on. Besides, everyone was already pissed at me but they will eventually come around. I don't know why but during the morning of a track meet, there is a lot of tension and everyone is in their own zone but as the day goes by and as we start to win events: everyone starts to joke around with each other and come out of their shell.

• • •

With our girl's team leading the meet by only 1 point, we needed to win the 4x4 meter relay. This is the most anticipating and most watched event at every track meet because it brings so much energy. Our girls' team has 110 points and our competition, Cerritos has 109 points so it all leads down to whoever wins this race. It can go either way so it will make or break us. We have more track meets ahead but we want to start the season off right. I did ok in the 400-meter dash and I came in first place in the high jump but I only cleared 5'2: which is not bad but it's not great either. I cleared almost 5'5 in high school but I just couldn't pull it off today.

I was disappointed in myself but I am very confident that I will clear 5'5 and higher before the season is over. Alex did ok today. Coach only had him in one event and that was 100-meter dash just to see where he stands. He came in second to last in his heat. His confidence was shot. I have never seen him so upset. But he knew what he was up against before he came out here bragging about how good he was in high school and at his previous college. I didn't care about how fast or slow he was or how many records he "Say" he has. I loved him and I was going to applaud him regardless. But I didn't know that I had a soar looser on my hands. I was at the finish line cheering him on but he was so upset that he didn't acknowledge me standing there. I'm pretty sure that a number of people get upset when they lose but Alex got furious. He literally turned his head the other way and kept walking.

But here we are down to the last event of the day and he still has not said anything to me or anyone else on the team, but at this moment, I couldn't focus on him. Coach put me on first leg so it was up to me to give our team a good lead. If that isn't pressure then I don't know what it is. I had no idea how I was going to pull this off, but I knew I had to do it.

I was told to gather the girls to stretch and warm up. I was trying to remain calm because if they knew how I was feeling right now, they would not choose me to start as first leg. We gathered around, prayed and got ready for lineup.

"Parker you up." Coach yelled. I was so nervous. I heard people cheering for their team. I heard individual names being called out, I heard coaches yelling at athletes to stop walking on the track because the race was about to start and above all, I heard a voice in my head telling me not to run this race but it was too late to change my mind because I was already in my starter blocks. I knew once that gunman raised that gun toward the sky that nothing else matters.

"Runners take your mark!" he yelled "Get Set!" I stood there sweating, trembling and waiting to hear the shot from the gun.

He pulled the trigger and I took off as fast as I could and suddenly, I was in a world of my own. I wasn't hearing anything but heavy breathing from the girls behind me trying their best to catch up to me. I tried to keep Coach P famous words in my head, "Sprint the first one hundred, tuck your arms in and kick your legs for the straightaway and once I get to the two hundred mark: give all that I have in me and more. I could hear Nene at the finish line cheering and screaming "Come on Parker, she is right on you. Don't let her pass you. Come on! We need you!" I heard her and I was trying my best to get up there but I felt my legs wobble with every step I took. "LONG BEACH IS GIVING OUT! SHE WON'T MAKE IT TO THE FINISH LINE!" Someone yelled out to one of the girls behind me.

The moment I heard that nonsense I pushed myself even harder. I was determined to keep these girls behind me. I finally made it to Nene who took off before I could make it all the way to her and all I could say was "Wait! Hold On Nene, You don't have the stick." She grabbed the baton and took off. I fell to the ground and was moments away from caving in and it seemed like no one cared. All I heard was "Come on Nene, Let's give them a run Nene, Don't let her catch up with you Nene" while I was over here laying outside of those white pearly gates. They love you when you out there on the track in first place but as soon as you hand that baton over; the attention is on that person running. By the time I got off the ground to cheer on my teammates, they were already on the fourth leg and Angie had the lead, of course. I could tell by the way she practice that she was going to come out here and show out. When we do the 4x4 run through at practice, she completes a 400 in about 53 seconds, so I knew she was going to give them a run for their money today.

We came in first, winning the 400 meter relay by six seconds and our girl team won first place overall by nineteen points. We received our medals and joked around with the other teams for a minute. Alex walked up and congratulated me. I started not to say anything to his stubborn ass but he was looking so cute with that puppy dogface that I couldn't resist. "I know I'm wrong for not coming down here to wish you Good Luck but I was so upset with the way I ran today." *Yeah, running like that you should be.* I thought. "Baby I understand that and if I would have done poorly (which I didn't) I laughed, "I still wouldn't have completely ignored you today the way you did me. But it's over now so we are not going to dwell on that. "Apology accepted." I said "Parker that's why I love you." "And that's exactly why I love you too but you are not off the hook. You will be making that up to me later on tonight."

Coach called a quick meeting to congratulate everyone on their success today. She was very proud of us. "Give yourselves a pat on the back because you all did very well. Now be safe for the rest of the weekend and I will see you guys and girls at practice on Monday. Let's put it up!"

Everyone stacked their hands on each other while Coach led the chant,

"1-2-3 LONG BEACH!!

Alright see you athletes later."

I grabbed Alex's hand and headed straight to my dad and step-mom because I didn't want them to try and run off. I needed my dad to feel Alex out for me and let me know if he sees anything that I couldn't see. Because believe it or not parents (especially dads) could smell a rat miles away. I am a daddy's girl so he is very protective: Which can be excellent and terrible at times. It all depends on the situation. I introduced them and then the handshake came. My dad told me before he came that if Alex gives him a soft and feminine hand shake that he was going to break us up because that will show him that Alex is not a man or some crap. I swear, my daddy comes up with all of these remedies that I have never heard of. I eased my way away from them just so they could get to know each other without me being around, but I couldn't go off too far.

I had to stay close and be nosey because I didn't want them running off at the mouth or scaring Alex away. Parents ask questions that we as females want to know the answer to but really don't want to come right out and ask. So it's kind of a good thing that dads grill the hell out of their daughter's boyfriend. We could really find out where their head is. But a minute or two was all my dad needed so I slowly eased my way back over to where they were standing to find the conversation coming to an end.

"Well ok. I really enjoyed you guys today. I already told her but be sure to tell your Coach and her assistant Coach P that I said, "Good Job. They put together a great team. Y'all gave em a run for their money today. Job well done Parker. Yes, job well done." My step mom added. "Well, we are about to get on this road and head back home. I'm not trying to be driving all night and besides, your mom here is hungry. She didn't want to go to the concession to grab a hot dog; too much fat in it and you know she has to keep that figure right." My dad said. She is a health freak. She really dont eat bread, definitely no fried foods or pork. Vegetables, lean meat and water is some her favorites. She wasn't big at all, as a matter of fact, she seemed to be in perfectly good shape but she still wanted to loose more weight. "Alex, it was nice to meet you" she said "and I trust that you are going to take care of my daughter while I'm not around." My daddy added

"Yes sir you have my word."

"Aight y'all. I love you and drive safe."

Thank Goodness that went well. No fireworks and no drama. Our team took first place, my daddy behaved and Alex passed the test. Today was good but I was ready to cuddle with my boo and lay down. We both agreed to stay at my house instead of Keziah and Mike's place. We're off of work tomorrow so we have no need to get up early. "Well let's get ready to get out of here. I'm just ready to take a shower and go to sleep: well let me rephrase that: take a shower, get a quickie and then go to sleep." Alex said

"Yea I bet you are."

Hell I was ready for that my damn self. I couldn't believe we went a whole night without it. But it was kind of a good thing because he sucked today and I barely made it across the line. The next time we have to go without sex about three days prior to the meet. I can't have him doing poorly because of my goodies. I can't be that selfish! Tonight I just wanted to cuddle up in that muscular body of his. We didn't have any plans for tomorrow and that's exactly when my job will call and tell me to come in to work. I said that I was going to put in my two weeks' notice soon or maybe the next time I clock in for work.

Working is not exciting to me anymore. I know it may seem like I'm lazy (which I am) but between Alex, school, practice and work: I really don't have time for myself.

Every girl needs time for herself. Besides, I don't need that job anyway. I could make it on the money that I have saved up, my dad and the aid that I am receiving from my school. They have cut my hours down tremendously so it already feels as if I have no job anyways. I talked it over with Alex the other day and he told me to do what I want but to also think about how I was going to make it when my money starts to run out. It was definitely a decision that I have to make but I was leaning more towards quitting.

Patrice L. Guyton

A Journal Entry

It's been a while since I've have talked to you. I have had so many things going but now I am settled so here you go.

April 24th 2008/ 8:30 p.m

First off, I can't believe that it's actually raining in California. I have been here for about eight months and this is the first time I have seen precipitation fall from the sky and that's pretty sad. All of the land out here is burnt. Everything looks like hay instead of grass so I am actually very happy to know that plants and trees are receiving their share of water right now. But I'm not too happy for myself. Lately, Alex and I have been arguing about some things that should be avoided.

He is very jealous and has a terrible temper problem. He gets mad at small things so quick. For instance one day at track practice I forgot to bring workout clothes. (Yea I know that was not smart) But coach was not trying to hear that. She told me that I was working out no matter what. If I didn't work out, I wasn't going to be able to run at the meet that upcoming weekend. I had two options, workout in the dress that I had on that day or our track uniform.

Our uniform is a short jumpsuit that's made out of 100 percent spandex. Well I wasn't going to run in my dress. A few of the teammates, including Alex, didn't qualify pass the District meet so they were out for the remainder of the season, meaning they didn't have to practice anymore. One of his homeboys saw me running in the uniform and went and told him: Mind you that my ass is very big and my pussy is super fat so my goodies were peeking through this thin as material. I had no other choice. We were getting ready for our Regional meet so I had to practice. I was barely done with my warm-up when I looked up and noticed Alex coming my way stomping as hard as he could with a look on his face like, "I'm about to fuck you up." He threw me a pair of big ass maroon basketball shorts. "Put these shorts on right now" he yelled. I looked behind me to make sure that someone was there because I knew damn well that this short, curly head, non running ass nigga wasn't talking to me. That was the first time that he had ever disrespected me. I was even more furious at the fact that he did it in front of my friends.

We stood there arguing until Coach P called me to come and practice. Like a fool, I eventually ended up with the shorts on. I later regretted it because all during practice everyone was teasing me saying things like "Put the shorts on Annie Mae" which was not amusing to me at all. I think someone told him that he somehow owns me and whoever that was provided him with false information.

Recently, I came back into contact with Marcus, an old boyfriend, from back in Mississippi. Every time he calls me, Alex will get so mad that I will actually have to get off the phone just to avoid an argument. I don't hound him like that when he talks to his girl-friends because he is always around me. We are with one another almost twenty-four hours of the day; except for when we have to work, so there is no need for him to be jealous. Marcus lives hundreds of miles away down in Mississippi and is only a friend. I knew him before I met Alex so I was not about to drop him just because he thinks that we still had something going on. Hell he would really want to blow something up if he knew that this was the same dude, that I lost my virginity to at the age of 14. I know, sad but true. We have moved passed that but we will always be friends. He has two boys and a potential wife. Besides, I don't see Marcus in that way anymore but I love to see Alex sweat, so I let him do his assuming.

Chanel, Dan, Alex and Teri got a job at this Chicken restaurant that just opened. They all went to fill out an application and were hired on the spot. Speaking of jobs, I quit mines simply because I didn't feel like working anymore. I was putting too much stress on my beautiful body. I was tensed every day and that job was not worth it. I don't miss it or regret my decision to leave.

I was very blessed to receive a 2003 **candy apple red Mazda Protégé** after a very emotional track meet I had about a month ago. I was trying to clear 4'10 in the high jump and I couldn't. 4'10: That's something an eighth grader could jump. I was so disappointed in myself because I know that I have done better and that I could do better. My dad and step mom was there encouraging me and telling me not to give up so easily but that didn't help at all. I cried every time I didn't clear that bar: I mean I was seriously out there embarrassing myself. Of course I was put out and that tore my heart into shreds.

I immediately walked away, found the nearest curb and sat there with my anging low to the ground. My dad and step-mom tried talking to me but I wasn't hearing anything they had to say; in one ear and out the other. I didn't even want Alex talking to me at the time. The only person that could talk to me and give me a few words of encouragement was my mom. I phoned her and told her how poorly I did and she didn't sound a bit worried. "Baby you can't win them all. Just last year in high school, you were a star athlete and now it's taking you a little longer to get adjusted but this is only your first year so give it some time. You just have to practice harder and stay focus, always keep God first and everything will definitely play out." Once I got off the phone with her, I was much better.

I was finally able to recoup my strength and say a few words to my dad and mom. After congratulating me on doing my best, they told me to take a walk with them and so I did. We ended up at the Protégé which was my step-mom's car at the time. "Parker can you get that coat out of the trunk for me?" my dad asked. He was standing right there so I was confused on why he couldn't do it but I obeyed him, opened the trunk and saw a yellow piece of paper with the words, "This car belongs to our angel 'Parker'. I was upset with the lack of success I had on my jump earlier but all of that left the moment I read those words. I was so excited. I wanted to cry but I had done enough of that already so I screamed to the top of my lungs. "THANK YOU JESUS!!" I no longer have to ask Dan, Keziah or Mike for a ride to get around. Even more so, I was able to see Alex whenever I wanted to.

Eventually my car started to establish more problems between me and Alex. I was late picking him up a few times from work and that gave him the perfect opportunity to tell me, "I knew was going to change once you got your new car." He claimed that no one else mattered as long as I got where I needed to go. I swear it's always something. Anyway, Track has been going good. This has been a crazy, fun, exciting and different season but I'm ready for a break. We have two meets left, North state this weekend and State next weekend and it's over.

After a track meet: Me, my dad and Alex walked past this guy who goes by the name "Buck". I know him from being over Mike's house, so when he saw me with Alex he said, "Parker, you looking good today. Where yo boyfriend?" and before I could get out "This is my boyfriend", Alex had already said "Her boyfriend is right here, who wants to know?" I was like Ooooh shit, because Alex has a smart ass mouth and Buck is in this popular gang out here called the Neighborhood Crips. I have heard some very disturbing things about them so even though they are cool to be around, I try my best to stay away from that crowd because gang bangers in Cali don't play around. If one fight then they all fight and Alex knows that because his brother claims to be a Crip and they are one of the biggest and dangerous gangs in LA, well California.

I remember going over his brother's house one day and it was about ten guys standing outside shooting dice on the sidewalk. Keep in mind that my car is red and red is not welcomed in their neighborhood so when I drove up, everybody jumped up reaching for their guns just because I was driving a red car in their "Blue" neighborhood. He had to tell them that I was with him. So yea, that's how serious gangs are out here. But anyway, Alex and Buck exchanged a few violent words. Buck was calling out his set and so was Alex. To me it was only a simple misunderstanding but to them it had gone to something serious in a matter of seconds. We were in Long Beach with all of Buck's bangers and Alex was alone because all of his people are in LA, well he had his god brother's (Dan and his brother) but hell they can't fight worth of shit and I know I was not about stand up against all of those men. I'm not a ride or die Bitch: I'm a smart chick. He wouldn't fight a gang of girls for me so it's sort of the same thing: I think. But that day was a day that I will never forget.

Alex and I starting walking my dad to his car and out of nowhere comes Buck and about 25 guys trying to call Alex on his bluff. He was furious. I think he actually thought that he could go against them all, but that's how it is when your adrenaline is pumping: You think that anything is possible. My dad was trying to get him to calm down and so was I but he wasn't trying to hear neither one of us. By this time a crowd came and Alex kept saying "If I don't fight him then I will look like a punk and we don't get down like that in my hood." The more we tried to calm him down the angrier he got.

He started to literally hit his head on a brick wall, banging it back and forth as hard as he could. I have never seen anything like that before. He seemed like an insane person and I have never seen an insane person. As my friend Melissa will say, "He's a damn fool". It shocked my dad so he came and pulled me away from Alex. I did what my dad suggested and let him walk all of that steam off. We didn't meet up again until later that night. He had to go to the hospital because he had given himself a concussion from hitting his damn head so many times. I've been asking myself if I should stay in a relationship with him because that was some freaky shit.

But he apologized to me. He told me that he hate I had to see him act like that. But as far as all of the mood swings that he has every now and then, we are doing ok.

We were on the verge of breaking up at one point because I went through his phone and noticed that he had been talking to two particular females on a regular basis. **Mistake # 1:** NEVER SNOOP AROUND because eventually you will find something that you really don't want to see and that also means there is a lack of trust somewhere. It's like this, I know he loves me but sometimes I just have to know for sure. I want to know that's it me and only me that he wants to be with. He didn't have their full names saved in his phone. One girl name was "Red" and the other one was "Shorty". I wasn't too worried about Shorty because they were having little everyday chit chat. "How was your day" and "How is work?" It was that Red that had my attention. She was telling him how she misses him and wishes he would stop by sometimes.

Without thinking twice I called her up from his phone but I blocked the number so she would not have his name on her caller ID. As soon as she answered all but who walks into the room which leads me to **Mistake # 2:** NEVER GET CAUGHT, but that's exactly what I did. I had the guilt look all over my face with his phone in my hand. He politely took his phone and walked out the door. He didn't call me for about three or four days and he didn't say anything to me at school. Every time I tried to call or text, he didn't respond. I took it that we were no longer in a relationship. I looked through my closet and found the shortest and tightest skirt that I owned. I picked out a tank top, tied it in the back and wore it to school. I be damn, that was the only thing I had to do. He was jealous of all the attention my ass was receiving and we started back talking right then. He explained to me that Red was a girl he went to high school with.

I love him so much even though we have our tiny flaws but what relationship doesn't? He hasn't gotten old to me yet and hopefully he never does. But yeah that's about all of the updates right now and as you could see I was a little behind. I have got to start writing to you every day or at least every other day because you have my damn hand hurting. But I have to get ready because he just called and said that he wants to take me out tonight so until next time, Peace and Love. -Parker

CHAPTER 25

The mistake that ruined everything

Well damn, that was quick. Track season was over and it seemed like it all happened with a blink of the eye this year. The girls did good overall but we only sent about three girls to state. Every relay lost except for the 4x4 meter relay. We won first place beating the number one 4x4-relay team in the state of California but we were disqualified because one of our teammates walked across the track to go shake someone's hand when the race wasn't over. We really deserved that title but it was snatched away from us because of a simple and stupid ass mistake. Everyone including myself was so pissed at her for doing something so irresponsible but we got over it: Weeks later, many weeks later.

I have moved out of the track house due to a lack of funds. I wasn't working anymore so that two hundred and ninety dollars a month was beginning to put a hole in my pockets. I had been talking to my grandma lately and she volunteered to let me come and live with her "Rent Free". God knew that I was not going to be able to pay rent another month. That was a huge blessing because either she was going to help me or I had to move in with my dad and step-mom, meaning I was going to change schools. I am still telling all of my friends back home that I have my own place and a job just so they could think I was out here in Cali, living it up. I wasn't doing bad: I just didn't have a job nor my own place anymore but hell they would never know.

I have been very exhausted lately. I haven't been practicing or working so I don't know what could possibly be wrong. My step-mom figured that my metabolism was low because of the small amount of daily physical activities that I was involved in. I've been sleeping and eating a lot these days but that's nothing new. That has been my lifestyle for years. Eating and sleeping are two things that I love to do so my body should be used to this.

I do not like the idea that I am not working so I have decided to go and look for another job. I love having my own money and having money gives me my own freedom.

As I lay in my bed, moments away from counting that last sheep, I hear my phone ring. I rolled over and tried to continue counting but the ringing didn't stop. My grandma is in the other bedroom trying to take a nap as well so I didn't want to wake her. I ignored the first call but whomever this annoying person is, keeps calling. My phone is on the other side of the room, on the charger. That means that I have to sit up, get up and walk over to answer. If you ask me, that's too much damn work. All but who has called me three times, Nene black ass. Before I could dial her number, she was calling back. *This better be important because she knows that I really don't fool with her scandalous ass anyway.*

"Hello" I said sounding irritable. "Parker get yo ugly ass up. I need you to take me to get me something to eat." For one, how in the hell can she call anyone ugly with that monkey ass face that she has and two, she didn't ask, she demanded. "Where is everyone else that always agrees to be your taxi?" I asked trying to hint at the fact that I didn't feel like being bothered with her. "I have called everyone but no one is answering." *Hell they were doing what I should have done and that was, Ignore Her.* "Damn Nene, I was lying down." "Parker please, there is no food in this house." "Yea, whatever, I'm on my way." I only volunteered because I was hungry myself and even though she is an obnoxious bitch, I couldn't let her starve. I didn't know where she wanted to get something to eat from nor was I going to ask her. I didn't feel like driving all over Long Beach and she wasn't offering any gas money. Once I picked her up, I took her to McDonalds and they have a dollar menu, so that was right in my range.

Once we arrived back at the track house, I decided that I would go in and eat. I wasn't doing anything at my grandma's house anyway. Nene does work my nerves at times but I was anxious to hear any new gossip that she had. Her messy ass always has the scoop on everyone. We are always at each other's throat but we can engage in a decent conversation every now

Fell Too Deep

and then. Alex was at work so I was in no hurry to get back to the house. Most of the girls have left the track house and moved into their own place or in with their boyfriends. The back room once was Keziah's room, but since she moved out, Nene and Teri has moved in.

After we ate: we popped in a DVD and relaxed. Before the movie began, Nene had fallen asleep and had started snoring. "Nene, Nene" I called her name repeatedly, but she didn't budge. I was going to leave but I didn't. I should have left but I stayed. As I grabbed my keys, Alex called. That's when I became sidetracked.

We are never lost for words when we are on the phone or in each other's presence. Six months into our relationship and I am still excited to see him walk through my doors. I still blush when I see his number pop up on my phone. I love Alex and the best feeling is knowing that he loves me just as much. When I told him that I was over here at the track house with Nene, he was shocked, mainly because we have bickered with one another this entire school year. Before we got off the phone, he told me that I didn't have to come and get him from work today because he was going over Dan's house to play video games. Typical Alex, but I was fine with that because I didn't feel like driving all the was across town to pick him up, but of course I would have.

Hell I was talking about Nene falling asleep on me but here I was about to do the same thing. I knew it would kick in soon because I was almost sleep when she interrupted me. There isn't any furniture in her room except for the tiny ass chair I was sitting in and the bed she was laying in. The chair was very uncomfortable; the floor wasn't an option so I decided to go get in the bed. She was already at the head so I went to lie down at the foot of the bed (it reminded me of when I was younger and there were about three or four people in one bed. Everyone was pushing, kicking and pulling covers off one another.) I was only lying there for a short period of time when out of nowhere, a vigorous chill went through my body. Immediately, I was horny. I started to rub on myself; from my thighs to my breast. This feeling shocked me. Why am I feeling so freaky and even more so, why am I rubbing on myself? Not thinking or knowing exactly what I was getting myself into, I place my hand on Nene's leg. I slowly rub my hand up and down her leg but then she moved her body. That was my cue to pull back. As I lied there in disbelief of my actions, I thought, "What am I doing? Why am I rubbing on this girl? This is so out of line.

Most of all, this is not me." Yes, I am horny but is it to the point where I can't wait until my man gets off of work? With that being said, I folded my hands in between my own damn thighs and tried to sleep those sexually hormonal feelings off.

It wasn't happening and there was no shaking them off. I took a bold step. I placed my hands in between her thighs and started to massage them gently. Oh, I was so wet and my hormones was really kicking my ass. I didn't care if she got offended. I was about to make her feel so good that she wouldn't want me stop even though, I am a girl. I could tell that she wasn't sleep anymore because she was slowly opening her legs giving me more room to play around with. Yeah I think she was feeling the same way I was feeling. I moved up to where she was so we would be face to face. Before things went any further, she stopped and asked if I knew what I was doing. "Do you really want to do this?" she asked. "Hell yeah." I said. "There is no sense in stopping now." No matter what anyone says, every girl has a little freak and bisexual feelings within. Since I'm a freak, why not try them both at one time. We started kissing and then she moved her hands down to my ass; trying not to squeeze it too hard, she gave me a grip that felt so good. She whispered in my ear, "Let me fuck you better than any man ever has," high off her aroma, I passionately said "Do it Nene". Tongue Kissing turned into a form of kissing that has no name. She outlined my lips with her tongue and then twirled that same tongue around in my mouth. With one hand, she rubbed her fingers through my hair and with the other hand; she went down my side with her index finger sending love spells through my spine. Her hands were so soft. It was something that I have never felt before. It felt so different. It's like she knew where to touch me. It felt so right.

Then I rolled her over so I could get on top and show her the magic that I had. I started with the most sensitive part on any person's body and that is, the neck.

Trying to keep her from squirming, I pinned both of her arms down beside her and made my way to her breasts, which were sitting so pretty. I licked my tongue around her nipples and eased my way down until her entire breast was in my mouth. That room was so heated but all I could focus on was her moans, "Yes Parker", "Damn Parker, Right there Parker." That let me knew that I was doing a damn good job. I placed my hands back in between her thighs and her cum was flowing faster than a waterfall. I gently placed my hand inside of her warm and moist vagina. I could tell that I had sent her to another planet. She placed her hands inside of me I damn near passed out.

We were finger fucking each other and it almost felt as good as a penis. I could feel cum sliding down my legs. I was on the verge of screaming. I tried holding it but I couldn't. We switched positions because she wanted to be on top. She starting riding me like there was no tomorrow. I laughed to myself, "Who knew that bumping pussy would feel this awesome?" She started grinding on me in every position possible. She said that she wanted to lick me down and not miss one single spot. By this time I could barely speak. I could barley move and it felt as if my body was about to lock up. I could not believe that a female was making me feel this way. She eased her mouth on down, and all I could do was shiver because I knew exactly what it was that she was about to do. She was headed down to eat me out. *Thank God, I shaved last night.*

I tilted my head back and grab her head to get ready for what I thought was about to be an unforgettable moment and then "Bang, Bang, Bang". Someone was knocking on the damn door. She jumped up and threw a blanket on me because I was completely nude, with the exception of having on socks. She threw on a pair of sweat pants that was on the floor and a tank top that laid on the chair that I was sitting in earlier. "Pretend like you are sleep" she said as she rushed to the door. Who of all people was it?

One of Alex's god brothers, Dean. He and Nene are close. I heard him tell her that he had been calling and didn't get an answer so he decided to stop by. "Damn". I thought. "Who is that over there sleep?" he asked. "Oh that's Parker" She told him. "We were both watching a movie and just fell asleep. But give me a minute to wash my face and I will be right out." She said. "Ok, I will go sit outside." He walked off and she closed the door. "I'm going out here to talk with him for a second because it seems like something is bothering him. I'll be right back and please stay lying in that exact position." She demanded. I waited for about ten minutes and finally, I came to my senses. I was lying in a bed waiting for a female to come and finish having sex with me. What did I just do but even worst; whom did I just do? Oh my gosh, Alex! I couldn't believe that I had just cheated on him. What am I going to do? As all of these thoughts flush through my mind, I jumped up and started putting my clothes back on. "Fuck." What if she tells Dean and he tells Alex? I was screwed but it wasn't a "What if" because she was most definitely going to tell him. If not him, she was going to tell her ace boom Teri and from there the news was going to travel. They were sitting on the curb outside. I was so embarrass to walk passed them. I said, "Bye" and drove off.

As I drove home, I repeatedly asked myself the same questions time and time again. Why did I enjoy that so much? Am I gay? Would I do it again? I was so confused because I love my boyfriend and he was the only person that I wanted to be with but then again, all I could think about was how good this just felt. I just betrayed a faithful person and I should be ashamed of myself. I knew that I had done a terrible thing. I felt sick as I replayed the moment in my head. I couldn't drive any further. I had to pull over.

Moments later, I was on the side of the freeway vomiting. I was dizzy and I saw my world crumble right before my eyes. What have I done? I prayed to God asking him to rewind the last hour of my life so I could do things a little bit different. Instead of going inside of the track house, I would have went back home. As I got back into my car, I realized that this was reality and as bad as I wanted to turn back the hands of time, I couldn't. There wasn't anything that I could do because the damage was already done. This is a secret that I must take to my grave. I can't tell Alex and I have to make sure that Nene never says a word to anyone. I have a feeling that the mistake I just made is going to affect me for the rest of my life.

CHAPTER 26

Word on the street is......

I had a craving for one of those chicken sandwiches from that restaurant that Alex works at. I think Chanel was doing drive-thru today so that means "Free Food." Alex was at his house waiting on me to come back. He didn't want to ride with me because they have been working him like crazy and he didn't like seeing his job, unless he has to work.

I pulled up to order my food and there was her little squeaky voice. "Welcome to Chicken –n- things, this is Chanel, how may I help you?" "Hey girl, this is Parker. Just give me the usual." *Meaning my normal free meal.* "Parker!" she said surprisingly. When she found out that it was me, her vibe changed. I could hear it though the speakers. Maybe she is having a bad day so I didn't think anything about it. When I drove around to the window, the first words to come out of her mouth wasn't "Hey" or "How are you?" "Oooh Parker, you are so nasty." "Excuse me?" I questioned. "The word is out. You are so wrong for what you did." By this time I was very confuse. Why was she beating around the bush with whatever she had to tell me. This isn't her. Something is wrong. When she handed me my food she said, "What happened with Nene the other day?"

I tried my best to remain calm and not break into a sweat. Chanel just said Nene's name. Could she know? Could the devastating news be out? I knew that fat, black monkey face bitch was going to run her mouth. I couldn't believe Chanel knew. If she knows then Dan knows, and if he knows, then his whole house knows meaning, Alex knows what happened. If there was a cliff anywhere around, I would drive off of it just to make this nightmare go away. As all of these emotions came out, the one I felt the most was hurt and disappointment. I don't know how Alex is going to react to this once he finds out but I'm praying that he hasn't found out.

As I drove, I tried to figure out some things; Was I going to tell him the truth? How am I going to tell him? How many ways am I going to curse Nene out? I can't loose my man over this bullshit. But I know how he is. He will never believe anything that anyone will tell him. If I say that it didn't happen then he will believe just that, even if the proof is staring him in the face. The trust and the faith that he has in me in incredible, making it that much harder to actually tell him the truth. So what do I do? Tell the truth or tell a lie: either way I knew someone was going to be hurt in the end. I was starving just a minute ago and now my appetite is gone.

When I made it to his house, he was in his bed calm and collect and watching TV so I knew he didn't know anything. So I chose to lie. "Baby you would not believe that it's a rumor out about me. People are saying that I slept with Nene!" "Baby! Nene!" he laughed "Are you serious?"

I tried to laugh with him so I could make it seem even more real, but deep down I wanted to cry. He had no clue that it really had happened. "Damn baby, you sleeping with females now? Wait, You aren't sleeping with females are you?" he asked.

"Boy stop. You know you are the only person that I want. Don't ever forget that." "Baby you know I trust you. Anyway, I don't want to talk about this foolishness anymore because the thought along is sending chills through my spine. Yuck!"

Now I have him convinced that it's a lie. The ball was in my court so I had to make sure that I didn't let it go.

Day's later people started to talk about what happened. I knew that it was only a matter of time before Alex found out. He was over his god parent's house chilling and playing the video game and I was out searching for a job. I hardly had money to keep gas in my car so Alex was helping out a lot but I didn't like depending on his money. He always say "My money is your money." When he didn't have it, I gave it to him but I hate asking other people for money, even if it is my boyfriend. If I fully depend on him, then later he will think that he has some type of hold on me and I will give no man that satisfaction. But he does take real good care of me. He is always there for me and he always put me first and this is how I repay him.

I haven't been myself lately and I know that it's because of what I've done. I've been so worried at the fact that Alex may find out. My guilt was eating me up but I had a feeling something more was wrong with me. When I go to use the restroom, I have noticed that I have been spotting a little. Though it has never happened to me, I figured it was normal. I wanted to call and ask my mom but I knew that she would start worrying and put more into the situation than what it actually was. When I was over Alex's house a few days ago, his aunt told me that her mom had a dream about fish. The old saying means that someone in the family is pregnant. Alex has a brother and a few cousins so someone was pregnant and just didn't know it. Pregnancy never cross my mind because I'm on birth control and I absolutely have too many positive things going for myself to get pregnant.

Alex insisted that I go the pharmacy right up the street and get a pregnancy test just to make sure that I wasn't. I ran in the store and left my phone in the car on the charger. Once I made it back to the car, I had three missed calls from Alex and two texts telling me to call him ASAP. Dean was with Alex at the house and being that he was the one that actually seen me in Nene's room, made me think that he had already spilled the beans and had Alex convinced.

After I gained enough courage, I called him back. I heard about three or four people in his background including that bitch, that I thought was my friend, Chanel. "Parker you might as well tell the truth. He already seen the texts and heard the truth from the main source herself." I know Nene didn't tell him. She doesn't even talk to him. I was so scared. I didn't know what to say or what to do. How was I going to get myself out of it this time? I didn't tell Chanel but I was hurt to hear her in the background talking about me. I could hear her say how wrong I was to cheat and how nasty I was to sleep with another girl. How could she switch sides like that? Chanel doesn't really like Alex. I didn't know what to do.

Alex finally spoke, "Parker did you or did you not have sex with Nene?" "No Alex I did not. I would never do anything like that to you. Baby I love you too much." I said "Parker, I am going to ask you once again" he said with such anger and hurt in his voice, "DID YOU OR DIDN'T YOU SLEEP WITH NENE?" Ok Alex, here is the truth. All we did was kiss and rub on each other. Baby I swear that is all that happen." Before I could apologize, he called me a Nasty Bitch and hung up on me. When I called back, he sent me to his voicemail. I tried calling Chanel, weak ass, just to explain to her what happened and she answered the phone talking total nonsense. "Parker how could you do that to him?" she asked . Chanel, fuck what you are talking about right now.

Is Alex there?" "Yes but he can't talk to you because he is outside crying and hitting the gate with his fists. How could you?" I didn't want to hear anything she was saying because I knew it wasn't going to get me anywhere. "Whatever, I'm on my way over there." "Parker, if I was you, I wouldn't come over here." I wanted to go by there but she told me not to. She said that she didn't want him hurting me in a way that he would someday regret. At this point, her opinion don't matter so I drove over there anyway. To my surprise, his car was gone so I kept driving. I knew his family was mad at me but I didn't give a damn. My only focus was to go and find my man.

I decided to drive over to Mike and Keziah's to clear my head, get some advice from them and take this pregnant test. I was praying the whole time that the Lord will give me a positive sign on this test instead of a negative sign. Maybe if I am pregnant then he would forgive me and we would be able to move on and raise our child together. Ten minutes ago, having a baby wasn't anywhere in my plans. I really don't like kids. They cry and must be attended to all day. My nerves are on the edge. I love my freedom, my sleep and being able to get up and go whenever I feel like it. I didn't know the first thing about a baby but I do know that maybe a baby would make things better for us or get me out of the mess I was in. A prayer was needed. "Lord if you allow me to be pregnant, I will faithfully serve you for the rest of my days. I will pay my tithes and forever live in your presence. Lord you have worked many miracles and I ask that you do one more. Please, God, Please let there be a baby in my stomach." Amen.

Once I made it to Keziah's house, she was leaving. She has a doctor's appointment: her baby is due any day. "Hey stranger," she said. I haven't seen you since you turned gay". She said jokingly until she saw my eyes filled with tears. "Parker! What happened?" I told her everything. "Alex found out what happened between Nene and I. It may be over between us." She couldn't believe it. She said that she could understand his pain but it wasn't that serious. She thinks that he should be more upset if I would have slept with another man, but that was not the case.

"Before you leave, can I run in the house and take this pregnancy test?" "Pregnancy test? Please tell me that you are joking? You are joking right?" "No, I am not." She threw me the keys, "I can't believe you. Lock my door when you are done and leave my key in the mailbox." She said.

While I stood waiting on the results from the test, I couldn't help but to cry. I was willing to give up my life and my career just to be pregnant by a man that just found out that I cheated on him.

I glanced down at the stick that laid on the sink. Pregnant! Can't be? I saw my heartbeat through my shirt. I just knew that I was moments away from having a heart attack. I thought about it for a while and came up with the conclusion that I was not going along with this pregnancy.

My parents will kill me! No, my dad will be torn. Oh gosh, he will be livid. He would literally go into depression. How am I going to tell them? What am I going to say? "Uh ma and dad: I'm pregnant. They always say that "You get what you ask for" and I asked to be pregnant just because I made an enormous mistake by cheating on my boyfriend. I want to tell Alex right now, so he could forgive me and we could move pass all of this madness but something was telling me not to do so. I broke his heart and now I don't know where he is or what he is doing. As I paced back and forth, I knew I had to make the best decision for me and not him. My mind was telling me to get an abortion and not to ever tell Alex or anyone about the baby. I am a smart and beautiful lady, not to mention how talented I am on that track. I have so many goals to accomplish. I have a long life to live. Pregnant at the age of 19? What type of shit is that? I wanted to have this baby so that I can keep my man but I wanted to kill it so that I can keep my life. I stood there for about an hour debating. "Should I keep this baby or should I get an abortion, ask GOD for forgiveness and move on?"

Patrice L. Guyton

A Journal Entry
August 12th 2006 / 10:00 p.m (Headed to a place far from here)

Guess What? I am 9 weeks pregnant. Yes, Pregnant. It's amazing that I am about to bring a human being into this world but I hate the circumstances that its under. I slept with a girl, Alex found out, I wished pregnancy on my life knowing that I wasn't ready and here I am. It's still not too late to get an abortion and believe me, it has cross my mind several times. I won't say that I regret that this has happened but I did make a stupid decision. The day Alex found out that I was pregnant was the same day that he found about me sleeping with another female. That was an emotional day for the both of us. So much happened at once. I left him feeling hurt, pain, disappointment and betrayal all in a couple of hours.

He rushed off from Dan's house before I could get there to talk to him. I tried calling his aunt's phone after he didn't answer his phone. She told me that he was at the house but she didn't want me to talk with him until he was calm. About two hours later she called me and gave him the phone. To my surprise, he wanted me to come over so that we could talk. My heart was beating as fast as two hundred miles per second. I knew that he wasn't abusive but I was just as scared. It was the fact that I had to go over there, look into his eyes and apologize. I used this pregnancy as a cover up for what I had done. I knew that it really didn't matter how severe my plead for forgiveness was going to be because karma was on her way.

At that time I couldn't worry about the future. I had to focus on "right now". I remember walking in his room and looking in his eyes, which were full of tears. He had a towel wrapped around his head and ace bandages wrapped around the both of his hands. Chanel told me that he was banging his head on the steering wheel and hitting the brass fence outside of their house. (I have never gotten so upset that I have actually hurt myself. He made himself bleed. I was dealing with a damn psychopath.)

We sat there talking and sharing our opinions on the situation. His aunt gave us a talk that the both of us needed to hear. She wasn't on his side and she didn't agree with the mistake that I made. She saw the love that was flowing between us. She knew that I loved him and she knew that he loved me. We came to a mutual agreement and decided to not bring that incident up ever again. I know that it's going to take him some time to get over it but at least he was willing to move forward. That night he wanted to hold me until we fell asleep. He said that he forgave me but he didn't want to hear or think about it anymore. I was fine with that. At that point, I didn't care if I ever saw Nene again.

However, I did want to call and let her know that she left a permanent scar on my relationship but I didn't bother. Alex told me to delete her number and never talk to her again, so I did just that. I gave him my promise that Nene will never be apart of our lives again.

Everything was good for a couple of weeks and our relationship started to heal, until his uncle wanted him to dance and model in a hair/fashion show. That's when he met Bria. A little young chick that was still in high school. Skinny with terrible skin but she has long, black and pretty hair. She was in this show so of course she had to be at every rehearsal. I went over there one day and out of all the females there, I noticed something different about her and the way she looked at Alex. So of course, I became suspicious and later there were questions that needed answering. I trust him but I just wanted to know if I should be worried about her. When I finally addressed him about "Bria," he got offended. He said that she was "Just a Friend." I had a lot of "Just a Friends" back in my day so I was already ahead of him with that lame game. Keep in mind that these two people had just met so him labeling her as a friend was just awkward to me.

He went on proclaiming on how he was not the cheater. He said that it was me and that I was only jumping down his throat about her because I was sleeping around on him, Again. One thing I hate is when the blame is on a person, the other switches the situation around so quick. Why is that? Are they covering up their actions? Are they really guilty and scared to confess?

After a few days of practice, his uncle came up with a rule that didn't sit well with me. He said that there couldn't be any extra people at practice so if you weren't in the show, you couldn't come. Damn asshole, well, he isn't an asshole but that was most definitely an asshole move. I wasn't able to see what was going on behind those walls. None of his family was going to tell me because it was obvious that none of them liked me. I didn't know why. Maybe he told them that I cheated on him or maybe they didn't approve of me. Either way, they have no real reason to dislike me. When I came around, I got the strange looks and the unfriendly ways. They weren't like his aunt and cousins on the first night that I met them, these people here were the total opposite. But what pissed me off even more was the fact that Alex didn't stand up for me. He knew that I felt like an outcast around them but he never mentioned it to his family. I hate when people judge me before they get to know me because I haven't disrespected any of them. I know he saw the way that they were treating me but it's like he didn't care and I know he didn't care. Maybe he felt as if I deserved the cruelty because I hurt him so badly.

A few days later, I learned that Alex went to practice and told everyone that I had cheated on him so now they definitely don't like me. I've heard that they also think that I planned this pregnancy just to keep him. It wasn't planned, I prayed upon it. They were starting to piss me off by placing their nose in business that wasn't theirs. I wasn't showing so that meant that I could still beat a bitch ass.

Anyway, since no one was willing to give me any details from Alex and this chick Bria, I decided to get it myself. I started to check his email without him knowing about it. Ever heard the saying "If you go looking you may find something that you don't want to?" It has happened to me once before with Alex but I still did it again. I didn't care because I was convinced that they were up to something. I found an email from this Bria bitch telling my man how much she enjoyed feeling his love. What? That sounds like sex to me. Did I mention it to him? No, but did I want to? Yes. I couldn't say anything just yet because I wanted to find out more. As the weeks went by, I felt us slowly drifting apart but I couldn't blame anyone but myself. It wasn't like he was treating me wrong intentionally but the mental and verbal abuse had arrived in our relationship. We started to argue about stupid things. Every time I spoke my opinion about something he would bring up Nene. It's like the agreement we had to leave her in the pass (**Meaning: not bringing her name up ever again**) was out the window. I made a mistake but he still managed to stick it out with me so he need to leave it alone or leave me alone. People will always make mistakes. It's up to us if we want to forgive them and move forward together or separately but he chose to stay in this relationship. Hell, I didn't make him and I'm getting sick of it.

I finally broke down and asked him about Bria. I needed to know if there were any feelings involve. Our relationship was hanging on by strings because of what I had done and I was trying everyday to show how sorry I was. When I asked him he said, "Yea I'm into Bri-Bri the exact same way that you were into Nene that day you were on top of her." I that is was Bria. Hold on, who the fuck is Bri-Bri? She has nicknames and shit? So of course we had this big argument and later that night, we agreed that this was not going to work. He told me that he would take care of his child by being in his/her life but he just didn't want to be with me any longer. I was pregnant by this stupid ass boy and it was obvious that he didn't care about it. We actually went three days without speaking to each other. Those days seemed like forever. I called and apologize, not knowing exactly what it was that I had done but I just decided to be the bigger person. He admitted to having feelings for this girl but he claims that he ended things with her because he was so in love with me. "Yea Right." He said that as a couple, we are going to go through problems but he was willing to make it work if I still wanted to. Of course I was willing but I went another day without talking to him. I wanted to show him that life is pointless without me. He got the point, came around and our communication, feelings and love has gotten so much stronger. His job was going good. I think someone up there found out that I was pregnant because he was getting more hours every week. Guess they thought he needed the extra money.

• • •

I have been talking to my mom and we both decided that I should go home and visit for two weeks before the Fall school year starts. My mom has finally accepted the fact that I was pregnant even though, it definitely took some time. I broke the news to her while my friend Melissa, was on the phone. She screamed as loud as she could. She was at a lost for words. She hung up on me and moments later, after getting herself together, she called me back. She told me that an abortion was out of the question and she promised me that everything will work out.

My dad and step-mom, on the other hand, was different. I was his little girl and his first born. He was at a family reunion in Mississippi when I made that call. This time my cousin Elise, was on the phone with me. I wanted her to be the one to break the news to him. I can tell by the tone of his voice that he was furious. I heard my step-mom in the background asking him what happened and if everything was ok. He hung up on me but unlike my mom, he didn't call me back. It was about two weeks later when I heard from him again. I didn't want to answer because at the time I didn't feel like hearing what he had to say. I knew that I was a disgrace and I knew that I had disappointed him but I didn't want to hear it. When I answered, he did the unexpected. He didn't yell and he didn't curse.

He simply told me two things. He said that I couldn't live with my grandma anymore because it wouldn't be fair to her to bring a child into her home. He said that she was allowing me to live there out of the goodness of her heart and now a baby was involved so he nor my step-mom wanted the extra burdens placed on her. Which was understandable. Then he told me that upon giving me the car, we had agreements that I would stay in school, keep my grades up and not get pregnant. I broke one of the rules so they took my car. I thought that since I was pregnant that they would be more considerate but as my friends back home will say: A lie.

My dad was acting like he hated me. I can understand his feelings but I really think that he hates me. He was so proud of me and now I have gotten pregnant. Our relationship after that has gone down hill. I've tried calling him but he doesn't answer. I leave voice and text messages on his phone but he never responds. As far as my step-mom, I didn't waste my time calling her. I knew that she wouldn't even say "Hello", to me right about now. She didn't care to hear an apology or anything I had to say. I let them down tremendously so I was ok with them ignoring me and treating me so badly. I must admit that it does hurt that I haven't spoken with them in a while but there is nothing else that I can do. I can't say I'm sorry anymore and most of all I can't take back what is done. My dad wanted me out of my grandma's house immediately. I didn't have anywhere else to live so I started living at Mike and Keziah's house. All of their rooms were filled and so was the couch so I had to sleep on the floor. That's right, on the damn floor. I was grateful to have that.

I felt abandoned and I barely had money in my pockets. Nicki moved in before me so she was sharing the other bedroom with Mike's daughter. Mike's homeboy, Omar was also staying there. He is from Florida but he came out to Cali to visit for a while. This was only a two bedroom house and they had five adults, a three year old and now a newborn because Keziah and Mike finally gave birth to their baby girl Kalean about two weeks ago.

    They had all of this going on and as much as they said otherwise, I know that having these people in their house was very overwhelming at times. It's like they never had or ever will have their house to themselves because they are always helping someone else out. My mom didn't like the fact that I was now pregnant and sleeping on the floor at someone house nor did she approve of my dad and step-mom taking the car when I needed it the most. She called my dad and tried to talk with him on how he and my step mom was treating me but he didn't care to hear her opinion. Instead he hung up and demanded that she didn't call him again.

Days went by and then weeks but he still wasn't letting up. I then realized how bad this situation had affected my father so I made up in my mind that it was best if I left for a while. I want everyone to calm down and think things through before something extreme was said or done. When I told my dad that I was leaving, the only thing he said was, "Before you get on that plane I want that car at your grandma's house with the keys in it." I gave the car back but I can guarantee you that I drove every ounce of gas out of it. I wanted the fuel so low that he couldn't make it to the gas station.

I told Alex that I was going to go home for a while to visit my mom and he reacted like I was moving away. He started interrogating the shit out of me. "Why are you going down there? You are probably just trying to go see another nigga. Why are you in so big of a rush to get home? He was acting like a lil bitch. He really flipped out when I told him that I wanted to stay for the entire summer. He went on and on talking about if I go then we was going to break up with me because he didn't trust me. So of course I flipped. "Hold up and wait a motherfucking minute. You don't trust me? So why in the hell are we still together? I know he wanted to say because of his unborn child but he didn't have the balls to say that. Instead he covered it up. He said that he was trying to trust me again but it takes time and if I left that he will only be suspicious of me. He promised me that we would move pass my past but for some reason that wasn't happening.

I have mention to you the reaction from my family but I haven't got around to telling you about how his. His aunt and cousins were happy for me but I knew they weren't going to shut him or myself out. I was over there one day and he came into the room where I was and said that someone wanted to talk to me. Once the other person on the phone told me who they were, I was speechless. It was his mom! I didn't know what to do or say. The first thing she said was that she was not upset with me; instead she insisted that we meet very soon. She told me that she had been praying for grandkids but she didn't think it was going to happen this soon. I was relieved to hear that she was not upset with me but I was eager to know more about her like her whereabouts, how she looked and why Alex never really wanted to talk about her. She sounded as if she was a very sweet lady. I still didn't pressure him into telling me anything about his mom. Whatever the reason may be, my goal was to improve their relationship and get them communicating again. I am all for family because their love and support is everything and needed in any situation.

Through all of the questioning from Alex, he asked if he could tag alone. His brother want us to move to North Carolina with him and his girlfriend but I'm unsure about that. He is a split image of Alex. They are six years apart but they look exactly alike well, Alex is short and wears curls and his brother is taller and wears a low cut fade.

• • •

Speaking of Alex, where is he? We are at the airport waiting to board this plane so we can head to Mississippi. Yeah, we are on my way back. He said that he was going to the bathroom but that was a while ago. This will be Alex's first time riding on a plane and leaving California.

As I glance up, there he stood, looking fine as hell. I was so happy that he forgave me and finally decided to move pass what I had done. I am realizing how good of a man he is; a hard-worker and goal-driven: I'm lucky to have him. Well it's our time to board. Don't want to miss my flight writing so until next time. Peace and Love. -Parker

Chapter 27

Welcome Back

It felt wonderful to finally have my feet back on this Mississippi soil. Riding down my streets, passing by my high school and actually feeling the love and southern hospitality that we have here in the South. The first night went swell. Mama wanted to cook some of her favorites to show Alex how we get down in our neck of the woods. She made fried chicken, corn bread, baked macaroni and cheese, lima beans and fried corn. That woman can get down in the kitchen on a bad day. Alex and my brother clicked automatically. They went and got their hair cuts together as well as played ball and video games.

My brother is completing his last year of high school at the best high school in Mississippi and that's Columbus High. Though he is in school most of the day, he and Alex still find time to kick it and talk about guy things. I have been trying to get Alex to open up more because he is extremely quiet around people he doesn't know and sometimes, he doesn't care to get to know people. He says "I'm my own person. I don't have to fit in." But I never said "Fit In" I just said open up. I tell you, dealing with him is a full time job and it shouldn't be because he is a grown man that is about to bring a child in this world in a matter of months so a lot has to change, and I'm speaking about the both of us. I'm not Ms. Perfect, no matter how much I think I am, so I can't judge him until I repair my own errors. I am happy with our relationship but lately I have been questioning his happiness.

I really feel that he is only with me because of our unborn child. I can feel the love but it is not as deep as it used to be. That could possibly be my fault but we both agreed to move on. If he knew that he couldn't get pass the mistake I made, he should have just left me when we were in California instead of taking me back and allowing me to fall deeper in love with him. I knew things weren't going to change overnight but I was hoping for our relationship to be better than what it is now. Who knows, maybe our child will make a big difference in our lives, for I have heard that "if there are already existing problem then having a baby would either bring a couple closer together or tear them apart". In my case, I'm hoping for the best case scenario. So until the true feeling actually comes out, I must wear a smile and hide behind this confusion, and doubt that I have. I do hope that I'm wrong. I hope his feelings for me are still there and that this is just a phase that he is going through.

• • •

We have been here in Mississippi for only about three weeks and many changes have occurred. Alex and I have been discussing a few things and decided that we would stay and have the baby here. He said that I seemed so happy here around my family and he was right. California is where everyone wants to be because you have the beautiful Palm trees, the perfect weather, the hot bodies and the entertainment but it's more challenging to survive if you are out there on your own. And I say on my own because neither my dad nor my step-mom has any words for me. He is a Pastor and my step-mom is a first lady so I figured that they should be the first ones to forgive and move on. That is what they tell their congregation every Sunday right? Be Faithful, Repent, Forgive and so forth. You would think that they would practice what they preach but they don't.

But I'm very happy to be back in Mississippi surrounded around my loving family and friends.

Since we were going to make this our home for at least the next year or so we had to get some things situated. I had to call Long Beach and withdraw. It feels like I'm losing myself just to be with a man. I am willing to drop everything: My freedom, my life and my education. I'm happy to be home but do I really want to move back here? Mississippi has the tendency to make people feel like they are stuck here. Am I going to be one of those people?

My mom was in the process of moving so that was a plus. She was staying in one of the most ghetto fabulous apartment complexes here in Columbus but it's cool. It was much better than the house I was in before I moved out to Cali.

(That house is located on the Northside of town and that same house is called the "Family House." My grandma lived there, my mom and her siblings were born and raised there so you could imagine how old it is. My mom nor her sisters and brother wanted to sell the house. My mom ended up being the last one to live there so my step-dad tore the house down and rebuilt it from the ground up. It turned out great but I expected that being that he is one of the best, if not the best construction worker in Columbus. He left a few things undone, but I still give him five stars on the remodeling of the house. Sitting here thinking back, that house had many, many memories. I had this boyfriend in the 9th grade and we were going out for about 2 years and I could still remember the first time we had sex. Another thing I remembered about that house was how my younger brother and I shared a room and a bed while we were teenagers. It was pretty irritating at times but somehow we got over it. It actually brought us closer together. We had rats and roaches very bad. All while I was in high school, I tried to keep that to myself and keep company away because it was very embarrassing. If you were to walk pass me in the mall or see me at school, you wouldn't think that I lived in a house that was the meeting spot for creatures. The bugs had gotten so bad that my brother and I started to joke and play around with it. *Hell it was either that or cry from the torture.* Being that most of the bugs comes out at night, we would turn off all of the lights, wait about ten minutes, turn the lights back on and go at them with the fly swatter as fast as we could trying to kill as many of those nasty ass bugs that we could. I could have been living worst but I wasn't. I had a roof over my head, food on my table and nice clothes on my back so I didn't complain too much, I just kept placing the rat traps on the floor (with cheese) and stayed with my roach spray by my side. *Ha,* but we had love in that small home of ours and that's all that matters. That house is still up and standing. My step-dad lives there now. He and my mom were going through a tough time so they needed there space.)

Alex was already up and out, handling his business. While I sat at home being spoiled, he was out trying to find a job to take care of us. Again I have to commend him on stepping up to his responsibilities. I volunteered going out to job search because I wasn't showing just yet but neither him nor my mom wanted that. They said that I should just sit back and enjoy my pregnancy so I was all for it. I didn't want to work anyway. I thought about going to a Community College here but I wouldn't have a stable ride back and forth to school every day. My mom's car was on its last leg so we try not to drive it as much. In order for it to start, you have to click two pieces of wire together until the car cranks up. It doesn't have any air so you burn up in the summer and the heat comes out very low and slow so you freeze in the winter.

The house that my mom was thinking about moving in was very nice. I mean it was the total opposite of where we are now and it wasn't an apartment. It was a house. A beautiful house in a nice neighborhood located in East Columbus. It has a big front and back yard. There are three bedrooms, two bathrooms, a nice size dining room and living room and the kitchen was huge. The home was perfect to me. My mom already had a meeting with Mrs. Roberts, the landlord so we were just waiting to see what happens. I hope and pray everything works out in our favor because that home would come at a good time.

Meanwhile, Alex was at an interview for a job working as bag boy at this local grocery store by the name "Mayflower." It was located downtown which wasn't too far from the house we were pray fully going to be living in. He was doing something that he wanted to do, no one made him get up and go search for a job. However, my mom made me swallow my pride and take a walk in the county office.

So here I am. I'm sitting here alone with all of the other broke people filling out a food stamp application. I thought I would never be in this situation. My plans were to go to college, graduate with a degree, get married and then prepare myself to raise a family. Not once did I ever think I would be on FBS (food benefits system). Those plans were cancelled so here I am sitting in the back praying that I don't see anyone I know. I was so ashamed but I figured the quicker I got in, the quicker I would get out. I filled out the necessary paperwork and turned it in. I dreaded every step I took going towards that receptionist. She was sitting there looking big and black as ever, her glasses kept falling down to her nose because of all the sweat on her fat ass face. "Thank you. We will process your information into our computer as fast as we can." She said. They take their precious time because they know we aren't going anywhere until the procedure was complete. They are basically saying that "We need them". By the time I made it back to my seat, my mom had this "You better straighten your act up" look on her face and before I could sit down she let me have it. "You think these people owe you? They don't owe you a got damn thing. You need their help and you are walking around like the world owes Parker. You better grow up before you bring this baby into the world. It's not about you anymore so deal with it. If you wanna claim to be this person that you aren't, leave out of this office and go get a job, that way, you wont need help from the system." I remained quiet because I knew getting a job was also out of the question. "Exactly now sit here, swallow that pride and wait for your turn." I have never seen her this upset with me. She made a lot of sense so I kept quiet the remainder of the time. Maybe having this extra help isn't that bad if no one knows. I could just go about living like we are doing it on our own. If my peers didn't know that I was about to receive "Food Benefits" then they wouldn't have anything stupid to say. From this day on out it would be our little household secret. I will do my grocery shopping either late at night or early in the morning so no one would see me. If anyone asked if I was getting help from the county, I would just tell them that my boyfriend didn't want us getting free money: that he wanted to pay for everything. Yep, that's what I'll say and I'm stick to it and take it to my grave. Some may say that it's not that serious but to me, it is. My reputation was at stake and I couldn't downgrade. Not Parker!

Upon leaving, my mom received a phone call from Alex. He was stunned to find out that he got the job. He was happy. This is not the best job but it is a start. He said he told the managers that he could work as many hours that they needed him to work and he would do whatever they wanted him to do. His main issue was moving to this small city where he only knew a few people and that included my immediate family. Columbus is small but I told him that mostly everyone here is friendly so meeting new people and trying to fit in will not be a hard thing to do.

    Alex had a job and I was approved for four hundred and fifty dollars in food stamps. I was very thankful.

On my ride home, I sat in the passenger sit, looking out of the window and counting all of the trees that we drove pass until I went into a deep thought. I thought about how fast things had gone and were going. I just left Mississippi last year and was headed to California to start a new path and begin a new life. It's crazy how things take a turn; sometimes for the good and sometimes for the bad. I wasn't out there a full year and I was already back home, pregnant and now on food stamps. In Cali, I had everything: a car, a place to live, money in my pocket, freedom and the list could go on for days. I didn't have to want for anything. My stepmom kept me with little thoughtful gifts, my dad tried his best not to let me go without anything and my mom: my poor Mom kept me going. She was one of the main reasons that I wanted to make a better person of myself.

She stayed with a positive word every day. I feel sick to my stomach thinking of the many people I let down. Track was my life. I felt a sense of relief when I stepped on the track. I was good at what I did. Now the only thing that I'm good for is sitting at home. I felt stupid and pathetic. I didn't have anything proud to say about myself but the fact that I had a high school diploma but many people had one of those. I was so much more than that. Myself and two of my other friends from high school made a pact to each other and that was: To come back to Mississippi successful, and both of them were still living out that dream. Melissa was in Alabama majoring in Accounting (with no kids) and Nina received a track scholarship to Baltimore Maryland, majoring in Sports Medicine (also with no kids). I believe my decisions and actions may have caused them to distant their selves away from me. Not saying that it's done intentionally but they have their future and career to worry about. I can't keep up with them anymore because I was no longer on their level. I still speak to Melissa but Nina and I haven't had a good conversation in months. I love them both and hopefully things eventually work out. If not, there isn't anything that I could do about it. But that's only one of the many adjustments in my life right now. But I'm slowly dealing with them.

. . .

Seven months pregnant and happy as ever. I am thankfully that I haven't had any challenges with my pregnancy thus far, only heartburns: My mom said it was because my child was going to have a head full of hair. You could usually find out the sex of the baby about four months alone and fortunately I was able to schedule an appointment on that very day. Alex took off because he wanted to be at the doctor's office with me. When the doctor told us that we were having a baby girl, we were so excited because that's exactly what Alex and I hoped and prayed for! Not only did we spread the news to everyone we knew, but we started shopping. We came home with clothes, diapers, socks and even a small dresser to put her clothes in. My mom said that we were taking it to the extreme but we were proud parents and full of joy, anxiety and happiness. But she did have a point because I hadn't yet had my baby shower so I wasn't sure who was going to show up nor the gifts that I would get so we didn't buy anything else, at least not on that day.

One day I woke up feeling wonderful until I walked into the bathroom and took a glimpse into the mirror. The further along I was getting, the worst my face was becoming. My neck was so black that it looked burnt and my face had a lot of bumps on it. I started to feel insecure thinking that if I continued to look this way; Alex will leave me once the baby was here. He is so handsome and slim so I knew that he wasn't going to want a fat girl walking by his side. I was trying not to gain so much weight so fast but I was. Alex was the type of guy that loves a girl with an ass, long hair and a flat stomach. Well I have the ass, my hair is medium length but my stomach was nowhere near flat: It was before but not anymore. Everyone talks about how I'm not going to have a problem loosing the weight because I was so skinny, but every time I put on a pair of my old pants, I noticed that it may not be as easy as they all say it will be. I was trying to become more active during the day and stop just sitting around , doing nothing but watching soap operas and eating. I tried for about a week but that plan felled because I was back in the house being lazy again.

We attended a Gospel Celebration at this Full Gospel church one night because my church "Divine Healing Temple" had to sing a few songs. I couldn't sing in the choir anymore due to the fact that I am pregnant and not married. The pastor felt that me being pregnant and in the choir didn't show good leadership. I was fine with his decision and I respected it 100 percent. I don't think we were at the celebration for five minutes and Alex was already clapping, jumping and singing these people songs like he has been attending this church for years. He got acquainted with a few dudes from the row that we were sitting on and after that, he fit right in. Alex was so excited about this church because it was very similar to his church back in LA. So he immediately wanted to join. He couldn't wait until Sunday so as soon as the preacher did the alter call, asked for candidates for baptism and opened the doors of the church for people to join, he ran up there. My mom agreed to drop him off every Sunday before we went to our church until he met someone that lived closer to us. The first day he showed his form of dancing, they fell in love with him. To this day he still loves his church and the people who have welcomed him with opened arms.

Meanwhile, Mrs. Roberts had given my mom a call to let her know that everything was good and that she could pick up her keys and start moving in. However there was one stumbling block. Her rent. Rent was only $275 while we were in the apartment but now her rent was going up to $550 a month. (If you are paying 550 a month in California then you are most likely living in the worst neighborhood possible.) My mom was hesitating on accepting this wonderful offer because she didn't know that rent was going to be that much. When she first spoke to Mrs. Roberts, my mom got the understanding that rent was going to be no more than 400 but once the real estate agency took a look at the house, they realized that the house was worth more. I understand that but having to pay this high rent and all of the utility bills were going to be another headache for her. Alex stepped up and agreed to help my mom out. He liked the house and he said that's where he wanted our child to be born and raised so he was willing to help my mom pay rent. Eventually, he was going to have to start paying something anyway because I wasn't working. You can't live anywhere for free well at least not long. Even family members probably won't ask you for rent right off but in due time, that conversation will come up.

As days passed, my stomach grew. Each doctor's visit that I went to made it feel that more real. I was walking around talking and playing but reality hadn't really sat in. I was actually about to be a mother. I'm still in disbelief and at times I am scared because I want to be the best mom that I could be. I would like for me and my daughter to have the same relationship as my mom and I have and even closer. I want the best for her and the best is exactly what she is going to get. I want to be mentally, physically and financially stable to take care of her because I honestly don't know the outcome of Alex and I.

Everything is going good now, but who knows: one day he may flip out and try to leave me so I can't be dependent on him or the little money that he has. It was hard because I wasn't putting anything into our relationship right now but love, I guess. Though love is the major part, I still felt like I needed to contribute more. I was too far along in my pregnancy to work so he and my mom was bringing in the income to support us.

We were finally in our new home enjoying every bit of it. Everyone had their own space and privacy so that kept some confusing to a minimum inside but on the outside: issues and concerns started to arise. Some were from my mom's friends, nosey Columbus residents and members from Alex's sanctified, holy filled full gospel church. My mom was being judged on having a man and a woman sleep under the same roof without being married. In other words, they were saying that she was allowing fornication to take place in her home. At Alex's church, he was being accused as the actual "Fornicator".

Never mind the things that goes on at all the other churches around this damn city like the preacher that is cheating on his wife, or the drunk deacons singing slow as hell on the front benches every Sunday, or some of the First Ladies that turn their nose up at everyone that doesn't have what they have (Which is sometimes nothing but a name). What about the choir members that are having sex for money. I think they call those people (Prostitutes), even those members that come to church running around shouting, looking like some damn fools when, before I got pregnant, was just partying with them the night before at the club. But I could go on and on about the problems and issues that everyone have even in their households but I won't.

My thing is, unless you are 100% perfect; which is no one but God; please don't judge me or my family. See I could care less what they have to say about me because I know that I have to see and answer to God for myself but when it comes to my family, especially moms, then we have a problem. She comes home practically almost every day telling me how she hears the snickering at work and in the grocery stores and it really kills me. It's not like she is saying, "Yea Parker, I'm ok with you and Alex having sex in my house or sleeping in the same room in." Damn, that's not the case. Yea we sin every day, even the Preacher whom you look up to. The one whom you think have no issues. The one who you run behind making sure his every need is met while your family and children beg for your attention. I swear, if they treated God that same way, then this world would be a better place.

But what's done is done. I'm pregnant; he is living here because he wants to be in his child's life. He is new to this city and no one was volunteering to let him live with them so, right in this damn house is where he is going to stay. Besides, we didn't have enough money to move into our own apartment. I told him and my mom to tell the next person "If they are willing to buy him a house or pay his rent every month then go ahead and do that but if not, Shut the Hell up. And that's that.

Chapter 28

Preparing for Delivery

I was fresh out of the shower and rubbing lotion all over this huge ass body of mines. I spoke to one of my high school classmates who recently had a baby. She told me a secret about having sex before a visit with your obstetrician. She said that it opens your vagina. She had the same doctor that I have and she said that if he sees that you are dilating just a little; he would go ahead and induce your labor. We have tried that every since I turned eight months and we always leave the doctor unsuccessful. Lately, we haven't been able to have good sex anyway because she is always in the way. We can't be as loud as we want to because my mom's room is right by ours. Luckily today we had the house to our self. My brother was at school, my mom was at work and Alex was on his hour lunch break so of course we were about to go at it. I wanted to be laying there naked, ready and waiting on my baby to come through those doors.

When he walked in we barely spoke to one another. Our time was limited so we had to get on with it. We made good love even though my big stomach was in the way. I laid there still trying to catch my breath and he was already up with his clothes back on. He gave me a kiss and said "Alright baby, I'll see you later."

Since we have been in Mississippi, Alex and I relationship was beginning to form back together again. At first, I was questioning his love for me but now I could actually feel his love again. I still don't think he loves me as much as I love him but his love for me is deeper than what it was before. I just cherish this guy. It's like I have fallen head over heels for him. I have had a few fall outs with my mom about him which was very surprising. She sees how much love I have for him and how much I am putting my all into our relationship and she somehow thinks that I am doing too much too soon. She loves him to death, don't get me wrong but she thinks I need to take it slow and focus more on the health of me and my baby.

I can love him and my child but she do not want to see me hurt again. When it comes to men, I have had bad luck. I don't know if it's been me or the guys I have been choosing but this time it feels different. I honestly feel that Alex is the one. My eyes light up every time I see his face. It's been over a year that we have been together and the fire was still burning strong for me. I have so much faith in him because I know that he will never cheat on me nor hurt me. I have never felt like this before with any of the many guys that I have been with it. I could see myself marrying this man besides, who else will date this 200 pound woman. I have hundreds of stretch marks on my legs and back and he doesn't have a single care in the world. In a very strange way he finds it very sexy. He said he loves them because his daughter was the one that gave them to me.

A few days ago Alex and I was having a heart-to-heart session and he finally opened up to me about his mom. One day he came home from school and his mom was gone. I thought gone meaning, at the store or at a friends' house. He said he went to his aunt's house to see if they had seen her and their answer was "No". Days went by and no one knew what to think because they didn't receive a call from her or knew of her whereabouts.

Finally one day, his mom called his aunt and told her that she and her husband had moved to Texas. He was heartbroken because he was still in high school and she was really all that he had. "How could she do that to me?" "What would cause a mother to leave her child?" he asked repeatedly. His aunt told him that she left because she was too stressed and she felt like a disappointment to them. She wanted to get away and provide a better life for herself and her kids so she thought that starting over would be her only option. I felt remorse for him when he shared this heartbreaking story and I could also relate to him.

My dad left my brother and I and we didn't hear from him for a few days but we were living with my mom so we actually weren't left on our own. Things happen in life but it's not until later that we realize that it is always for the best. I didn't know her but I was willing to give her a chance instead of judging her. Besides, what matters the most is that they are speaking again.

The doctors said that I could have this baby any day now so she and her husband packed up their things to head here from Texas. She wanted to be there to see her first grandchild born. I was excited for Alex and his mom because this will be the first time they have seen each other since she left California, which was about 3 years ago. I knew this was going to be a very special moment.

・・・

I glanced at the clock and the time said 8:00 pm: that's when Alex got an important phone call. His mom was on the line when I answered. "Hello" "Hi sweetie, how are you and my grandbaby" she asked. "Hey mom, we are doing good. Everyone is sitting around waiting on your arrival." "Uh, about that, I was wondering if you could ask Alex to step outside!" "Alex!" I yelled even though he was sitting across from me. "Dang baby, I know you see me right here in your face." "Well this is your mom of course and I have some disturbing news …….She said that she and your step-dad was outside." I joked. Before I knew it, Alex had jumped up and ran outside not thinking twice about putting on shoes. I heard them screaming and just carrying on out there. I wanted to be a part of this reunion but I didn't bother getting up because by the time I would have made it off of this couch, she would have already been in the house. When they walked in, they were holding hands and both of their eyes were red and full of tears. I was happy for him because I couldn't stand the thought of not seeing my mom pass a few months and here they were reuniting after not seeing each other in years. I was speechless! What a memorable moment! She finally looked toward my way and started crying again. "So you are Parker? Aw, Alex she is beautiful with her big stomach." I wanted to say "woman stop lying" but she was being generous. I knew I wasn't anywhere near beautiful but I took the compliment and said "Thank you." As I struggled to get up, she walked over, gave me hug and kissed me on the forehead. Her and my mom really connected and by the time we ate dinner, they were acting as if they were high school friends. We were all sitting around talking when his mom, said that she couldn't go on another minute without apologizing to her son. At times, she could barely get a word out because she was crying. They caught up on times and he gave her his forgiveness. After that it was like they were never separated.

I wanted to know a little more about Alex like: how he was as a child and how he act during his teenage years. A few things I already knew was if he doesn't get what he wants: he pouts and he thinks he is right about everything when most of the time, he is not. She commended me on putting up with him and his attitude. Then she laughed and said, "Hell I applaud anyone that puts up with any one of my sons. They are good men so don't get me wrong but they do have tempers that will make you want to knock their heads off." I spent a few days around his brother while in California and he seemed like he could be cordial but I didn't know how he acts when he is upset or when things aren't going his way. I couldn't speak on his behalf but I do know how my Alex acts so I couldn't argue with her on that. We all decided to go to bed and leave some conversation for tomorrow or else we would have been up all night. Alex and my mom needed to get to bed for work, my brother had school and I had an appointment with my doctor as well. We decided to let his mom and step-dad sleep in our room until I had the baby. So to the couch we went!

The doctor's office was filled with pregnant women, as usually. I thought it was going to take forever for them to call my name but luckily as soon as I sat down: I was called to the back. Alex insisted that his mom take his place and be there right by my side. The nurse checked my blood pressure, asked me a series of questions and checked my weight. The normal routine before the doctor comes in. I knew by me sitting at home every day and not being as active as I should, that I gained a few pounds but I didn't know actually how much until I asked the nurse who looked surprised when I stepped on the scale. "Exactly how much do I weigh" I asked her. "According to the scale here," she said sarcastically "It says 210." I yelled "210". What the hell? I was 145 pounds before I got pregnant and now I'm in the 200's. I never in a million years thought I would weigh that much. I knew I was big but damn. Mrs. Judy claimed that my weight was coming from the baby. BullShit ! Unless I was about to pop out a 65 pound baby, which was totally impossible, then my fat ass was overweight. I was officially ready to have this baby and start my workout plan. After sitting there waiting and listening to Mrs. Judy try to convince me that I wasn't fat, the doctor finally gave him and checked to see if I had dilated any. Just when I thought I had enough news for today, he pulled his hand out of my vagina and told me that he have to induce my labor tomorrow since I have dilated two centimeters. I had spoken to soon because what I just wished for has come true. I was very excited because there was a big possibility that I would be united with my first born tomorrow. He gave me my paperwork and told me to be at the hospital at 5 p.m. and prepared for labor. Upon leaving, of course the first person I called was Alex. He was at work and ecstatic. I heard his friends in the background yelling, Congrats. He was ready to come home right then but I said "No sir honey, we need that money." I'm pretty sure that he was going to take a few days off once the baby got here so he didn't need to leave today. Later that night, his mom and my mom prepared a big dinner for me to eat, meat loaf, fried chicken, mashed potatoes, baked macaroni and cheese, greens, yams, home-made rolls and of course to keep the meal healthy, we had to throw in a side salad. I just complained about my weight but here I am about to eat all of this starch, carbs and fat but I didn't care. The doctor strongly recommended that I didn't eat anything in the morning so I had to gobble down as much as I could that night.

After Alex and my brother got home from work, we all ate and sat around to watch a movie until everyone fell restless and was ready to take it in for the night. I took my shower first and then Alex took his. We knew that this was going to be the last night, for at least six weeks that we would be able to have sex so we have each other as much as possible. After about three times ,we laid there naked until the both of us fell asleep.

Patrice L. Guyton

Labor:

Ten hours into labor and the pain was really kicking my butt. I was trying my hardest not to get the epidural but those contractions felt as if someone was poking the inside of my stomach with a razor blade. I could barely move. I was lying there asking God, "Why me" and cursing everyone that was asking me some of the stupidest and craziest question that I'm sure every pregnant girl in labor hates to hear, "Are you ok? Does it hurt?" I wanted to say "NO, this is the best feeling ever" but I didn't have time for the sarcasm: I needed all of my energy for those contractions. Alex's mom was up; pacing back and forth crying and I believe more scared and nervous than I was and then she started snapping pictures. My mom was praying asking God to give her the strength to make it, when I was the one in pain. Instead of me, her stingy self was asking for strength for herself. Alex, my baby, my love was right there holding my hand and guiding me along the way.

He was looking at the screen preparing me for every big contraction that was about to come. He was being so supportive. I was in a lot of pain but I couldn't think about anything but my daughter moving around trying to find the right time to come out and bless her parents' lives. We were so happy.
    Things were a bit rocky for us but as the time went by, we were able to grow closer together and build a stronger bond before we had our child. I looked around and saw all the love in my room and had no choice but to smile and Thank God for truly blessing me with a loving family. I was able to live in that moment for only a few more minutes when the biggest and sharpest pain hit me directly in my side. I became weak.

I couldn't speak a single word; all I could do was cry. Alex had been telling me to go ahead a get an epidural because the contractions was only going to get worse but I kept pushing it off. But that instant pain changed my mind. I got out the words "Get me the shot" the best way I could. Alex knew exactly what I was trying to say and arranged for the nurse to come in stick that 12 inch needle in my back. When she entered the room, she made everyone leave, including Alex. She discussed with me the process and warned that if I moved for a split second, that I could be paralyzed along with many other terrible side effects. I gave her my approval and she and another nurse went on with the procedure. After a few minutes, the pain was gone and I was relieved.

Fifteen hours into labor and our baby girl still wasn't ready to come. She hadn't turned around, nor was I dilating as much as I should. Finally the nurse came in and told me that they were preparing to give me a cesarean. What the hell is a cesarean? "It's the medical term for a c-section." The nurse said. I thought "NO." anything but a c-section. I wanted to live in the moment of actually giving birth to my child not being cut open.

Since I was only entitled to one person in the room, I chose Alex even though I wanted my mom with me every step of the way. They were moving me so fast that I only got the chance to wave good-bye and then I was headed down to another delivery room.

"Parker, we are going to lift you up and transfer you from this rolling cart to a table so we can perform the surgery." The doctor said. Once I was on the table they place a half cut board on top of me separating the top and bottom of my body so I couldn't see anything pass my breasts. Secondly they gave me the shot that was suppose to make me numb. The doctor told me that I was going to feel the pressure of the knife but I was not going to feel the pain.

Alex and I were looking at each other with happiness and excitement in our eyes. Only about ten minutes later the doctor yelled, "I'm done cutting. Now all I have to do is flip back this flab of your stomach and flip this side over and….", He then pulled out the most precious, loud and beautiful gift that was ever given to me. "I welcomed you"… he cleared his throat, What's her name?" the doctor asked "Samiyah Janice Jones" Alex said in a Proud father tone. "Here is "Samiyah Janice Jones." The doctor finished. He spanked her butt and she cried for only a few seconds and that was it. I could barely see what was going on because I was still lying down but Alex told me that they were washing her off and checking her weight.

They then wrapped her and gave her to her dad. She was 8 pounds, 10 ounces, 21 inches, healthy, bright skin and beautiful with a head full of hair. The feelings that were running through my body were indescribable. Happiness was flowing through my veins. Alex leaned her over to me so I could kiss her because I wasn't able to hold her just yet. Then he kissed me. "We did it baby", he cried. After the doctor took my baby to the back for check-ups, Alex left to go tell the family the good news but I had to stay and be stitched up. I laid there with the biggest smile on my face trying to remember every moment of this life-changing experience. I was overwhelmed. I was now a Mommy! Who would have ever thought that I would have a child?

Patrice L. Guyton

A JOURNAL ENTRY

APRIL 8TH 2007

The last time I talked to you, I was pregnant but today make 2 months that Samiyah has been born. Every since February 8th, my life has changed tremendously. Many things has happened and many issues has come. For one, I have a job. Yes a job. I'm a cashier at this grocery store by the name of Southern Planet. If you would have told me to go work at a grocery store or restaurant a year ago, I would have laughed to your face but here I was doing it simply because I had to. Alex's income was cool but I felt like I needed to be a better help and bring in some extra money.

Since I wasn't pregnant anymore, I wanted to bring my sexy back because during the pregnancy, it was only a t-shirt or some leggings and I no longer wanted to dress like that. I didn't want to let myself fall apart even though my weight was still in the 200's. I am very insecure about that and I'm sure that everyone around me could tell. I would have never imagined myself being this big. I keep trying to go about things the normal way but this weight was really affecting me. Alex was being supportive and telling me that I wasn't fat: Which was all a lie. I knew I was big but he somehow didn't see what I saw. I knew he loved me know matter what. *If only I could love myself that much.*

Once I started working, I had to get my shirt in an extra-large and that was a major disappointment. I went from wearing smalls and even some extra smalls to extra-large. Many people told me that I was going to lose my baby fat very quick because I was so skinny: Been 2 months and still no progress. The nurses gave me a stomach band before I left the hospital. They said it was supposedly going to flatten my stomach. I know it takes time because losing weight the healthy way is not done overnight. I just didn't want Alex to become turned off with my overly large body. I ask him daily if I'm still pretty and attractive to him and he continues to say yes but he has started to get quiet irritated because I am thinking less of myself. I can't help it. I think it's natural to feel this way after having baby so he is going to have to deal with the complaints and insecurities until I'm fully loaded again. He is always by my side but at times I still find myself questioning if he really loves me or is it just a show.

Is he only here because of our baby girl or do we have something deeper than that? I trust him, Lord knows I do, but I must admit that our relationship isn't 100 percent just yet. I know in order to have a good and healthy relationship that you have to learn how to trust your partner but every since I cheated: I've felt guilty because I believe in Karma and that dirty bitch don't play. I don't want him to turn around and cheat on me so I had to be on my shit. I had to make sure that I was being a good girlfriend by making sure that he was happy at all times. I know he is faithful and I know that he loves me but I still had my doubts and those thoughts in the back of my head. I'll give you a few examples; both happened during the night around the times that I thought he was asleep.

It was around one something in the morning when I just so happened heard him texting. My back was towards him so I rolled over so that we were facing each other. I pretended to snore to make it seem like I was still asleep. He dropped the phone and closed his eyes and now he was the one pretending to be asleep. I continued to fake snore to see if he was going to pick the phone back up and damn it he did. I couldn't see what the text said so I tried to focus my eyes on who he was sending the text to and that way, I could ask him about this chic or whoever it was later. I waited to see exactly how long he was going to text this mysterious person and it went on for another twenty-five minutes.

Anger was taking over me because if I was to pull some shit like that, there would have been a World War III. I hopped out of the bed and went into the bathroom to throw him off. When I came back into the room I was very pissed but instead of lashing out at him, I decided to ask questions first before assuming the worst.

"Uh, Alex". "What now Parker?" he answered me as if I was bothering him but he was the one texting a bitch in the middle of the night. "So what's up? Who are you chatting with this late?" I asked getting straight to the point "Oh that's my friend, Red, from high school". He said with no problem. "You remember I told you about her a while back." I started to think *Red, Red*. Nawl I don't know no damn Red. But suddenly I remembered a story he told me about him and some friends starting a group in high school. They called themselves "The Berries". He was "Thorn berri" why? I have no idea, "Wildberri" because she was the wild one. I heard she had five tattoos, a couple of piercing in her face and she changed men like she changed draws. Talking about Wild! "Strawberri", because she loved strawberries and some more shit. Then there was "Redberri" aka "Ms.Red" because she was a redbone. She had long black silky hair that stopped in the center of her back. She was half Belize which meant she spoke two languages and her stomach was as flat as an ironing board. She was made up sorta like a white girl, meaning she had no ass. But she is a very nice and pretty young lady. The group thing seemed stupid to me but he shared with me how close they all were. They had each other's back. I met the lil Red girl at church one night. Alex was invited to come to her church and share a dance at their youth extravaganza and he wanted me to come along for support.

We didn't actually greet and shake hands because once we walked in; the service had already started so I spoke, as we walked to the back row. I don't know why but as soon as a woman finds out that her man's previous friends (specifically females) will be any place that we are attending: we put on our best clothes, best shoes and make our faces up so good that sometimes we are looking like a damn mannequin. We start to stare them down and compare ourselves. "Oh she doesn't look better than me, Oh her eyebrows need to be waxed" or "that earring and necklace set does not match with what she has on and so forth. This particular woman could simply be nothing more than a sister figure to our man but yet and still we judge. Hell I was and still is an example of doing just that. But once I actually looked at her, I realized that she was a pretty decent looking girl. She had on a dance uniform because she had to perform right before Alex went up. Overall, I didn't see any physical signs of them being high school sweethearts or lovers so once we left I didn't think twice about her.

Now here she was texting my man in the middle of the morning talking about God knows what. When I asked him what it was that they were talking about, he said that he was telling her how happy he was with his newborn baby. I heard him say "newborn" but I didn't hear him say anything about me. I didn't believe a word he was saying so I have been suspicious of him every since.

On another night things were similar but this time when I woke up, he wasn't in the bed. I walked to the hall and down to the den where I found him sitting on the floor in Indian style right in front of my brother's laptop. Now instead of walking my dumb ass over to see exactly what it was that he was doing, I asked him and of course, he grabbed the mouse, clicked a few times and said, "Nothing." Things seemed skeptical that night and I was going to get to the bottom of it. "Alex, tell me the truth. Why are up here instead of in the room with your family?" He responded with the wackiest answer ever, "Because I didn't want to wake y'all up." When he knows I am the hardest sleeper ever.

Fell Too Deep

If I don't roll over, I can literally sleep through him having sex in the room with me. He said that he couldn't sleep so he decided to play a game on the internet but once I finally walked over to the computer, the screen was blank. That definitely led to an argument because he didn't have to shut the computer down if he was only playing a game. There was no way in Hell I was going to let him just get away with feeding me that bull shit.

We started arguing and he was talking over me while I was trying to talk over him. He even accused me of cheating on him again. He said I was having a guilty conscience. He kept screaming, *"YOU WAS THE ONE WHO CHEATED, NOT ME. I HAVE BEEN FAITHFULL THIS WHOLE TIME BUT I CAN'T SAY THE SAME ABOUT YOU."* I know what I did but how many times was he going to remind me? He kept trying to use reverse physiology but it wasn't going to work: Nawl, I wasn't letting that one pass me by. I told him that he could blame me that whole night but he weren't going to sleep until he told me the truth. Simple words turned into curse words, low pitch turned into high pitch until he finally broke down and told me the second wackiest answers of them all. "Fuck It" he shouted. "It was a surprise but since you are accusing me of something that I am not doing , that leaves me with no choice but to tell you that I was about to buy your Engagement ring!" My reaction was yeah fucking right. I told him to knock that shit off because he knew damn well that he was not trying to buy me a ring. Are you kidding me?

My next questions were, what website did you go to and where is your debit card to purchase this ring? His ass couldn't say shit. We started calling each other every name in the book until he "Supposedly" got upset and called his brother. He was asking him to drive to Mississippi to get him because I didn't trust him and he couldn't take it anymore. He told him about his engagement ring scam and yadda fucking yadda. I was furious because I knew he was lying but I didn't have the facts to prove it. I didn't want him to leave me because he was my partner. At that point, I didn't care if he was cheating on me. I was going to strive and become a better woman and stop accusing him because he may actually leave me one day and that will be the last thing that I need. So of course I pulled out my drama skills and started crying and apologizing for things that I didn't even do. I just knew that I didn't want my man to leave me so we kissed, made up and went to sleep. I haven't mentioned that night since but I still wonder what it was that he was doing. But like always I believe him. Whatever he say is right. If he said he wasn't doing anything then I believed just that.

Besides my baby girl, he was my all and I was not going to lose him over my assumptions.

Any who, we decided to name our friends, Jessie and Kevin, Samiyah's god parents. They were now married, in school, working, doing positive things and living a happy and stable lifestyle. They are very loving and caring and the ones that often have to help us get through our arguments so we figured they would be the perfect candidates for the job.

His mom and step-dad packed up and went back to Texas. We all hated to see them go. In the couple of weeks that she was here I could tell that she would go up and beyond for her family and I loved that. She got word from her job that she had to be back at work within the next week or she was going to be fired, *Hell she was gone for almost three weeks: what did she expect*. But she was definitely a huge help around the house since everyone else was back at work. Alex was saddened when he found out that she had to leave so soon because he wanted more time to spend with her. She has met her first and only grandchild and when she saw Alex, she had a glowing spark in her eyes and a smile as big as my behind. I assured him that this was not going to be the last time that he sees her.

Alex quit his job at the grocery store and is now a Mentor at a corrections facility for troubled teenagers. He really loves this job because he come home every day with different stories about those kids. Some of them don't have parents and if they do; they care nothing for them, some are gang bangers, and some are plain out disobedient and disrespectful. He said despite all of their problems, he loves to go to work and be a help and an older brother to them.

Many changes are occurring in my life but there is one that I am the most pleased with. I am finally communicating with my dad and step-mom again. I went my through my entire pregnancy without speaking to them. I called a few times but they never answered, so I stopped calling. I knew that they were still upset with me so I decided to give them their space. The night my baby was born, my brother said that they were ringing the phones off the hook asking how I was doing and if I needed anything. My dad only wanted to know if my daughter looked like him, for some odd reason he thought that she was going to be his twin. They do have similar features but I think that's mainly because we argued so much. Since her birth, they have been very supportive and I am very thankful for that. They sent her a

3-in-1 bassinet, a pink and green Jeep stroller with a matching bag, diapers, clothes, shoes and a Birth bracelet that provided a bible verse of the day she was born. Samiyah is too small to ride in her stroller right now but when she is big enough we will be cruising through town showing off.

I couldn't ask for a better baby. She doesn't cry like normal babies. She may moan or whine when she is hungry or needs her pamper changed but that's it. She seems to be very friendly because she will let anyone hold her. She was already the perfect child so we couldn't ask for anything else.

On a sadder note, we got news last week that my mom have to travel to Birmingham, Al to have open heart surgery. At her job the supervisors always try to keep their employees up to date on their health and physical exams. My mom has being feeling nausea and out of breathe lately so she mentioned it to the nurse. When my mom told her that she hadn't been eating healthy nor exercising as much as she should: the first thing that came to the nurse's mind was "Overweight". But that wasn't the case. My mom's heart beat was unusual. When the nurse listened to her heart it made the sound of a rage wind. Enlarged hearts ran in our family so without going any further, she referred my mom to the first available heart specialist. When she went in for her appointment, the doctor did confirm that her heart was making that whooshing sound because it had a hole in it. He wanted her to have surgery as soon as possible because her heart was tearing. He also warned her that she could die if she didn't choose to have the surgery and she could die if her heart failed during the surgery. Sort of a lose-lose situation. Family and friends were terrified because we already knew the outcome from both my aunt and my grand-mom. No one knew about their heart condition until they passed away. We were blessed enough to have found out about my mom before it was too late.

 My brother was not only devastated by her having surgery but also shocked because she was going to miss his graduation. He was already down in out because of the lack of help that he was getting from our parents. When I graduated from high school, my dad and step-mom both had really great jobs. I'm talking $30.00 an hour, so they were able to help me financially as far as buying my cap and gown, going half with my mom for my prom dress, invitations, senior book, shirts and other little senior nix, naxs. My mom was also a huge help. She tried her best to buy me a new outfit every Friday. Unlike my brother, I basically had it made. I didn't have to work or buy anything and here he was working his senior year at a fast food restaurant instead of enjoying it the way I did.

Patrice L. Guyton

    I feel guilty because he thinks that no one cares for him as much as they care for me and that's not the case. They had the finances with me. He always used to say that I am constantly being treated better than he is and that our parents love me more than they love him and certain situations make that assumption seem true but it's not. Now my dad is jobless, my step-mom is trying to make all the ends meet, and my mom was about to be off of work for God knows how long due to her surgery leaving him to fend for himself with little or no help. I had a job but I wasn't getting paid as much but when I did have extra; I tried to help him out. Everyone was doing good but now they were barely making it. Prayer always changes things so I'm hoping and believing that everything plays out with my brother, my mom's surgery, Alex and I relationship and my dad and step-mom. It has to.

Chapter 29

HAPPINESS

We are up, getting ready for church and as usually on Sunday mornings; everyone is running around and getting into each other's way. But for some reason, things felt different. My best friend Cherell is coming to church with us today so besides the other commotion that is going on, she is nagging and asking me unnecessary questions: "What time are you guys coming? What are you wearing?" Hell she has never been this excited about going to church so something is up! Alex taught the drama team a new dance at his church and insisted that we all come and support him. Kanetra, a good friend and a member from the church, stopped by and picked him up. She wanted to make sure that he was on time and prepared. My mom is working her second job at New Breed Baptist church, babysitting toddlers during church service and she demand we be ready once she got off. Well of course I was running late: It wouldn't be me if I wasn't. Before my mom left she specifically said, "If we miss this dance, I am going to be highly upset." She was acting like she had never seen him perform. He has danced at our church on several occasions and is always dancing around the house so I didn't know what made today so special.

They were dimming the lights and about to close the doors when we arrived, so we made it just in time. He was home practicing and going over this dance every day. Because dancing is his heart, he gives his all whenever he performs whether it's a full house or a handful of people. But in this case the church was pack, just like every Sunday. Some of the members have seen him dance at a Youth Day program but some haven't.

When the dance was over the crowd cheered, the musicians played and I stood up about to say, "Yea, that's my man" but I forgot that I was in a church. Afterwards, a number of people stood up and told testimonies. I knew it wouldn't be long before Samiyah started getting cranky. I noticed that her diaper was wet so I left out to change her. "Hurry back Parker." My mom whispered. I told her "Ok" but as I walked out, I thanked my daughter for cutting up at a time like this. Don't get me wrong because I love to hear how the Lord has worked miracles in people lives but sometimes they can go on and on and on and I wasn't up for it today. As I walked back in I noticed Alex get up but I didn't think anything about it until I saw him grab the microphone. I turned towards the door to walk back out but somehow I ended up at my seat. As he started to talk I could hear how nervous he was because he kept fumbling his words and saying "Uh". *Oh hell, he is about to get up here and embarrass the both of us.* I wanted to make myself disappear so badly. He has never spoke in front of a body this big and here he was about to give a testimony.

"I would like to thank God for all of his blessings and the many people that he has put in my life. My daughter is one of those people. She has blessed me abundantly since the day she was born." I knew where this was going but Pleeeaasse don't say my name. I mumbled "and then there is Parker." He said with much glee. I glanced around the room and all eyes were focused in on me. *Damn it.* "Before I move on, I would like to ask Parker if she could come up here." He asked. I'm in church but in my mind I am cursing his ass out. He could have warned a sister that I was going to be the center of attention because I would have worn a prettier dress and shoes that I can actually walk in. We weren't sitting that far from the front but it felt like it took me ten minutes to get to where he was standing: which was in front of hundreds of people. Some I knew and some I didn't.

He knew my ass was shame because the minute our eyes met, he gave me this little smirk. He then proceeded with his speech. "Parker, you have been here for me when no one else was. I can talk to you for hours about any and everything. I want to thank you for putting up with me because I know sometimes we don't see eye to eye but you are always there to make me smile at the end of our arguments. I may not say it a lot but I cherish you, I respect you, you are the perfect mom and I honor you, I love you and most of all…" He pulls out a box and goes down on one knee. People were screaming in disbelief and clapping. I looked at my mom and Cherell and the both of them were crying. Everyone was saying "Yes" for me but I didn't know what to do. As I looked down at my man, I felt my body about to go into a shock. I couldn't move. I couldn't speak. Two ushers

Fell Too Deep

walked up behind me for support in case I fell out because that's exactly what it felt like I was about to do.

He went on to say…, "Parker: would you do me the honors of becoming my wife." I fell to my knees so that we could be face to face. I am now sitting here crying my eyes out. He asked again and I nodded my head "yes." We both stood there for a minute or so taking in the cheers from the crowd and then we were escorted to the back. As we walked out the pastor said, "Did we just have a proposal in church? Let's give that young couple a hand clap of praise one more time." I was so happy. Here I was just questioning his love for me while he was out saving up money to buy me a ring. I felt so special. I was literally floating on cloud nine. I called my dad first because I was excited to tell him that he was about to have a son-in-law. When he answered, all I heard was he and my step-mom screaming saying "Congratulations". They already knew because Alex had to call and asked my dad for his approval. Everyone knew what was going on except for me. I was wondering why Cherell wanted to go to church with me so badly. I knew it had to be something major going on to get her in a church. I am so happy because I am finally engaged to the man of my dreams !

• • •

As the days went by there was no drastic change in me and Alex's lives. We were still arguing about petty shit and I must admit that some of it is my fault. I am always accusing him of cheating on me. And every time I ask he says, "If I didn't love you or if I was cheating on you, why would I propose to you?" He does have a strong point so I am just insecure with myself I guess. I am always second-guessing his love for me. I have the mindset that men are going to be men no matter how faithful they portray to be. I'm not exactly where I want to be in my life. I am bigger than I have ever been with only a high school diploma at the end of my name. Due to that, I will always have that voice in the back of my head telling me that I aint shit, never going to be shit and that he only wants to be with me because of our child. He says all of the time that trust is everything in a relationship and if I don't trust him then we have nothing and he is right. I know I have a good man but why can't I put away my insecurities and see him for who he is? Why can't I look in a mirror and see the beautiful queen that I once saw before I had my daughter?

Chapter 30

I'm leaving....

While at work one day, all of the employees were standing around with hardly any customers in the store due to a terrible thunderstorm. My brother and Alex walked in and by the look on their faces, I knew something had happened. Since we were already slow, my manager said it was ok if I stepped to the side to talk for a few minutes. He shared with me that he had to quick his job. He began to tell me this drawn out story about how his boss asked him to dance at the skating ring one night and that he was going to pay him with the next check. Well today was pay-check day and to make a long story short, his boss was short on his cash. In a separate envelope from his check was a 10.00 bill with a letter saying thanks. The reason he quit his job was because his boss tried to "Play" him. He kept saying that he was going to take care of Alex but then he turn around and give him ten dollars. They got into this huge altercation, he walked out and there was his job; gone out the window. As if that wasn't enough to get me going, he then had the nerves to hit me with more news: He is moving to North Carolina. The first person he called once he quit his job was his brother and they somehow came up with this decision without me nor my opinion. He told Alex that there are better opportunities there than it will ever be here in Mississippi. I didn't have the strength to go further with this conversation because I felt myself getting very upset. It's best to leave your personally problems at home and I couldn't deal with this right now. So I walked back to my register and focused on the two hours I had left. I prepared myself for later because there was really no way in hell that he was about to up and leave us. Hell No!

Fell Too Deep

Once I made it home, I changed out of those wet clothes and grabbed my beautiful baby who was waiting patiently on her mom. Alex was sitting on the floor playing his video game so I gave him the signal to come to the back. "Now explain this absurd story to me again." I started. "Well first it's not absurd, while you trying to use big words it's just this simple word they use now a day's call "Respect." He said. "Alex, regardless of how you put it this decision to just quit your job was nonsense but since you swear I never listen to you, I am all ears. I sat there trying to hear and understand every word he was trying to get out but he kept loosing me when he said he was leaving in a few days to go to North Carolina to "Supposedly" start a new life for Samiyah and me. "I'm going to go out there with one thing on my mind and that is "Providing for my family. I am going to start off with a job and then save my money, get a car, get an apartment and then send for my two favorite girls." This goal seemed impossible to me especially when he said that this will all happen in two months. "Damn Alex, you making it sound easy to do so why couldn't you do all of that while you were here." "Now Parker you know as well as I know that there are no good paying jobs in this town and besides, Mississippi ranks the lowest when it comes to education." "And LA has the most homeless people so what are you saying? That has nothing to do with you packing up your shit and moving." He was trying to drift away from the main topic but he wasn't getting out of this one. He continued, "I am only looking out for my daughter's sake because I want nothing but the best for her and I don't think that she will receive that in Mississippi." "Damn Alex, you act like many successful people haven't made it from here. Have you forgotten about Oprah and Morgan?" Of course it's harder to achieve major goals here because we lack the opportunities but it doesn't mean that we can't go out and become just as successful as anyone from LA or any other popular city. Now we can sit and go back and forth about which state is the best but this is where I'm from and I am a very proud native so you can take it or leave it.

If I chose to stay here, my daughter stays and I can guarantee you that she will be more humble than you ever will be." "Baby you have a point but I can't be here anymore. Besides the two of you, nothing here excites me." I mentioned to him the agreement he and my mom made about going half on the rent because if he leaves, she will be left to pay all of the bills by herself. I am not making enough money to help her out and take care of things with my child. He was about to be jobless so I have to take on the major responsibility with Samiyah. "I know y'all wasn't depending on my money every week." He said "Alex it's not that we were solely depending on your income, you made a promise that you will help her out but if you knew that you couldn't hold up to that then you should have told her in the beginning. That's the main reason we moved in this house. And if you didn't notice: she is about to have an open heart surgery so she will be off of work for at least a couple of months. What about then? What are we suppose to do." The moment he opened his mouth I stopped him in the middle of his sentence. "Fuck it Alex. Just go to North Carolina and don't worry about a thing." I didn't feel like hearing his response because he was on the verge of pissing me off. He wanna cry about his boss not giving him more money so he decides to quit his job and run.

What type of shit is that? What other way was I suppose to react? He always tell me to find ways to resolve a problem before giving up but here he was doing just that. It didn't seem to bother him because he was about to leave and live stress-free for a while but I am the one left with the mom about to have surgery with a 95 percent chance of not making it. I have to be the one to find a good babysitter for my daughter while working and keeping the house intact. He tried having his brother give me a talk about how better life will be out there and all the opportunities lying there ready to be taken, but that didn't make things better.

All I knew was that my fiancé was about to leave me here with a pile load of stress to take on by myself and all he could say was "Everything is going to be ok." I felt like I was being selfish because I didn't want him to leave. He promised that he wasn't going to party every night nor cheat on me so I eventually gave in. I have no choice but to believe him when he says that he is not going to let us down because he hasn't yet made me think otherwise. He also promised to send for us once he got situated and I believe just that.

• • •

Later that day, his brother and his girl drove down to get Alex. I wasn't sure how I was going to react to him leaving but it really felt like a ton had been lifted off my shoulders. I had other things to focus on like my mom and getting her ready for Birmingham in the morning. I have been so busy with dealing with Alex that I really haven't thought about her surgery but once reality sat in, I then realized how serious it was. I ask God every day to watch over her as she lye on that table. The doctors always think that they can predict their patient's future but really they have no say. My mom made sure that the bills were situated for this first month so that could be the least of my worries.

Our church was very supportive. Many of the members stopped by to bless my brother and I with food for the week while some dropped off money to help us keep up with the bills. A few stopped by, prayed for us and gave friendly reminders that everything was going to be O.K. The choir director, Mrs. Stewart and her entire family were, always there for us in our time of need. Their family went over and beyond to provide for us and we did the same for them. I used to refer to them as "church members" but that doesn't seem appropriate being that we were practically raised with one another, so they will always be considered as our immediate family. I will never forget the days she volunteered to cook, clean and watch Samiyah when I needed that extra help during the day and besides, she is the grandmother of my best friend Tony so she will always be respected.

Chapter 31

And we all said, "Amen"

Everyone was up and moving slower than normal. The day has finally come where we have to take my mom in for open heart surgery. My brother and I were both trying to hide our feelings because we didn't want this worrying spirit to rub off on my mom. We wanted her to think that we were Ok and in it 100 % with her but we weren't. As always she was up singing and talking as if this situation wasn't effecting her. We have to love her because of the amount of faith that she has.

You could have a gun to her head and she will say "if you shoot me and I die, then it was meant to be but I will stand on faith until I leave this earth." She always tries not to think the worst and I give her two thumbs up on that because if things aren't going as plan, I stress out. I looked out of the window and noticed my step-dad pulling up in his jeep. He took the day off to drive us up to Alabama. She gathered the last of her things and before she walked out of the door she looked at my brother, Samiyah and me and said, "The same way I'm walking out of this house, will be the same way I walk back in. I claim a full recover right now in the name of Jesus. I need you two to get along, take care of the house and just continue to pray because everything is going to work out. I love y'all and we are going to make it. Parker don't you worry about Alex. Y'all will meet up again, if it's meant to be and D.J, don't you worry about graduation. I'm sorry that I'm not able to make it but you know I will be there in spirit. I'm so proud of the both of you for even graduating high school because many kids don't. I love you guys and I really need you to be strong for yourselves and for me." My brother couldn't help but cry because as easy as she made it sound, deep down we felt and thought otherwise. We prayed and walked out of the house.

CHAPTER 32

Recovery

My mom is alive and well! She was hit with a few complications but with the grace of God she made it. After surgery the doctors walked out and told me that she actually died for nearly a minute but they were able to recover her. He also shared with me that they had to perform not one but two surgeries. They found out that her heart had more damage to it than what he had expected. Thankfully and pray fully, she made it through. Her heart is very fragile so they warned us to keep stress and bad news as far away from her as possible so we followed the doctor's orders and did just that.

My brother finally graduated from high school! I knew without a doubt that he was going to graduate but I was concern about him staying focus those last few days of school. The incident with my mom took us by surprise because it not only affected her life but it affected the family as well. He has been through a lot and I'm proud to say that he made it. He will not give up especially if it's something that he knows he is capable of performing himself. He is the youngest but I look up to him in many ways. You will not run over him and get away with it. You will respect him. He doesn't give a damn about what other people have to say about him. We have the same personality but when it comes to being a "Pushover" we are total opposites but not for long because I'm working on being that "Woman" that stands up for herself.

It has been over a month since Charlie, Alex's brother, came and snatched my fiancé from me and still, there have not been any progress with him. He told us about the many opportunities that were lined up for him and how better life was in North Carolina but Alex still doesn't have a job. Every time I talk to him he is in a club or at the studio dancing. His brother is a local producer and keyboardist in Charlotte. He is currently working with a young artist/rapper who is trying to become a rising icon. Alex let me listen to some of his music over the phone and it did sound pretty appealing but I didn't know him and really didn't care to know him.

All I knew was that Alex was out partying instead of looking for a job to bring his family to be with him. On top of that, he had to get his phone turned off due to a lack of funds. That along had me very upset because we could no longer talk and text each other all day. He had to wait until he was around his brother to call me. Maybe I am being a little too hard on him but I feel that I have to because he could easily loose his main focus.

Finally, I am having some excitement in my life. I really don't do the club thing because I am still insecure about my appearance but every now and then, I'll chill with a few friends and drink a couple of mixed drinks. I just recently celebrated my 21st birthday so my cousin treated me to the Silver Star casino in Philadelphia Ms. We walked the strip and ate at the buffets. I didn't win anything, not even the money I played but I was very happy to get out of boring ass Columbus for a while.

Lately Terica, Charlie's girlfriend, and I have been communicating quite a bit. He wants us to get acquainted so once I move there we would already know a little about one another. When they came to get Alex, I was on my 15 minute break so I wasn't able to really sit and chat with them but from the looks of things she was a pretty young lady and seemed to be really nice. She just turned 26 so that puts her five years older than me. She stood at about 5'6 and had curly hair. We have clicked after carrying only a few conversations so that's a good thing, being that she will now be able to keep an eye on Alex for me.

Meanwhile, I am starting to get discourage with him because he hadn't yet found a job. I am trying my best not to put pressure on him and over step his boundaries but I was becoming very impatient. It seems as if he doesn't know how serious this is. I have to be with him and it has to be soon. My mom just had heart surgery but she is much better now so I'm able to leave whenever he is ready for us. That's very selfish of me but I can't risk him going out there, finding a "playmate" and Samiyah and me not seeing him again. Temptation is a motherfucker and all it takes is for him to walk pass a beautiful girl with long hair, waist as thin as a rope, a big ass and apple-shaped breast and I will be history. He claims to still love me but I have to be there to make sure. Some say "If it's true love then being thousands of miles couldn't keep the two of you away" but I don't believe that not one bit. I am still insecure about my looks and my weight and this stress isn't helping. I don't love myself so how will my man ever love me?

Patrice L. Guyton

Days later and in the midst of me nagging, he still managed to be faithful and finally get a job. Hell that's a huge relief. I knew that he would eventually find something because of his determination. He is now working as a cashier at this big retail store called "Sam's Town". If his work is quick and accurate after his 90 day probation, he will be qualified to move up to a better and higher paying position. I am very happy because this is a huge start for me and my daughter. We are now paychecks away from moving to North Carolina.

A Fool for Love

A fool for love is exactly who I am.
I know that I'm not wanted, because he sometimes considers me as Spam.
But I love this Man. I have faith in this Man.
He is more than anything to me, though to him, I maybe Less than.
His love is so sweet, yet so bitter like an rotten pecan.
I have to make this work, I have to a take stand.
I have to take this move to North Carolina, yep that's the plan.
I'm leaving my mom behind during a critical time in her life.
But I have to make this move, though the feeling of disappointment, digs deeper with a knife.
I'm a fool for love but this feels so right.
It happened so fast, like a thief in the middle of the night.
I'm a fool for love and this is right.
I'm going to stand by my man, I won't go down without a fight.

CHAPTER 33

Two Months Later on I-20

As I look out the window, I think about how fucked up my life is right now. We are on our way to Atlanta to meet Alex. He has found an apartment so Samiyah and I are moving to Charlotte, NC. I can't get established if my life depended on it. I'm back and forth. I finally drove Alex to the edge because he has broken off our engagement. He was right when he use to say that my guilty conscience will be the thing that ends our relationship. I was too busy worrying about him, his new job and the parties that I didn't stop to realize that he could actually be one of the guys that will never mistreat his girl. I was always questioning him about where he had been and why does it always take days for him to call me.

He keeps telling me that he is too young for stress but hell so am I. His favorite phrase is "If you are doing all of this interrogation now then it will only get worse the moment we become married." That's total bullshit because if I have a question or concern about something it's normal to ask for clarity. Right? I was faithful and I needed to know that he was doing the same. I failed to realize that I was maybe accusing him of cheating when in actuality, he really wasn't. I thought that maybe if I knew his whereabouts and exactly what he was doing every second of the day, I would feel some type of relief. But it didn't. I am left without the father of my child. Through the tears, hurt and the pain, I still managed to keep this hurtful news to myself.

I didn't bother telling my mom or anyone that we were no longer engaged because I figured that I could eventually make him change his mind. My mom would not have approved of us going there under these circumstances. We made an agreement to live two separate lives once I made it there. The only reason that he wanted me to move with him was because he wanted to be in Samiyah's life. He also agreed to help me find a job so I could later move into my own place. It was clear that he didn't want to have anything to do with me. For some reason, I didn't take him serious. I just thought that once I arrived in North Carolina that things will change.

Maybe it was the long distance that kept us arguing all the time but since we are going to be face-to-face, hopefully everything will get better. We shall see!

• • •

I walked into an apartment totally different from what I imagined. He explained to me that it was a studio apartment but hell I'm from Mississippi: I have never heard of actually it was. There was only a living room, a bathroom and a tiny ass kitchen. As I glance around the room, which only took about 10 seconds, I noticed Alex pull a long cord; and connected to it was the bed. I be Damn! I was going to be sleeping on a bed that comes out of the wall. I placed Samiyah in her playpen and took a seat while I tried to recuperate. Alex and I were walking around as if we were strangers. He barely said a complete sentence to me and I'm very stubborn so I played along with his game. But this was our little spot so I didn't complain too much because I knew, I could have easily been back in Mississippi by my lonesome. I knew that it wouldn't be long before we got on each other nerves because there is not enough space for us to go and shut off to ourselves. If we had any problems, we had the choice to step outside or sit there and deal with it. Not many options but that's about all we have at the moment.

After a few days, we realized that an extra income was needed in order for us to really make it. We lived across from this shopping plaza that had a grocery store, a cleaners company, the dollar market, barber shop and a fast food restaurant by the name of "Carl's." They sold burgers, fries, hot dogs and etc. We were living in a pretty good spot because we had everything we needed all in one area. It was even better because we didn't have a car, so that meant we didn't have to travel far, by foot, to get our necessities! I sent Alex to the grocery store and he came home with groceries and an application. As I read over it, I noticed that it was an application for that fast food restaurant. "Alex, what's this?" "What does it look like? It's an application" He almost pushed that "Do you really wanna fuck with me" button but I counted to 3 and proceeded with my conversation. "I understand that Alex. I'm asking because you know damn well that I am not about to work in a fast-food restaurant." "Well we need an extra income so just feel it out, turn it in and just see what happens. They may not call but just give it a shot. Please?" he asked. "Ok" I replied. At least by this time we were carrying a decent conversation and not getting smart every time one of us spoke a word. The next day I pulled out some jeans, a nice screen tee and walked across the street to turn in my application. I was surprise because once I walked in the restaurant, I noticed how clean it was and the employees were not ghetto-looking.

I guess you can never judge a book by its cover. I handed my application to the manager, who was the sexiest white man I had ever seen. I went off into a dazed about the two of us kissing on the beach just before Sunset but suddenly, I came out of that fantasy world when he asked, "Are you available for an interview now?" Now? With me looking and dressed like this? Was he serious? "Yes I am prepared for an interview." I lied! After about ten minutes and 20 sexy eye blinks, I was hired right there on the spot. I was now back in the working world. But I thought about it. Damn, did I really stoop this low? Am I about to be flipping burgers and weighing tables for a living?

As I dropped my head in shame I wished that I wasn't here. But I was in a city where no one knew me, so again; I swallowed my pride and did what I had to do. Lying was becoming a huge part of my life and I had to continue doing it to keep up my reputation back at home. Once again, If anyone asked if I was working, I'll tell them that I work at some fancy restaurant or a clothing store. I will just make something up because they will never know. I was able to lie to everyone about my happiness, my employment, having a car and etc.

I was too embarrassed to speak the truth which was that I didn't have shit and that my life was fucked up in too many ways to count. I am now in North Carolina stunting like I am doing it BIG and I am living with a man, the father of my child, who didn't want to have anything to do with me. I was the mother of his child so he just dealt with it. It is very true when you hear someone say, "Having a baby by a man won't keep him with you if the love isn't there." I figured that having Alex's child would improved our relationship and made him love me more but that wasn't the case in this weird ass relationship. He made it clear that there were no strings attached and that I was only out here to supposedly get a job and strive to do better than I was doing in Mississippi. "Bullshit".

His brother Charlie and Terica helped us out as much as they could as far as providing us with transportation but they had their separate lives. Our first choice is always the bus but if there was a place where the bus didn't run or if we had to do our big monthly shopping, we would ask them for a ride. After about 3 weeks, we were finally able to get cable. That was definitely a plus because now I was able to watch my soap operas. We also had a house phone, with free long distance, so I was able to call my mom as often as I wanted.

Before I moved here, he told me that we weren't going to have sex. Let's just say that he couldn't last one night. Needless to say that the sex was good and my job was great but I still had a feeling of emptiness. We still didn't have a title between us so I looked at it like, "Damn, he's using me," but I wanted it just as bad as he did so I went with the flow. On his way home from work one day, he stopped at the Dollar Market and bought a prepaid cellular phone: he said that he wanted to be able to check in on us while he was at work or away from home.

Just the other day he was getting dressed to head out with some of his co-workers so of course I was pissed because I am always left sitting at home with the child while he went out for the entertainment. I noticed his phone over on the counter so I went into my investigation mode to see if I could find anything interesting. Once the phone was in my hand, I hesitated. I didn't know if I should go through his phone or let it be. Not trusting him is why I am in the predicament that I am in now. He doesn't want to be with anyone that is always on his back about something. He had proven to me that he wasn't a cheater so I knew that I wouldn't find anything but the suspension was killing me.

As much as he said that it was none of my business: I felt like I had a right to know if he was sleeping around with other females. Hell we were having sex practically every night so why couldn't I snoop around. If a motherfucker was to give me a std, I needed to know who ass, besides his, that I had to whoop. It really irks me how men think that they can have the cake and eat it too. Here we were making good love every night, cuddling, laughing and enjoying each other like we were an couple when in actuality we weren't.

He keeps reminding me that this is only temporary and that he is only helping me out until I got my own spot. He told me not to let my feelings get involve but how can I not get attached if he is sending the wrong message. His words were saying one thing but his actions were saying something completely different.

As he turned the knob: I heard the water from the shower head hit the bottom of the tub. If I was going to do anything I had to move quickly because this dude takes a 5 minute shower and not one second over. My scheming skills have improved so I only needed about a minute or two and I was done. I quietly snuck over to his phone trying to remember the exact way it was laying so I could put it down that same way. I grabbed the phone and saw that he had one unread text from a girl name Shelly. Either I was going to read the message and delete it or not read it all. Of course I chose to read and delete it because not reading it was not really an option.

I had a gut feeling that I was on to something because I started to tremble. The text read,
    "I really like u 2 and I really hope dat u keep your promise when u said things r not goin 2 change just cause your babymoms is here."

My eyes became full of tears as I scrolled them back and forth reading the text over and over again. I was trying to make sure that these were the exact words that I just read. I stood there contemplating on my next move. He was playing with my emotions and that was definitely not a good thing. I wouldn't have come out here if I knew that he was going to be disrespectful. How could he? I promised myself that I wasn't going to say anything but I wanted to hear what he had to say. Then again I sort of already knew how this was going to play out and I wasn't in the mood to hear him lash out at me for going through his phone so I threw it on the bed and said to hell with it. I wanted to pack me and my baby's things and move back home but I couldn't.

I decided to sleep on the couch that night to avoid having to look in that bitch ass face of his. I was given signs after signs that this wasn't where I was meant to be but I kept holding on and I kept praying. There was a child involved so I had to stick it out. I didn't want to be another statistics where the girl gets pregnant and the guy leaves the girl. I wanted the family and most of all, I wanted the love. I need this to work!

Meanwhile, my job was cool. I was hired as a cashier and silly me for thinking that taking orders was the easiest job. This was a well known restaurant in the south so we were busy nonstop. We had customers from sun-up to sun-down and that was mostly because we were the only fast food restaurant on the block. When there weren't as many customers, my duties were to fill the ice machine, sweep and mop the floor, clean the tables, stock the lids and napkins, clean the windows and make sure the bathroom was clean. This was definitely not my ideal job but it was helping out with the bills so I was very grateful for that. It was a lot of cool people working there, including some of the managers, so besides us being filled to capacity: joking and playing around with them made my long work hours fun and quick. This guy name Courtney was forever flirting with me. He was one of the cooks but not really my type. He was very short, about 5'5 and 32 years old but he looks more like 25 or 26. He would always say, "I'mma take you from your boyfriend," but I tell him every day that Alex and I was not together. He couldn't believe that we were living together and sleeping in the same bed and still didn't have a commitment to one another. He had a very good point and that's what I was trying to get Alex to see. We were doing everything couples do without the title. Courtney tried to get me out the house a few times to go and chill or maybe hit up a few clubs but when I ran it across Alex, he would get defensive. Later he changed his answer and said "If you go out, don't say anything to me when I go," and he knows that's all bullshit because he leaves with or without my approval. He was doing what he wanted to do but when it came time for me to go out and try to have some fun: he was against it. If I'm not at work, I'm sitting up in this damn apartment everyday tilting my head trying to look at this 13 inch TV. If it wasn't for Terrica coming over every now and then to take Miyah and I sightseeing, I wouldn't have a clue as to what Charlotte looks like.

When Alex and I got along life was good but when we didn't, our days together seemed long and stressful. When the both of us are off of work we try to rent a movie and relax. We are both stubborn so sometimes after a heated argument, neither one of us wants to admit our mistakes nor apologize. But sooner or later, he is always the one to say "Let's work it out or let's talk about it." Sometimes I still want to hold a grudge for a few more days and be the childish one but he always find a way to make me forget our bad times: At least for the moment.

LONELY

A bad case of loneliness
Gives anyone a good reason to give up.
I feel abandoned.
I feel alone
What's going on?
I'm in a relationship but it feels like I'm stuck.
My feelings, he doesn't give a Fuck.
Damn,
What do I do when there is nothing to do?
What do I say when my man keeps walking away?
He say that we aren't together
So,
I really need to accept these feelings.
But I'm tired of being broken-hearted and lonely
Come on God,
Where are the healings?
Pour them out.
I need an overflow.
Show me the light.
Which way do I go?
A relationship is nothing without Stability.
He needs to be a man
And handle his responsibility.
I have my daughter but it's nothing liking being held by a man; your man.
I'm lonely....

Chapter 34

Day after day, I realize that I am always stressed out about something. I mentioned it to my mom and she said that I made a drastic move without praying about it first. She believes in praying on situations and waiting until God sends an answer back telling you which way to go. Now coincidentally, my job scheduled me to work the same hours and days that Alex's job had him working. We were fortunate enough to have his brother watch our baby for a couple of days but suddenly he was offered a job and Terrica was now working nights so she was sleep during the day, leaving us without a babysitter. We called around to local daycares to find a price that fit in our budget but the lowest amount we came across was about 300 a month. We couldn't afford that even with the two incomes.

With no question about it, I had to be the one to quit because Alex was making more money. I just hated the fact that I had to loose my job. I was enjoying working and bringing home my own earnings but now I was dependant on his money: yet again. Yes I was pissed because I was back to square one which meant I had to get back on food stamps. When I agreed to come out here, all of this extra drama was not in the plan. I wanted to make it work with Alex and try the whole family thing again but those plans were being shifted all over the place. When I went and applied for assistance, I was granted only 200 dollars this time. It wasn't much but it did help. Yes we were receiving free food but I still wasn't happy. I felt like I had no purpose in life. I wasn't doing anything but sitting at home all day. I couldn't work because we didn't have enough money to pay for childcare and I couldn't do school online because we didn't have a computer and I couldn't go on campus because again, we didn't have a babysitter. Every time I came close to something I would fall back to nothing and I was sick and tired of it.

If I move back home, I would be in the same predicament but I would be happier there than I am here simply because I would have more help and more love but of course that wasn't an option due to my level of pride.

Alex has been doing a little back-up dancing for an artist that his brother found. When they saw how great he could dance, they wanted him dancing on stage with the rapper to make the show more entertaining. He was able to find more excitement while I remained locked down in the house.

One night they had to perform at a birthday party for a teenage girl. It was going to be at the skating rink so I asked if I could tag along. He hesitantly said "Yea" as if I was asking him for something out of the ordinary. Of course I had to bring Samiyah but that wasn't a problem besides, I figured that the environment would be pleasant enough for a child. Alex didn't actually come out and say it but he really didn't want me to go. My thought, "Oh fucking well". It was raining so that gave him the chance to say that he didn't want our baby out in that type of weather: Oh please! He wanted me at home for a reason but I wasn't giving him. So I calmly packed her a bag and prepared to leave the house. I was so excited to get away from those same four walls that I dreadfully look at every single day of my life. If it wasn't for me walking downstairs to the mailbox, I would have started to forget what the outside world looked like.

Once we finally arrived at the party, I saw the real reason why Alex didn't want me there. He didn't give a damn about our baby getting sick; he just didn't want me to know that he had invited Shelly. He literally disrespected me to my face and there wasn't a thing that I could do about it at the moment but take it. I was very upset but I couldn't show it because Shelly would have thought that I was intimidated by her. Bitch! The whole night he flounced back and forth from me to her. He didn't seem to care how I felt about this fucked up situation. The only thing his curly head ass had on his mind was going out there to dance. He was acting totally different around me than he was around her. I got dryness and was kept at arm-length but she got smiles and hugs.

When the show was over, I overheard Alex tell his brother to take Miyah and me to the house because he was riding with Shelly. He wanted his brother to lie to me saying that he was going to ride with some of the other guys, but his brother refused to lie to me. I strapped Samiyah in and as I got in the front seat, only seconds from pulling off; I coincidently looked over and there was Alex and Shelly kissing in her car like they were true lovers. The look on his face was familiar; it was the same way he looks at me when we are kissing. Charlie also saw them but he couldn't say anything but "I don't know what's going on with my brother." As soon as those words came out of his mouth, I burst into tears. I didn't know why I was sitting there and allowing him to disrespect me. I felt like I was the only one trying to make this relationship work. Alex kept stressing the fact that we weren't together so I was able to go out and do whatever I wanted as long as I didn't bring a man to his house. I couldn't possibly talk to anyone else because my heart was with him. I was in love with him so why would I go out and date someone else when I knew I wasn't going to be in it 100 percent.

Once I made it home I put Samiyah to sleep and tried to cry myself to sleep but I couldn't do anything but pray and ask God "Why Me"? Why was this happening to me and why was I allowing it to happen? We were doing so well before and now I was being treating like fucking slum and for what reason?

A JOURNAL ENTRY:

November 11th 2007

I wish that I am happy with where I am in my life but I'm not. I'm sure if you looked up the word "Depressed" in the dictionary, you will see a picture of my fat ass face beside it. Things aren't going well at all. I wish I could talk to someone but I can't because I don't want them knowing what I'm going through. I try my best to sound uplifting and happy when I'm on the phone with my mom or dad because they can always tell when something is wrong. We were evicted from the apartment that we were living in when I first moved out here. We got behind on the rent and wasn't able to catch up. He tried to pay as much on the rent as he could before asking for an extension but eventually the manager got fed up with that. Besides rent, we had the light bill, cable, phone bill, diapers and a number of other miscellaneous things that we needed and we had to take care of all of those things off of his income.

Samiyah loved the new home and adapted to it very well because it was more room for her to crawl around. As always, I wasn't able to help out with anything but the food. I am still receiving food benefits but sometimes we barely make it through the month with enough to last the three of us. We often had to lean on his brother to help us out and he did what he could, when he could. Sometimes we would only have hot dogs and a few bags of noodles and there were times when we didn't have that. One night we had only one bag of noodles left and we knew that wasn't going to be enough for the three of us. We didn't have a vehicle to go and get food and we didn't have anyone to call on to bring us food. We figured if we went to sleep that we wouldn't be as hungry so being that our child comes first; we fixed that pack of noodles for Samiyah. Many times we went to sleep without having anything to eat but as long as our child was fed, we were ok.

Just recently I sat down with Alex to see exactly where we stood as a couple. I had to know if I was out here just to keep him company or if my life served a better purpose. Once that conversation started, things got heated and things were said. He mentioned to me that he and Shelly had gotten closer and that she had gained very strong yet confusing feelings for him. He told me that she wanted to be with him but she didn't know exactly what to expect being that he and I was living together. I didn't know what to think. I didn't know if should cry or beat his motherfucking ass for coming to me with such nonsense. When I asked him how he felt about it surprisingly, he told me the truth. He shared with me his true feelings.

"Here is the thing. To tell you the truth Parker, there are three girls that I truly care about and that includes you, Red and Shelly." I started to walk off but he grabbed my arm and said, "Wait, Just hear me out." At that moment I didn't want to hear anything else because I could feel where it was about to lead to, this was his way of breaking up with me.

He continued, "Red was my high school crush, a club member and my best friend. We talked about everything and had a good time together. Shelly is like the good girl. She's in college, with no kids, very smart and pretty with beautiful brown eyes. When I'm around her we can chill for hours without all of the drama. Then comes you."

"Then comes me? How dare you call me last and say my name as if it hurts for it to come out of your damn mouth?"

"Can you please let me finish? You had my first child so we share something greater than what I share with the other two girls. I love you but we argue entirely too much about things that could easily be avoided."

I was speechless: just absolutely lost for words. I couldn't believe that he had the balls to confess all of this to my face but I think what hurt me the most was when he had the audacity to say that I was only one of the three girls that he was in love with. He admitted that he and Red had been communicating via internet and over the phone lately so that's how he regained his feelings for her. I thought back to when we were living in Mississippi.

I confronted him about texting her late that night and he brushed me off. Now the truth was out and I couldn't get upset because I had a feeling of what was going on way back then. I had a gut feeling that they were doing more than catching up but like always, my ignorant ass just let shit slide. He told me that he needed time to think about it and once he made his decision, he was going to tell us which one he was going to choose to be with.

Which One He Was Going To Choose To Be With? Are you fucking kidding me? I couldn't believe that I was going to actually sit there hoping and praying to God that I would be the one he picks. I was so much more than that and I deserved even more.

SETTLING

Ever settled, just to be with who you thought was your
    True Love?
Ever settled, just because you didn't want to see your
Loved one fly away like a Dove?
Ever settled, because you thought you and your mate fit
Perfectly like a glove?
Every settled, just so you can have someone to Hug?
Well,
I have…
As a matter of fact, I think I'm settling now.
He is my Rock, my Life, my World;
Did I mention that he's the father of my baby girl?
I be damned if another bitch take my spot.
She will not wear my clothes
Nor will she sleep on my couch.
So, I'm in it to Win it,
But this relationship feels like a competition.
I'm fighting for his love
But "his love' is my opponent.
I can't separate myself.

I'm attached like a tick.
With a broken-heart that only he can fix.
But, I know I deserve better.
That's like wearing pleather when you are used to leather.
If I ever push through this desperate love letter.
He will be the Footer,
And for once, I'll be the Header.

But,
I can't,
Well, I don't want to move on.
I hate the thought of being lonely.
So scratch what I said earlier,
I won't have an empty home.
So for now,
I must Settle.

Eventually he chose to be with me because apparently he liked the fact that we had already established a family. I thought "What the hell", I've been here this long so I might as well stay. Only people from the outside looking in will judge me. No one knows how much I love Alex and how bad I want our relationship to work. I would go over and beyond for him and to be with him. I can't stand the idea of another female being with my man so if it takes me changing myself to make him love me more then that's exactly what I'm going to do. As long as he loves me, I know that we will be ok. If I continue to put him first then he will see that I will do anything for him and that I am here to stay. After that decision I can assure you that things didn't seem right anymore. His love was there but not as strong as before. I knew then that the only reason he was with me was because of our child and at that point I was thanking God for her every day because if it wasn't for her, I may not have had the man of my dreams standing beside me. Some may say that I have my priorities screwed up but I don't care. I am only trying to find ways to keep the man that I long for right here in my arms.

His mom wanted to be a bigger help to us so she offered moving here, to Charlotte. Once this plan was confirmed, I was able look for jobs again! She and her husband will be staying here in our home looking after Samiyah basically whenever we needed her to. We were going to have a babysitter and since she was driving her car, we will now have transportation to get around instead of leaving the house two and three hours early to catch the bus.

It seemed like things were starting to look up for me as far as income and employment. The same day Mrs. Judy and her husband arrived in Charlotte was the same day that "Wall-Home" called and ask if I could start working immediately. Wall-Home is a huge retail store and I am working as a cashier. Prior to Alex's parents coming, I had an interview and I also completed the first level of Orientation. So after I prayed, I pretty much knew I had the job. This will be my second job in retail and even though it has been a while, I was more than happy to start.

My mom and step-dad wanted to come and spend the holidays with us this Christmas so I talked it over with Alex and we both agreed that would be a great idea since his mom and step-dad was already here. When we moved into this apartment, we were sleeping on comforters and sheets on the floor. We just recently came into some extra money so we decided to go and purchase a blow up mattress. Pretty sad huh?

His mom was able to bring a table and two small chairs from her home in Texas. I was very thankful but we needed more furniture in our home. We were at a place in our life that we couldn't splurge a single dollar but Alex still found the time and money to go and invest in a play station 3. He is always complaining about how bored he is and that he needed a stress reliever. I would have been more open to the idea if he would have ran it by me first but like always, he never does. He figured since he was the "Man" of the house that he didn't have to ask my opinion on anything and that is total bullshit. But due to our lack of funds, he had to end up taking it back so purchasing that game was a waste of time. Just a few days ago, we went to a few rent-to-own furniture stores and purchased a sofa, loveseat, flat screen TV, computer and a center table. So we practically went from a dead apartment to a place that brought things to life the minute you opened the door. We held off on buying a bedroom suit and just continued sleeping on the floor. We were young so it didn't bother us as much. Ok, I have to go for now. So until next time, Peace and Love –Parker.

Chapter 35

Bells will be Ringing

You already know when it's Christmas time because you can feel the love and smell the sweet aroma of good food cooking. Everyone was here, well almost everyone. My mom and step-dad finally made it in around 3 this morning. They stopped a few times due to bad weather on the outskirts of Atlanta but thank God they were able to make it through safely. Unfortunately, my brother wasn't able to come due to his job. He is a kitchen crew member at the hospital and unless there was a death in the family: they had to be at work everyday. I hadn't seen him in a few months so I was looking forward to hanging out with him, especially now because this is the time for family and laughter. He always has something foolish to say every single time he opens his mouth. He makes my day even when I'm at my lowest so I really hate I couldn't see him this time. Alex's mom and step-dad was here along with Charlie and Terrica. Besides today being Alex's birthday, this Christmas was a special one for us. Even though our baby girl doesn't have a clue as to what is going on and probably never will, this is her first Christmas so we are overjoyed. She is ten months and not quite walking but she is crawling around and trying to get into everything. All of us were amazed at how fast she was growing. It seemed like it was just the other day that she came into this world and in only two months, she will be a one year old.

I was so proud of Alex and the relationship that he had with Samiyah. He has been the best father since the day he found out that I was pregnant. When she gets up early crying for a bottle, he will wake up and go and fix it for her without me asking him. When I come home from work, I find my daughter in one piece and very happy. He allows me to have time for myself so every other day he will take her to this park by our apartment and they would spend that quality time together. I'm very grateful to have a man in my life that loves and cares for his child because there are quite a few that doesn't. This was his first born and she was a girl so he cherished her with all of his heart and soul and I loved that.

Everyone had finished eating so we sat around to play a few board games and continued to enjoy each others' company while we had most of our family here. Suddenly, Alex stands and says, "I have an announcement to make." That's weird because he isn't the type to talk in front of anyone, not even his family, but I was sure that it wasn't anything major. He is probably about to thank everyone for coming over to spend Christmas with us.

He continued, "I'm going to make this short and sweet. None of you may know but Parker and I have been struggling with a number of things within this past year. We have been evicted; we don't have a car, sometimes no food in our refrigerator, we sleep on a floor (which is sad to say) and for a moment I really didn't think that we were going to make it as a couple.

Every now and then I would go out and hang with girls and have fun but when I come home I am unhappy. Parker, I have put you through a lot and when I think about it, you should have left me months ago. As for me personally, I wouldn't stay with a woman if she were treating me like I have been treating you. I can say that the only thing that held us together this long was love and love is going to keep holding us on until eternity. Shelly and Red are girls that I thought I wanted to be with but when I think about the struggles that me and you have made it through and when I think about the good times that we have, I will choose to be with you any day. I know where we have been and I know where we are going. Parker, I said all of this to say that I love you and I am truly sorry. I love our family and I want this to last forever so will you please do me the honors of putting my ring back on your finger?"

"Wow!" was all that I could say. "That was deep and very well said. Hell that was almost better than the first proposal."

I wanted to let him in on a few secrets of my own but I didn't. Shelly and Red once accused me of calling and playing tricks on their phones a few times but neither Alex nor those slum bags had any proof. I wanted to be a woman and admit that I did call their phones a few times but

NAH! I just let their minds continue to ponder. Red was miles away over in California but she stayed heavy on his mind so I played on her phone out of hurt and anger. Shelly, on the other hand, was nothing to me. I played on her phone because it was something to do. I don't know; maybe it was hearing the anger in her voice that gave me adrenaline rush. He has questioned me about it over and over again but to this day, I still deny it. I promised him the very first time that I wouldn't call and play on these chics phone but yet in still, I did it anyway. It wasn't the time to confess all of this. He has just made it clear to me that he no longer wanted to look back, only forward, so I was willing to do the same. I happily said, "Yes" And placed the ring back on my finger.

My mom was shocked because she didn't know that he called the engagement off nor did she know half of the things that we were going through. His brother facial expression didn't show too much of anything because he is so damn mean that you wouldn't know if he was happy or upset. But I could tell that he was wondering if I was the perfect fit for his brother. Terrica on the other hand, was sitting beside him with that envy and jealousy look but trying to portray as being happy. I can assure her that Charlie was never going to ask her to marry him just because he didn't understand the type of woman he had. She had her own place, own car, very pretty and worked a 12 hour shift five days out of the week.

They go out and have fun every now and then but for the most part they're arguing and it was worst than Alex and I. What they did was their business and I had nothing to do with that. On the other hand, I was happy that we did hit rock bottom because now we can be grateful for each other and move pass that devastating time in our lives. I didn't cry this time but I was definitely filled with joy on the inside. This is where I was trying to get back to. I wanted us to have that thrive and love that we had when we first met in college, before all of the drama and before all of the pain. We both had good jobs, we were getting alone, had food in the fridge and just living life. At the end of the day, that's what it's all about, Happiness.

• • •

A couple of days later we said our good-byes to both of our parents. My step-dad and mom was getting ready to head back to Mississippi and his mom and step-dad got a call from the manager at "Cypress Place" giving her the approval for them to move into their own apartment. It was good news for them because they finally had their own place. Their apartment was about fifteen minutes from where we live. They were our babysitter whenever the both of us worked the same hours on the same day and they were our transportation to get back and forth to work. Eventually, we got used to the new change. It felt good to be happy again and living the independent life. When we weren't working, we were home as a family and we caught up on our good love making that we used to have before his parents moved in with us.

At that moment, life was great and we had no complaints. He started to clean up more and sometimes he would attempt to cook a meal. He isn't the best chef but he did know how to scramble some eggs, cook some bacon, make a home-made burger and cut up some fries. Sometimes I sit back and observe the positive changes that we have made. My daughter is so beautiful and happy; I have a place to call my home and I am stress-free. I know this is going to work. I could see us in that beautiful house with the white picked fence and my kids running around playing. Finally, happiness is here to stay. Thank you GOD!

A JOURNAL ENTRY:

FEBRUARY 7TH 2008

I only have a few minutes left before I clock back in so I have to clear my head before I go back out there dealing with those crazy customers. Alex works in the same plaza as I do so today; we decided to have lunch together. He has advanced at his job so he is able to take his lunch break whenever he wants to. He is now a full-time stocker. He recently received a pay raise that includes full benefits so the both of us were happy about that.

He had a lot of friends at work and most of them were females. When I first moved here, that bothered me but now it doesn't. I knew he loved me and that I was the only person that he wanted to be with so I didn't worry about that anymore. I've learned to have faith in him so I'm trusting that he will not hurt me again. At this point in my life he was my all and everything. All I seemed to find myself thinking about was him, and my daughter. My mind, body and soul is in this relationship and I can honestly say the same about him. He promised to never leave me and he knows that I'm not going anywhere. We are like two peas in a pod. You barely see one without the other. We had family night at least four times a week and those times are solely dedicated to our baby and each other.

Income Tax season had finally rolled around so that means; Money, Money, Money! For some strange and ridiculous reason, Charlie thought that he was going to claim our child this year on his taxes. He barley worked last year and besides, this was our child. Alex told me that Charlie called and he figured that it was an emergency because he hardly ever calls. I could hear him now, "Alex, man it would really help me out if you would let me claim Samiyah this year on my taxes. I would give you a few hundred dollars." Damn, I wish he would have asked me. Alex was upset because he knows that his brother was out of line for asking that dumb ass question but I would have laughed it off. His brother never comes to visit us nor does he ever volunteers to come pick up Samiyah and spend quality time with her. Alex and his brother does not have that type relationship or that connection that you have known for brothers to have but there he was trying to claim our child on his taxes. Boy he is something else!

    Even if Alex hadn't already file his taxes, he still wouldn't have let his brother do it. I know that I may come off as if I don't like his brother but it's really not that. I just hate his ways. He has a very bad temper and you can't tell him shit because he thinks he is right about everything, all the damn time. He has helped us, in so many ways so don't get me wrong but not enough to get thousands of dollars off of our child. But he's cool.

Not to long ago, he and Terrica invited the three of us over to his house for dinner for the very first time! The night was supposed to have been a relaxing night until something very drastic happened. I'm sort of embarrassed to tell this story but I can always rely on my journal to keep a secret. I tell you everything else so there is no need in stopping now. You are the only one that will ever know this, well besides Alex, his brother and Terrica: Samiyah is too young.

(Charlie cooked spaghetti; we drank some wine and listened to music for a few hours. I had been stuck in the house with nothing to do so when I saw Liquor; I went for it. I remember sitting on the couch talking to Terrica and waiting on the food. While no one was looking I snuck in a few shots of Vodka. Alex and Charlie was gone to the store to buy more wine. By the time they came back I was very tipsy and on the verge of being totally wasted but I still found the strength to drink more wine and take more shots. Finally, the food was done and placed on the table for us to eat. I had so many drinks that I could no longer hold my piss. I had to get to the bathroom and I had to get there quick. My period was on that night so I remembered trying to keep my eyes open long enough to grab a tampon out of my purse. That was all that I remembered about that night).

I BLACKED out. I woke up to bright lights and a beeping noise. I was in the hospital being asked my name and if I had been sexual abused. I was scared and I was nervous because I didn't know what was going on. Moments later, Alex was standing over me. His eyes were the color of fire and I could tell that he was very pissed.

"Alex, what's wrong? What happened?" He looked at me and said, "Parker, what didn't happen?" The story supposedly went like this:

(He told me that I went into the bathroom and stayed there for a while. He called my name several times because everyone was waiting for me to eat but I never answered. He had his brother unlock the door and there he found me on the floor passed out. My pants were down to my knees and there was blood on my clothes. He pulled up my pants and he and Charlie carried me to the car: to go home. Once we got outside, some neighbors were talking and drinking (something I should have never started). Those neighbors must have thought that I had been raped or beaten because before they could get me inside of the car, the ambulance arrived. He said they examined my body and took me to the hospital.)

"So now we are here waiting on you to be discharged. My brother and Terrica are in the waiting room with Samiyah." I didn't know what to say. I was so ashamed because I allowed myself to get so drunk that I couldn't remember anything. I was even more embarrassed because my menstrual cycle was on and not only did Alex see it: His brother and the nurses noticed it. I felt trifling and stupid. It was a little after 5 in the morning and Alex and Terrica both had to be at work at 6. Once I was released, I didn't want to ride home with them. I didn't have enough guts to face them after everything that I had done. Once we got in the car, things seemed so awkward. No one was talking and the radio probably wasn't passed the volume #2. I apologized to everyone but that still didn't make things right. Charlie said that he was cool and that he wasn't too worried about it. I still couldn't believe what happened. After that day, no one brought the issue up again so I'm guessing that I was officially forgiven. Charlie showed me a different side of him and honestly it was a side that I had never seen.

Maybe there really is some love in that black heart of his or maybe that was just a one time thing.

• • •

Finally, our money from Alex's taxes had come so that helped us out tremendously. He received 3100 dollars which exceeded the amount that we thought we were going to get. It was our first time doing taxes so we both figured that we would receive around 1200 dollars or even less. We were overly excited and exceedingly thankful because with that money we were able to catch up on bills, buy a 50" flat screen TV and of course he bought another play station 3. This time he didn't have to take it back because we had extra money to splurge with. He gave Samiyah and me seven hundred dollars so we went on a little personal shopping spree. I hadn't been shopping since I've been here so of course I didn't know how to act. We went to store after store while he sat at home and played the game. Once we finally made it home: the three of us put on our best clothes, went to take pictures and then out to eat dinner. Meanwhile, our lives seemed to be moving along pretty fast. Samiyah is turning one in less than two weeks so we had to prepare for her birthday party. It seems as if my mom was just here and now she and my youngest brother will be traveling here again for the party. Many children say it but I mean it when I say that my mom is the best. She is always there for me whether I'm right under her nose or miles away. Well that's it for now. I have to go back to work. I'm already running late. Peace and Love –Parker.

Approximately Three weeks later

Chapter 36

An Opportunity to Dance

Samiyah's birthday party was a blast. She is officially a one year old but sometimes she acts five. I can already see that she is going to be an Independent girl. She thinks that she is the Boss of the house and that Alex and I are her kids. She is so cute and tiny so we have no choice but to let her have her way and that's exactly what we did on her birthday. It was a small birthday party simply because we didn't know any kids her age so the only people that celebrated with us were, my mom and brother and later that night, Charlie and Terrica finally showed up. Mrs. Judy was offered a job and she had to start the exact same day of the party. That was understandable so we gave her a rain check.

We song Happy Birthday and just like any other one year old: we allowed her to eat her birthday cake however she wanted to. She had it in her hair and nose and not to mention her face and clothes. She knew exactly what was going on because she started to act like a spoiled brat. You would think that a child that young wouldn't know how to fight for attention but she did just that the entire day. Instead of blowing out the candle, she spit over the cake. Instead of keeping her hair pretty with the little bows that I neatly placed in her head, she pulled them out and threw them on the floor.

Instead of being cheerful, she cried when she couldn't get her way. I tell you: that child of mines is definitely a character but I never get upset at her because I know that one day, she is going to make me a lot of money on Broadway with those acting skills that she already has. We took her to the park for a while and we figured out that being pushed in a swing is one of her favorite things to do. If it was up to her, she will want you to push her in a swing for hours at a time.

My mom bought her all sorts of toys, as many as eight outfits and about two pairs of shoes.

She received a bike from her uncle Charlie and aunt Terrica. The bike looks like it could be for a five or six year old but maybe she can get some practice out a little earlier. "Yea Right", they knew damn well my baby couldn't ride that bike anytime soon and I'm sure that when that time come for her to learn how to ride a bike, she will have a new one. I'm not saying that anything is wrong with this one and I'm not bothered by the idea that the bike is "Blue" but come on. They could have bought a Barbie doll or a shirt or a bag full of sweets: not something that was probably giving to them. However, I am grateful because it's the thought that counts right? "Yea", right.

As we sit around in this apartment I sometimes have no other choice but to sit back and think about life. North Carolina is great and my job is flowing like it should but is this really where I am supposed to be? Is this how I am going to live the rest of my life?

At this moment, I really don't know what God has ordained me to do. I haven't been to church since I moved out here and that is a very sad thing to say. I have lost touch with myself and the person that I am. I know exactly where I am physically but mentally I am lost and emotionally; I'm drained. I love Alex to death and I can't see myself with anyone else but I'm really getting sick of the same routine that we perform on a day to day basis. We go to work and then we come home to do nothing.

I guess this is apart of the "Growing Up and being Responsible" life but I know a lot of adults that still go out and have that special time to themselves. Like now, Samiyah is asleep so we should be having some "Alone" time but of course he has his curly head ass on the floor, sitting in Indian style, playing those video games. When he plays that game, nothing else matters. That's sort of how I am with my Soap Operas but they only last about an hour or thirty minutes, if you have the DVR, so that doesn't compare to the hours he spend on his game. It wouldn't change things if I talked it over with him so I am learning to save my breath and let it be.

A few friends from back home sometimes call and entertain me on the latest gossip or rumor that is going on. Everyday is full of drama in Columbus but you can either make something out of it; meaning rise above it and find something positive to do, you can move away like I did or you can just sit and entertain the mess. As much as I used to hate all of the nonsense, it at least made the days go by. I have no friends here and at times like these, I hate it. I don't have anyone to go to the movies with or walk the malls with. All I have is Samiyah and Alex but my mom somehow believes it's a good thing. She always tells me that, "Girls always leave a scent of blood and too much blood can lead to complications". For that reason I try to keep a small circle and I have even learned to keep some woman at arm's length. Many people have wondered over the years why I like to hang around dudes and that's because they don't run around town spreading confidential information but lately, some men are more bitches than the women so you have to be careful either way it go. Now don't get me wrong because I know a lot of men bitches but the ones I cling to, is not like that. They tell me what's right, what's wrong, how men act and how to react to men. They keep it real instead of sugarcoating an issue to make me feel better so I choose to hang out with a dude instead of a chic but I wouldn't trade my female friends for anything in this world. I do wish that there was at least one girl out here that I can relate to but for now it's just the three of us. As I sit here contemplating on the facts of life, my thoughts are interrupted by a phone call. Of course Alex didn't move from in front of the TV so I went an answered the phone:

"Hello".

"Hello, this is Richard with BBC. I'm trying to reach an Alex Jones."

BBC is the most popular TV station. They are based out of Los Angeles California and I was puzzled as to why they wanted to speak to Alex. Maybe this is a joke but they are calling from a California number. I didn't hold him any longer because I wanted to know what was going on.

"Could you hold please?" I gently asked

I placed the phone on my thigh and whispered out to Alex.

"Alex…Alex…Alex Jones. Would you please get your nose out of that game for a few seconds? There is a guy on the phone by the name of Richard. He says that he is calling from BBC. Do you know him?"

"BBC? You mean the TV station?"

"Well he didn't exactly say that he was associated with the TV station so I don't know. Here, just take the phone and see what's going on!"

"I can't believe this! This phone call may change our lives forever" he yelled.

I didn't know what the hell he was talking about. If anything, I was confused. Alex wasn't even a minute into his conversation when I heard him scream louder than a man being punched in the balls.

"Thank you so much and I look forward to seeing you guys in a couple of days".

"Alex! Tell me what's going on. Why do you have this huge Kool-Aid smile on your face?"

"I didn't tell you this but I sent in a thirty second audition tape to "America's Talent" and that was the casting director calling to let me know that I had been selected to go out to LA and audition."

"That's amazing! Congratulations baby! Oh my gosh, we are about to be famous! So um, when do we leave?"

"Uh about that, he stated that we had to find our own transportation to and from the auditions. We don't have enough money to buy all of us a ticket and barely enough for me so I am going to ask my brother if he could get his company to purchase me a plane ticket."

"Can they do that?"

"Yea, that's how he goes back and forth to LA to promote his music."

"You better hope that he can pull this off for you because this is a once in a lifetime opportunity."

"Exactly, I need him to come through for me."

He immediately got on the phone to call his brother. I couldn't hear their conversation and I couldn't exactly tell by his expressions what was being said on that phone. I saw his face go from a smile to a frown and then a smile and frown again and seconds later, the conversation was over.

"Ok, this is how it is going to happen. My brother said that he could get me a one-way ticket to California and work on a one-way ticket back here to Charlotte."

I wish we had enough money to buy him a roundtrip ticket and we wouldn't have to worry about him running into any complications. Hopefully, his brother can get both tickets and bring my hubby back to me quick but safe with no problems. But we all know how his brother can get; he will say one thing and later totally forget that he has promised someone a favor. I think we have enough money to maybe get him a return ticket but we would definitely have to manage the rest of our money. The cable and the phone bill are both due in about two weeks which is the exact same time that he will be coming back. He has ordered all of these damn sport channels because he didn't want to miss a football or basketball game this season and because of that our cable bill is 300 dollars this month and our phone bill is about 90 dollars. The cable is in my name so that definitely has to be paid. Even though the bills were coming in at one time, I really wanted him to go out there because I knew the moment they saw him dance, he was going to automatically advance to the next round. He could possibly win the entire show so he had to at least go out there and give it a shot. He is a great dancer and I do believe that he will prosper even if this does not work out for him.

Once he makes it out there he will need money for food and gas so we discussed it and figured out the things we need and the things we can do without. We ended up taking from our bill money and I wasn't pleased with that but I have to keep in mind that this audition could possibly change our lives forever. I have heard many stories about families giving up everything that they had in order for their child or loved one to go off and better themselves such as leaving for college, going on singing, dancing and even modeling shows. This is a great opportunity so I wanted to support him in every way that I could. My dad used to do it all of the time for me. I would need money while I was in college and sometimes he and my step-mom would have bills that were due but he would still find a way to get me what I need.

My family as well as his family and friends were very excited. I updated my status on my web page and everyone started to comment and many wished us Good Luck.

He had to be at the airport in less than four hours so of course we had to make some good loving before he left. I can't have him going to LA with sex on his mind. There are a lot of beautiful girls out there and even the most faithful man can sometimes be tempted. My goal right now is to have him come as much as he can. I'm still so amazing in my bedroom. He ate the hell out of my pussy and I sucked the hairs off of that dick. We made that good old fashion love that you only have when you are truly in love.

About two hours later, we had to end our lovely rendezvous because the airport was about an hour drive from our house. Once we made it to the airport, I parked instead of dropping him off at the gate. We sat down and talked for a few minutes but the time seemed to fly by so quickly. It was time for him to head through the security check point. As he prepared to show his boarding pass and ID at the security check-in, the tears immediately started to flow. Samiyah starts to cry because she sees her mommy crying. He allowed one tear to drop but that was about all.

"Would you stop acting like I'm not coming back?" He said. "Alex I know that you are coming back but I'm going to miss you. Is it ok for me to miss my fiancé? You are going to be away for a week and you know that we can't be away from you that long."

"I know and I understand because I am going to miss my two favorite girls as well but you have to remember that I am going out here to do this for us. I want to see you and my daughter happy so if that means that I have to leave the two of you to hopefully make some money, I will do just that. I will call every day and we will definitely instant message each other all of the time. This week is going to fly by very quick so just be strong for me. My mom will be back and forth over there checking on you two and make sure that you let her know your work schedule so she can watch Samiyah."

"Ok Alex, I have all of that."

I was nervous about him going back to his home-town. I wanted him to see all of his family and friends but I didn't want him to forget about us. He promised to come back and besides, he loves us too much not to. We said I love you, gave each other one last kiss and Samiyah and I waved good-bye as he walked off.

Chapter 37

"No Soaps for you"

As I wake up and wipe the drool from my face, a feeling of discomfort came over me. Samiyah was still asleep so I decided to start cleaning up this house and then fix me something to eat. Alex has been gone for four days and I have started to get lonely. I already have no life as it is but now my days are definitely long with him being gone.

24 HOURS AND 10 MINUTES AGO:

I'm sitting here on this couch and suddenly the phone rings. I assumed it was Alex because his audition was this morning and I have been waiting on him to call and tell me the good news. I looked at the caller ID and it was him. I answered the phone as excited as I knew how.

"Hey baby it's me."

Oh Gosh! He didn't sound too pleased. Maybe he is trying to fool me.

"Hey Alex, how did it go?"

"I didn't make it through."

I quickly took a gasp of air because I didn't believe him. I didn't want to faint while he was on the phone. This couldn't possibly be happening.

"Alex!" I screamed. "No! What happened?"

"They didn't give me enough time to really dance. They cut my music off after about twenty seconds into the song."

"Alex, you knew that was going to happen and that's why I told you that you have to start off blowing their minds away. You can't wait until the ending of the song to put your all into it."

"I know babe and I'm so sorry."

Hell it's too late for him to apologize. What's done was done and there was nothing we could do about it. I hate this and I hate it bad. I know how bad he wanted this but I think I wanted it more.

"Well Alex, I know you did your best and there is no sense in crying over spilled milk. I'm glad you had this opportunity. So, when do you come home?"

"My brother is working on another ticket as we speak so hopefully I would be back early in the morning around 6 or 7 if so, my brother will pick me up from the airport and bring me home."

"Oh, I wasn't expecting you for a couple of days but I am definitely not complaining. Your daughter and I miss you so much."

"Man, I miss y'all too."

"Hey, how about I make you a dinner tonight so you can enjoy it once you get here. I know it will be early in the morning when you arrive but we can save it for tomorrow night. I really want to do it because it will make the time go by quicker tonight."

"Yea, that will be good because all I have been eating is fast food."

"Well you go ahead and enjoy the rest of your day with your friends and family. I love you."

"Thanks baby. I love you too."

I slammed the phone on that table as many times as I could. I am so pissed but I was trying my hardest not to let him hear it in my voice but the truth is that I am furious right about now. Yes, he experienced something new in his life but now we are broke. I was very supportive of the idea but now that we have these bills that are due tomorrow, I am P-I-S-S-E-D. Now what do we do? I don't get paid until next week and his check will not have that many hours on it because he is in California. The money that he got back from his taxes is gone and I am officially broke.

That explains the headache that I woke up with. But that was yesterday so today marks a brand new day. What's done is done and now we have to find a way to get some money. I bet if I was at that audition, Alex would have made it through. Sometimes you have to put your foot down and let the world know how bad you want something. But oh well, everything in life happens for a reason so let's just hope that there is a damn good reason for why he didn't make it through.

Samiyah is finally up so we are sitting here looking at each other, eating grits. I woke up thinking about a fully cooked breakfast that included maple sausage links, biscuits, eggs, grits and bacon but I realized that Alex wasn't here. Hell I can't eat all of that by myself: well I can but I am seriously trying to loose as much weight as I can right now. Summer is approaching and I have to get back in that two piece bathing suit so, I decided to only cook the grits. We ate, I re-cleaned the kitchen and we both took a bathe. Moments later, I found my lazy ass on the couch ready to go back to sleep.

As I placed Samiyah in her play pen, I realized that my stories were about to come on and suddenly I had energy again. (Victor has gotten himself in more trouble and today determines if he is going to get caught or not.) I kicked my feet up, took a sip of my orange juice and press the Power button. "Hmm" I thought. That's weird, there was no picture and there wasn't a red dot beside the time on the cable box meaning that my soap opera wasn't recording. I got out of my comfortable position and went to beat on the TV screen. (You know how you used to do when you were bootlegging cable and suddenly it goes out. You try to beat the TV senseless hoping for the station to come back up.) I still didn't get anything. I changed channels and still nothing and suddenly that fucking light bulb clicked on in my head.

"THE CABLE IS OFF!" I screamed so loud that it scared my child but having no cable scared the shit out of me. This can't be happening and definitely not now. I can't survive without a TV. The cable bill isn't due until a few days from now so I couldn't understand why it was off. I tried to think back to the negative things that I have done in my life because God was definitely punishing me by taking my stories away. Friday's are the best days because it's the last day of the week and it leaves your mind wondering over the entire weekend. I immediately dropped to my knees and started asking God to forgive me for whatever I had done. I even promised not to do whatever it was that I had done again. I said "Amen", ran to the TV to turn it on and it was still off. DAMNIT, my prayer didn't work! I realized that the cable and phone bill was due around the same time so if the cable was off then I'm pretty sure that the phone was off. I took a deep breath and walked over to the phone; I picked it up and heard "dunnnn". I have never been so excited to hear a dial tone in my entire life. I called Alex on his God-brother's phone but no one answered. Samiyah was hanging over her play pen trying to figure out what was going on with her mom but she had no idea.

This day couldn't get any worse even if it tried to. I can deal with going to hell and back but I can't deal with missing a day of my soap operas. I hate for people to tell me what happen because it's not the same as actually watching it. As I sit here in denial, another light bulb clicked on; What if I pawn his play-station? I could get about 200 dollars because they are worth at least 400 in the store. I glanced over to the floor where he usually keeps it but I noticed that it wasn't there. I know damn well it was here before he left so maybe he put it in the bedroom to make sure Samiyah didn't touch it. It wasn't in the bedroom so I assume the worse. "We had been robbed!" That boy loves that game to death so I didn't want to tell him but I figured that it's better that I tell him now than for him to come home looking for it. He didn't answer the phone when I was calling him about the cable being off so why should I try and call back? I felt bad so I gave in. As I walked over to the phone to call him; again, he was calling me. I didn't prolong,

"Alex the cable is off and your play-station is stolen."

"The cable is off? But the bill isn't due until a few days. Have you called them?"

"There is no sense in calling if we don't have any money to pay them but did you hear the second part of that sentence? I said the cable is off and your play-station is GONE." He sighed,

"Yea I heard you. My game is not stolen and it didn't mysteriously vanish."

"So where in the hell is it?" "I pawned it before I left to have extra money." "Extra money?" I asked. You took our bill money for extra money and now you are telling me that you had more money on the side." "Look, I know that you are mad and I know what you are about to say but let's just discuss this when I get home in the morning." He said.

I slammed the phone on that table once more. I could give a damn if it breaks or not but I remained calm. There was no reason for me to get upset because he wasn't here to hear me curse him out. But he is most definitely right, we will talk about this the minute his conniving ass gets off of that plane. I knew that he was too calm for a reason.

Meanwhile, I started re-cleaning the house even though I hadn't messed anything up. When I'm upset I clean up so by the end of the night this is going to a squeaky clean house. I was going to fix him a nice dinner but he has just ruined that. I could care less if he eats for the next few days because he has had enough money to stack up on food.

Samiyah was getting sleepy so I gave her a bath and put her down for the night. I played on the computer until I my eyes started to hang low. Since Samiyah was in her play pen I decided to sleep on the couch, again. The blow-up mattress needed air and I didn't want to disturb my daughter with the sound from the air pump. I laid there thinking of everything that I was going to say to Alex but more importantly, I wanted to know his reason for pawning his game without telling me. I fell asleep with questions un-answered.

Chapter 38

First Cable and then…

When I opened my eyes, I noticed sunlight outside of my window. The sun does not rise until seven but it felt later than that. I glanced at the cable box and it said 10:15. Damn, I do not think that I have slept this late since I gave birth to Samiyah. I was on the couch so I was surprised that I did not at least roll over. I looked over to the playpen and to my surprise; my daughter was sleep with an empty bottle in her mouth. I grabbed the bottle, placed it on the kitchen counter and ran into the bedroom hoping that I would find Alex sleep on the blow-up mattress but I didn't. "This is very weird", I thought. Where is he? He was suppose to be here around eight but he is two hours late. I started to think the worst as if he had been in a plane crash or something but if that was the case, someone would have called. Speaking of calling, I went to grab the phone to call his God-brother to see if everything was Ok when he left but this time there was no dial tone. I placed the phone on the receiver and picked it back up, still no dial tone.

Yesterday was terrible and I had a feeling that today was not going to be any better because now I have no cable nor do I have a telephone and to top things off, Alex is not here. I opened the door to see if someone had left a note because maybe I was sleeping too hard to hear him knock. There wasn't a note in sight. I couldn't do anything but go back in the house and wait for him to come home. As I was about to close the door, I heard footsteps coming up the stairs. Our apartment is the only one on this floor so those footsteps were coming to my house. "Alex? Is that you?" I yelled. Nevertheless, it wasn't him. It was his mom and by the look on her face, something had happened. "Don't tell me. Is he hurt? Where is he?" She didn't budge. "Let's just go in the house." She said. "Mrs. Judy please tell me what's going on." I asked as I closed the door behind her. She then gave me her cell phone, "Call Alex and he will tell you himself."

I was confused on how I was going to call Alex when he is supposed to be either on a plane or at this house. But without further a due, I grabbed the phone out of her hand. "What number am I suppose to call?" "Oh it's the same number that he has been calling from." "The same number? You have got to be kidding me. Alex is still in California?" This was not about to be pretty.

I started not to call. Something was not right because I felt the anxiety running through my body ,as I dialed the number.

"Alex?" "Yes this is me." "I'm glad to hear that you are Ok but what's going on? Why aren't you here with us?" "Look, I'm going to come straight out and tell you because there is no other way to say it. At first I was trying to surprise you and sneak home but we ran into some complications." "Who are we Alex?" "Me and my brother." "Ok, go on." "He gave me my confirmation number and I was scheduled to leave Cali at eight o'clock last night but once I got to the airport, I realized that my brother had the wrong last name on my ticket so I had to wait for them to change it. "So are you trying to tell me that your brother doesn't know your last name?" "Can you please let me finish? Damn, I hate when you do that. You always try to finish my sentence for me. As I was saying, I ended up missing that flight. They tried to get me on the next one but it wasn't until I was about to board the plane when I realized that my flight was going to New York instead of Charlotte. I tried one last time for the 3 a.m. flight that was leaving to go to Charlotte but we went back home and overslept." My brain puzzled as I tried to figure out all of this nonsense he just fed to me. I didn't understand it and I'm pretty sure that he really didn't understand what he was trying to say.

"Ok Alex, you said all of that to say what? You still haven't told me anything. When are you coming home?" "And that's what I'm trying to tell you. When I say this, please don't look at it as a negative thing. I have tried not once but three times to come home Parker; three times. If the same thing fails three times then it's not meant to be so I have decided to stay out here in California. I'm going to try and get a job and move you and Samiyah out here since there are better opportunities." I didn't give him the opportunity to finish his make-believe "I think I'm talking to a dummy" bullshitting ass story. I had to stop him and let him have it and at the moment I could care less about his mom sitting beside me. Enough was enough. "BETTER OPPORTUNITES? BETTER OPPORTUNITES

Fell Too Deep

WAS THE REASON WE MOVED TO CHARLOTTE FROM MISSISSIPPI AND NOW YOU ARE TELLING ME THAT YOU ARE NOT COMING BACK BECAUSE OF SOME FUCKING SIGN. YO ASS IS PROBABLY LYING ABOUT THAT ANYWAY JUST SO YOU COULD STAY OUT THERE. I CANT BELIEVE THIS SHIT. YOU TOOK THE LAST FEW DOLLARS THAT WE HAD, WENT TO CALI, SPENT IT ON BULLSHIT, SNUCK AND PAWNED YOUR GAME, SPENT THAT ON BULLSHIT AND NOW YOU HAVE THE NERVES AND BALLS TO TELL ME THAT YOU ARE NOT COMING BACK TO CHARLOTTE. IF YOU DIDN'T KNOW, THE CABLE AND PHONE IS OFF AND RENT IS DUE NEXT WEEK SO WHAT AM I SUPPOSE TO DO? I GET PAID IN A COUPLE OF DAYS BUT IT'S NOT ENOUGH TO COVER ALL OF THESE BILLS. WHAT ABOUT YOUR JOB? ARE YOU GOING TO JUST UP AND QUICK LIKE THAT? WHAT ABOUT YOUR DAUGHTER?"

"Parker I know that you are mad but I promise you that everything is going to be Ok." "I'll call my job and have them send my check to me. I'll cash it and try to help you out as much as possible." "As much as possible? Are you fucking kidding me right now?" I don't have anything else to say to you Alex. Good-bye." I had to hang the phone up because I was very upset and I didn't want to say something that I may regret later because right now I can call him everything but a child of God and that's not a good thing. I need to clear my head for a while because this is too much to take in at one time. I knew that this was only the beginning of a big disaster to come. My fiancé is thousands of miles away from me and now he has decided not to come back without first discussing it with me. His mom was about to leave but she left me her phone. She was only feeling sorry for me because of what her son has done but I don't care. I need a way to communicate with him until we could figure this thing out.

Later on, he called and said that he had a proposition for me, and that was to pack up all of our things and move in with his mom until he gets situated out there. I am fed up with moving back and forth. I am also tired of having my daughter get used to one place and then after a few months move her to another location. Now he wants me to pack up everything in this apartment and have it out by the 1st, which is only a few days away. This is so stressing and I am confused. What are his motives? What is he thinking? Why would he do something like this? Moving in with his mom is my only option right now. I love my freedom and I love the fact that I have my own space. There has got to be another way.

CHAPTER 39

"His mama's a Bitch"

Another dreadful day gone and a day closer to rent being due. I'm looking in the mirror trying to finish curling my hair before Mrs.Judy makes it here. I have to go to work today so she will be watching Samiyah for me. Speaking of her, she was knocking at the door. "It's open! Come on in." "Parker, it's me. My husband is with me today because he didn't want to stay at home." "Ok, that's fine. Y'all can have a seat and I'll be right out as soon as I throw some make-up on my face." "It's raining out there so we should leave earlier than normal. You know some of these people in North Carolina cannot drive."

Hell some of them can't drive and neither can she. She drives like a turtle and during the rain, she moves like a rock. She panics when an eighteen-wheeler passes her. I mean who does that. But yet in still she wants to talk about these other people. This state needs to pull their license as well as hers but not until I am off of work.

"Since it's raining outside and Samiyah doesn't have on any clothes right now, she can just stay here with Al and I will drop you off and come right back home." Judy suggested. But this is my child so I should have some say so. It's not a problem with her staying here but I like to kiss and hug her before I walk into that stressful job. I hope that was ok with her. "Oh that's fine. I will just throw her on a sleeper and her little raincoat then we can leave." As we got in the car and pulled off, I noticed that her whole mood had changed. She was now on the phone so I didn't know if that person had said something to her or what but her vibe was different. The radio is low and I feel a lot of tension in this car; even the windows were fogging up so I don't know if that's from the heater in the car and the cold weather outside clashing or if it's from the steam off of her ears. She asked me yesterday if I could buy her a case of water the next time I went to work and I told her yes. So I asked.

"Hey, did you still want me to get the water today?" "Parker you can Shut the hell up talking to me right now?" "Uh, excuse me? Did I just miss something?" "You can stop acting so innocent and acting like the victim. It didn't make any sense for Samiyah to ride with us to your job in this rain. You don't like her being around my husband because you think that he will probably do something to her." "I didn't say one time that your husband was going to…." "Oh just shut up." She interrupted. Oh now this bitch done snapped. She is my future mother-in-law so I tried to remain calm but this was about the second time that we have been in a conflict.

She was upset about me wanting to bring my child with us. How stupid is that? I can't do this with her right now because as she knows, I have a lot of shit on my plate and it has to do with her terrible parenting skills. We were a stop light away from my job so I kissed my daughter on the forehead and jumped out of the car. Yes, I was in the middle of the street but I don't care. I have to walk off this steam before I clock in. I already have to deal with these ignorant ass customers so their ignorance plus my anger equals me being fired before the day is over. I glance down at my watch and notice that I have five minutes left. There was a hot dog stand set-up outside of my job, so I went to grab a soda. I turned around and then noticed her car pulling up on the curve but now her husband was driving. As he illegally parked the car, she hopped out and grabbed my baby out of her car seat. I was confused on what she was doing until her fat ass starting wobbling towards me. She took all of her strength and threw my baby in my arms and said, "Since you want your baby so bad, take her" and she wobbled back to her car and they drove off.

As I stand here minutes away from being late, I start to cry. I took a seat on the bench to try and gather myself. If she didn't know, I need this job. I can't afford to miss any days due to foolishness. Alex claims to be staying in California. He didn't have any money so I had to try and make ends meet right now: Not take off of work. I couldn't call anyone because I didn't have a phone. I couldn't take the bus back home because I didn't have any money nor did I have a key to get in my house. This is fucked up and it's all because of her. I waited outside for exactly thirty minutes and I realized that she wasn't coming back. I took my daughter's raincoat off in the car because she had the heat on and it had gotten a little warm. She didn't have a cup, no diapers, her hair wasn't comb and to top things off she had on a sleeper pajama set. I never take my daughter outside unprepared and looking like this so I am even more pissed at the stunt that this woman has pulled. I didn't know where to go. I didn't know what to do but the first thing that came to my mind was to go inside and explain to my boss what had just happened.

"Parker, I am so sorry to hear that. You can have the day off with pay. Is there anything that I could do?" "I don't have any money so could I please use the company's' phone to call home to Mississippi and see if my mom can wire me some money through the money gram here in the store." "Of course you can. Just press *99 then the phone number starting with the area code." "Thank you so much and again I am sorry that I couldn't make it in to work today." "Well, you actually did make it to work today, you just can't work." He laughed. I wasn't in the mood for laughing but that corny joke sort of made me feel a little better. Hell at least he wasn't mad. I prepared to call my mom. I knew she wasn't going to like this.

"Are you serious? Did she really do that? Tell me that you are lying to me because I can take you lying to me but I can't take a Grandmother treating her grandchild in such a way." "No mom, I wish I wasn't lying. She literally threw my baby to me and left us standing there." My mom tried to call Mrs. Judy's phone on three-way but she never answered. "She better not answer because the moment she does, I am going to let her have it. Now you are telling me that my grand-daughter doesn't have a sippie cup, diapers or a coat. "Isn't it like 40 degrees up there in Charlotte?" "It feels colder than that." I had my mom call Alex next. He finally answered after about the third time. He couldn't believe what happened. He then asked, "What did you do to make her so upset?" I answered, "How in the fuck do you suppose I did something to her? Why wont you accept the fact that your whole family is screwed up from her down to your brother and then you? I didn't do anything but ask a question and she snapped so I jumped out of the car instead of snapping back. My mom jumped in the conversation and that didn't make things any better. They argued, he hung up and he never answered again. Now what am I suppose to do? Where am I supposed to go? I don't know Terica's or Charlie's number by heart so I'm stuck. My step-dad was calling my mom from the other room so she told me to hold on as she placed the phone down. As I sat there waiting, my boss walked in with a bag and said, "You are one of my most faithful employees. I have never had any problems out of you and I really hate what you are going through right now." He then gave me the bag and on the inside was three sippie cups, two pacifiers, a bag of diapers and wipes, a gallon of milk and some crackers and a pink coat. He went out to the floor and got those items for my daughter.

He was the manager so I am sure that he didn't have to pay for them but I was so grateful. "I am so Grateful to you sir. I knew you were a great man the day that you hired me, Literally. Even though you own this entire store, you didn't have to do this and I appreciate this so much. You have no idea how you have saved our life right now." "You are welcomed and it was no problem at all." I held back my tears but the moment he walked out, I opened up. I was mainly worried about my daughter and the things she needed right then and suddenly somehow GOD made away in minutes. My good friend, whom is now one of the youngest yet most faithful pastors back in my home-town once told me "If you are going to Worry; Don't Pray but If you are going to Pray; Don't worry." He may have forgotten that he ever told me that but it has stuck with me to this day.

My boss is a lifesaver and the timing couldn't be any better. He will be blessed for blessing me.

Finally, my mom was back on the phone. I told her what GOD had just done and she was overwhelmed. "There are still some nice people in this world." She said. "Baby, I know you don't want to hear what I have to say but I am going to say it anyway. You have been through enough stress. It has been nothing but hell the moment you moved out there and I feel that your time in Charlotte is up. Alex has already said that he isn't coming back so why should you stay? How are you going to keep paying the rent every month as well as these bills when you don't have a way to work nor do you have a stable babysitter. Alex doesn't give a damn about y'all because if he did he would be there instead of California. The whole idea about you moving in with Judy is out of the question because of what she just did.

I know you hate Columbus and I know you hate being here but it's home and really there is no place like home. There aren't many jobs here and some of the people are messy and negative but there is some good out of this. You have your family, a few friends and your church family who have been asking about you every Sunday. We all miss you and your beautiful spirit and it's time for you to come back home. You know your cousin works for a car rental company so just say the word and we will be there." I thought about it for a only a few seconds but that was all of the time that I needed. She was right but she is always right. I hate Columbus. There is nothing to do there so to make the time go by, everyone stays in everyone else's business. Mostly everyone there is trying to figure out ways to leave but like my mom said, that is my home. I don't know what the future holds but right now, I think it's best that I go back and in a weird and scary way: I sort of miss it. Don't tell anyone I said that.

I hung my head in disbelief and asked, "How quick can y'all come and get me?"

"Halleluiah!" she yelled. I get paid Friday and your cousin is off this Saturday so we can leave Friday night when she gets off. Hold on baby, I think this is Alex calling back." I wonder what he wants. "Parker?" "Yea mom I'm still here. That was quick. Did he hang up again?" "No, he was calling to tell me to tell you that his brother is outside your job waiting on you. I guess he had him to come and pick you girls up so I am going to let you go. Do you still have the computer?" "Yes I have it." "Well your brother is going to stay in contact with you through the email thingy. I'm going to wire you $60 dollars so that should last you until we get there. You stay strong and we will see you Saturday. I love you." "Ok ma. Thanks so much and I love you too."

Chapter 40

Another Departure

I can not believe that I am actually leaving Charlotte tomorrow. I haven't been out here for a year and I am already on my way back. All of our things are packed and I'm ready to get this show on the road. Well, I actually have a house full of shit but I can't worry about that. The furniture, the TV and the computer are all still here. The furniture isn't paid off but I couldn't do anything but call the rental place and have them come and pick it up because we weren't making anymore payments on it. The computer is ours to keep because it is paid off. I had too much stuff and not enough time. I mainly packed the things that Samiyah and I needed. I even packed the entire bathroom furniture that we bought. I loved it so it wasn't staying here. Alex's clothes and shoes were everywhere but I didn't bother collecting them. The apartment manager said that he will be here in the morning to put a lock on the door because we were many days late on the rent. He said that whatever is left in the apartment will go out on the street. There wasn't anything that I could do but he didn't want his clothes anyway because if he did, he would be here right now. I know that me saying that a hundred times a day is not going to bring him back but it sort of soothes things. About two hours later, all of our things were packed up and off into a corner.

    I was disturbed by a loud bang on my door. The clock said 4 a.m. so I was not trying to get up to see who it was. They continued to knock and then I heard, "Girl it's cold out here. You better get up and open this door!" It was my mom, my cousin and my brother. I was so happy to see them. "I wasn't expecting y'all until this morning." "Well technically it is morning." "I know that but I was thinking more like 7 or 8. You know around the time that the sun comes up. What are y'all some vampires? Done scared the shit outta me earlier this morning." "Outta is not a word." My cousin said. She was born and raised in Mississippi but she speaks nothing like the majority of the people there. You would think that she was from up north or the west coast. "Well I'm sorry but it's a little too early for me to give you the right pronunciation of words. "Enough of that, we all need to get some sleep because that was a long eight hour drive and we have to do it again in less than three hours." My mom said.

I tried to close my eyes but I couldn't. I was excited to see my family but I wasn't ready to go home. Samiyah heard the commotion so she woke up and then everyone else woke up because she was the main person that they wanted to see. After my mom played with her, we packed the car and got ready to head out. They didn't get much sleep but they were ready to go. Charlie came by and gave me one hundred dollars. He said that Alex told him to give it to me. A hundred dollars ain't shit when you are broke, moving and have a daughter but I took it with no problem. Everyone was down stairs waiting on me but I had to do a run through and make sure that I wasn't leaving anything that my daughter and I really needed. They were only able to rent a small jeep so I had to leave a lot. Before I walked out, I placed my hands on my hip and took one last look at this apartment, my apartment. Of course, I cried because even though we are leaving, this was my house. I helped purchased everything in here. This was my own place, my palace. I set and broke my own rules. I was going from independent to being a dependent all over again and that shit really pisses me off. I adore my mom and I love being around her but there is nothing like having your own shit. We had bad moments in this house as well as good but like always, the good out weighed the bad. Things happen for a reason and like I always say, "Let's just hope that there is a damn good reason on why all of this is happening." They blew the horn once more so I knew that it was time for me to lift my head and walk away. There is always an ending to every story; whether it's bad or good. Unfortunately, this is a bad one but I must learn from all of this and make sure that my next story has a happy ending. I closed the door, wiped away my tears and walked down the stairs to the car.

As we head down the road, I continued to hold back my tears. They know that all of this hurt me but I didn't want to show it. I had to show them that I was a strong woman that can handle anything. But what am I going to tell everyone back home? What will they think of me? I wish words didn't bother me as much. I wish that I can stand tall to someone that talks down on me but right now I can't. I have changed because things that didn't used to bother me is now bringing me down. At one point in my life, I didn't care what anyone had to say about me but now it's like I live off of people's opinion. I don't know how I got to this point but I'm working my hardest to get back to that Bitch that I was once before.

    I should not have moved up here but I did. Before I left Mississippi, my cousin said that this move had "Disaster" written all over it, but like always I never listen to her. She is only one year older than I am so I feel there is nothing that she could tell me. But, as much as I hate admitting it; she is always right. I looked around and realized how much I love my family. They are always here in my time of need and I am forever grateful for that.

Chapter 41

I'm not living without you..

My cousin Elise is getting married soon and today we have to go and get fitted for our dress. I was afraid that I will be looking like a big balloon in the wedding but now it won't be as bad because I have lost a ton of weight; unintentionally. But, she looks absolutely adorable standing there in that white dress. She have waited long enough so I'm happy for her. I still pray daily for my special day but I'm sure that isn't coming anytime soon.

My mom walked in the room where all of the bridesmaids were and gave me her cell phone. "Who is this?" "I think it's Shelby from the gas station." "Hello?" "Hi Parker, this is Shelby, the manager at Tex-a-go. You recently filled out an application and I wanted to know if you were available to come in today at 5 for an interview?" "Yes I can. Thanks so much for calling me back." "You are welcome and we will see you at 5." That was a major relief. Alex has been straight bullshitting out in LA and claims to be broke so the moment I made it here, I went job hunting. I have never worked at a gas station but I'm sure that this job will be a breeze. It was already 4 so I changed out of this dress and waited for my mom to take me to the interview.

Because of my charm and class, I was hired there on the spot. She wanted me to start tomorrow and I didn't have a problem with that. I went home and prepared myself for what was to come.

It's funny how early you get to work on your first day. I didn't have to be there until 9 the next morning but I arrived at 8:25 with my new shirt on and a nice pair of pressed jeans. I was happy to be working again but most of all I was ready for my checks to start rolling in. I became frustrated a few times while trying to learn how to work the cash register and turn the gas pump on and off but eventually, I got it. I'm quiet around people that I don't know but I seemed to be fitting in Ok. I really didn't have any other choice if I wanted this job to last me for a while.

• • •

The first few days have been cool. One girl wanted the night off so I volunteered to take her schedule. I had already worked that morning but I decided to come in and work for her. I pulled some cool points and made extra cash in the same day. How great is that?

I haven't talked to Alex in a few days so I don't know where we stand. I tried calling but no one ever answers the phone. I have even sent text messages but still nothing. He is probably telling them not to answer. Hell he better be working or at least out looking for a job. He knows that he has a responsibility so I don't know if he is trying to avoid me or what. I can feel the distance between us and I wasn't talking about the miles.

Samiyah had dosed off and my best friend Cherell had come over to visit with me. I hadn't seen her since I made it back home so we have a lot to catch up on. I talked her into getting on this new website that everyone have been talking about. It's called Myplace.com. We were sitting there doing nothing so I volunteered to make her a page. We had a lot of mutual friends so I sent a friend request to them all. I got to Alex page and decided to snoop around before I sent him a request to be her friend. Cherell is just as nosey as I am so she wanted to look on with me. I noticed that he still had that he was engaged and happily in love with me on his page. That was a relief because if any chic read his page or tried to get at him, they would see that he is taken. I scrolled down to his chat box and found him communicating with Red. They have been carrying on a conversation for exactly three days. "Oh Shit." Cherell said. Oh shit, was right because I knew that this was not going to be good. They were talking about meeting up at a party this coming weekend. "You said that it's been a few days since you talked to him right? Do you mean over the phone or in general?" Cherell "Girl, I have texted and called that phone and even sent messages to his page but he hasn't returned anything." I don't know if he overlooked it by mistake or on purpose but there he was, communicating with Red but not me.

My woman's intuition told me to log in under his name because I still had his password. I knew that I was putting more into this situation than what it really was but I had to make sure.

So I logged into his page, clicked on his inbox messages and guess whose name I see first: That's right: Red. What is it about this girl? He just can't seem to shake her. There was thirteen messages between the both of them. He sent seven and she sent six. Hell yes, I counted how many times they talked to each other. Cherell is beside me shaking her damn head as if I was some sort of stalker or something. Maybe I was ,but did I give a Damn? Hell NO! She knew if she was in my position that she would do the same thing. Hell she was the one that showed me how to figure out someone's security answers and change their passwords. She is a Pro in this. I'm telling you, the girl has talent. But when I go to Alex with this information, I need to have everything memorized. The times they talked, how long, the time he logged off and so on.

I clicked on the messages and we started to read away. Cherell was reading too slow or either I was reading too fast because she kept telling me to go back to the previous message. The first messages were basic. You know, "How have you been and what are you up to?" But as I read on, things began to get a little deep. "Why are you in California and where is your daughter?" she asked. "My daughter is in Mississippi with her mom and I have decided to move back out here to provide a better life for me, my daughter and my future wife. "See Cherell, I knew it. I was worried for no reason. I couldn't believe that he had actually told her that we were getting married. Well he did in so many words. I started to log off but I wanted to see her response, so I continued reading. "Red, you and I were good friends in high school and I miss you so much. When I got with Parker, I had to loose all contacts with you because she was so jealous and insecure with herself. She knows how pretty you were so she was intimidated by you."

Damn, for him to say that I was going to be his future wife; he was down talking the shit out of me. I didn't want him to loose contact with her or any of his friends. I just wanted him to realize that I was his girl now so he needed to focus a little more on me.

"Red, what if I asked you to be with me? What if I told you that I didn't love Parker anymore? What if I told you that there wasn't a day that went by that I didn't think about you? My time with her is up. What if I told you that I am out here to find you and make you my future wife?"

I can't explain my feelings right now. As I fall low with shame, Cherell leans my head on her shoulder and tries to comfort me. She didn't say a word and neither did I. All I can hear is silence and then my mom's house phone started to ring. I didn't feel like moving so I sat there with my head still on my friend's shoulder. Seconds later, the phone started to ring again. "I'll get it." Cherell volunteered. She walked in and asked, "Do you feel like talking?" "Who is it?" "Its Alex bitch ass." How ironic is it for him to call me right now? Could he have known that I just logged in to his page? He has not called in days and now he is calling. I didn't care for what he had to say but I was going to ask him about Red. "Hello." "Hey, how is Samiyah doing?" I noticed that he didn't ask how I was doing. "She is good but you would have known that if you would have been calling. Speaking of which, why haven't you called?"

"Look Parker, there is no easy way to tell you this so I'm going to just come out and say it. I'm in love with Red. The truth is that I have always had feelings for this girl. Since I have been here, we have came in contact with each other again and I really want to make it work with her. I will still be in our daughter's life so you don't have to worry about me not taking care of her. I just can't deal with the drama from you anymore. I'm sorry Parker but we can longer be together".

"Alex please don't do this. Please don't leave me! What do I have to do? What must I change? You can't just walk away from me like this. I won't let you!" "I'm so sorry Parker that I wasted your time. My heart just isn't with you anymore. I will be in touch." "You will be in touch? Are you kidding me? Please say that you are kidding right now. Hello?.....Hello?" This motherfucker has hung on me.

Tears filled my eyes as I tried to gather my thoughts. Oh my gosh Cherell, is this shit really happening? Here I was assuming that we were still engaged and that he was in Cali to settle down, find a job and fly us out there. He was definitely trying to settle down but obviously not with me. How could this be over? What happened? We were doing so well before he left to go to California. We weren't arguing or fighting. It feels like a car had just hit me. How could he hurt me so bad at a time like this? He just called me a few days ago and told me that he wasn't coming back to North Carolina. He took all of our money and blew it on bullshit. I had to move back to Mississippi because I didn't have enough money to pay our rent and bills and now this bitch is telling me that we can no longer be together because he is in love with another girl. Now what am I suppose to do? How am I supposed to make it? He found the perfect opportunity to get back out there and he took it. He knew all along that he wasn't coming back to us. He even said that he wasn't feeling me anymore so why didn't he say something before now? Why didn't he prepare me for what was about to come?

I cheated on Alex last year with Nene and now karma bitch ass was biting me in the ass. How could I think that I could hurt him and get away with it? But no, this is different. This is very different.

WHY

Why am I sitting here crying my eyes out
Because I loved and cherished you so.
Why didn't I see this coming?
Because I'm a fool: A fool that just don't get it.
Why did you lie and lead me on?
Because you are a Man and that's what y'all do.
Why does my house not feel like a home?
Because the Love of my life is gone
They say when you are down, to just pray
I tried…..
But all I could do is continue to cry.
What does this mean?
When my thoughts about you
Are not so clean
Yet they are dirty
Because you chose to be so flirty
But I still can't go on pretending
Like what you did, didn't hurt me.
I'm still in denial Because I THOUGHT what we had was real
I thought it was Mission Accomplished
And Goals Fulfilled
I'm shaking my head
Because those were the lies you fed:
To me
Now I'm in this empty ass bed
Still shaking my head,
Trying so hard to figure out if things were really that jacked up
What the Fuck?
You left me and fell in love in less than a month.
Huh ?
What's that?
She was your high school crush?
Nigga Hush !
How dare you leave me for a Chick name "Red"
Well now you call me "Red" because I'm hotter than a motherfucker.
Oh I get it,

Patrice L. Guyton

You thought I was a sucker
But I still ask,
How could you not tell me that she always had a major part of your heart?
That she was the Aorta
And I was just being pushed along like a shopping cart.
Damn,
I hate you
Because you did me so Bad
But Damn,
I still love you
Because of what we Had
Yea, yea I know
Had is past tense
You made me feel dumb
And I have never been dense
So does that explain why my heart no longer feels so immense?
But I blame myself
For not having common sense
I should have known when she used to call
That right there was a major hint.
To pack up and leave your ass
But you kept me there and fed me lies
I admit, you did that shit with class.
Why didn't you tell me that she came first and I came last
And that she was the Gold and I was the Brass
Well the truth is out and I can't change the past.
But I want you to know that this hurts terribly
Yea,
this shit hurt BAD.

CHAPTER 42

First and last check......

"Damn Cherell, would you please hurry up?" I swear, this girl has been moving slow every since high school. I'm about twenty minutes from being late and we haven't even left the house. Cherell has moved in with us because of some family issues that she was having and I couldn't be any happier because I can talk to her all day and every day. If she got tired of me, the only thing that she could do was go into another room. She was already like a sister so this made it official. I love the fact that she is here but at times like these, I wanna make my mom throw her ass out (not literally) but damn. I specifically told her that I wasn't driving to work today. She have to drop me off because she had to go and get my mom from work. Somehow, she didn't understand that because she is just now about to put on some clothes.

"I'm ready bitch so calm down." "Whatever, yo ass is going to have me late. You know they already don't like me up there." "Girl, don't nobody care about those women. Just go there, work your hours and come home."

I try to communicate with them but most of the time, I just sit back and listen to them talk to one another. They have been there longer than I have so I try to stay in my space. I have ran across a lot of old classmates and friends. I didn't know that gas stations were busy like this. They sell cooked food so lunchtime is the busiest. It's right across the street from the country club, down the street from a school and around the corner from the projects so you know that its people coming in and out every single day. When I'm not behind the register, I have to stock the beer coolers, mop the floor and clean the bathroom. That's something that I wouldn't prefer doing but it's a job and right now it is paying the bills. Speaking of bills, today is payday! I get my first check and I know that it's going to be a good one. I have been working like crazy but I know that it's going to be worth it. My drawer came up short a couple of times and I think they take that money out of your check. One time it was $5 and the other time is was like $15. To this day, I still can't figure out where the money went. I don't know if I gave a customer too much money or what but I knew damn well that I didn't take it.

"See, you were worried for nothing. You made it to work safely with two minutes to spare." "Yea, whatever. Yo ass still move too slow. When you pick up the girls from your mom's house, don't forget to do Samiyah's hair for me." "Ok, have fun at work." "I get my check today so you know today is going to be a happy day. Bye chick." Like always, I inhaled and then exhaled, I thank God for the good day that this is going to be and I walked in.

I walked towards my timecard so I could clock in but Tiffany, the assistant manager stopped me. "I have your check right here, but let's go and have a seat. I have something to tell you." I wonder what this could be about. "I really hate that they chose me to do this but Shelby, the head manager, has fired you." "What! You have got to be getting me." "She said that your drawer keeps coming up short. Last night, when you got off, she re-counted your drawer and this time you were short $239." "You have got to be kidding me. I would never steal. True, the money was right there in my face and probably easy to steal but not once did I ever think about or actually take a penny out of my register or anyone else's. Please don't do this. I need this job." I couldn't help but to cry.

"This is not a good time for me to be without a job. Someone from that store stole money from my register and I didn't know who it was. I was the new girl so I would be the first one to leave and that's why the thief used me, to get the money". "I'm sorry but she have decided to let you go." She handed me my check and a sheet of paper. The paper read, "You are responsible for paying $239 back to the store. Please sign and return this to the manager." I wasn't about to sign a damn thang.

"I'm sorry Tiff but I am not signing this paper because I didn't steal that money. One of these snakes took that money so they are going to pay it back; not me. As a matter of fact, I would like the number to the owner of this store." He was a rich white man that owned about ten gas stations throughout the south of Mississippi. "I don't have his number but you can call up here in an hour or two and Shelby should be here. You can talk to

Fell Too Deep

her about it then. Again, I'm sorry that this has happened." I called Cherell to come back and get me. I waited patiently outside for her to come but when she arrived; My mom and my brother was in the car so before we pulled off, I told them what happened. I knew that fireworks were about to explode. My mom plus my brother plus Cherell is a terrible combination. They all have that "Beat a Bitch Ass" mentality but I'm more of the crybaby. My mom demanded that the head manager and the owner come to the store immediately to resolve this issue. "My daughter doesn't have a reason to steal from this damn store because I have raised her better than that. How dare you fire her when you have no proof?" "Proof?" I thought to myself and then the light bulb popped on. "Wait a minute ma, there is a camera that overlooks the entire store including the cash registers. How about we take a look through that tape for your proof?" Shelby, the head-manager, stepped up and said, "I'm sorry but that camera doesn't work. We left it there to fool the customers." "The camera doesn't work?"

My mom and Bob, the owner, yelled. "Why didn't you contact me about the camera when it stopped working? You know that there is a rule in my code book about the camera working at all times." She didn't have anything to say but, "I'm sorry." I then added, "How in the hell are you sorry. You just fired me because I was coming up short, you don't have any proof and you didn't contact the manager when the camera stopped working. Y'all are up to that sneaky shit up here and I'm glad that I was fired." Bob said that I could continue working if I wanted to because there actually wasn't any proof, but I denied his request. I wouldn't dare work in that store again. They always looked at me funny anyway. I wouldn't even purchase my gas from there. Somebody set me up but they are going to be the ones that have to live with it: Not me. So to hell with all of them! I grabbed my check, my angry clan and walked out the store.

Chapter 43

One month later:

I have been home for exactly two months and once again, I feel that my time is up. I don't think that I serve any purpose here. I was talking to the first lady at my church and every time I tell her that I am leaving Columbus, she says, "Girl I need you to get yourself together and stop running back and forth. You need to get stable for yourself and your daughter." I get tired of hearing her say that over and over again but she is right. I really don't know what direction to head in and I don't know what the future holds but something has to happen and it needs to happen now.

Alex have started to call Samiyah a little more than what he used to do. It went from once every two weeks to about once a week. That's still terrible, being that I wouldn't be able to go a day with talking to by daughter, but its an accomplishment. He has finally landed a job. He is working as a cashier at another retail store. He claims that he could only send about twenty dollars every week because they haven't been giving him any hours. I don't give a damn about the lies he is trying to sell me, but what I do care about are those funky ass twenty dollars that he is sending. If that is the only money that he has then I can understand but Chanel has been telling me that they have been going out, partying and drinking. You can't go out if you don't have any money. He told me the other day that he has been thinking about joining the army and he is going to take the necessary steps to see if he is qualified. I personally don't think that he is going to do it simply because he doesn't seem like the Army type. The only thing that I can see him doing is sliding across someone's church floor. But who am I down his dream when I don't have any dreams of my own.

Right at that moment, I came up with an idea. I am going to move back to California. I don't know how we are going to get out there and I don't know what I'm going to do once I get there, but I'm leaving. I am tired of taking my daughter from state to state but she is still a baby so she doesn't understand what is going on. I haven't been back to California since I got pregnant with Samiyah and that was two years ago. I asked my dad if I can move out there and he said yes without a problem but I'm sure that's only because he hasn't seen his granddaughter in person. But I knew that things were not going to be as smooth with my step-mom. I dreaded calling her but my dad said that she had to be on board with this decision. When I left California two years ago, everything was a mess. I wasn't speaking to her or my dad and I remember telling her that I wouldn't care if I ever saw her again. I have always heard people say, "Don't EVER bite the hand that fed you," and in this case I hate I ever bit that motherfucker. I really need her right now. My life will practically be ruin if she says that I can't move back. I also have a child now so that means that she will have to deal with a crying baby and that is something that she wouldn't be used to.

I gained enough courage and called her. She said that I should wait because they are in the midst of trying to buy another house so they wouldn't be able to afford it. That wasn't the answer that I wanted to hear so I took matters into my own hands. I called my dad back and fed him some bullshit because I knew that he would believe it. I told him that California is a better environment for Samiyah. I told him that I was going to school online and that I would look for a job as soon as I get there. I even volunteered to help pay rent or utilities.

This whole scheme was about me getting back to Alex. I'm not over him. I haven't forgot the shit he pulled a month ago but I can't move on and forget that he ever existed. I mean we were engaged for crying out loud. I have tried to date and I have even got on some of those dating websites but I can't stop thinking about him. I can't stop thinking about the life we had. We were happy and very much in love and that's why I don't understand how he could be in love with someone else. The only way I see that being possible is if he was never in love with me. He would literally have to tell me that our love was a fake. I can't let him go to the army without seeing if I could make things right with us. If I put on his favorite outfit, wear his favorite perfume and beg him to get back with me then maybe, just maybe, he will come running back. Red thinks that he loves her but the moment he see us step off of that plane, he is going to change his mind and my life is going to be complete: Again.

Journal Entry:

This is going to be my last journal for a while and that is only because I have a lot of shit on my plate. Thoughts are constantly going in and out of my mind and its becoming to be overwhelming. This is really the time that I should be writing but I can't. My mind is so flustered that I can barely think. I talked Alex into buying my daughter and I plane tickets to go back to Cali. I don't know where he got the money from and really, I didn't care. We are going to be united soon and I couldn't be happier. He kept telling me over and over that he was only buying the tickets because he wanted to see his daughter before he left for basic training. But I knew that he wanted to see me also. He didn't actually say those words but I knew that he was only trying to play hard. He still wanted me and the moment I step off that plane, he will come to his senses. But I still couldn't believe that he was actually about to leave us. This all seems so strange because he never talked about going to the army. If you ask me, this has "RED" written all over it. He was allowing this girl to come in his life and change him. I never tried to change him because he was perfect the way he was: except for a few minor things like his fucked up attitude and those overly sprayed jerry curls. But besides that, he was cool.

I was only here in Mississippi for two months and now I am leaving, again. My first lady was right. I need to get myself together. Once I make it to California, my daughter and I would have lived in three different states in only a year. That is insane. I am so busy trying to run behind a man that probably doesn't want to have anything to do with me. What is wrong with me? Am I that deep in love? I have and is willing to drop my entire life in seconds just to follow him and that is not healthy. As much as I say that all of this is nonsense, I continue to do it. I think that he is just confused on what he wants but I know that he still loves me. He has to.

I have to take my daughter away from my mother, yet again, and though I am not happy about it: I still have to go. She loves me but she loves my daughter more. She is going to be torn when we leave and I hate that I have to be the one to hurt her but, me getting back with Alex is far more important than my mom looking at my daughter everyday. I have a cellular phone now so she can call as often as she like. My brother will eventually get over us leaving because he has such an active life. He goes to school, he sings, mimes at our church and he works. Cherell is going to be affected by this as well. We wake up to each other and we go to sleep to each other every single day. She has the choice of moving back with her family or stay here. Even though my mom looks at her as a daughter, its going to be hard for her to continue living here because I will be gone. But that's life and if I don't move now, I will never move. I will eat my life away, gain one hundred pounds, go to sleep lonely and live misery ever after.

I'm starting to think that unpacking is something that I shouldn't do because the moment I unpack, I have to repack everything all over again. In the morning, we will be off to the airport again and living the same sad-story but hey, somebody has to live it.

The next time you hear from me I can guarantee you that I will be a changed, new and improved woman. This is the last stop because I refuse to move again. I plan to mature and worry more about my daughter than anyone else. I can't keep doing this to myself. I can't keep falling in love with these men that thinks that they can do me any kind of way. Alex had better be glad that I love him because if I didn't, I wouldn't try to get back with him. Shit, why can't a man ever chase my ass? I'm sick of this shit. But until next time. "I'll Holla". Peace and Love –Parker.

CHAPTER 44

Get adjusted and Welcome to Paradise

"Samiyah! Let's go baby. Mommy have to get you to school. You have been late this entire week. Today is Friday so let's try and get you there early. I unfolded her stroller and quickly placed her in it. "Ouch mommy," she said. I pinched the skin on her leg while trying to fasten the buckle. "Mommy is sorry, I said as I kissed her on the leg. I'm always late and moving fast. I have about ten minutes to get to the end of the road to catch the bus.

(This stay is not going how I had envisioned it to go. As much as I wish that it wasn't true, I had to face reality and realize that Alex was really over me. He and his god-brother picked us up from the airport and he showed no excitement towards me at all. On the ride home, he was on the phone with Red the entire time. He didn't have one word to say to me. He was acting like I had done something to him. I am the one who always drop everything and run to him but now, all of that was in vain. We are out here in California and I still couldn't get him to come see his daughter or even call for that matter. I knew that I had made a mistake but there isn't anything that I can do about that now. I called him everyday and if he didn't answer, I left messages threatening to put him on child support if he didn't come to see her. I'm guessing that he didn't want that to happen because just a few days ago he showed up but he wasn't by himself. I opened the door and to my surprise stood a tall dark-skinned man with a baldhead that was dressed as a soldier. "Parker, this is my recruiter Rick and Rick, this is Parker." Why was a recruiter at my house? To my understanding, a recruiter, dressed in army gear, is a person that persuades men and women to join the army. Was he trying to get me to come aboard or what? Well come to find out, he was there because I had to sign some paperwork. I had to sign an agreement form stating that he will send my daughter 250 dollars on the 1st and 15th of every month and then there was a form that stated "I, Parker, will not put Alex on child support in the future." Let's just say that paper didn't get signed. Hell, he will never have me looking stupid. Who ever typed that letter up had just wasted ink and paper because that was a bunch of bullshit. Even though he signed that paper telling me how much money he was going to be sending her, I didn't trust him.

He was upset because I didn't sign the child support paper but I didn't care. If he ever decides to stop taking care of my daughter, Child Support will be notified. He has lied to me and lead me on for years now so I don't believe a single word that he has to say. Before he left, he kissed Samiyah and gave her a hug. I know that must have felt weird being that he hasn't done it in months. "I leave for basic training tomorrow", he said "so I will not be able to call until I graduate." But he never calls so it will be the same as before. He wrote down my dad's address because when you are in basic training the only communication that you have with the outside world is through writing letters. "Please write me back when you get my letters. I want to know her every move. I want to know her favorite foods and I want to know how she does at daycare. Please Parker, tell me everything." I wasn't planning on telling him a got damn thang but I told him I would just because that's what he wanted to hear. Samiyah waved bye and that was it. He was out of my life again and so I regret coming back out here but there is nothing that I can do about it now.

My step-mom still wasn't talking to me nor was she talking or playing with my daughter, who is her grand-child. Me and my step-mom already didn't have the perfect relationship so by me coming out here without her 100 percent approval made things worst. She was upset so that made my dad upset because he didn't want to take sides. (If he had to choose sides, of course he was going to take hers over mines.)

After I dropped my daughter off at school, I rode on to the mall. I am tired of sitting in the house doing absolutely nothing so why not window-shop. The moment I stepped off of that bus, I realized how much I hate riding it. You are on there with all sorts of people. They all have different looks and some even have very disturbing smells. Sometimes, I have to sniff myself because some of these nasty motherfuckers will have you thinking that you done shitted on yourself. However, I do appreciate the bus services because though it takes you forever to get to your destination, you get there for a cheaper price. In Columbus, if you don't have at least 10 dollars to give someone for gas, you are stuck. Whereas here, I can ride as long as I wanted to for only 4 bucks a day. You can't get any better than that. As I continued walking, I looked to the right and saw "JSS", my favorite shoe store. They sell the most and latest fashionable shoes. It's also very pricy but the shoes here are worth every dollar. I didn't have any money but I wanted to try on a few pair anyway. There isn't any harm in dreaming right? You can find anything that you want from hooker boots to stilettos.

    I spotted a teal snake skinned pump that I just had to try on. I looked on the bottom of the shoe and they were $200. "Hot Damn," I yelled before I knew it. But I still couldn't resist them. I knew that I wasn't going to buy these shoes but I at least had to see what they would like on my feet. I rung the service bell and out walked this "dark-skinned chick who had jet black hair that flowed down to the center of her back. She had on a pair of 6 inch black hooker boots that came up to her thighs. Her body was bad. I mean calling her a (Coke bottle) would literally be an understatement. She had on a black and white stripe dress that fits tighter than spandex. I stare at her while she stare back but neither one of us could get a word out.

    "Well are y'all going to say something to each other or are you going to act like zombies for the rest of the day?" Suddenly, I came back to earth. "Uh, excuse me?" I turn around to a tall, black and sexy young fellow that stood behind me. I whispered, "Could this be my lucky day?" "I believe you were going to ask Tiffany here if she had that shoe in your size." Shit I forgot about the shoe and no longer cared about it. I had to figure out who these sexy ass people were. "Yes, I was going to ask her if she had this shoe in a size 10." "Tiffany, would you go check in the back for this beautiful young lady?" I looked around to see if anyone else was in the store but it wasn't. Could he be calling me beautiful? "So what's your name?" "Parker, and you?" Tiffany walked out. "Yes we do have them in a 10 and this is my last pair." I was embarrassed because I knew that I wasn't going to purchase them. Hell I just wanted to try them on.

Fell Too Deep

"Benjamin." "Excuse me?" I said. "You asked for my name and I just told you. My name is Benjamin but people call me (Top Dolla)", he said as he pulled a wad of hundreds out of his pocket. "Top Dolla huh? I see that you are one of those niggas that like to stunt. Why did you have to pull all of your money out when you told me your name?" "No sweetie, you have me confused. I don't stunt at all." He said. He walked over to the cash register where Tiffany was standing. "How much are the shoes Tiff?" "Uh, lets see, with tax included the total comes out to $224.60." He gave her three of the hundred dollars bill that he was holding. "Give the change to Miss.Parker. It is Miss.Parker right? You aren't married I hope?" I didn't know what type of game these two were playing but I wasn't down for it. This is some playa/pimp tight shit and I didn't want to be apart of it. "Yes it is Miss.Parker but what do you think you are doing? My mom taught me to never take anything from strangers because they always want something in return and whatever you want, you can't have." "Whoa, be easy little mama." I don't want you to do anything but walk. "Walk?" I asked confusedly. "Yes little mama, walk." Shit, who wouldn't walk for three hundred dollars? I threw my hands on my hip and started walking my ass off. But then they both laughed. "Nawl lil mama. I want you to walk at my club." "Yo club?" I asked. Then Tiffany spoke up. He owns a strip club about twenty miles from here. He is asking you to come strip at the club." Hold the fuck up. Are they serious right now? I looked at both of their faces and they were definitely serious. "Strip club. I ain't no stripper!" "Baby you don't have to be. All I want your fine ass to do is wear a bathing suit and dance. You don't have to take anything off. My crowd will be satisfied if you just shake your big ass booty. Tiff here is one of my specialists. She gets the job done and go home every night with about how much Tiff?" "I make at least $2,000 a night." "WHAT? When do I start? After hearing that number, I jumped in and didn't ask any questions. This is so out of my character. The love of my life doesn't want me so I don't give a damn anymore. I am broke and bills have to be paid.

 We arranged for Tiffany to pick me up tonight because Top Dolla had to get there earlier. She seems like a cool person so I trust her to get me there safe. I gave her my address, grabbed my shoes and my left over change, and walked out.

 It was already time to pick up Samiyah from school. As I walked toward the bus stop, I couldn't believe what I just agreed to. Am I really going to be working at a strip club? My stomach wasn't flat but neither did I have a muffin top. Top Dolla liked what he saw with my clothes on so I know the crowd will love me even more with the clothes off. I was about to degrade myself but I had to do what I had to do. However, no one could know about this, not even my closest friends. This was going to be another thing that I am taking to my grave.

Oh my gosh, Samiyah. Who will watch her? I can't just tell my dad and step-mom that I wanted to go out tonight because they will become suspicious of me going to a club every night. I got it! I will tell them that I was offered a night job. Literally, it was a night job. I will tell them that I'm going to train to become a bartender at this club in Long Beach, making five hundred dollars every night. That will be great news to their ears and pockets because I will be able to help them out on the bills. I hate living off of people because that means that person has some type of hold on you. I just need a place to lay my daughter's head until we get situated. If this works out for me, I will have my own place and a car in less than a few days or a couple of weeks.

• • •

The doorbell ranged. I kissed Samiyah and ran as fast as I could to the door. I didn't want her to see me leave the house.

We arrived at club "Paradise". When I walked in, I realized where the name came from. It was like walking into Paradise. There was ass and breasts hanging out everywhere but of course no one's ass was bigger than mines. "Parker just follow me. We are going to the back." Tiff said. Once we made it to the room where all of the strippers were, Tiffany walked to her locker and I tried to maintain myself. For one, I was nervous as hell and for two, these chics were walking around butt ass naked and no one seemed to be bothered by it. As I glance around this room at all of these beautiful women, Top Dolla walked in, "Ok, listen up ladies. We have a new girl tonight that goes by the name of, "Juicy P." I am so happy that I am not going to be the only girl that is starting tonight. Then he said, "She is over there standing beside Tiffany." I was on one side of her but as I looked on the other side; I noticed that no one was standing there. "Parker, introduce yourself." What the hell? Juicy P? Where in the hell did that come from? I wanted to make up my own stripper name. Something like, "Mississippi Fat Kat or Big Booty Intruder." I didn't blame him for calling me juicy because I am juicy indeed, so I took the name and owned it. "Hello everyone, my name is Parker. I was born and raised in Mississippi and I just recently moved back here to Cali. This is my first time so I will be looking to you all to show me the ropes." They all welcomed me and some went out to the floor. Top Dolla walked over to me and gave me a sexy pair of red lacey boy shorts and two red stickers that were shaped like stars. "No bra for those little A-cup breasts tonight." He said. "Just put the stars on your nipples and you will be good to go and before I forget, here is a key to your locker.

Go ahead and get dressed and I will be back to get you in a few minutes. Oh and there is a surprise in your locker. Enjoy." I waited until he walked out to see what this surprise was. Before I even open my locker, Tiff said, "Damn Juicy, you have gotten a lot of gifts today. I didn't get any treatments like that when I started working here." Was she jealous? Top Dolla had bought me another pair of shoes. They were fiery red and stood about six inches tall: definitely the type of shoes that are strictly for a stripper. "Well girl good luck out there and I will see you in a bit." Tiff said and walked off. It didn't take me more than about thirty seconds to get dressed being that I didn't have shit to put on. I did a few ass shakes in the mirror just to see how I was going to look from behind and boy was that ass on point. Top Dolla walked in and I became even more nervous because I knew that it was time. He made me take three shots of "Vodka" and after about four minutes; I was in there. There are a lot of sexy ass women in here but I wasn't intimidated. I am the new girl and I am about to take over. I have stepped out of my character so I might as well make it worth it. "They have a (No Hands) policy here. That means that the men or woman can't touch the dancers. They can lick and moan all night but they can't touch; Absolutely no exceptions. When I found that out, I was down for whatever because I knew that they couldn't put there hands on me. The shots were kicking in and I was ready to put on a show for these animals. We paced the floor a few times just so I can get the feel of this club and the environment. The minute Dolla unleashed me, the lions came running trying to see who would be the first one to get the fresh meat. I tried to check out these niggas and their swag so I would know who had the most money and who was willing to give it all to me. "I'll take you first." I said to the guy that stood about 6'3 and weighing about 220 pounds.

He had a perfectly lined haircut and was dressed in Polo from his head to his feet. I whispered in his ear, "Damn, you look good. Wont you come over here and have a seat."

"Lil mama you fine as fuck ya damn self." He replied. "Well I hope you have enough money to keep up with me. This is my first night and

I'm trying to make a statement." "Do yo thang shawty cause money ain't a issue." That's exactly what I wanted to hear.

I knew that No Hands was the policy here but I wanted to take the rules into my own hands. I grabbed his fingers and stuck them in my vagina. "Now keep them still." I said "Damn lil mama, you wilding out already." "I told you. I'm here to mark my territory." I reached down to my knees and starting bouncing my ass up and down on those four fingers that were inside of me. I then hopped up, turn around and placed my breasts in his face and licked the cum from my pussy, off his fingers. He was rock hard but who wouldn't be? He reached in his pocket, pulled out some bills and placed them in my beautiful laced panties. I was enjoying myself so I didn't want to stop and look at how much he actually gave me. I kept dancing and he kept throwing out the money. Tiff walked over, "Aye Juicy. Dolla wants to holler at us in the back." "What? Now? Damn!" "I guess that's it for tonight handsome." "Damn shawty. Aight. I'll be back to look for you and only you." He said and I walked off. "I see that you are fitting in just fine huh?"

"Girl yes, I love this damn place and I've only been here for an hour." We made it back to the changing room. "Where is Dolla? I thought you said that he wanted to talk to us?" "Oh, girl I just said that to get you away. But I have to leave and head home for my other job at the mall." Damn, already?" "Yea. I would stay longer but I have to pull a double and I need to get some sleep. You can stay if you can get a ride home." She knew damn well that I didn't have a ride home. Besides, there was something more to this story. Her attitude changed right after she saw those shoes that Dolla bought me. She is definitely jealous because all of the attention is now on me. I can bet any amount of money that she has never left the club within three hours.

But she is my ride for now, so I have to deal with her. Speaking of money, I walked over to the other side and pull out the money that the gentleman had given me. 100,200,300,400,500,600,700,800,900,1000 ,1100,1200,1300,1400 and 1500. DAMN! Ain't no way this nigga came off of that much cash in minutes. "That guy gave you that much money?" Tiff asked. I rubbed it in her face. "Yes, I guess he loved the new meat very well. Imagine if I was here a few hours longer." "I'll be in the car." She said and walked off: Jealous Bitch.

I got in contact with Dolla before I left because I wanted to tell him what was going on. He volunteered to pick me up from now on because he didn't want things to go sour with Tiff and I. But to me, she was already a nobody. She is a bad bitch and now that I am here, she can't see that. I'm insecure about myself as well but when it comes to the money, I won't let anyone get in my way. This isn't the last of me. I'm here to stay or at least until I can save up thousands of dollars. I have a kid at home that has to eat. Her daddy isn't doing shit so I had to do it.

Chapter 45

"I don't want to see you"

"Parker! I have another letter from Samiyah's sperm donor." My dad said as he walked in the house. I knew that this letter was going to be about Alex's Basic Training graduation. I just recently wrote him a letter telling him that I wanted to bring Samiyah to his graduation. I told him that he didn't have to worry about financing the tickets because I had money to do so. I wanted it to be a surprise but I knew that I had to involve his mom in this plan because his graduation was taking place in Fort Knot, South Carolina. I haven't spoken to her since the incident she pulled, but I was ready to move pass that, well I was willing to use her because we needed a place to stay. Charlotte is only about forty-five minutes from Fort Knot, South Carolina so I knew that she was going to the graduation. I have been communicating with Terrica but not Charlie so I did not want to stay with them. I still can't stand his ass anyway.

Alex has been keeping in touch with Samiyah through letters but that still wasn't the same as actually being here with her. At first, I didn't read any of them to Samiyah because of the hurt that I was still feeling. I still can't get over him leaving us. The more I think about it the more it hurts. I figure that the pain will go away as the days go by but it didn't because I am still hurting. I have a lot of rage towards him but everyday, I pray that God protects him and continue to lead him in the right direction

I always write him back even though I said that I wasn't going to. I let him know when she has her doctors appointment, her favorite foods and her favorite cartoons. He was my ex-fiance and my daughter's dad so I can't be mean to him even if I tried to. Everyone wants me to put him on child support and stop all communications with him but I can't. He has hurt me time after time but I just can't do the same thing to him.

I sat down and opened the letter. It read as follows:

"Parker, I don't want you to come to my graduation. Red is going to be there and we both agreed that you should not be present. However, I would love to see my daughter. We were thinking that Samiyah can maybe ride with my mom to the graduation and you can stay at her house until they get back. I don't want to see you and neither does Red. To be honest, I wouldn't care if I ever saw you again. But just know that if you try and come out here, I will tell my mom to leave you at her house because I don't want the drama that I know you are going to bring. Kiss Samiyah for me. Holla".

Wow! Shit just keeps getting worst with him. I can't believe this letter. He is acting like I was the one that left him with a child and that I was the one that called him and said "I no longer want to be with you because I am in love with someone else." Now this motherfucker has the audacity to tell me that he don't ever want to see me again? I don't understand this sudden change. He is mistreating me when I should be the one mistreating him. Get the Fuck outta here! As I wipe away my tears, I come up with a plan. He wanted drama so Imma give it to him. I wrote back and told him that I already bought the tickets to fly out there and that I couldn't get a refund. So whether he liked it or not: He is going to see us in a couple of days.

I had to purchase last minute airplane tickets so they were extremely high. Samiyah was still flying free because she was under the age of two. I looked online, a roundtrip from Los Angeles to Charlotte is going to be $700, and I had about $900 in all. If I buy this ticket, I will definitely have to make a lot of money tonight at the club because I'm going to be damn near broke. I have to buy food once we get there and whatever else that we need so I had to go there with plenty of cash on hand. I immediately purchased the ticket and ripped that letter into shreds. I didn't tell anyone about this because I knew that this wasn't going to sit well with them.

The next day, I lied and told my parents that Alex bought a ticket for Samiyah and I to fly to Charlotte to attend his graduation. My mom thought that I should go but my dad and step-mom said that this could be one of the worst things I would ever do. I didn't care about anyone's opinion because the ticket was bought and my mind was made up.

CHAPTER 46

A Near Death Confrontation

Mom! Daddy! I gotta go! I'm running extremely late. Samiyah is upstairs in the bed sleep. I will see y'all in the morning." "Ok, Be Safe." They said. Tiff was outside waiting on me. She stopped picking me up for a while because of the fucked up attitude that she was having. I didn't want to be around her at the club and especially not in the same car. She knew that I was taking over and that I wasn't going anywhere so eventually, she started to come around. Usually, Dolla comes to get me but tonight she called and said that he had something to do so, she will be by to pick me up instead.

We arrived at the club and I knew that I had to go in and shake a lot of ass because there is a lot of money that has to be made tonight. Alex didn't want me to come to North Carolina for what ever reason, but it was too late because our plane leaves tomorrow afternoon. What's done is done and I wasn't giving in.

"Juicy, I have to go in because I perform in ten minutes so grab your shit and lock my doors when you get out." "Just wait on me." I said. "Here I come, Damn." "No, I have to go." She tossed me the keys and walked in the club. See, that's why we can't get along now, she always thinks that everything has to go her way. I'm the new bitch around this motherfucker so what I say goes. I grab my clothes and got out of the car.

As I placed the key in the door, to lock it from the outside, I hear footsteps. I turn around, but no one is there. It's dark as hell out here and I have seen too many movies to know that you don't go outside by yourself, especially at a club. I'm out here procrastinating with these keys and I need to get my ass in the club. I threw my purse over my shoulder and headed towards the door.

Suddenly, someone comes from behind and puts their hands over my mouth. "Aye bitch, what about a quick fuck before you go in?" I mumbled threw his hands, "Look, I don't know what type of games you are trying to play but you better get yo damn hands off of me." "Nawl Juicy, you see, I have been watching you since you started and now it's my time to get some pleasure from you. I tried to remain calm because reacting was only going to piss this mystery person off but then my daughter flashes before my eyes causing me to scream for help as loud as I could. "Shut up bitch." He said as he threw me on the ground. "No one can hear you." I tried to fight him off of me but his body is too strong to move. "What do you want from me? Why are you doing this?"

He grabbed both of my hands and pinned them to my side. I can't believe that no one is hearing the tussle back here but I forget that we are outside of a club. He was using all of his might to hold down my hands so I used the bottom of my body to squirm, kick and try to move him off of me. "After I rape you, I'm going to kill you. You took the spotlight from my home girl Tiff so she paid me to destroy your nasty ass." She is the head bitch around here. "Let me go!" I yelled. But he didn't. "Shut up, you stupid bitch." He screamed. "Help, somebody help me. Please". He grabbed my throat with one of his hands and slapped me senseless with the other.

I fought until I couldn't fight anymore. I knew that this wasn't going to end pretty, so I gave up. He pins me down by sitting on my legs. As he rips off my skirt, I can feel the burns on my body that came from being tossed around on this rocky cement. He pulls out his dick and painfully forces his way in. I continue to scream but still no one answered. He tries to shut me up by banging my head on the ground. I start to feel faint but I can still feel the pain from this man torturing me. He is violating me and the only thing that I can do is take it. Why won't he stop? Why is he doing this? I continue to lye on the cold ground with bruises over my body. I realize that this is it. I know that no one is going to come to my rescue. I close my eyes and begin to pray aloud but I felt the energy leave my body. All I could say was, "Lord Help Me."

I woke up to the sound of an IV machine. I tried to move my arm but I was strapped to a hospital bed. "Juicy! Juicy, its me Dolla. Are you OK?" I tried to talk but I couldn't so I nod my head. "Do you know what happened? Do you know why you are in the hospital? I nod my head again. "Good, I'm going to bring in the Police officers. They are outside of your room. Is it ok for them to come in and ask you a few questions?" I nod my head.

"Hello ma'am. I know that this is a bad time but we have to ask you some questions. A man called 911 and said that he had just raped you and had orders to kill you. Once we arrived, you were completely naked and blood was everywhere.

For a minute, we thought that you were dead." I tried to gain enough strength to give the police a statement. "All I can remember is him telling me that Tiffany paid him to take me out. As I think about it now, she went ahead in the club and made sure that I came in after her. This whole thing was a set-up." "That's exactly what it looks like to us." The police said. Then Dolla interrupted, "If Tiffany had anything to do with this, she will regret it for the rest of her life". Dolla tried calling her but she never answered. "But what about the guy that did this to me?" We don't know anything right now." The officer said, "But maybe this Tiffany girl has a few answers for us." The doctor ran a test on the sperm they found on you so, if we can find a guy that matches what we have, we will have our Rapist. You can believe that we will investigate this until we can find out who did this to you.

I glanced at the clock on the wall and noticed that it was 6:00 a.m. This means that I only have a few hours before I leave. They didn't want me to check out so quickly but I had a plane to catch. I have a black eye and bruises on my arms and thighs. If my dad sees me this way, he is going to flip out. So, I guess I'll just tell him that I got into a fight with one of the girls from the club. I couldn't tell anyone about this tragic situation. Dolla agreed to drop me off at home. I was very sore and could barely walk but nothing was going to keep me from getting on that plane. Maybe this is God telling me that I did not need to go to Charlotte. Maybe this is a sign and maybe it isn't. It's too late now because no matter what, Samiyah and I are boarding that plane.

CHAPTER 47

Welcome back to Charlotte

Things felt strange the moment I stepped off of that plane. I was still in pain from the attack but this was a different feeling. I walked down to baggage claim and there stood Charlie, waiting on us. I thought Mrs. Judy was coming to get us but obviously not because Charlie was here. This is not a way to start my vacation but oh well. He didn't speak to me, Instead, he walked over to Samiyah, picked her up and gave her a hug. Of course, she starts to cry because she didn't remember him. Maybe this was a mistake after all.

It was quiet in the car before he started interrogating me like he was someone important. "How are y'all going to eat? Do you have money? Where are y'all going to be staying? Not once did this ignorant ass man ask how we was doing or how was the plane ride. "Uh, I have my own money. I don't need y'all to do anything for me but provide me and my child with a place to lay our head." He knew where we were staying at because he was taking us there. It damn sho wasn't going to be with him.

Once we finally made it to Mrs. Judy's house, I got out of his car without saying bye or thank you and slammed his door. Maybe I was a being a little disrespectful but he has been disrespectful to me since we met each other, so fuck him. Here we are a year later and his mouth still irks the hell out of me but I guess that is something that will never change.

Mrs. Judy greeted us at the door being as fake as she knew how. "Oh my Gosh! You girls are so pretty and dang Parker, you have lost a lot of weight." I wanted to say, "And dang Mrs. Judy, you have gained it all, but I didn't. I can't trash talk the woman that is allowing us to sleep in her home. But she shouldn't be surprised at my weight loss being that her son was the reason. She knew that he fucked up but she never wanted to admit it. We started carrying on a conversation like nothing had ever happened between us. Every time I replayed her throwing my daughter into my arms, I wanted to cut off a piece of that fat on her body and cook it, never mind cook it, I wanted to burn it. That maybe a harsh thing to say but I mean every word. It takes me a while to forgive someone when they have hurt me or anyone in my family, for that matter. I don't like when people say, "Just move on and forget about it" because they know that in reality, you can't forget what someone has done to you. Besides, it seems better to hold a grudge because it shows them that you are really hurt by their actions. Sometimes you can't move on and be the bigger person. I'm not saying that it can't happen, I'm just saying that I won't be the bigger person in this situation.

Samiyah has fallen asleep so it is time for me to take it in as well. We have a long day tomorrow so I need my rest. I brought along my best clothes because I had to impress Alex and show that Red chic how to dress. I could care less about this graduation and I could definitely care less about him not wanting me to come. I just want to see him, give him a hug and reminisce about old times. Red isn't more than a friend to him so I didn't care about her. I am the one that had his baby, not her, so she is dumb if she thinks, that Alex and I aren't going to work this thing out.

GRADUATION:

We stayed at the security checkpoint for damn near thirty-five minutes; they wanted to make sure that everything was legit with the car, such as the registration and car insurance. Once we made it on the air force base, we drove to the building that he was supposed to be at but no one was there. When Judy called, he told her that he was walking around with some of the guys until we came. We rode around until we found a parking space and waited for him. Today is "Meet and Greet" day so there are a lot of people out. I could only imagine what the graduation is going to be like tomorrow.

We were all sitting on the car admiring the scenery when suddenly I drifted off into another world. I went to a place where it was only Alex, Samiyah and I holding hands and enjoying life. The soldiers are walking around with their families and loved ones laughing, talking and looking so happy and blissful. I, on the other hand, was at a place where no one wanted me to be. Alex made it clear to me that neither he nor his girl wanted me come but I'm here. I knew that this was a mistake but I was ready to deal with the consequences. Besides, there isn't any more damage that Alex and his family can cause in my life so this is a chance that I'm willing to take.

The officers blocked some of the roads making it hard for the traffic to maneuver quickly. Alex called his mom and told her that he couldn't get through so he wanted us to meet him at the food court.

I became so nervous. I am about to see Alex. What is he going to say? Is he going to give me a hug or a handshake? Will he still have feelings for me or will he hate me for coming? Well the time is up. Once we pulled in to the food court, I got out of the car and walked around to the other side to get Samiyah out of her car seat. Miss. Independent wanted to walk so I put her down.

As we start to walk, I hear,

"Samiyah!" Alex yelled as he ran towards her. He tried to pick her up but she started to cry. She no longer knew this person. I mean he did walk out on her just a few months ago. "No Alex, don't make her cry. Just give her a few minutes to remember you." Mrs. Judy said. He put her back down and gave his mom and step-dad a hug. "Oh Alex, it's so good to see you." Judy said. Since he was in the mood of giving away hugs, I had to take advantage of it so I reached towards him to get me one. "Hey, how are you?" I asked. Instead of saying fine or giving me a handshake, this bastard lean back and says, "You know we don't get down like that. Anyway, mom I would like for you to meet someone very important in my life. I know that y'all have been communicating over the phone and the internet but here she is in person. Mom, this is Red. Red, this is my mom." They both said, "It's very nice to finally meet you."

I tried to maintain my composure because I know damn well that they are not about to go on with their day and pretend that I don't exist. He just disrespected me when I was only trying to be nice and his fat ass mom didn't have shit to say about it. I even spoke to Red but she didn't part lips either.

I remember seeing her, about two years ago, at the church but now she looks different. She has on a blue jean skirt that come down to her knees, a black v-neck shirt that looks like it was made out of polyester and a pair of black flip-flops. Her hair was in micro braids but it was synthetic hair, instead of real human hair. Who does that? The only thing that she has going for herself is her physical appearance. She is a red-bone, weigh about 135 pounds and her stomach is as flat as a pancake. She is very old-fashion but also very beautiful so I guess that's why Alex is so in love.

I said that I was going to do this and say that but seeing her kills everything that I said. He will be a fool to leave her and come back to me. I have his child but that's all I could offer. He isn't in love with me anymore and there isn't anything that I can do to change his mind. I'm not as thin as I was when we first met nor do I stand up to Red and her beautiful qualities. It's true, he went from rags to riches. All I ever wanted to do was make him happy when I should have been making myself happy. I fell… I fell terribly.

They continued to stand to the side talking and laughing. They were enjoying each other's company and I was just there to humiliate myself. I wanted to scream better yet, I wanted to cry but I couldn't let them see that they were getting to me. I grabbed my daughter and headed towards the bathroom.

"Parker is Samiyah hungry?" Alex asked. I can't believe it! He actually said something to me. I didn't want to turn around simply because I didn't exist to him a few minutes ago, but it made no since in stooping to his level. Besides, I'm sure my daughter is hungry but so was I. What about me?

"Yea, she probably is but I'm going to the bathroom to change her diaper." "Ok, we will be inside at the Café so just look for us when you come out." I said "Ok" and walked off.

When I came back, I spotted them in line and walked over to where they were standing. "So, what does she like to eat?" Alex asked. "She is a picky eater but she usually eats what I eat?" Well you have to tell me what that is because I'm not buying your food, I'm only buying hers." He said.

Ok, once again, I must maintain myself because this dude is really tripping. How many times do I have to tell these ignorant ass people that I have money? I don't need anyone to do shit for me or my daughter. What part of that does his family not understand? It was time to let him know how I felt because like my friend Tony always says, Enough is Enough.

"Alex, you have been very disrespectful to me and I don't appreciate it. I really don't understand why you are treating me this way. I don't need you to ever buy anything for me or my daughter so remember that."

"Parker I do not want the drama with you today so just tell me what to order her.

What about the chicken nugget combo? Does she eat nuggets?" My thought, "What fucking child doesn't eat chicken nuggets?"

"Yea Alex, that's fine. I can't deal with you right now." This man has just ruined my appetite. I seriously went from starving to not being hungry at all. I can't believe him. I really can't. I had to go and sit down because I was feeling like I was about to have a mental break down.

I placed Samiyah in a booster seat and prepared her to eat. Alex walks over and pulls her food out of the bag. She loves to eat so the moment she saw her fries, she started bouncing up and down. That's her, "I'm about to eat," dance.

As he placed her nuggets and drink on the table, I noticed something. I then looked over to Red and noticed the same thing. They each had a ring on their married finger. I know DAMN well........Hell no! That would be nonsense. They couldn't be married after meeting up only five months ago. I glanced at it again…No, he couldn't be that stupid. I'm sure that its nothing more than a promise ring or maybe its just a coincidence because I always put fashionable rings on my married finger and I'm not married. Besides, she just flew into Charlotte this morning so there was no way that they could have gotten married this morning.

After they ate, they took Samiyah to one of the toy stores here on base. The both of them were holding hands, kissing and laughing the entire time and they did it right there in front of my face. I could no longer stomach them anymore. Mrs. Judy took on to the fact that they were really getting under my skin so she agreed that the best thing for us to do, was to leave for today and come back to the graduation in the morning.

Alex gave Samiyah another hug and asked his mom if he can talk to her for a second. I stood there because I wanted to hear what he had to tell her but they knew that I was trying to be nosey, so they walked off. Slick Bitches.

After crying the entire ride home, I became drained. I wasn't playing or talking to my daughter simply because I didn't have the energy to do so. I have never placed my problems in front of her and here I am doing it now. I called my mom to tell her how they treated me today and of course, she was upset. I also told my dad and honestly, I thought that he was going to get smart and say, "I told you so," but he didn't. He was actually trying to find a way to get out here to blow some motherfuckers up.

Yes, he told me not to come but then again, he wasn't going to have anyone disrespecting me. I hope everything will be a little better tomorrow. His mom told me that she was going to call and talk to him for me but who knows because she is a compulsive liar I hope that she pulls through for me. I would like to talk to Alex just to find out where we went wrong so I can possibly have some type of closure. I have to know something. I will never be the same if I never know why the love of my life walked out on me. Before I went to sleep, I wrote down a list of questions to remember for tomorrow. I needed answers and I was ready to hear what he had to say.

Chapter 48

This Is It

I woke up feeling refreshed and ready to take on what this day has for me. But wait, why is the sun beaming outside and why does my phone say 9:20 a.m.? The graduation started at 8. Oh shit, we overslept! I jumped up as fast as I could, tripping over my luggage on the floor and ran into Mrs. Judy's room to wake her and her husband up. But she wasn't there. I looked out the window and her car wasn't there. Hmm, that's strange. I thought.

I went back into the living room, where my daughter and I were sleeping and there was a note on the table.

It read...,

"Parker we went ahead and left without you. Neither Alex nor his girlfriend wanted you to come. He said that you said some terrible things to him yesterday so he didn't want to see you today. I didn't want to argue with him because today is his day, so I just left you guys. We should be home around 5'o clock this evening. I left the keys to my car outside. I'm in the rental car. I'm sorry -Judy.

I read that letter at least ten more times to make sure that I wasn't dreaming. I can't believe that I was sleeping so hard that I didn't hear them moving around. I'm guessing that is what Alex told her yesterday. This fucked up family has no balls. Alex broke up with me over the phone and now his mom has written a letter. Am I that intimidating? No one can ever man up or woman up and tell me the shit to my face, and that is what pisses me off the most. I hate when people go behind my back and do sneaky shit. Damn. I spent my money to fly out here and bring Samiyah to her dad's graduation and this is what I get in return?

I needed someone to talk to. I wanted to curse but I couldn't so I called Melissa, no answer. Next, I called Cherell. Besides the fact that she is one of my best friends, she sometimes does me justice just by cursing someone out for me. After I told her what happened yesterday and this morning, I had to ask her for a favor. I knew that I was about to step out on faith by asking her to do this for me. The answer wasn't going to be "No", it was going to be a "Hell No." However, I asked her anyway.

"Cherell, do you feel like renting a car to come and get Samiyah and me?" "What?" she said. "How am I going to do that?" "Would you really consider it?" I asked surprisingly. "Girl yes, I want to slap me a bitch anyway for the foul shit that they have pulled."

(I wanted to ask my mom but she just bought a new van so I knew that she didn't want to put that many miles on it this soon. Besides, she can't drive that long without first, getting enough rest. Her friend, Mrs. Harris, husband passed away and his funeral is tomorrow. If she comes to get me, she will really be pushing it with the time. So I didn't bother asking her.)

"Ok, call my mom and ask her if she can rent a car for you?" While I waited for her to call back, I started packing our clothes even though the distance from Columbus to Charlotte is about eight hours. That wasn't just around the corner and down the street, this was a long ass ride and I couldn't believe that Cherell volunteered to drive it. It's almost 10 A.M. so if it's going to happen, I want it to happen now because I would love to be gone when Mrs. Judy gets back; I wanted to leave her fat ass a note to read.

Cherell called me back, "Your mom told me not to worry about it. She said that she and your brother are about to put on some clothes, and come and get you.

I couldn't believe it. I could not believe that my mom was about to head up this highway. She came when Samiyah and I first moved Charlotte, she came for Christmas, she came for Samiyah's 1st birthday, she came when Alex left us and now she is on her way, Again. There is no way that I could thank her enough for everything that she has done for me within a year's time. She is the true definition of a mother. She puts her kids first so I have no other choice but to cherish her the way that I do.

Cherell decided to ride with them and I wanted to warn Mrs. Judy for what was about to come because neither one of them takes bullshit from anyone, especially when it comes to me: But I didn't. Fuck Mrs. Ruby and her psycho ass family. My mom finished handling some business, gassed up and they headed out.

Fell Too Deep

Due to my mom getting a late start, Mrs. Judy beat them to the house. I didn't want to talk to her nor did I want to see her. The moment she walked in, she apologized. I didn't care to hear what she had to say but I felt like she owed me at least that much.

"I would like to apologize for how my son is acting. I didn't raise him to act this way. I am very upset because I found something out today and he suggested that I should be the one to tell you. He didn't want to hear or see your reaction so, here it goes: Alex and Red are not girlfriend and boyfriend: they are married. They got married at the courthouse on July 5th of this year, 2008, right before he went to basic training. I'm sorry that you had to find out this way but there it is." She walked in her bedroom and closed the door.

Married? Did she just say "Married?" The rings that I saw on their hands yesterday were wedding rings! How could I be so stupid not to see this? He left us in February, called it off with me in March and got married in July. How is that even possible? I have been stressing my life away worried about someone that doesn't give a damn about me. Some of my hair has fallen out and I have lost a ton of weight. I don't deserve this. How could Red marry someone who just got out of a relationship? I see now that my heart and love didn't mean anything to Alex.

I kissed Samiyah and placed my hand over my face. I don't know what to do next. I thought about suicide but that wouldn't solve anything. I wanted to run far away but I wasn't going to leave my daughter. I didn't have any other choice but to sit there and take this devastating news that was just given to me.

My mom was lost but they eventually found these apartments after riding for nine hours. I applaud them for coming to my rescue at the last minute. I don't know of anyone else that will drop everything that they are doing to spend half of their day in a car coming to get us. I was so happy to see them and for a minute, I had forgotten all about how crazy these two days has been.

I called out to Mrs. Judy's room to tell her that we were about to leave but she did not say a word. She couldn't come to say good-bye to her grand-daughter? Is it that serious? I hate it for her because this will be the last time that any of them see my daughter. They don't deserve to be in her life. She is a dead-beat grandma and Alex is definitely a dead-beat dad. She hasn't done anything for my child so we will never need her. Well forgive me, she once sent a ten-dollar money order and told me to buy Samiyah whatever she needed. I started to rip it but I used that money on some chips and cookies; which was the only thing that I could buy. Her broke and emotional ass does not matter to me nor is she important. Alex was willing to sacrifice seeing his daughter just because his chic, well excuse me, his wife didn't want me to come to his graduation. He helped me to understand who was more important in his life.

Once we realized that Mrs.Judy wasn't going to come out of her room, we got ready to leave. She had a glass vase on her table with a dozen of red roses in it, so Cherell picks up the vase and throws it in the kitchen, hoping to get her attention. I heard glass splatter everywhere and she still didn't budge. My mom said, Ok that's enough. Let's go."

The plan is for me to finish off my vacation in Mississippi. My stepmom is going to change our return tickets from Charlotte to Alabama and that way, we won't have to drive up here to catch the plane.

• • •

I am on my way back to a place where I always end up in the midst of a trial and that is, Mississippi.

None of this is making since to me. How could he love and move on so fast? I can't stop blaming myself. If I had done some things a little different, maybe this wouldn't be the outcome. I still had my list of questions that I never got answered. I called him a few times but he never answered so I had no other choice but to send him a few texts. I just wanted answers. I wanted to know why and how could he hurt me the way he did. Then he finally text back:

"Parker, every since that day you cheated on me, things for us went downhill and you know that. I wasn't able to trust you again and that ruin our relationship. Keep in mind that you never were the Picture perfect girl. You complained a lot, you were lazy and you never had a solution to any of the problems that we had. I did love you but when I went back to Cali and looked into Red's eyes, I fell in love. I looked at Red and said..

"You are going to be my wife."

For once, I have the love I deserved. I am married and I am in love. Parker, I need you to realize that there is nothing that can be done about it. I'm with the woman of my dreams and I'm sorry that it didn't work out but I do wish you the best and I will still take care of my child. Its late so I'm going to sleep. Holla."

"Wow"! was all that I could say.

And that was that. He was gone out of my life and this time for good. I was distraught. I no longer wanted to be alive. I thought that it would be better and easier to take myself out of these miseries now instead of going on living and getting over this heartbreak the hard way. I never want to hear or see the words Charlotte, North Carolina ever again.

I was glad that I had the tickets switched because I was able to spend a few days at home with the family before I got ready to go back to California, again. Alex left me and right before I went to Charlotte I was raped and put in the hospital, disrespected to my face by Alex at the graduation and then finds out that he is happily married.

How do I suppose to live after that? I feel like a "Nobody". I have always put myself so high on the peddle stool because I didn't want my peers to look down on me. I have been pretending to be someone that I am not. I am always so quick to say, "Yea, I live in California, yes I have the perfect man in my life and yes I have my own money. I wish that I could tell the world that I don't have shit, I used to strip for money and that I am never going to be shit, so accept it or leave it. I have went broke at times trying to keep up with the latest fashion and I am tired of it all. I can't take it any longer. I feel like going under a rock and hiding out; Forever. Many girls look up to me because they think that I have so much going for myself. But if they knew my situation and if they knew my thoughts at night, I am sure that they wouldn't think so highly of me.

If only I could accept the person that I am, I wouldn't have to have a man to tell me how beautiful I am. It's like I fight for attention when I shouldn't have to. How will I ever overcome this?

Patrice L. Guyton

PIECES OF ME…………..

Underneath this Oil of Olay, Cover Girl and Mary Kay
Lies alligator skin, acne, blemishes.
Inside of this beautiful six inch pump shoe,
I have aches and bruises.
Behind these colorful clothes are a few scoops of gain
Because right here once was a stain.
But I covered it up, just like I cover up.
All of my problems and all of my pain

See, these are the pieces of me.

This Red hair was once brown
And that brown hair was once long
And Nappy,
I couldn't get anything to straighten it, not even a hot comb.
But after a guy took his love from me and told me to
Run Alone
I cried and became stressed
Because To him I thought I belong.
Then,
All of my hair fell to the sink
And suddenly I fell weak.
But I boastfully stuck out my chest.
I couldn't let the world know that he got the best of me.

See, these are the pieces of me.

I've decided not to go out of my way to keep up with the latest fashion
To Hell with it.
Give me garbage bag and a pair of scissors
And watch me get sick with it.

I'm a living example of "Everything isn't as good as it seems"…
Now don't let this beautiful gap smile fool ya.
I wasn't always this happy.
I had a terrible attitude and was very sassy.
I had a heart

But,
It was barely beating
From the way it was treated
The lies and cheating

I don't tell my secrets
Because
I once put my trust in friends
And they broke the silence and told
That's why I'm so fearless,
that's why my heart was so cold.
My pastor once said, "A person always in mess, is lacking something that they
need
I was lacking the most important thing and it was the size of a mustard seed.
....Faith
So,
As I erase the feeling of shame
Replace my failures with fame
Embrace the meaning of GOD's name
I will no longer be the same
Because
I finally realized the pieces of me

Before I hoped on that plane, my mom said a few words that will stick with me forever.

"I want you to go back to California and keep your head held high. You have seen what type of person Alex is so, I hope that you are really done with him. Everyone will definitely get what is coming to them but don't you ever wish anything bad on anyone. You have changed into a different person, thought about suicide and even lost all of your hair due to stress. I want you to continue to pray every day and ask God to give you the strength and faith to make it through this tough time. I know it doesn't seem like it right now but one day you are going to look back at this and laugh your ass off. Mommy loves you and I need you to take care of yourself and my granddaughter. You are a smart, beautiful and intelligent young woman and you will overcome this."

As we stood in that airport saying our farewells; yet again, I was no longer devastated. I wasn't sad anymore. I had a feeling going through my body that I have never experienced before. Was it hate? Was it betrayal? I tried to cry but I couldn't. I tried to be sad but I wasn't. No one should ever go through the pain and suffering that I have been through. I must say that this whole love experience has taught me a lot. The main thing that I have learned is to never put your all into another human being because they will put your heart on a platter and serve it to the lions.

I really feel like Alex has ruined my life. I am only 22 years old and I have already been through a shit load of problems. GOD has been with me and I know that even in this season, he is still with me. I would ask, "Why me" but I have learned that all things happen for a reason. GOD has my life already planned out, so no matter the consequences, I have to accept it and live it.

CPSIA information can be obtained at www.ICGtesting.com
Printed in the USA
LVOW040526010512

279752LV00001B/9/P